SET SAIL FOR MURDER

A POLLY PEPPER MYSTERY

RICHARD TYLER JORDAN

OLIVER-HEBER BOOKS

Cover art by Dar Albert at Wicked Smart Designs

Published by Oliver-Heber Books

0 9 8 7 6 5 4 3 2 1

"Working in Hollywood does give one a certain expertise in the field of prostitution."
—Jane Fonda

"Hollywood is where they shoot too many pictures, and not enough actors."
—Walter Winchell

1

"If I see one more ESTATE FOR SALE sign planted on our street, I swear I'll develop hysterical blindness!" griped Polly Pepper, legendary TV star from yesteryear from the back seat of her Rolls-Royce.

As her adult-but-still-living-at-home son, Tim, maneuvered the family car up serpentine Stone Canyon Road to Pepper Plantation, their fabled home in the ritzy hills of Bel Air, California, Polly continued her rant. "You know who's swooping in like carpetbaggers and buying up these foreclosures, don't you? That's right. Bling-laden rap music producers driving humongous bulletproof, carbon-emissions-choking Hummers with smoked-black windows. I saw 'em on *The Real Housewives* show. They pick up pricey suburban palaces like ours and treat a star's mansion as if it were little more than Barbie's Hampton's Holiday Playhouse. Music people are the only ones left in Hollywood who can afford the bazillion-dollar-shocker sticker prices that Realtors are pasting on everything from Nimoy's old cruddy tear-down to that cardboard box over on Mulholland that the widow McMahon has been trying to unload since her meal ticket expired."

Tim ignored his mother as he pumped the brake to second-guess an indecisive suicidal squirrel that was playing Russian roulette with the traffic.

Seated beside Polly was her maid and best friend, Tiara, who rolled her eyes and made a low growling noise as she tried to ignore her boss's tirade. Looking out the window at the mansions they passed, she agreed, "Agents from Vultures21 have been circling our place for months. And I've never seen your business manager cry as hard as he did this afternoon."

"Never mind Eeyore," Polly said, waving away Tiara's recall of the solemn financial meeting from which they'd just come. "Doom and gloom. The sky is falling. It's the End Times. Whine, whine, whine. Honestly, the way he carried on, you'd think this was World War III, Armageddon, and the final episode of *Succession* all rolled into one big black plague. I promise we'll survive, kids! I'm a star, for heaven's sake. An icon. A great job with tons o' moola will come along soon. Just like Carol Burnett, I always land in clover."

But for the first time since emerging as an international entertainment star forty years ago, Polly Pepper was personally feeling the heat from a global financial meltdown. The value of her investments had dramatically plunged. Her 401(k) was more a 01(k). Most of her Hollywood chums were downsizing and laying off their personal fitness trainers, ditching their doggie hypnotherapists, and negotiating lower compensation for their pricey mistresses and/or boy toys. Rodeo Drive was as deserted as a Diana Ross comeback concert tour.

As the tall black wrought-iron PP monogrammed gates to Pepper Plantation came into view, Polly momentarily felt a sense of dread about her beloved home. Featured a dozen times in *Architectural Digest,* the house was almost as famous as Neverland Ranch and Graceland—but without the dead masters of the manse. Polly could never imagine moving from the estate, any more than the Hunchback could leave Notre Dame Cathedral. She'd sooner be hit by one of the ubiquitous tourist buses that hogged the narrow streets in the hills than hand over the keys to the bank in a foreclosure and have to live in a common condo in Riverside.

She straightened her back. "I still have my champagne wishes and caviar dreams! They brought me to where I am today," she affirmed.

"Nearly out of champagne in the wine cellar," Tiara reminded Polly.

"As long as my account at the Liquor Locker is still active."

As the gates to the estate parted, Tim guided the car along the cobblestone-paved driveway and stopped beside the granite front steps of the Norman-style mansion. Built during the silent-screen era for long-dead and longer-forgotten star Carmel Myers, it was the house Polly had dreamed of owning ever since she was a little girl selling maps to the movie stars' homes. Back then, while waving down cars with out-of-state license plates, and wearing the skimpiest halter top her mother would allow, she had promised herself that the house would one day be hers. And in the 1980s, for what was then a staggering fortune of five hundred thousand dollars, she'd made her dream come true. All these decades later, she was still proud of her twenty-seven-room mansion, its manicured gardens, and Olympic-size swimming pool.

Polly stepped out of the car, but instead of following Tim and Tiara directly into the house, she walked to the three-tiered water fountain gurgling in the center of the car park. She admired the large, ornate, carved stone bowls resting beneath a topper finial of a stone cherub—fat, naked, uncircumcised, and grinning mischievously as it urinated into the shallow water, which overflowed from the uppermost basin down to the lowest and largest pool. She peered into the water and reached in to retrieve a penny. "My lucky day! Something amazing will happen!"

Polly turned around and took in the full view of her magnificent home. Bombarded with memories of her nearly four decades living on this property, Polly could feel tears well in her eyes. She recalled the glamorous star-studded parties, many of which her son, Tim, had personally conceived and designed. She thought of the years of Tim's growing up: his pony, which roamed the estate and ate her roses, the relief she felt when he fell in love for the first time. "A mother's happy moment," she said to herself, holding her hand to her heart. "Thank God he didn't turn out straight! That would be so Bo-*ring*!"

Polly caught Tim and Tiara watching her from the steps and decided there were too many happy memories to risk losing the house. It was time to do something about her potentially dire financial situation.

When Polly entered the house, she set her clutch purse on the Lalique foyer table, exhaled loudly, and said, "Listen up, it's pow-wow time. Meet me in Paradise"—the name she'd bestowed upon her bathroom/spa "in fifteen minutes. Wear your Mr. Wizard caps, 'cause we're about to become captains of our own destinies. We need to reinvent ourselves. To make Kool-Aid!"

"I hope you mean lemonade." Tim gulped. "If you're planning a Jim Jones suicide pact, I'm joining AA."

"I'm a survivor," Polly called back as she ascended the Scarlett O'Hara Memorial Staircase, the name she'd affectionately bestowed upon the grand steps leading to the second story of her famous residence.

As her hand caressed the carved mahogany banister, Polly was conscious of the simple parts of the house that made up the sum total of her mansion. The plush carpet under her feet felt softer. The crystal chandelier, which hung from the two-story ceiling in the stairwell, seemed brighter and more elegant. When she arrived on the landing, her attention was drawn to the showbiz memorabilia that adorned the walls and illustrated her long and illustrious career. "It's been a great ride," she proclaimed as she passed framed photographs of herself with other legends, including Sammy Davis Jr., Julie Andrews, Edie Adams, Eva Marie Saint, Fred Astaire, and even Princess Diana rolling her eyes at the queen of England. "Something will save us from debtors' prison," she whispered, and headed for her bedroom suite and the anticipated luxury of taking a bubble bath in her mammoth sunken Jacuzzi.

In her bedroom, Polly stepped out of her heels and kicked her shoes across the carpet toward the French doors of her walk-in closet. Polly entered her ginormous bathroom—complete with every modern and futuristic plumbing amenity and skincare product a cover girl could wish for. From the plush monogrammed bath towels to the wine cooler stocked with champagne and chilled glass flutes, to the rain shower, bidet, steam room, and spray-on-tan chamber, this was the one place on Earth where she truly felt that spending eternity in heaven would be a comedown by comparison.

Polly turned on the water taps to her tub and dumped a half jar of green tea and peppermint bath beads into the torrent. As the bubbles churned and frothed, the scent of a candy store filled the room. Polly removed her clothes, draped them over the leather chaise lounge, and then dipped a toe into the water. Slowly adjusting to the preset temperature-controlled whirlpool, she submerged her entire body, leaned back, and let out a long moan of satisfaction. "Thank you, Jesus!"

With the Jacuzzi whirring and its magic jets pulsating, Polly picked up the phone beside the tub and pushed the intercom button. "I'm ready," she said, then closed her eyes and rested her head against the soft built-in cushion behind her.

In a moment, Tiara made a halfhearted knock on the door before entering Polly's inner sanctum. "Timmy's here too, Miss Water Sprite, so you'd better drag those suds up to your throat," she said as she headed for the wine cooler and withdrew a bottle of champagne.

In tandem with Tim, who set three glasses on the marble sideboard, Tiara popped the cork and began to pour the bubbly. When each had their own glass, Polly raised hers and began to make up a song using the most positive lyrics she could think of. The melody was discordant, and the meter made no sense. Still, she rambled, "We're in the money... Put on a happy face... Look for the silver lining... Dance all your troubles away..."

Tim bobbed his head and snapped his fingers to the beat of Polly's ad-libbed tune.

Tiara harrumphed. "Someone's been sniffing the Maybelline."

"Spring is busting out all over..." Polly continued. "I am sixteen going on seventeen... Before the parade passes by... Put on your Sunday clothes when you feel down and out... Don't worry, be happy... And don't bring around a cloud to rain on my parade!"

Tiara tossed Polly's rubber ducky into the suds and said, "Okay, already. We get it. The world's chaos is only half bad. We're luckier than anybody else. I'll be Pollyanna, and Tim can play Doris Day."

"Um, I'm more the Hugh Jackman type," Tim protested. "He's always smiling."

"And with damn good reason," Polly said as she backhanded a splash of bubbles at her son. "But seriously, folks, we're at a crossroads. We have a choice to make. We can accept the lousy cards we're dealt or reshuffle the deck and cheat. Cheat fate, that is. I refuse to go along with the pessimists." Polly knocked back her glass of champers and waited for a refill. "I believe in Polly

Pepper! Always have, despite my mother telling me I'd end up a failure like her. Ha! I only wish she could still talk so I'd know what she was thinking whenever I park her wheelchair over my star on the Walk of Fame."

"Leaving Grandma there for hours at a time isn't such a nice thing to do," Tim said.

Polly pooh-poohed Tim's concern. "She'll never admit that she gets a thrill out of seeing tourists point to my star and talk about how much they love me. Not to mention the semi-fresh air she takes in on Hollywood Boulevard."

Tim and Tiara both agreed that it didn't help to fear their financial future. "We can take in boarders for extra money," Tim suggested.

"I don't cook and clean for strangers," Tiara objected.

"You don't cook, period," Polly mocked.

Other than the muted whooshing noise of the Jacuzzi jets, the room settled into a torpid unease as unexpressed thoughts about their potentially dire situation hung in the air and mixed with the steam rising from Polly's bathwater. A financial crisis was new territory for the threesome, none of whom ever considered that a day might come when they'd have to add the word *austerity* to their vocabulary.

As Tiara reached for the champagne bottle and refilled all three flutes, the telephone rang. Polly splashed like a baby in an inflatable pool as she listlessly said, "If it's JJ, I've definitely reconsidered the offer from Depends. And I'll take any voiceover work—including that commercial for the Tourette's syndrome convention he tried to suck me into last week."

Tim looked at the caller ID. "Just your luck. It's Laura Crawford."

"What the heck could *she* want?" Polly said, making a bigger splash in the tub.

Polly Pepper was famous for being able to find something to

like about almost everyone. Laura Crawford was the exception. Laura was Polly's least favorite cast member from *The Polly Pepper Playhouse,* her long-ago-canceled musical/comedy variety television series. Polly and Laura could go years without seeing or speaking to one another, and when they did communicate, it was always Laura who instigated the overture. Without exception, every conversation came with an agenda. After transparent faux pleasantries, Laura got to the root of the reason for her calling. It was always a variation on one theme: how they could all make money using Polly's name and international prestige to take advantage of autograph hounds or collectors of celebrity memorabilia.

"Don't fall for any of her schemes this time," Tim said as he answered the phone and ignored his mother adamantly waving away any interest in speaking with Laura. "Auntie Laura!" he exclaimed. "Oh, status quo. Mending another broken heart. Polly? Couldn't be better. She's soaking in a boo-blee at the moment. But I know she'd love to chat." He smiled evilly at Polly's icy stare and pushed the cordless phone into his mother's hand.

Polly moved her lips and closed her eyes as she silently counted to ten. She then morphed into her Polly Pepper persona. "Sweetums!" she cooed. "You're picking up my thought vibrations. I was just thinking about you. Um, a couple of weeks ago."

For the next full minute Polly lied about her busy schedule. She feigned boredom with having to schlep through airport security, and the increasing lack of amenities in the first-class cabins of the dozens of different airlines she claimed she had to take en route to untold numbers of personal appearances and special-guest-starring roles on sitcoms. "Mainly abroad, dear. I'll send a tweet when *Muhammad and Me* airs on Al Jazeera's new comedy night," Polly said.

In Hollywood, like bringing a bottle of imported wine to a dinner party in Paris, it's boorish to ask an out-of-work actor to talk about their latest projects. No one ever tells the truth. "My agent wants to put me up for the new Christopher Nolan film" was code for "I'm a humongous failure!" And when one said, "I'm writing my memoirs," everybody knew they were totally washed up in the biz.

Laura was smart enough to know that Polly was in the same boat as every other onetime major female star in her age range. When Polly became silent for a long while and listened intently to Laura, Tim and Tiara knew something had caught Polly's interest. "A cruise? As a matter of fact, I do have some time off coming up."

Tim nudged Tiara, and they both nodded their full support to Polly for a high-seas adventure.

"Alaska?" Polly winced. "Isn't that the place where that moron who ran for Veep puts lipstick on her pit bull? I remember donating to Actors and Others for Animals to have her tongue removed... or was it to have her daughter spayed?" She listened for another moment. "I hear she's a humanitarian at heart. Where did I read about her support group for unwed teenage girls with sexy but irresponsible sperm donors?"

Trying to get off the line, Polly finally said, "Yes. Uh-huh. I'll tell JJ to call you first thing in the A.M. No, stop being afraid of him. He's really a kitty cat, albeit a saber-toothed one. Yes, ciao to you, too, dear. *Arrivederci.* Bye-bye. Gotta go now."

Polly hung up the telephone, picked up her champagne flute, and took a long swallow. "Refill, please," she said, looking at Tim. "We have something to celebrate. And I won't say I told you so about landing in clover!"

Over the next few days, a volley of calls between Polly and her reptilian agent, JJ Norton, ensued. They hammered out the details of the cruise that Laura Crawford had instigated, and finally signed contracts that provided for two extra guests to accompany Polly, albeit with less-than-stellar accommodations for her companions.

True to her nature and desperate for a job, Laura had somehow convinced the talent booking agent for Astral Cruise Lines—who ran the popular Kool Krooz Xitement ships—that she could get the legendary Polly Pepper to host a weeklong series of lectures with the original cast of her famous TV show. Although Polly was a piece of cake to convince to go along for the ride, the other two members of her comedy troupe, Arnie Levin, and Tommy Milkwood, weren't as eager to join in the promised fun. Especially since it meant sharing a stage again with the scene-stealing Laura Crawford. For the two male costars, twelve seasons on television with Laura had been as painful as watching the fluke of Timothée Chalamet getting leading man roles. Almost.

As hysterically funny as both gifted men could be, like most comics, they also had their dark sides. Arnie Levin could be as cruel as he was amusing—as the restraining orders from five former wives, and Sophia Vergara, attested. While audiences adored him, for twelve seasons *The Polly Pepper Playhouse* staff had scuttled out of Arnie's path in the hallways at the studio. The writers had to endure his weekly visits to their offices, where he held hair-tearing tantrums whenever he perceived that Polly or Laura or Tommy or a guest star was getting a higher percentage of funny lines in a sketch. He was a brat with a temper that would make famously frightening Jerry Lewis look like the grandfather in the Werther's Original candy commercials.

Tommy Milkwood, too, had a flair for dragging negative vibrations onto the set. Often, when his *ego-meter* detected that audiences were responding more favorably to the others, he sabotaged a sketch in order to draw attention to himself. A master of mean-spirited practical jokes, he knew that snails were the only things that terrified Laura Crawford more than her recurring nightmare—the one in which she was reduced to working as a sales associate behind the Clinique cosmetics counter at Macy's. Armed with this fear-factor knowledge, Tommy once maliciously sent Laura a Christmas gift of stuffed escargot from an epicurean mail-order catalog. Her nightmares escalated, and she became addicted to sleeping pills.

The two comics were in agreement that they'd rather have appendectomies performed by Homer Simpson, without anesthesia, than have to work with Laura Crawford again. However, the reality of their own economic downturns made them reluctantly agree to the cruise. They rationalized that the horror was only for a week. Surely, they could put up with a putz like Laura for that amount of time. Plus, they'd get an all-expenses paid holiday and have an opportunity to mug for live audiences again.

When Polly heard that Arnie Levin and Tommy Milkwood were ready to set sail, she decided that a celebration was in order. She telephoned her beau, Beverly Hills police detective Randy Archer, and suggested dinner at Spago—and a much-needed sleep over at his condo.

2

Polly, Tim, and Tiara stepped from their hired limousine onto the curb at the cruise embarkation gate at pier 35, in San Francisco. They were awestruck by the sight of the enormous ship berthed before them and grimaced at a motley group in the check-in queue. "Tank tops?" Polly said, looking at several young men.

"This is what they call a Kool Krooz," Tiara mocked. "Neanderthals. Jerry Springer guests. Southern state governors hiding out with their mistresses. Just pray to God that we aren't assigned to the same dining table as the bald guy with shorts, missing front tooth, and hairy watermelon where his stomach should be, showing below his sleeveless T-shirt!"

Polly turned to Tim. "When your second father and I made the crossing aboard the *QEII,* I wore furs—before PETA, of course. For the men, suits and ties were de rigueur!"

Tiara pointed to a large banner and read, "WELCOME ABOARD THE KOOL KROOZ. *INTACTI!* NO SHOES. NO SHIRTS. *NO SHIT!*"

"Kool Krooz, eh?" Polly echoed ruefully.

"*Intacti*?" Tim said. "Um, does anybody else realize that's an anagram for *Titanic*?"

The trio looked at each other with wary expressions as the limo driver deposited their luggage with a cruise ship attendant and waited for Tim to hand him a tip.

"Kool Krooz, indeed!" Polly said again, but this time with enthusiasm. She predicted that the following seven days were going to be filled with many memorable experiences suitable for embellishing out of all proportion at dinner parties and in the autobiography she constantly threatened to write. "Much relaxation, and most of all a payday from my lectures and selling millions of units of *The Polly Pepper Playhouse* DVDs."

"Look around," Tiara retorted. "I'll bet this group only watches reality TV. *Biker Bitches' Conjugal Jail Visits,* is my best bet."

As the trio moved toward the check-in line, a solid woman in a flowing muumuu and sombrero abruptly barged into the space between Polly and Tim. "Hold it, Polly," the woman barked, recognizing the TV icon. "Don't move!" She looked at her companion. "Shoot her fast, Larry!" The woman wrapped a thick arm around Polly's neck and yelled at her friend, "Make it snappy! And don't mess it up. This is going up on eBay."

Polly smiled for the camera, but instead of saying "cheese," she muttered, "I'm gonna make Laura pay for this."

While the flash was still a spot before Polly's eyes, Muumuu Woman grabbed the digital camera out of her companion's hands and looked at the image he'd taken. "Yep! That's her, all right. No mistaking that famous chipmunk overbite. An easy five bucks. Ten if she signs the print later," she said as if the star were invisible. She made no attempt to share the picture with Polly. "Hey, we'll get the whole collector's edition: Laura Crawford and the other two clowns who used to be on that old show." The woman waddled away with her friend, still talking amongst themselves.

"Bon voyage to you, too," Polly called out. She looked at Tiara. "Chipmunk? Bet she thinks I'm Leslie Caron."

After Polly and her posse had gone through the Homeland Security checkpoints and were finally on board the ship, a smiling steward, the poster boy for the "after" pictures in a teeth-whitening ad, was assigned to escort them to their cabins. Dressed in a white uniform with gold braiding on the sleeves, he was at once professional and personable. Tim eagerly sized him up, looked at his name badge, and decided that Keith could be a cool Kool Krooz diversion.

As Keith led the way from the check-in desk and out through the ship's enormous ten-story-high center atrium en route to the glass elevators, he explained that their luggage would be promptly delivered to their cabins. He also discussed the many recreational amenities of the ship: casino, cinema, disco, spa, all-you-can-eat Taco Tuesday. "If you brought your laptop, there's an internet access fee. And your cell phone will work as long as it's compatible with the phone tower on the ship." He then explained that it was mandatory for them to attend the safety drill, which would occur just before departure. "The captain doesn't feel bad when one of his passengers ignores his drill, then falls overboard."

"I'm not ready for my final exit," Polly assured him as they stopped in front of a cabin door.

"Lately, our ships and suicide pacts—or murders—seem to go together," the steward continued. "Old couples especially tend to get on this very ship and disappear before we arrive at the first port. Voila!" he announced as he inserted the key card into the lock and led the way inside.

Polly's smile instantly vanished. "Sweetums," she cooed, "there's been a teensy mistake. I've been assigned to a lovely deluxe veranda penthouse suite." She looked around. "This is no bigger than Jo Anne Worley's boa closet. Where's my ocean?"

"This is an inside stateroom," Keith explained. "You have a virtual view. It's on the television. Channel 3."

"Miss Pepper doesn't want to see a *movie* of the ocean, she wants the Pacific outside her very own, very expensive, and completely comped deluxe veranda penthouse suite," Tiara said.

"This is like a cheap motel in South Central LA," Polly pouted, spying a single Hershey's chocolate kiss on the bed pillow. "I've never been to South Central, and this cabin may make their cheap motels look like a room in the Playboy Mansion, if you get my drift."

Tiara snatched the key card and printout of Polly's reservation from the steward's hand and carefully reviewed the details. She matched the cabin number on the door with that on the printout and shook her head. "This will not do. Miss Pepper was promised a suite. You'll have to make other arrangements for her."

Until now, the steward had been as cheerful as a Disneyland ambassador wired on ephedrine. Now, he stiffened and crossed his arms. "I'll see what can be done," he said, struggling to maintain the advertised high level of decorum required of all employees of the ship.

Tim stepped forward. "We know this isn't your fault, Keith, but my mother really was promised a suite. After all, she's the star on the ship."

"Aren't they all," the steward deadpanned.

"Beg pardon?" Tiara growled.

"What I mean... that is... everyone aboard the ship is treated like a celebrity," the steward corrected himself as he apologized, quoting the company motto.

When Keith finally left the cabin, and with no promised satisfaction, Polly sat down on the bed and sighed.

Tiara groused, "Betcha that Laura Crawford's got a great suite, and you'll be stuck right here for the duration of the voyage."

"Get her cabin number," Polly said, and pointed to the telephone. When Tim obtained the information from the operator, Polly ushered everyone out of the stateroom and down the corridor to the glass elevators.

The Galaxy Deck, where Laura's cabin was located, was more like a wing of the Ritz-Carlton hotel. Crystal pendants dangled from sconces on the corridor walls. The carpet was a mural of underwater sea life. "Dolphins and whales and starfish." Polly pointed to the floor. "We have barnacle-print linoleum on our deck!"

Polly knocked on Laura's cabin door and called out her onetime protégée's name. It took a louder second knock before they heard Laura's weak voice.

"Who?" Laura whispered through the door.

"Just us sea urchins, sweetums," Polly said.

The door opened a crack as Laura peered into the corridor. "I'd invite you in, but—"

"We'll only stay a second." Polly blithely nudged the door and Laura aside. She stepped into the cabin, and her jaw dropped. The suite was more like an elegant New York Fifth Avenue penthouse apartment than a floating hotel room. The stateroom was dominated by a sunken living room, which was four times the size of Polly's own accommodations. Straight ahead was a stunning view of the Pacific Ocean seen through floor-to-ceiling sliding glass doors that led to a private terrace. A fifty-inch flat-screen television adorned one wall, and an elevated dining area, wet bar, and kitchenette were on the opposite side of the cabin. A separate bedroom contained a queen-size bed. The bathroom was marble and travertine and boasted a large glass shower.

Polly picked up a small ceramic bust of Nefertiti set on the coffee table and examined the shape of the queen's nose and headdress. "A fitting tchotchke to symbolize this stateroom is meant for royalty," she said.

Laura closed the door, then listened with detached interest as Polly wandered around and described her own small room. "I rather think they accidentally gave my suite to someone else," Polly suggested.

Laura picked up a copy of her reservation. "Sorry, Polly. Someone else may have your stateroom, but this one was definitely assigned to me," she said, pointing at the cabin number and her name on her key card and itinerary. "But don't tell anyone I'm here. I'm trying to avoid... um, well, you know... um, fans."

"Fans are sorta the point of you being here in the first place," Tiara said.

Polly looked askance at Laura. "I'm sure the captain or someone will realize they've made a gross mistake and will reassign me to the proper stateroom."

"No doubt," Laura said. "Until then..." She opened the door to signal that Polly and her troupe should leave.

"I suppose you need to get some rest," Polly said as she took one last look at the magnificent cabin. As she was reminding Laura that their first show was scheduled for four o'clock that afternoon, Polly spied a bottle of Moet beside a welcome basket of fruits and chocolates wrapped in cellophane. "A decent bottle," she said, and glanced at the card. "'Welcome aboard, Polly Pepper,'" she read aloud.

Laura giggled. "Yeah, your bottle was misdirected to *my* suite. You'll save me the trouble of bringing it to your cramped space. Ciao!"

Back in her tiny stateroom, Polly was seething over Laura Crawford lying about the accommodations that were obviously meant not for a second banana but for a star. "She's a lying little slut!" Polly spat.

"Something you never knew before?" Tim scoffed.

"I would like to know how the little conniver arranged the swap," Polly said, and held out a champagne glass to be filled. "It's entirely my fault. I have always let her get away with the crap she pulls because I felt sorry for the little no-talent loser." Polly clinked glasses with Tim and Tiara.

"She was born with titanium *cojones* the size of heavy-duty construction equipment," Tiara mocked. "Even your agent and your Sterling Studios' nemesis, Stephanie Hough, don't treat you with as much disrespect as Laura Crawford does."

"Never mind," Polly huffed. "I'll take this up with the captain later. I can't wait to see 'em haul her body out of that gorgeous suite. In the meantime, we'll attend the safety drill, then stroll along the Lido Deck before my first lecture."

"I suppose it's time for you to see more of the riffraff that Neptune has barfed up from the ocean for this cruise." Tiara grinned. "The embarkation was just a small sample."

After Polly and her troupe found which lifeboat they were assigned to in the event of an emergency, they made their way up to an outside deck, champagne glasses in their hands, and marveled at the number of people who were sailing with them. "How, during this sucky economy, can so many people afford to take a cruise?" Polly asked as the trio wended their way through a sea of bodies roaming the deck. "Heck, if it weren't for the fact that this is a freebie—with a paycheck to boot—I wouldn't waste *el dinero*!"

"The sycophants who take this type of cruise can always scrape up the bucks for a chance to rub elbows with celebs," Tiara said. "Star stalkers will do almost anything for memorabilia and to boast of having met a famous person. Heck, Matt Damon's gardener told me that someone paid fifty thousand dollars for a jacket that Matt wore in his latest *Bourne* movie."

"That's ridiculous!" Tim scoffed. "Fifty grand for a Matt Damon hand-me-down? Hugh Jackman's T-shirt, fresh off his back after a sweaty workout at the gym, maybe."

"If Billy Bob Thornton auctioned off a vial of his blood, some fans would cut off payments to their mothers' rest homes in order to get the bucks to place the winning bid," Polly added.

Polly bathed in the idea that many people had turned out for an opportunity to see her in person. "But if these darling fans are so eager to see Polly Pepper, why have I not been accosted by the great unwashed? We've had only one dubious encounter. I've been walking the deck for ten minutes, and no one else has asked for a selfie picture or an autograph."

At that moment, Polly saw a large group of people huddled by the outdoor tennis court. She veered off course and made her way toward the throng. "Perhaps they're giving away free samples of Ryan Seacrest," she said. The crowd was too thick for her to see what everyone was interested in, so Polly tapped the shoulder of a corpulent woman squeezed into a tight-fitting two-piece bathing suit. "What's all the excitement about, sweetums?" she asked.

The woman turned and looked blankly at Polly. "It's only Dr. Beverly Crusher!" the woman said, and instantly turned back around.

Polly tapped the woman again. "Is someone ill? Or is she demonstrating cardiovascular surgery?"

The woman saw Polly's eyes wander over her rolls of flesh. "Sheesh, lady! It's Gates McFadden, for cryin' out loud. Ya know, *Star Trek: The Next Generation*."

"So, she's not a real doctor. She just played one on TV." A smile played across Polly's face, and she turned to Tim and

Tiara. "Another celebrity on board! Thank you, Jesus! Never heard of her, but we'll have one of our own kind to share some fun times with. We'll invite her over for Lush Hour—no, she can't see my cabin. Still, she'll be thrilled that we're here too. Birds of a feather and all that."

As Polly continued strolling along the deck, she spotted another group of people taking photographs. "They should be saving their pixels for when they come to my show," she said. "Now, who on earth?" As they grew closer to the mob, Polly stepped up onto a deck chair, the better to see over the heads of the other passengers. In the very instant that she saw who was at the center of attention, she lost her balance and fell into Tim's strong arms. They both dropped their champagne glasses as Polly squealed, "You'll never believe who's here."

"Famous?" Tiara asked as she picked up the stems of the shattered flutes.

"Big star?" Tim asked.

"On parole?" Tiara added.

"Once, and not at the moment," Polly answered their questions as she whisked away shards of broken glass with the toe of her shoe. She took Tiara's glass and drained the contents. "You'll never guess."

"Hints," Tim demanded.

"Still blond after all these years."

"'Years' being the operative word?" Tiara suggested.

"Curly hair."

"Bernadette Peters?" Tim said.

"Married Hollywood royalty."

"Mia Farrow," Tiara said.

"We have the same gynecologist."

"TMI." Tim frowned.

As the trio continued their futile game, a voice emerged through the crowd. "Look what the autograph trawlers hauled in with their nets. It's everybody's favorite international legend from 20th century television, recordings, theater and now, apparently, ocean cruises. The iconic Polly Pepper! And looking better than the photo on the ship's newsletter, I might add!"

Polly, Tim, and Tiara looked up to see a familiar face squeezing through the throng of admirers. As the woman drew closer, Polly opened her arms for an embrace. "Deena Howitzer! Sweetums, your figure hardly ever shifts—much."

Deena Howitzer had appeared on a Broadway when she was fresh out of drama school and quickly landed the lead role in a television sitcom about a single mother of three daughters, trying to make ends meet. She'd raked in a fortune for the five seasons the show aired, but had pretty much faded from view and the public's consciousness afterward.

As Tim and Tiara exchanged hugs with their old acquaintance, Polly looked puzzled. "Deena, dear, you're not a celebrity stalker. What the heck are you doing on this rust bucket?"

"I wouldn't miss a freebie week on a Kool Krooz." Deena sniggered. "Hell, I'm here for the same reason you are, honey. And the same reason she's here." Deena pointed to Kate Jackson. "And him." Polly followed Deena's gaze to Bronson Pinchot. "And there's the all-grown-up Cori Berman, that little rat, but looking very sexy, I must say."

"Haven't seen him since his series *Highway to Heck.*" Tim recalled the hit sitcom on which Cori had starred in as a child before moving into a series of forgettable teen horror movie roles.

"He could have had a decent career if he hadn't been such an evil little twerp," Deena added. "It didn't help that he had a bad-boy reputation. He poked out the eye of one of his costars on *Heck,* and he got that Becky Thatcher actress pregnant when they were doing that crummy feature about Tom Sawyer and Huck Finn." Deena's eyes caught a few other famous guests on the ship. "Look over there. It's Arnie Levin and Tommy Milkwood."

"They're with me," Polly said almost apologetically. "We're the stars of this fantasy cruise for TV land couch potatoes."

"Aren't we all," Deena deadpanned.

"We? All?" Confused, Polly looked around and saw that the ship's deck was as thick with pseudo-celebrities as roaches in a Chinese restaurant's kitchen. She let out a moan and began ticking off the names of the old-timers she sort of recognized: "Is that... Jonathan Taylor Thomas? Ouch, that's Peggy Lawton—I think. That used to be Cybill Shepherd."

"No one in Hollywood, except Chevy Chase, is too old, obscure, or on trial to be hosting their own Kool Krooz shipboard event," Deena announced. "You didn't think you'd be alone, did you?"

"You've been duped," Tiara said. "Laura Crawford has seen to it that you're sailing away on a voyage of the damned."

"Oh, God, Laura Crawford is on this cruise to?" Deena realized.

"She's holed up in her cabin, afraid of fans," Tim said.

When Polly found her voice, she said, "In other words, we're on a 'has-beens' cruise. The ideal vacation for starstruck autograph hounds, and the last ship to sail toward the end of a showbiz career."

"Just look around," Tim said. "Bottom of the barrel *Dancing with the Stars*-caliber celebrities outnumber the passengers two to one!"

"I'm stuck on a ship of fools, and I'm the biggest one of them all for having trusted that duplicitous Laura Crawford!" Polly lamented.

"You're in shock," Deena said. "I know the one thing that will set things right." She looked at Tim and Tiara. "Take her arms."

Deena steered Polly to the elevator and took the car up to the Polar Bar.

As Polly and Deena played catch-up over a bottle of champagne and agreed that there were more washed-up divas and divos on this cruise than had ever appeared on *The Love Boat, Murder, She Wrote,* or at the drive-through window at Dr. Rinkle's Freeze Frame Discount Botox Center in Rancho Cucamonga combined, it became obvious that both stars had fallen on difficult times. "We're of an age," Deena explained matter-of-factly. "This is the only lousy job I've had in a year! I used to be on a pin-up poster, for crying out loud. Millions of teenage boys nailed me... to their bedroom walls, that is."

"Next port o' call. potluck dinner theater in the basement of the Church of the Born-Again Virgin," Tiara suggested.

Polly wasn't surprised that Deena's career had faltered. She was never much more than a pretty face. But she was shocked to learn that the fortune left to Deena by her late, great husband, Grand Devlin, one of the true legends from the golden age of Hollywood, had vanished.

"*Vanished* isn't quite the right word." Deena retracted her statement. "I'm a spendthrift. I admit it. I like pretty things, especially if they're young, hot, just off the bus from Omaha, a little rough around the edges, and will do anything to become a star. And I mean *anything*—like that reality show you judged last season. However, pretty things are expensive. After a while it takes more cash to keep 'em happy." Deena gave Polly a tap on the arm. "Another reason to reclaim my virginity. What about you? You're an international icon with boatloads of moola! You don't need to be here. What's your sad-sack story?"

Polly took a long swallow from her champagne flute and heaved a heavy sigh. "Sure. Boatloads," she repeated. "Well, at least oodles. Frankly, I took this gig to help out my old costar Laura..."

Deena instantly put up her two hands. "Don't even mention that shrew while I'm trying to have some fun with an old friend."

Polly took Deena's left hand and studied it for a moment. "I seriously doubt that Laura purposely cut that fingertip off," she said, recalling the tragic week that Deena was a guest star on *The Polly Pepper Playhouse.* "Laura slammed her dressing room doors on everyone from Elizabeth Taylor to Rock Hudson to Mary Martin. I'm sure that she didn't know your pinkie was in the way."

Deena shrugged. "Please! I've almost forgotten about *that* incident. I'm referring to what she did to Aaron Hanson and me."

"I remember him!" Tim smiled. "The sexy star from that dumb Disney Channel musical *Remedial Rapper.*"

"Laura Crawford came along and ruined a very beautiful thing!" Deena added.

Polly nodded, remembering the scandalous headlines. "Honey, stage mothers tend to keep an eye on their meal tickets," Polly said, referring to Aaron's parent/manager/publicist/agent, who made a public fuss about Deena's relationship with her teenage son. "But I never quite understood how Laura got involved in the first place."

Deena took an extra-long sip of champagne. "It's no secret that Aaron isn't exactly academically gifted," she began.

"With those deep dimples, he'll get all the straight A's that life has to offer," Tim said with a laugh.

"Right you are." Deena smiled. "Still, he should have known better than to let his dialogue coach take compromising pictures of him in the shower. Why wouldn't they turn up on eBay? After the dialogue coach got busted, the studio hired Laura to take his place on set. I'd already been tutoring Aaron—"

"So to speak," Polly interrupted.

"But when rumors found their way to Laura Crawford, she

raced to the rags and made a small killing selling me out. Oh, I was so ready to slice 'n dice her!"

"On that salacious note," Tim said, looking at his wristwatch, "we've gotta run. Show starts in half an hour!" He gave Polly's Zip 'n Sip alcohol package pass to the cocktail waiter, then looked at Deena. "Hope you're going to be in the audience. You can still take a shot at Laura."

Tiara smiled. "Polly Pepper meets Jerry Springer. What a hoot!"

"Nah, I'll catch her when she least expects it. One day she'll be indisposed, and I'll be right behind her. Of course, it'll never happen! I'm too old to get used to a flea-bitten mattress in San Quentin."

Deena walked out of the bar with Polly, Tim, and Tiara, and before blowing air-kisses, she said, "I know I'm on a very long wait list to take care of Laura. I'll leave it to someone with a more inventive way for doing her in than my primitive idea of slitting her throat. Ta!"

The quartet parted and walked away in opposite directions. Polly went to her theater, and Deena to the casino.

3

When Polly and her family arrived backstage at the Big Players Little Theater on the Promenade Deck, Arnie Levin and Tommy Milkwood were already waiting. Polly trilled, "Déjà vu!" as she embraced her two former costars.

"I don't see the lovely and talented Laura Crawford," Tommy Milkwood said snidely, looking at his watch and tapping his foot. "Where is that goof-off? She'd better not hold up the show just to make an entrance! She wouldn't even rehearse with us earlier."

As Polly scuttled about, peeking out through the curtains into the nearly full auditorium, she called back, "It's my fault that we didn't rehearse. A gazillion apologies. I figured we'd do the same shtick we did at UCLA last year: tell stories, let the audience ask questions, and kill 'em with funny answers. Then we run home and pop a cork."

Arnie Levin sassed, "I'm not putting up with Laura the way I used to. If she dares to step on my punch lines..."

Tommy added, "After all these decades, she still remembers the best behind-the-scenes anecdotes about our old sketches, but instead of feeding me intros, she tells the stories herself. A simple straight line to lead me in to telling about that day when all of the Polly Pepper Prancers couldn't leave the bathrooms. That story is golden. It's my story!"

"Actually, it's my story," Polly said. "What a disaster! I'm sure it's what finally killed dear ol' Fred Astaire. He never recovered from having to waltz with Laura on camera after rehearsing all week with real dancers."

"That's a perfect example of how Laura steals the spotlight," Arnie snapped.

Tommy gave Polly a hard look. "To this day, whenever I run into any of those dancers, they insist that it was Laura who spiked their salads at lunchtime."

"I hear that the plumbing in the studio's bathrooms never functioned properly again!" Arnie said.

"Every single one of those dancers still talks about wanting to die that day," Tommy continued, "but they had a stronger will to live, in order to kill Laura Crawford for depriving them of their once-in-a-lifetime opportunity to dance with the great Astaire! That little publicity putz made sure she had Fred all to herself."

"Sticks and stones!" The voice of Laura Crawford suddenly issued through the backstage area as she ambled up to her former castmates. She looked at Tommy, then at Arnie. "Stop churning up the past, for cryin' out loud. I'm a more mature person than I was when we worked together. I've learned a lot of life lessons the hard way, from watching *Oprah*. I realize now that I could sometimes be a pain in the backside for a few people. But let's start fresh. Please?"

"Absolutely! Fresh!" Polly chimed in.

Tommy and Arnie looked at Laura with contempt.

As the cast assembled and prepared for their entrance, the

stage manager asked if anyone needed something stronger than water before they stepped before the audience.

"Hey!" Laura barked. "Are you insulting Miss Pepper? The stories about her blood components being equal parts plasma and champagne are totally false!"

The stage manager held up his hands to guard himself against Laura's vitriol. "It was just an offer. No offense intended, ma'am," he said, looking at Polly.

"None taken, sweetums." Polly smiled and touched her hand to his warm cheek. "Laura was just looking out for me. Like the time she brought her entire AA meeting to Pepper Plantation, unannounced. She thought I had a problem. I had to borrow extra cans of coffee from Dean Martin across the street." Then, as an aside to the stage manager, Polly whispered, "I could use a teeny-weensy flute of anything that sparkles. Something medicinal."

The stage manager winked at her and rushed into one of the dressing rooms. He returned with a split of Andre champagne. Upon seeing the label, Polly's smile disappeared. "On second thought, I'll just have water," she said. "The audience is the only intoxication I require," she said with her famous wide smile. "On with the show!"

The stage manager lined the cast up in order of their entrances. "You'll go out boy, girl, boy, Polly," he said, placing Tommy in first position, followed by Laura and Arnie. "I'll announce your names, and one by one you each walk out with great big Kool Krooz smiles. Bow and wave to the audience. Pretend that they're your guests. You're honored to have them in your homes. Then, when I introduce Polly Pepper, join the audience in a rousing ovation. After the crowd settles down, each of you takes one of the chairs. Save the wingback in the center for Miss Pepper."

Polly looked at Tim and Tiara. "Wish me luck, dears. And swipe a bottle of Cristal from the Polar Bar for me, please!"

Suddenly, *The Polly Pepper Playhouse* theme music began to play through the speakers and the audience applauded with eager anticipation. One by one, the cast was introduced, and each moved out onto the stage. When Polly's name was announced, the theater reverberated with a standing ovation and thundering applause, and the star made her grand entrance.

After a full five minutes of blowing kisses and holding her hands to her heart and dabbing at fake tears with a Kleenex tissue, the cheers and bravas subsided. Polly sat on her throne and welcomed her admirers as well as the old cast from her classic television show.

Over the next hour, the laughs and giggles from the audience came every fifteen seconds. They had come to see and be entertained by the great Polly Pepper and were not disappointed. Only once, when Arnie Levin took off his shoe and threatened to "beat the crap out of you, Miss Laura effing Crawford," did the audience sit in silence until they erroneously decided that the appearance of hostility was a funny sketch routine.

"'Can you feel the love tonight?'" Polly sang a cappella to the crowd as Arnie chased Laura off the stage, with his shoe held high in the air. "We're just like any other family—the Roys on *Succession* come to mind." She laughed, and the audience laughed with her. Laura and Arnie eventually returned to their seats, and both stuck their tongues out at each other.

"What's a mother to do?" Polly teased as she looked at her costars and concluded her performance. She thanked the audience for their generous love and affection. "And don't forget to take me home with you!" The stage manager walked out and handed Polly the boxed set collector's edition of the most popular sketches from her legendary television series. "I'm all yours for $159.99," she said. "I also make a great gift for all occasions!"

Laura Crawford spoke out and said, "Don't forget, the supporting players always make a star look good. Buy these freakin' DVDs; we need the money!"

As the audience laughed at Laura's famous potty mouth, Polly's theme music played again, and the cast took more bows. "Come back anytime... every time," Polly called out. "We're trapped, er, staying here all week! Lucky you!"

As soon as the cast was backstage and out of sight from fans' eyes, Arnie roiled with furor at Laura. He walked up to his old costar and gave her a shove. "You miserable... no-talent... thieving... You stole my best lines! So help me, as God as my witness, the next time..."

Laura shoved Arnie back. "Your comic timing stinks like the monkey cage at the zoo on a hot day in July," she said. "You were never anything more than *third* banana, so thank me for getting you a job. I'm your meal ticket, and don't forget it!" She looked at Tommy Milkwood. "The same goes for you, you whiney little sissy. If we don't all do this show, none of us gets paid. It's in the small print in your contract. So don't think about quitting," she spat, and flounced away.

By now, Tim and Tiara were finished telling Polly how brilliant she had been and were now wondering how the performers would ever be able to get through another show together. "Never fear," Polly said. "Laura needs the money. We all do. She'll be back onstage tomorrow, even if I have to kill her and prop up her body in that chair!"

The next morning Tiara knocked on Polly's door and used the spare key card to enter her cabin. "There aren't any windows in this darn place," she said, and turned on a light. "It's ten o'clock, but you can't tell if it's day or night!"

Tim followed with a serving cart. "Is this what they mean by Kool Krooz cuisine?" he asked. "Your breakfast's been sitting outside in the corridor for God knows how long. The pancakes are cold, and the Bloody Mary is warm. The steward simply abandoned the tray."

"Perhaps he joined the suicidal geriatrics. Did he remember the Tylenol?" Polly asked as she stepped out of bed and slipped into her pink silk monogrammed bathrobe. She reached for the drink. Tiara handed her the headache tablets. "I trust you all slept better than I did," Polly moaned. "The neighbors in the stateroom next door were certainly enjoying their first night out." She gave her son a lift of her eyebrow.

Tim started to explain, "Keith and I—"

"Never mind," Polly said as she washed her Tylenol down with a large sip of her Bloody Mary. "Keith's giggles weren't the only reason I couldn't sleep. It occurred to me that I'm being taken advantage of by Laura. Again."

"D'ya think?" Tiara cracked.

"Just because Polly Pepper is supposed to be everybody's favorite legend and a good ol' sport, too, doesn't mean that I have to play the pushover!" She looked around the room. "This is where being pleasant has gotten me."

A knock on the door interrupted Polly's martyrdom. "Good God, I haven't finished my moldy breakfast, and they're here to take it away already," she complained.

Tiara opened the door and was met by two of the ship's uniformed security officers. "May we come in?" Tiara shrugged and stepped aside.

Polly continued her tirade against Laura. "Laura Crawford has used me for the last time. She was always an albatross around my neck. But it takes two to tango, so I'm fifty percent guilty."

"Guilty, Miss Pepper?"

"Another BM ASAP, sweetums," she said to the ship's representatives. "You may take away the tray and bring a double..." Polly's was suddenly more aware of the two inordinately attractive men in uniform. "You're welcome to finish off my muffin," she said seductively.

The taller and more dimpled of the two men announced, "I'm Sergeant Skyler. This is Officer Brown." They simultaneously held up ship security badges.

Tiara stepped forward and snatched the identification away from Brown, the more menacing looking of the two men. "You're obviously not here for an autograph," she said. "What's up?"

"The captain wants to see the three of you right away," Sergeant Skyler said.

Polly's look of confusion instantly turned to gaiety. "It's about time! I knew I could trust him to do the right thing about this horrid situation!"

"It doesn't get much worse," Officer Brown agreed.

"Darn tootin'!" Polly said. "Laura Crawford finally gets what she deserves!"

Sergeant Skyler looked at Polly with undisguised horror. "I know you're from Hollywood, and you're used to debauchery of every variety, but nobody deserves this!"

"It's either her or me," Polly said as she finger-combed her hair and reached for her Bloody Mary. "I may be famously pleasant, but I couldn't let that little slut get away with what she was doing."

Sergeant Skyler reached out and took away Polly's Bloody

Mary. "I don't think you should say another word until you see the captain," he admonished.

Tiara instantly stepped in between the two and wrenched Polly's BM away from Skyler. "If the star wants an innocent breakfast energy drink, you're the last person to judge where she gets her protein from," she snapped.

"Oh, I can't wait to see the look on Laura's face!" Polly giggled as she finished off her drink and handed the empty glass back to Skyler. "She'll simply drop dead when she gets what's coming to her."

The two security men looked at each other, then looked back at Polly.

"Um, I think we'd better get to the captain's quarters right away," said Sergeant Skyler.

Tim looked at Sergeant Skyler. "This isn't about Laura Crawford's stateroom, is it?" he said suspiciously.

"Not unless you count the fact that Miss Pepper's fingerprints are all over the place," Officer Brown said smugly.

"A thorough cleaning before I move in?" Polly hedged.

"Preserving potential evidence," said Officer Brown.

"Evidence?" Tim managed to say.

Polly, Tim, and Tiara each looked at each other with growing apprehension. Tiara swallowed hard. "Has there been a crime?"

"You should know. You just stated that the victim got what she deserved," Officer Brown said.

"Victim?" Polly brought a hand to her lips.

"Is Laura...?" Tiara couldn't bring herself to complete her thought.

"Yep."

"I was going to say, 'Is Laura going to miss a show or two?'"

"Same answer," Officer Brown said.

"How many?" Polly asked, remembering Laura's comment that if the entire troupe wasn't onstage, they wouldn't get paid.

"How many shows are you doing?" Skyler asked.

"Seven."

"That's your answer," he said. "Get dressed. The captain is waiting."

4

A big cruise ship is like a small town, and soon the details of Laura Crawford's death swirled like gossip and hairspray at the Clip 'n Curl beauty salon. Word quickly spread throughout the ship that Laura's body had been discovered on a massage table in the Starfish Spa. Her carotid artery had been slashed. The weapon of choice: a DVD, the edge of which had been filed to the sharpness of Sweeney Todd's razor. The bloodied title on the disc: *Season Six of—The Polly Pepper Playhouse.*

Despite being associated with the implement of execution, no one would ever suggest that the universally beloved Polly Pepper was in any way connected with, or capable of, a murder. In fact, there was an outpouring of genuine compassion for the legend in her own time/mind. As her colleague and onetime costar took up space in the crisper section of the morgue's refrigerator, strangers queued up to buy Polly as much sympathy champagne as she could swallow.

In exchange for picking up the bar tab, Polly left her fans with a souvenir sheet of damp Kleenex. It wasn't easy coaxing compassionate tears for Laura Crawford. To put on a plausible performance of grief, Polly had to dig deep into her actor's bag of tricks and retrieve genuine moments of genuine sorrow in her life: the day Karen Carpenter died... her mother spitefully throwing away her copy of *How To Become a Famous Movie Star*... the earthquake that rattled one of her Emmy Awards off the display shelf and cracked its cheap-o base. When she thought of those experiences, her eyes welled sufficiently to imitate heartache.

"You survived those two dreadful husbands and the horror of Vicki Lawrence taking *your* Emmy Award home the year that the Academy made a mistake!" said a female fan who was comforting Polly with a bottle of Piper-Heidsieck. "You'll get over this tragedy, too, sweetie."

With each new passenger telling her how sorry they were about Laura's death, and how she must be feeling the terrible loss more deeply than anyone, Polly became genuinely morose. She realized she wasn't responding appropriately to the tragedy. "Why do I have to force tears?" she complained to Tim and Tiara.

"Probably because you know that Laura Crawford was a mean-spirited harridan who used you and your fame to get ahead in her own career," Tim said. "She diminished your stardom by convincing you to perform on this has-beens cruise."

"Maybe you're not as nice as you and the whole wide world think you are," Tiara stated matter-of-factly. "A friend is dead. Murdered. It's not natural to be as unmoved as you are."

Polly was silent for a long while as she considered Tiara's words. Finally, she nodded. "What's wrong with me? Although I feel bad about how Laura died, I'm not sad that she's gone. You're right. I'm not nice!"

"That's not altogether true," Tim said, comforting his mother and handing her a flute of champagne. "You're very nice—for a diva. I'll bet Alec Baldwin and Christian Bale and Vanessa

Hudgens and Lindsay and Shannon and... well, everybody who isn't you, wishes they had your reputation. Laura Crawford pretended to be the girl next door with a Mary Tyler Moore turn-the-world-on-with-a-smile personality. You saw through her. She was a phony baloney. How many times have you told me that Laura's sole agenda in those early days on your show was to get her own variety series and to become a bigger international star than you? It's not your fault that her post-PP life was a mess. Her career stalled because she was difficult to work with. The *National Intruder* only kept her in the public eye because people got a sick giggle out of reading about her multiple divorce wrecks, and that bank-draining palimony suit filed by that lady golfer, and the stints in celebrity twelve-step basket weaving clinics."

Polly shook her head and said, "Tiara's right. I have no feelings. Subconsciously I must be holding Laura responsible for making me feel washed up in the biz." She took another sip from her glass. "I'm going to make it up to her."

"It's a little late to become girlfriends," Tiara said.

"There's nothing to make up," Tim said. "Heck, when she was really down and out, you purchased a few pieces from her art collection to help her get by. So what if you bought the Warhol, Bachardy, and Hockney at garage-sale prices? She needed the bucks, and you came through."

Polly looked at her son and Tiara. With sudden resolve, she knocked back the champagne in her flute with one long swallow. "There's still one more thing I can do for her," she said.

Tim and Tiara exchanged looks of unease. "The best thing you can do for that dead woman is to let her chill and allow the ship's police or the Coast Guard or whoever handles crimes on the high seas to do their job without your interference. Say something genuinely heartfelt about her at the beginning of your next lecture. She doesn't rate anything more than that."

Polly wasn't listening. "How does my skin look?" she asked as she opened her purse and looked at her reflection in a hand mirror. "It's been ages since I had a facial. Hear that sound?" She waited a beat. "It's my pores begging to be exfoliated. I could use a full-body massage, too. My back's been aching from sleeping on that god-awful mattress."

Tiara poured more champagne into Polly's flute. "I know what you're thinking," she said. "Drink this, and a couple more. Tim and I will rub your back and your neck and your scalp and your toes. I'll even dust your navel."

Polly reached for the telephone beside her bed and pressed o for the information operator. "The Starfish Spa, please and thank you," she said. In a moment she was making an appointment with Rosemary.

Polly hung up and looked at the two faces giving her reproachful stares. "What?" she asked. "I'm simply going in for a little R&R. While I'm trapped on this floating cemetery, I may as well enjoy the amenities."

Polly took the glass elevator from the Coral Deck to the Anemone Deck and stepped out into a quiet corridor. She followed the engraved placard that pointed to the Starfish Spa. At the frosted-glass door, she turned the knob and was instantly met with the scent of flowers and the soft plinking sound of Celtic harps. The music instantly made her miss the time she toured Ireland in *Spuds: The Musical*. And the aroma took her memory back to one particular warm spring night in the Hollywood Hills—a time when she had been deeply in lust with the chief makeup artist on her show. The air outside his home was filled with the perfume of night-blooming jasmine, and Polly now sighed as she remembered their furtive assignations and how much she missed his physical touch.

While thinking about her long-ago lover, a door to the inner sanctum opened. A young woman with short-cropped dark spiked hair and lips the shade of bubblegum reached out her hand. "It's a pleasure to meet you, Miss Pepper. My name is Rosemary Thyme. Please come in."

Polly eagerly followed Rosemary into a small room. "You're only missing parsley and sage," she joked.

"They're my middle names. It's what comes from having parents who worshiped Simon and Garfunkel."

The room was the size of Polly's tiny stateroom. A massage table was covered with a starched and ironed white sheet. The lilting music filled this room, as did the seductive floral scent, which she could now see came from glowing candles.

"Hang your clothes there." Rosemary pointed to a hanger on the back of the door. "Rings or other jewelry can go there." She pointed to the colorful abalone shell on a stand beside the massage table. "Get comfy and push this button when you're ready." Rosemary left the room and closed the door behind her.

Polly took off her clothes while looking around for any indication of Laura Crawford having been there. Disappointed that the place seemed to be evidence-free, she slipped under the sheet, which felt as though it had just come out of a warm clothes dryer.

Rosemary entered and instructed Polly to lay face down on the table, with her arms over the sides. As she rubbed warm scented oil into her palms, she said, "If I'm too rough, let me know. I'm stronger than I look. Some people like to be nearly pummeled. Others want a sensitive touch."

"The harder, the better," Polly said as Rosemary began her treatment. With every stroke of Rosemary's hands, Polly moaned in ecstasy. "I'll take you home with me."

"I'm available for adoption or foster care," Rosemary joked. After a moment of quiet, she whispered, "I trust you won't mind me telling you how much my grandparents loved you and your show."

Although her face was deep in the well of the massage table's headrest, Polly rolled her eyes. *Would another murder in the spa make any difference?* she thought.

"You can't imagine how that makes me feel," Polly managed to say. "I'm sure they're proud of you and your talents, too. You make me feel as though I've died and gone to heaven. Just like Laura Crawford. She hasn't a clue about what she's missing. Or does she? I hope that her masseuse gave my dear dead darling the special VIP treatment."

Rosemary went from the warmth of sunny Ann-Margret to the coolness of a senator under judicial questioning. "Yes, such a waste of life and talent," Rosemary said in a steely tone. "No doubt the good Lord Himself joined St. Peter in the golden welcome wagon."

Just as Rosemary was about to knead Polly's lower back, a quick rap on the door was followed by an uninvited head peeking in. "Sorry 'bout last night, hon," a female voice said to Rosemary. "That crazy Crawford creature waltzed her chubby calves into my room and expected me to evict the client I was working on. Said she was in a hurry. I knew you wouldn't mind one last customer. We all need the tips. Frankly, I'm surprised she heard me, what with her barking at her cell phone, and me giving her the bum's rush out the door. I noticed you couldn't get away quickly enough. Can't blame you! After that bloodcurdling scream, I thought someone was being murdered. Oh! Ha! I guess they were! Gotta go. Call me. Ciao!"

As the door closed, Polly lifted her head and opened one eyelid to look at Rosemary, whose face had turned red.

Rosemary explained, "That was Talia, the nosy masseuse. She loves to start gossip. Yes, Miss Crawford was my client—she screamed like someone had stuck her with a white-hot poker. After I washed her face and slathered her flaking and puffy skin with my own special revitalizing emollient, she pinched her nose as if she smelled rotting eggs and demanded to know all of the ingredients. That's when she had a major meltdown."

"Cream of fish entrails and red tide seaweed?" Polly asked.

"Garden variety hairy tree snails. Fresh from the Florida Everglades," Rosemary said. "I shell a couple of dozen of the critters, mash their gummy little bodies in the Cuisinart, add a few other secret natural ingredients to the paste, and voila! The way Miss Crawford yelled and slapped me—like she was swatting at a swarm of bees—you'd think I'd just plastered her puss with leeches! That's a whole other recipe. She was so scary that I threw her a wet towel and scrammed out of the place! That's what Talia heard and saw."

Drats! Polly thought. *A semi-plausible story!* "I'll buy a big jar of your snail pulp before I leave," Polly said and lay back down to continue her massage. "You have to understand something about Laura Crawford. She was terrified of snails."

Rosemary liberally sprinkled sea salt crystals over Polly's back, and with a circular motion of the palms of her hands, she scrubbed the top layers of the star's skin. "This will make you tingle for days," Rosemary bragged.

Although Polly wanted to completely give in to the sensual pleasure of the treatment, her thoughts were divided between snails and a killer loose on the ship. As Rosemary rearranged the sheet over Polly's body to expose her left butt cheek, Polly asked, "Doesn't a murder in this very room make you nervous about being alone with a client?" Polly felt Rosemary's hands squeeze her bottom just a bit harder than necessary as she worked her thumbs into the tender flesh.

"As a matter of fact, I am being extra careful," Rosemary said. "I'm only accepting appointments from celebrities I know. Or in your case, who my grandparents can vouch for."

Polly's buttocks involuntarily clenched.

"Sorry. Too hard?"

"You think that celebrities are incapable of murder?" Polly asked.

"Nah! I watch *E!* just like everybody else." Rosemary sniggered. "I know you all have your share of maniacs out there in La-La Land. But you guys are more likely to kill each other. Oh, and Miss Crawford got the ax in the room next door. It's been sealed until we get to port, and the police can do a thorough investigation."

For a moment, Polly felt gypped that she wasn't recreating Laura's massage experience in the same location as her demise. "What if the killer thinks you saw him... or her? Doesn't that scare you?"

Rosemary stopped and thought for a moment. "As I told the captain and the chief of security, I didn't see anything. I left the room because I felt in danger from Miss Crawford."

"Did you report the incident to anyone?"

"Not at the time. The spa was actually officially closed. I was leaving when Miss Crawford arrived. I only agreed to accept her because she tried to pull rank with one of those 'Don't you know who I used to be?' threats and said she knew people who knew people. How many times have I heard that line? Anyway, when she had her little fit about the face cream, I skipped out as fast as I could and went for a walk. And no, I didn't see anyone I knew along the way. Then I came back and found..."

Polly raised herself up on her elbow and pulled the sheet over her bosom. She looked at Rosemary. "So, you don't have an alibi. Tell me, did you smear Miss Crawford's face with that smelly junk on purpose because she was a difficult patron?"

"It's not smelly, it's not junk, and I don't need an alibi. You're insulting me."

Polly continued gazing at Rosemary, who was wiping her hands on a towel. "Of course you aren't the killer. I never thought so. But what about that Talia person? D'ya think she saw anyone who might be suspicious?"

Rosemary chuckled. "As I said, the spa was closed. The so-called 'client' that Talia was with was some rich guy. With every voyage she finds someone new to have an affair with. Cameras are everywhere, so she can't go to their rooms. It's easier to have her rendezvous here. Talia makes so much noise on her own, it's a miracle she even heard Miss Crawford scream."

Polly sat up and set her feet on the floor. She immodestly dropped the sheet as she reached for her clothes and began to dress.

Rosemary reiterated, "I swear, I had nothing to do with Miss Crawford's murder. Maybe the killer surprised their victim, and she didn't have time to make a sound."

Polly finished dressing and remembered to take her rings from the seashell. "Dear, I'm not insinuating anything about you and Laura Crawford. I just want to get my facts straight. A friend is dead and getting freezer burn down in the meat locker, and I want to know why she died and who committed the evil deed. If you say you had nothing to do with it, I totally believe you. I'll even give you an extra-large tip."

Polly handed Rosemary her key card and said, "Charge it. And add enough to buy the new boxed set of *The Polly Pepper Playhouse*. You'll make Nana's and grampa's Christmas."

5

A successful massage should have the effect of making one relaxed and lethargic. Polly, however, was ramped up as if she'd guzzled a four-pack of Red Bull with a double espresso chaser. As she strutted her way back toward her cabin, her attention was divided between recalling Talia's testimony of witnessing Rosemary running from the scene of the crime, and wondering what miracles the snail pulp cream might perform on the wrinkles under her eyes.

Could Talia be a killer? Polly wondered as she moved along the corridor. She was certainly a pushy person, popping into the massage room during a private treatment. "Utterly unprofessional and probably unethical as well," Polly muttered. "She never apologized for the interruption." Was Talia pointing a gossipy finger at Rosemary? Could the disruption have been her way of planting the seed for a theory that Rosemary was involved in the death of Laura Crawford? Perhaps she needed to deflect any thoughts of her own involvement.

Or maybe the paramour Talia was reported to have been entertaining sliced the life out of Laura. Was this supposed rich passenger also famous? God knows the ship was crawling with more bottom-of-the-barrel celebrities than the contestants on *Dancing with Chopped Liver.* Suppose Laura had recognized Mr. Moneybags when she tried to get him booted out of the salon; he might have gotten scared, especially if Mr. Wealthy knew of Laura's penchant for making extra bucks as a spy for the *National Intruder.*

As she envisioned Laura's last moments, Polly imagined her former costar settling down on the massage table, waiting for Rosemary to return, calm and collected, to finish her treatment. Perhaps the door to the massage room opened, and Laura, with her face down in the headrest, mumbled an apology for her venomous sputum. But suppose, instead of the healing touch of an understanding masseuse, the killer yanked Laura's head up by a fistful of L'Oreal *I'm worth it* tresses and then quickly and deftly drew the sharpened DVD deep into the soft flesh on Laura's neck. Although Polly hoped for a mercifully rapid demise for Laura, the images in her head triggered horror stories of eighteenth-century guillotined French nobility still blinking their eyes in shock and confusion and babbling, *"Mon dieu! Que la baisef!"* as their disembodied head dropped into a basket to the cheers of the bloodthirsty, cake-deprived citizens. Polly shuddered at the horror and closed her eyes in deep revulsion.

In that instant, she suddenly collided with another passenger who was exiting a stateroom. Polly wailed, "Sorry! My fault... Do forgive... I'm a clumsy..."

"Mother!"

Polly looked at Tim, then at the cabin number, and smiled evilly. "Cozier accommodations on this deck, sweetums? Or perhaps you're just out for a stroll. God knows both our heads have been turned by more than a few points of interest on the ship," Polly said as she continued walking toward the elevator.

Tim fell into lockstep beside his mother. "It's not what you think," he said.

"Silly boy. It's *exactly* what I think." Polly sniggered. "We've both come from a massage... in a manner of speaking. Anyway, I'm far too busy to be envious of your fun and games." She stopped and looked at her son. "Is that a bald patch I see on your crown, darling man? I think you're receding."

"Bald! What? No!" Tim protested. "I'm too young..."

Polly shrugged. "Perhaps it's time to have the Rogaine talk with your doctor."

As the pair continued along the carpeted hallway, an image in the distance suddenly caught Polly's attention. She stopped short and grabbed hold of Tim's arm. As she peered down the corridor, Tim followed her gaze.

"Tiara!" they both called out in surprise as Polly's maid and best friend closed a cabin door behind her. Tiara turned toward the voices as Polly and Tim sidled up to their friend. For an instant, she looked embarrassed. However, she quickly crossed her arms and raised an eyebrow. "As Miss Mae West said, 'To err is human, but it feels divine.'"

Back in her stateroom, Polly gave Tim and Tiara a rundown of what she'd discovered during her hour of massage therapy. "Laura's only been dead for a day and already I have three possible suspects!" she beamed.

Tiara huffed. "Get a copy of the passenger list and you'll probably find a dozen more," she said, pouring three flutes of champagne. "I've already seen Peggy Lawton, Macauley Culkin, and Jane Curtin in the gym. They're nice, but I'll wager that Laura wasn't on their Facebook friends lists."

"What about Deena Howitzer?" Tim said. "We love her to pieces, but she did threaten to kill Laura. And she wanted to do it with a knife."

"I chatted with Deena. She wasn't in mourning, but she also

had a reasonable alibi. Drinks with the captain all evening long."

Polly accepted the champagne that Tiara handed her. "My last sip. I have a show to do in an hour," she said as she lifted her glass. "I'd say Daddy Bigbucks is the most promising of my suspects."

"You don't even know he exists," Tim said. "And why would he kill someone he doesn't know? Furthermore, why do you think Talia might be a suspect? What's her motive? Even Rosemary doesn't have a good enough reason, that you know of, to hurt Laura."

Polly ignored Tim. "If I could find out who he is, the gazillionaire I mean, I'll wager that we'd be closer to solving the crime.

"By the by," Polly said, "since when do we keep secrets from each other about our carnal diversions? Who the hell were you two making whoopee with at this relatively early hour of the day?"

Tim and Tiara both exchanged smiles. "You go first," Tim said.

"No, you go first," Tiara countered.

"Ladies before gentlemen," Tim insisted.

Tiara sighed. "I swear I was minding my own business. Sort of. You know I'm a sucker for a man who—"

"Has a pulse," Polly interrupted.

"Who has musical talent!" Tiara snapped. "I was walking through the atrium this morning, on my way to Cartier to pick out what you'll be buying me for Christmas, and I was drawn to the piano player. He was cute. Played unusual chords." Tiara's thoughts drifted back to seeing the pianist dressed in a tuxedo, with a white silk handkerchief in his breast pocket. "His fingers were long. The backs of his hands were as smooth and white as the piano keys."

Tim interrupted. "Short, featherlight hair? Prematurely darkish gray and combed just so? Sort of an aristocratic face, with a deep cleft in his chin? British accent?"

"Er..." Tiara said warily.

"Lawrence Deerfield." Tim dismissed the man. "Been there."

"This time he smiled at me, not at you!" Tiara continued. "At first, I thought he was just happy to have someone pay attention to his playing. But then..."

"He played 'Love Is a Many *Splintered* Thing,'" Polly teased her maid.

"At least there's still one man alive who notices that I'm alluring," Tiara said. "And he's only one degree of separation from us. That is, he once worked with Laura Crawford. Actually, he *almost* worked with her. The witch had him fired from a production of *Follies*. According to Cute Stuff, er, I mean Lawrence, Laura couldn't memorize the songs, so she took her frustration out on her accompanist. It's been months, and he's still upset."

"Sondheim's lyrics can be a bitch," Polly agreed.

Tim chuckled. "Same thing almost happened to D'Angelo! The getting-fired part. He worked with Laura, too. Sorta."

Polly and Tiara both looked at Tim. "Beverly D'Angelo is aboard?" Polly said, excited by the prospect of seeing another old acting friend.

"No. D'Angelo Vincente. One of the deck officers. Italian." Tim smiled and winked. "It's strictly forbidden for crew and passengers to interact—in a playful way—if you get my drift, but he couldn't help himself."

"You'll corrupt the entire Kool Krooz fleet before this voyage is over." Polly nudged her son.

"D'Angelo said he learned English by watching reruns of *The Polly Pepper Playhouse* in his village. He became a huge Laura Crawford fan. When he discovered that she was on this cruise, he disregarded the rules and went to meet her in person.

He just wanted to tell her how much she meant to him as he was growing up. But she wasn't the fun-loving clown he expected. According to Mr. Modesty, when Laura got a look at him, she threw herself at his biceps. When she was satisfied, she threatened to have the captain put him out on the first iceberg that floated by."

Polly frowned. "Laura? No way, Jose. Unless he was ill equipped."

Tim shook his head. "Trust me! The problem was that he took a snapshot of her."

"One stupid picture?" Tiara said.

"A variation on Britney Spears's vagina monologue. Every star, even one with Laura Crawford's less-than-stellar place in the cosmos, knows that a salacious sexual tryst with photo-ops can be a career breaker. Laura had enough of those in her lifetime, and she wasn't about to let another opportunist sell her down the river to the *National Intruder*."

"Are you hearing each other?" Polly looked at Tiara. "Being fired from a job is one of life's most humiliating experiences. A lot of people go nuts when it happens to them. Laura Crawford got your boyfriend's tushy canned, and you said he's still holding a grudge!"

"He's not my..."

"Ding! Ding! Ding! Motive for murder!" Polly called out like a carnival barker awarding a cheap plush-toy prize. Turning to Tim, she said, "And, now that Laura's dead, your latest BFF still has a job. Bingo! Bull's-eye! Bonanza!"

"I guess death can be a good thing for some people," Tim admitted.

Polly polished off her glass of champagne and poured another. She looked at her watch. "Just a teensy taste," she said, filling the flute to the brim. "Ten whole minutes until showtime. We now have five suspects!" She reconsidered.

"Actually, we're down to your two. Mine are pathetic," Tiara exclaimed "Lawrence couldn't—"

Tim interrupted. "D'Angelo wouldn't—"

Polly said, "They're men! Make no mistake. No Y chromosome can stand a bitchy X, especially if the X humiliates the Y—or thinks she has the upper hand." Polly turned to her family and said, "Skip the show tonight. It's your duty and responsibility to get back to your respective *chromies* and suck out as much info as you can!"

Polly Pepper was used to the miasma of whispers that occurred when she entered a room. The Tsunami Grill was no different. Heads turned, and the star nodded in acknowledgment of their attention as she and her entourage walked past tables of fans. As Polly, Tim, and Tiara seated themselves near the outside deck, a waiter quickly arrived with a bottle of Moët immersed in a bucket of ice. He set three flutes on their table. "Perfect timing, sweetums!" Polly trilled, and affectionately touched the waiter's arm. "We'll need another in about ten minutes."

The three lifted their glasses to each other. "Lovely audience tonight," Polly said, "with the exception of that little pisher Cori Berman."

"Making trouble again?" Tiara said.

"What else?" Polly complained and took a long swallow of her champagne. "He made a big deal about not being able to see the entire cast from *The Polly Pepper Playhouse.* I sorta lost my PP persona and yelled out, 'One of us is dead!'" Looking at Tiara, she added, "You're supposed to vet the damn question notes before I reach into the fishbowl for the completely spontaneous and totally improvised spur-of-the-moment Q&A's."

"I had another 'mission accomplished,'" Tiara reminded her,

and set her flute down. "You should have used the cards from yesterday's appearance."

"I didn't appreciate Mr. Berman bringing up that old *Tiffany & Co. vs. Pepper lawsuit*," Polly said.

"Are you sure it was Cori who wrote that question?" Tim said. "He's probably kind of young to remember all that collection agency stuff."

Polly waved away the old problem. "Anyway, Tiffany & Co doesn't mean much anymore. They're in shopping malls, for crying out loud. I'm forever devoted to my dear Louis-François Cartier. And soon, when royalties from the new DVDs start pouring in, I'll be able to shop there again."

Suddenly, a forced whisper from behind Polly startled her and nearly made her drop her glass. "I see everything," the voice insisted as the trio instantly turned around.

"Sorry, hon, did I mess with you?" A smokey-voiced woman holding a martini glass pulled up a chair. Uninvited, she joined Polly and her crew. She reached out her hand to shake Polly's. "You probably know me as Madam Destiny. The ship's fortune-teller and clairvoyant." She shook Tim's hand and then Tiara's. "You can call me Marsha. Marsha Scott. That's the name on the measly paycheck they deign to hand me."

Marsha was one of those people who instantly made friends with strangers, and Polly was no exception. From the way Marsha carried herself, it was obvious that very little impressed her—except Polly Pepper. "As I said, I see everything that you do. On-screen, that is. Even that dreadful *Detention Rules!* musical mush you did with those slutty Miley and Vanessa clones."

Polly gave Marsha a warm smile. She clinked her flute to Marsha's martini glass. "Yeah, that was a flop waiting for financing. You'd think the nut jobs in charge of green-lighting films at Sterling Studios could tell from the damn script that no amount of preteen sex on the screen can save a story about high school football stars who sing and dance and lay the most seductive cheerleader, while being voted valedictorians too." A thought occurred to Polly. "As the kids say, 'OMG!' Since you're such a well-respected—or at least employed—clairvoyant, tell me something interesting about Laura Crawford's murder case."

"Oh, that old saw?" Marsha said. "Literally. No offense. I know that she was a friend of yours. At least an acquaintance of long standing. Madam Destiny knows a heck of a lot more about a heck of a lot of things than she ever tells any living and breathing soul. The idiots who run this fleet of rust buckets pay me to be a novelty act. If I ever revealed what I really see when my gifts kick in, I'd be fired and sent back to the phone bank at the Psychic Network. Nobody wants to hear the truth about their fate unless fame and fortune are involved."

"I know I'll have a happy ending," Polly said, and gave Marsha a friendly nudge. "We'll get you another drink. Then you can tell me all about that incredibly lucrative job that's coming my way, and name the tall, dark, and handsome stranger who is about to enter my life."

Marsha smiled as she raised her hand to attract a waiter. When the foursome were once again set up with fresh drinks, Marsha looked at Polly and said, "As a matter of fact, you are going to meet someone who will change your life."

Polly smiled. "Smart? Sexy? Sense of humor? I'm not too old for Tom Holland."

Tim choked as he accidentally inhaled champagne.

"Shush," Marsha said, glaring at Tim and taking another sip of her drink. "This is exacting work. I need to concentrate." Returning her focus to Polly, she said, "This stranger isn't the romantic type."

"Oh, good God, he's not one of Liza's ex-husbands, is he?" Polly pleaded.

"You're not that idiotic." Tiara chuckled and gave a fist bump to Tim.

Marsha was now looking past her hosts, staring into a future that only she could see. "You have a perfectly fine relationship with another man. He's a guy's guy. Likes sports. Hunting. I see a badge. Boy Scout maybe? Hmm. I saw the same thing when I did a reading for Deena Howitzer. No, the man who is soon to draw your attention is serious about you, Polly Pepper."

"Goody!" Polly enthused.

"Maybe goody, maybe just good," Madam Destiny said.

"In other words, not exactly soulmate material?" Polly said. "Another fan? I love 'em all, but I was hoping for something a little cuddlier than the pandas and koala plush toys they send me."

Marsha was silent for a long moment. "I also feel that Laura Crawford was in deep stinky doo-doo long before she died."

"It was snail paste," Polly said. "But it did have the faint smell of bad breath."

Marsha the mistic came out of her trance long enough to give Polly a condescending look and take another sip of her martini. Back in her reverie, she said, "I mean Laura Crawford did something to piss someone off."

"No kidding!" Polly, Tim, and Tiara called out in feigned incredulity.

"She knew her killer, all right. I see swimming pools and movie stars," Marsha said in a distant voice.

"Your reception is picking up *The Beverly Hillbillies,*" Tim said, and shared a chuckle with Tiara.

Marsha twisted her mouth and gave Tim an exasperated sigh. "I also see leather. And the number three is a very significant sign."

Tiara nudged Tim. "Movie stars and leather. Sounds kinky.

Like most of our friends. And some of the publicity staff at Disney."

Marsha came back to the present and took one last long sip from her glass. She looked at Polly and said, "Laura Crawford was in serious trouble. Soon you will be too."

"Worse than doing seven shows on this voyage of the damned?" Polly said.

"Laura convinced you to come along for one reason."

"What reason?"

"Ya got me," Marsha said. "But my impression is that Laura Crawford's death was retribution. She paid the ultimate price for double-crossing the wrong person."

Tiara huffed. "Oh, dandy. That could be anyone she ever met!"

"My vision's gotten fuzzy," Marsha said as she stood, a little unsteady on her feet. She held on to the back of Polly's chair and looked at the star. "Doris Day used to get puppies left at her doorstep. You get dead people. It's a gift that you'll just have to live with." Marsha turned and slowly wended her way through the maze of tables.

Polly watched as the ship's clairvoyant left the room. "A drunk psychic," she said. "Not a very reliable source for eyewitness news from the future!"

6

Polly turned her attention back to her champagne and grumbled, "I'll bet that I can read distant signs on a dark and foggy road more clearly than Madam Motor-mouth can see what's around the corner of life... and death. What good is being tuned in to the future if it isn't in HD?"

Tim added, "Ms. Black Magic Woman said it herself. She's a novelty act."

"Accent on the word *act*," Polly said. She looked at Tim. "Hard physical evidence trumps ephemeral psychic symbols any day. And speaking of... evidence, any luck with your amore, Dan Jell-O?"

"D'Angelo," Tim corrected.

"That's what I meant. And please keep any vivid descriptions of romantic tidal waves rolling in your stateroom to yourself—at least until we need to scare off your grandmother the next time she begs to move in with us," Polly said.

"Hard evidence—not so much," Tim said. "However..." Tim scanned the lounge to determine if anyone looked suspiciously like Marlee Matlin, prepared to read his lips, and hand-sign the private conversation to the *National Intruder*. He leaned in toward his mother and Tiara. "Three strikes," Tim whispered.

Polly's smile faded. "TMI, sweetums."

Tim rolled his eyes. "I meant D'Angelo got a third and final demerit for fraternizing with a guest—no, not me. Laura Crawford called the captain and blew the whistle on her little afternoon delight. D'Angelo explained that the company has a semi-zero tolerance policy for a lot of things and sleeping with a guest and/or photographing them in the nude—although indecent photography isn't specifically in the employee handbook—are biggies. His contract was going to be terminated as soon as we dock in Juneau."

"Going to be?" Tiara said.

"Dead passengers don't complain much," Tim said. "The captain figures since Laura expired, so does her grievance. D'Angelo told me he always knew he'd never be fired."

Polly took another sip from her champagne glass and pondered D'Angelo's confidence. "He sees the future too, eh? Anyone so reckless with the company rules, and who thinks that he's untouchable by the HR department just because he's pretty, is either a narcissist, deluded, or has friends in high places to protect him. Or maybe his superhero good looks come with superhero powers to demolecularize problem passengers."

Tim shook his head. "People who resemble a Renaissance statue come to life get away with murder."

"Precisely!" Polly said a little too loudly and slapped the tabletop to punctuate her pronouncement.

"I was being facetious," Tim said.

As other passengers looked in Polly's direction, Tiara said, "Mr. Tim isn't suggesting literal murder. Heck, if I had a dollar for every time you said you were going to *kill* your agent, JJ, I'd be able to bail out Washington."

"Maybe so," Polly said. "But with all due respect to dear

Sophia Loren and Sofia Coppola, as well as Armani, Cavalli, Fendi, Gucci, Prada, and Versace, this Dan Cello fellow *is,* after all, Italian. Those people are infamous for dealing with others who rat on them."

Tim and Tiara gave Polly condescending stares. *"Those* people?" Tim derided.

"Be careful of cultural generalizations," Tiara warned. "You don't want a repeat of that Tony Bianchi situation."

Polly rolled her eyes as she remembered a Saturday afternoon, years ago, at Sonny Bono's Palm Springs hacienda. "All I did was quote some long-dead famous wit."

Tim had heard the story a gazillion times and recited, "'Scratch the surface of any actor...'"

"'... and you'll find an *actress.*'" Tiara completed the quote.

Tim and Tiara joined Polly's laughter. "That doesn't go down too well when you're in the company of a paranoid, lunatic macho stud screen legend who thinks everyone is talking about him and can't take a joke," Tim said. "I thought ol' Tony was going to knock you in the pool!"

"For a supposed tough guy, he was such a sissy," Polly said of *The Blob* star. "Everyone else at the party had a sense of humor —even my dear, sweet, dead-too-soon *Brady Bunch* dad."

"Loved him," Tim and Tiara sang together.

"Me thinks that Mr. Bianchi doth protested too much," Polly said. "Even his name reeked of West Hollywood!" Tim poured his mother and himself another glass of champagne. "D'Angelo is certainly a man of mystery," Tim said.

"All the really sexy ones are," Tiara agreed.

"But a killer? Hardly," Tim said as he pinched his mother's cheek. "However, just for you, and for the sake of investigating every inch of D'Angelo, I'll become his best bud—at least for the week. It's certainly my pleasure!"

Polly patted Tim's hand and offered a sly smile. "You're a

trouper—and so unselfish." She turned to Tiara. "You, on the other hand, are a both-feet-on-the-ground adult, and when it comes to matters of love and lust, I know I can count on you to—"

"Nuh-uh! Not this time!" Tiara instantly countered. "I know what you're going to suggest. I won't become a spy. The man who tickles my ivories, er, plays the eighty-eights, isn't anywhere close to being a natural-born killer! So what if he's held a grudge against Laura? Who hasn't? Her picture on the bathroom mirror in his cabin means nothing!"

"Laura's picture is up in his cabin?" Polly said eagerly.

"He gave her devil's horns and a mustache and blacked out her front teeth." Tiara giggled.

Tim chuckled. "When I designed Garry Windsor's last big party, his personal assistant told me that one of the important rules at the house is that whenever Garry returns from his *Gold on Ice* figure skating tours with that Austrian harridan, Helga Bruder, a fresh photo of Helga has to be on his dartboard. He'd love to kill her, but of course he wouldn't."

"See! Defaced pictures mean zilch," Tiara said.

"Polly Pepper never judges anyone lest she herself be judged," the star said. "I'm simply suggesting that both of your new friends have had unpleasant encounters with Laura Crawford, and both have semi-plausible motives to eliminate her. I want you both to keep an open mind about your paramours. Let your beaux spill their guts and get confessions out of 'em!"

"The only confession I want from my Lawrence is that he can't—as the song says—smile without me," Tiara said. "If I play my cards right, he might take me away from Hollywood. I'd kill to have a normal life!"

Polly took a small sip from her glass and gave Tiara a serious look. "Darling. Honey. Look around. This ship is ground zero for *normal*. Would you really consider giving up being one degree of separation from Jennifer Aniston's latest mating mash-up? She needs your double chocolate fudge brownies whenever she gets dumped. And what about all those fab invites to Ellen's and Portia's parties? You'd miss those for sure. And what about the fun of getting firsthand and completely unethical but totally reliable trashy dish from Dr. Hooper?"

"Only the really dumb stars still go to that scurrilous shrink," Tim said. "But the stories about Rob and Julia and Ben and Adam are too bizarre not to be true! He's more fun than *Access Hollywood, E!* and *TMZ* all rolled into one gossip convention."

"You couldn't give up living at Pepper Plantation either," Polly continued. "Or having Barry Manilow over for drinks at Lush Hour and playing Texas Hold'em with Wanda Sykes twice a month. Could you conceive of a life in which a manufactured Disney vacation satisfied your spirit of adventure?"

Tiara hesitated. "I once knew someone who was normal."

"Once is quite enough, dear."

"She seemed happy," Tiara continued. "Mary worked for an insurance company. She had a two-bedroom, one-and-a-half-bath townhouse in downtown Detroit."

"What good is half a bathroom?" Polly pooh-poohed.

"She married her fitness trainer... even though he had a wandering eye..."

Polly screeched, "The bum!"

"No. He really had an eye that wandered all over the place," Tiara corrected. "You'd talk to the man and couldn't be sure that he wasn't looking over your shoulder or at your chest or at a bit of something lodged in your teeth. His left eyeball just sorta randomly moved, like a glob of that stuff in lava lamps."

Tim crossed his arms over his chest and shook his head. "I hate to say it, but Polly's right. You wouldn't last a week if we reintroduced you back into the wild. You've lived among eccentrics for too long. You're one of us now."

Polly clicked her tongue. "Everyone thinks that beds are warmer on the other side of Beverly Hills. Trust me, that's only because *normal* people are bored with their lives. They use sex and drugs and porn and these pseudo-celebrity cruises for escapism from dreary jobs and kids they may love but don't necessarily like. They'd kill to be in your shoes as much as you think you'd kill to be in theirs."

Tiara rolled her eyes, then stopped a waitress who was passing by with a tray of smoked oysters. "We'll take those off your hands, dear," she said.

Tim said, "'Normal' people don't like smoked oysters!"

Tiara looked at Polly, whose vacant eyes now seemed to be staring into the abyss of Madam Destiny's domain.

"Daydreaming about a shipload of suspects?" Tiara asked after she'd swallowed two oysters.

Tim waved his hand in front of his mother before she blinked and returned to the moment. Polly suddenly bolted upright, picked up her champagne glass, and knocked back the remaining bubbly. With a river of adrenaline gushing through her system, she gloated, "I'm brilliant! I should get one of those Genius Awards! I've been waiting for an amazing idea to come to me, and it just did! I know where to get the name of the killer!"

In the next moment, Polly and her troupe were racing out of the lounge and tearing along the Upper Promenade Deck to the glass elevators. As Polly impatiently jabbed at the call button, Tiara nervously tapped a foot, and Tim cracked his knuckles. "You'd think this was the Sears Tower instead of a fourteen-story ship," Polly complained, impatient for the elevator to arrive. Soon, the doors parted. They smiled to conceal their irritation as they waited for the packed car of ancient passengers to shuffle out and argue about whether or not they were on the correct deck.

"You're an idiot," said one old woman to a man who was probably her husband.

"It's this way."

"You're turned around."

"I have a sixth sense."

"It's called dementia."

Just as another old man with more liver spots on his bald head than bruises on an overripe banana peel convinced his partner that indeed they had gotten off too early, Polly, Tim, and Tiara slipped into the glass box and frantically pushed the button to close the door. One of the women in the group tried to step back inside. "What goes down must come back up. Like heartburn," Polly trilled as she nudged the lady out and pushed away the flailing arms of a dozen octopuses trying to keep the door from closing. The others looked on with dumbstruck faces as the door panels slipped across the threshold and cut them off from Polly.

Swiftly dropping to the main deck, Polly, Tim, and Tiara exited past another queue of withered old-timers eager to ride up to the casino or dining rooms. Polly's son and maid were in lockstep behind the star as she flew past the Armani, Cartier, Dolce & Gabbana, Ferragamo, and Montblanc boutiques. Ordinarily, each of these shops would have lured Polly away from whatever appointment to which she might have been en route. But not this time. Halfway down the main concourse, Polly came to an abrupt halt in front of the All Bound Up bookstore. "This is it," she said.

There, in the display window, was a giant poster of the famous Hirschfeld caricature of Polly with her exaggerated large eyes and lashes and prominent overbite. Below the poster was a pyramid of boxed sets of *The Polly Pepper Playhouse* collector's edition DVDs. Polly smiled.

As they entered the store, Polly instantly spied a young woman wearing the uniform of a ship's employees. The girl was leaning her elbows on the counter as she read a book. Polly sized up the clerk and figured she looked nerdy enough to perhaps have been friendless as a kid, and therefore might have had time to watch reruns of *The Polly Pepper Playhouse* instead of being chased by boys. Polly placed her hands on her hips, tilted her head to a forty-degree angle, smiled brightly, and cheerfully called out in her well-known Polly Pepper falsetto, "I'm hee-eere!"

The startled employee recoiled. When she recovered, she

instantly recognized Polly. "Oh, my stars! It's... um, you... from the DVD box! Wow! Your hair really is that color! Does Bozo think you copied him?"

Despite her annoyance, Polly maintained her famous and infectious smile and moved into the store. She reached out to shake the young woman's hand. "I'm a terrible guest on this adorable little boat of yours. I should have dropped by sooner to introduce myself. I'm Polly Pepper, of course."

"Tiffany-Amber. Of course."

"Is Tiffany-Amber responsible for taking such good care of my babies?" Polly pointed to the large display of DVDs. "They look dusted and as fresh as the day they came out of the factory."

"They don't require much care and feeding," said Tiffany-Amber. "Anyway, nobody touches 'em. In fact, we've just slashed the price. Again. You'd think there'd be at least a little interest. 'Specially since that star who got sliced and diced in the spa is—or was—on the ship."

Tim and Tiara simultaneously reached out to steady Polly.

"You'll think I'm an empty-headed, vain, and ego-driven legend, but I'm simply dying to know who is gobbling up my precious body of work," Polly said.

"As I said, the fish aren't biting." Tiffany-Amber closed her copy of *Killer Cruise* that she was reading.

"Still, I must thank each and every person who purchased my collection. They'll naturally want my autograph, for sure," Polly said. "Would you be an incredible doll and provide me with a list of all the passengers whose journey I'm helping to make extra special by their selecting this amazing and historic bit of television memorabilia?"

Tiffany-Amber paused. "Gee. Um. Cashless cruising is how it works on board, so we probably have a record of the sales. But I think passengers' purchases are, like, confidential or something. Like ATM PIN numbers or sins you confess to a priest."

Polly surreptitiously nudged Tim. He reached out to Tiffany-Amber and introduced himself. Instantly, his blue eyes, deep dimples, and warm smile cleaved Tiffany-Amber's rapidly pounding heart. "Hey ya," he said in his most seductive voice. "Listen. Here's a grand scheme. Mom—Polly Pepper, I mean—is giving an intimate private cocktail soiree before her show this afternoon in the Lusitania Lounge," he lied. "Just a bunch of used-to-be-semi-famous and now totally forgotten has-beens hanging out and wondering what happened to their lives and careers. It'd be cool to be with someone like you to keep me from slitting my wrists when they start counting who had the most guest appearances on *The Love Boat.*"

Tim had Tiffany-Amber's heart at first drool. Not only did she eagerly accept the invitation, but she decided that she could indeed call up an inventory of purchases from the store's database. In moments she accessed an Excel spreadsheet on which the names of every passenger who purchased Polly's DVD collection were entered. She printed out a copy and handed it to Tim, who folded the paper and gave Tiffany-Amber a warm smile and a thank-you that practically melted her plastic name badge.

Tiffany-Amber reluctantly took her eyes off Tim for a moment and looked at Polly. "You won't get writer's cramp signing from this list. If you start now, I'll bet you finish before the flavor's gone from my gum." She snapped a wad of Bazooka.

"I'll give it my best shot," Polly said, trying to suppress her irritation at both Tiffany-Amber and the four thousand plus passengers' apparent lack of interest in buying her DVD collection. As the trio left the store, Tim backed out slowly, smiling and maintaining eye contact with Tiffany-Amber. As he blasted her with enough megavolts of sexual energy to keep her awake with an all-night fever, Polly teased her son. "Heartbreaker!"

"Every girl needs a platonic BFF." Tim smiled.

Soon, the trio was back in Polly's cabin, and Tim was unfolding the passenger information. Looking at the short list, Polly's eyes instantly went to the column on the far right-hand side and shouted, "$59.99?! The bonus booklet alone, with never-before-published photos of me with Cher and Bette and Rock and Barbra, should cost more than that!"

When she finished being indignant, Polly focused on the names listed on the sheet. She called out, "One. Two. Three. Bingo! Look at that. The last name on the list."

"Lawrence Deerfield!" Tim said.

Tiara grabbed the piece of paper and looked at the name. Her heart sank. "The date of purchase was the day we set sail," she said. "I will not believe that a man who finds me desirable is Laura Crawford's murderer!"

"Maybe you're next!" Polly said. "What if this nut job is a celebrity serial killer?"

"Lawrence is not a nut job. And I'm not a celebrity."

"You're practically radiant with my reflected glory!"

"Any radiation from me is the stored-up heat of finally canoodling with an attractive and talented man!"

Tim wrapped his arms around Tiara. "Heck, even the other two names here don't mean anything—yet. They could all simply be people with the sophisticated sense to own Polly's classic shows."

"Sophisticated? On this boat?"

"I'm going to the captain!" Polly announced.

"Why?" Tim said.

"There's a killer on the loose!"

"He knows that."

"But he doesn't know who committed the crime!"

"Neither do you!"

"It's probably Lawrence Deerfield."

"Probably?" Tim countered.

"Where's your evidence?" Tiara added. "A defaced photo of Laura? A piano accompanist who said he didn't much care for Laura Crawford because she was responsible for getting him fired from a job? A purchase of DVDs at the bookstore? Unless you find something in Lawrence's cabin with Laura's blood or DNA on it, you'd better think twice about potential slander."

"I'll bet he saw Laura and then flipped out," Polly said. "He's at the piano. Laura Crawford walks by and doesn't acknowledge his playing—like most everyone else. It's another insult from her. He decides that the ship is too small for the two of them. Anticipating being afloat for a full week with the shrew in close proximity was way too much for him to handle.

"Under a spell of animosity, he planned the best way to get rid of his nemesis. He considered throwing her overboard. But cameras are everywhere. He'd have been videotaped and quickly arrested. He's been on this ship long enough to know that there aren't any cameras in the spa. Oh, and to make the murder especially symbolic—like the Zodiac Killer—he bought the DVDs specifically to slash her with a disc on which she appeared."

Tim said, "Your ideas are farfetched, to say the least. For one thing, he's playing piano almost nonstop."

"I presume he takes a potty break."

"He would have had to know that Laura was going to the spa, and that her masseuse would walk out during the treatment."

"Not a stretch since she alienates everyone. Guessing that the masseuse might quit is an easy one."

"You're getting mental," Tim said.

"I'm being intuitive." Polly tapped a finger to her temple.

"You mentioned cameras," Tiara said. "They're everywhere.

If Lawrence was performing in any of the lounges or the atrium, we could match the time that Laura was killed with any time that he may have left his keyboard to take a murder break. We'll be able to definitively prove if Lawrence was working during the time that security thinks that Laura was rubbed out. Let's see those tapes. I want him exonerated!"

Polly looked at the other passenger names on the list. "Sarah Stratton. Rachel Lashton. First, let's find these other passengers and see how many reasons they had to knock off Laura Crawford."

Locating Sarah and Rachel was not as simple as calling for them at their respective cabin doors. Neither was in her room.

"The casino!" Polly declared. "They're probably blowing what's left of their paychecks or some pitiful government stimulus cash." The trio raced to the Promenade Deck and entered the ship's gambling parlor. Colorful neon strobes swept the room. Revolving red and blue police cruiser lights on top of slot machines cast an eerie glow. The miasma from hundreds of ringtones announcing gaming winners, as well as dour-faced poker players and scantily clad cocktail waitresses bearing trays of watered-down drinks, instantly put Polly in mind of the time she performed her nightclub act in Las Vegas. "It's like the Sahara," she said.

"It's more like bingo night in the basement of St. Alfredo's in Norwalk," Tiara charged.

"Remember when I used to do two weeks a year on the Strip?" Polly said. "God, they paid a fortune. Fifty grand a week! Now only Bette and Cher and Barry get the big bucks. Maybe I should think about reviving the old act. I'll talk to JJ."

Tim looked at Tiara with eyes that said, "Let her have her fantasy." He then looked at Polly. "How do you propose to find these two trees in this forest? You don't even know what these Sarah and Rachel people look like."

"They're fans. They'll find me," she said. Just then, an elderly woman and her thin-as-a-pipe-cleaner husband shuffled up to her. "Sarah or Rachel?" Polly asked.

The woman grimaced. "We just want to tell you how much we loved your show when you were on the television."

"Sweet, adorable fans. Thank you!" Polly gushed.

"When are you coming back?"

"I'd love—"

"Do you still talk to Ethel and Fred?"

Polly gave the woman a momentary look of puzzlement. "Every Memorial Day. And Lucy and Ricky, too. I'm the other legend. The one with the famous musical/comedy variety show —syndicated in forty-two countries and now available on DVD with special commentary by Liza and Barbra and even Michelle O. And me, of course."

The Gumby doll husband gave his wife a look of exasperation. "I told you it was Dinah Shore!" he said and shuffled away toward the ringing slot machines.

Just then, a shapely cocktail waitress in a black skirt and a brocade keyhole bustier, bearing a tray of drinks, approached the trio. She smiled at Polly. "I couldn't help overhearing those two passengers," she said. "I hope you weren't offended by their lack of knowing that they were speaking with the iconic Polly Pepper."

Polly beamed at the waitress. "They were sweet to think that I might be Lucy or Dinah."

"Although you'd have to be a ghost." The waitress laughed.

Polly was instantly smitten with the woman. "We'd love some bubbles," she said, and paused to look for the server's name badge.

"Michelle Most. No name tag tonight. I'm new in the casino."

"Well, Michelle, we're all very happy to meet you."

The cocktail waitress smiled. "I, for one, am very excited that you're in my casino." She turned to the other two. "You must be Tim, the legendary Beverly Hills party planner." She reached out to shake his hand, then turned to Tiara. "And you're Polly's best friend. I read the *National Intruder* when I'm in line at the store." Michelle looked at Polly. "My mother wanted me to be you when I grew up."

Polly reached out and touched Michelle's smooth cheek. "I hear that a lot. There's only one me, but you're a beautiful young woman, and I'm sure your mother loves you even though you aren't a household name. I'll send her an email and rave about how well you perform delivering three flutes of Cristal to us. Nice and cold, please?"

Michelle laughed. "You're much nicer than that rude and mean-spirited Laura Crawford."

"Not really," Tiara said. "If her awesomeness doesn't have a taste of something bubbly soon, you'll see."

"Coming right up," the cocktail waitress said with a smile. "In the meantime, here's a free one-hundred-dollar gambling card. Take a seat at one of the slots and win a fortune. I'll be back in a jiff."

Polly looked at the card. "Let's give it a shot," she said, and wandered over to a computerized poker machine. She sat on a stool in front of a multicolored, blinking screen. Tim showed his mother where to insert the card and how to start the game. As icons of playing cards appeared on the touch screen, and she tapped at the images, she started to hear the electronic sounds of invisible coins proclaiming that she was winning. Soon, Polly looked at the tally on the screen to see how much she was raking in. She giggled; then she slipped into a zone of complete concentration.

When Michelle returned with champagne for the trio, Polly showed zero interest. She was glued to the electronic poker game and screamed with delight every time she won a hand and heard the coins and saw that her free one hundred dollars had transformed into three hundred, then four hundred, and five hundred dollars.

"Quit while you're ahead!" Tiara begged. "You tell her, Michelle. She'll end up losing everything."

"It's my job to make sure our guests have fun," the waitress said with a smile. "Keep tapping those cards on the screen, honey!"

Tim could hardly believe his mother's good fortune. "Beginner's luck," he said, and swallowed a good portion of his champagne.

Polly shushed him and Tiara. "Now look what you've done! You've broken the spell. You jinxed my winning streak!" Polly's hundreds of dollars soon drained into twenties; then, finally, she was broke. She looked at Michelle. "Good times and bum times, eh? I'll take that drink now."

Michelle handed Polly a flute. "The important thing is that you had fun. After all, it was a freebie. It's not as if you really lost anything."

"I never know when to stop when I'm having a good time," Polly admitted. She reconsidered what had just happened. "Actually, it's a good thing that I lost when I did. We didn't come here to play. We're looking for a couple of fans."

Michelle looked around the cavernous room. "You'll find more than a few in here, I'm sure. At least the ones who are over fifty and don't confuse you with Shirley Jones."

"Two specific fans," Polly said. "Maybe you can help us. I haven't a clue what they look like, and they may not even be in the casino. But their names are Sarah Stratton and Rachel Lashton."

Michelle shrugged. "They could be anywhere. It's a big ship. The fastest way to find 'em would be to page their names."

"Duh!" Tiara said. "Why didn't we think of that?"

"Just tell me where you want to meet these two, and I'll make the call," Michelle offered.

Polly looked at Tim. "The Blue Dolphin Bar?"

Tim nodded.

"You got it," Michelle said, and scurried away. Soon the trio heard the names of the two passengers they were seeking. When the waitress returned, Polly raised her glass to Michelle and drank what was left of her bubbly. "By the by," she said, "what time did Laura Crawford visit the casino on her last night alive?"

Michelle shrugged.

"But you said she was rude and mean-spirited," Tiara reminded her.

"I used to be the hostess at the Tsunami Grill," Michelle said. "Miss Crawford came to the restaurant, but she wasn't scheduled for the first dinner seating, and we were booked solid. She got angry when I suggested that she'd have to wait at least an hour or that she could get a fast bite at the Starlight Bistro. She threatened to call my supervisor. I did the unpardonable. I told her she was welcome to do so. I even dialed the phone and handed it to her. I wasn't in the best of moods that night."

Polly frowned. "You got into trouble?"

"As I said, I *used* to be the hostess. My supervisor relieved me of my duties, and I collected a demerit. As I walked away, Miss Crawford gave me a look that I'll never forget. It said, 'You're a nobody, and don't let anyone tell you otherwise.'"

Tiara shook her head. "The truth is, at this stage in her career, *she* was the nobody!"

"In Laura's defense, her ego was incredibly fragile," Tim said. "She needed to be treated like a star. Of course, she had no right to behave as she did toward you, but that's how she convinced herself that she was important. She looked down on anyone who wasn't in show business."

Michelle nodded. "But I really didn't appreciate being

dressed down in public, especially since my mother was in the dining room and witnessed the whole scene. It was humiliating. I was miffed that my boss offered the same resolution to the problem as I did, but she accepted his suggestion to seat her with another group. She just wanted to throw her weight around."

"Is there any way to know with whom she dined that evening?" Polly asked.

"Talk to the maître d'. His name is Marco. I'll bet he remembers Slaughtered Crawford... oh, sorry... as vividly as I do."

Polly embraced Michelle and promised to return before the end of the voyage. "If my two fans don't show up, I'll have another go at the poker machine later tonight," she said, and left the dark cave of the casino.

Sotto voce to Tim and Tiara, Polly said, "Don't discount a waitress who has a grievance."

8

As Polly, Tim, and Tiara raced toward the elevator, Tim asked, "How could you have remained friends all these years with someone whom everyone else despised? Even strangers disliked her. You're judged by the company you keep."

Without breaking her pace, Polly said, "Laura Crawford and I were *never* friends. Colleagues, yes. How many times do I have to repeat this story? It's all in that horrid and ridiculous unauthorized biography."

"*Pickled Polly Pepper*," Tiara said.

"The one thing that moron writer got right was that hiring Laura was your first father's fault. I got the little squirt in a package deal. I should have known at the time that she weaseled her way into my show via your father's pants zipper."

Polly continued her brisk pace along the corridor. "It goes all the way back to the time when we were casting the show. Mr. Pepper #1 insisted that I needed to have someone younger and edgier, and of course sexier—but he wouldn't say it—to spar with on the program. He said it would make me stand out more and give me an opportunity to show the public how generous I was to new and less talented performers. I thought that was why we hired guest stars, like Valerie Bertinelli."

When the trio arrived at the elevators, Tiara shook her head and tsked, "The politics of Hollywood. Laura Crawford brought a negative vibration to the set of *The Polly Pepper Playhouse*. She helped kill off your calamitous first marriage. Yet, because the ratings were high, and audiences got a kick out of her, you let the diva walk all over the place as though she were the Taylor Swift of the Sterling Studios lot. Did anyone ever sneeze as loudly?"

"Only Jay Leno," Polly said, and pushed the call button for the elevator car. "Mr. Pepper #1 was right about me looking saintlier next to her. The public loved me more than ever."

Remembering what the sleazy celebrity biographer had written in his book about Polly, Tim quoted from memory, "'Only Polly Pepper has fans as ardent—and demented—as dear dead Elvis.'"

When the elevator arrived, the trio stepped inside and offered paper smiles to the other passengers. They remained silent until they reached deck six and stepped out into the corridor. Tiara added, "Yeah, and that nasty book revealed that a lot of fan mail had to be sent to the FBI. Remember the one who offered to rip Laura's vulva out through her nose?"

Polly nodded. "And that lovely man in Iowa who wrote to say that he'd invite Laura to his pig farm and accidentally on purpose knock her into his bottomless manure pit. People can be so darn sweet!"

Tiara said to Tim, "The fact is, whenever the *National Intruder* cooked up stories about Polly's and Laura's supposed catfights, the ratings zoomed. When they fingered your first father for having an affair with Laura, Polly got another Emmy."

Polly stopped in her tracks. "There was no connection!"

"I'm not saying that you didn't deserve to win that year, but Lana Turner was totally convincing as Ethel Rosenberg in that Hallmark special *Fried*. The electrocution scene was so convincing, I swear I could smell her burning flesh!"

Polly lifted an eyebrow. "Are you insinuating..."

"That the Academy doles out sympathy Emmys?" Tiara said. "Is there another explanation for why Kirstie Alley took home Bette Midler's Emmy for *Gypsy?*"

As they continued down the corridor, the raucous sound of drunks floated out to meet them. "God, I hope we're not seeing those two killers in a sports bar!" Polly complained as they arrived at their destination. To Polly's relief, the revelry was coming from a table behind which a banner announced HAPPY 70th ANNIVERSARY! A very old couple looked dazed and nearly catatonic as they sat hunched over plates of barely touched cake and melting ice cream.

Tiara pushed Polly toward the group. "Make their day."

Polly strolled up to the table and was greeted with immediate recognition and awe by the younger—although still old by anyone's standards—members of the party. She smiled at the honorees and said, "Such a long marriage! You must be the only people left on earth who were around when Edison invented the light bulb!" Polly spied a glass of champagne. She picked it up, took a long swallow, and made a face. Raising the glass in the direction of the anniversary couple, she said, "A wise woman once said, 'The first time you marry for love. The second time, for money.' I hope you've got plenty of dough, because neither of you is in any shape to start over again."

The entire bar erupted with gales of laughter. Spoken by anyone else, the words might have been considered caustic and insulting. But Polly Pepper had a way of letting the targets of her jests know that everyone was in on the silly and innocent fun, and that no offense was ever intended. She kissed the elderly couple on their foreheads. "Bravo! Brava! Toodles!" she said before turning around and seeing Tim and Tiara seated at a table with two women who were probably about Polly's own age, but who appeared older and certainly less well cared for.

Tim stood up when his mother arrived. "Miss Polly Pepper," he said, "may I introduce Ms. Sarah Stratton and Ms. Rachel Lashton."

Both women had radiant smiles and reached out to shake Polly's hand. "I was thrilled beyond my wildest dreams when you paged me!" Sarah Stratton gushed. "The Lord made this my lucky day!"

"It's *my* lucky day!" Polly countered. "Lord knows."

"Imagine, being invited for drinks with the famous Polly Pepper! Is this the prize I receive for getting sixty-five percent on the *Days of Our Lives* trivia contest?" Rachel Lashton said.

"I'm the winner. And good for you for knowing your *DOOL* trivia—sort of!" said Polly. "Pop quiz. Bo told Hope about his latest psychic vision. True or false?"

"Um..."

"EJ is the only one who saw Sami kissing the former body-guard, Rafe!"

"Er..."

"Never mind. I prefer *General Hospital*." Polly raised her hand to get the attention of a cocktail waitress passing by. "We'll have a bottle of something cold and bubbly and expensive. *Tout de suite, por favor,* sweetums."

Tiara looked at Polly. "Are you sure the ship company is picking up the tab?"

Polly dismissed Tiara's concern. While she waited for her champagne to arrive, she made small talk with Sarah and Rachel about the fun time she was having on this Kool Krooz.

Both women were quickly revealed to be movie star fanatics and had booked reservations on this cruise a year in advance. "This is my annual vacation," Sarah said. "I've already seen Andrew McCarthy, Ally Sheedy, Tom Wopat, Joyce DeWitt and that dead actress from your old show!"

Not to be outdone, Rachel added, "I saw Justine Bateman in the pool, and Soleil Moon Frye was walking around without bodyguards, just like an ordinary everyday person. Oh, and I hear that Dr. Ruth and Tina Yothers are aboard! I saw Laura Crawford, too."

"Before, during, or after her spa treatment?" Polly asked.

"But the biggest star, by far, is you, Polly Pepper!" Rachel said, ignoring Polly's query.

When the cocktail waitress returned, she set five champagne flutes on the table and uncorked a bottle that was nesting in a bucket of ice. "Barbara Eden and Craig T. Nelson were on the last cruise," the waitress said.

Tiara knitted her eyebrows and gave her a look.

"But it's true, Polly Pepper is the biggest name we've had in quite some time." She looked at Tiara again. "Okay. The biggest name *ever*. Jeez."

The waitress then poured champagne into each of their flutes. Polly was first and didn't wait for the others to be served. She drank her full glass, then held it out for a refill.

When at last they all had been served, Polly raised her flute and offered a toast. "To new friends, and to the one dear person missing from this amazing moment, my darling former costar and very close confidante and trusted friend, Laura Crawford."

"The *National Intruder* said that you two couldn't stand each other," Sarah said between sips of champagne. "I didn't like her because you didn't like her. That's how much of a fan of yours I am!"

"Laura was easy for some to dislike—perhaps even to wish a

Hollywood death similar to that Phil Spector victim, Lana Clarkson," Polly said. "Poor baby. Even I know not to clean a shotgun with my tongue, especially one belonging to that wig-wearing freak-o music producer."

"Also, the *Intruder* said that Laura had a potty mouth," Sarah continued. "As a good Christian, I don't know if I could ever invite her into my home. My friends wouldn't understand."

"You'll never have that problem," Tiara said with an edge to her voice.

"Good Lord, the *Intruder*!" Polly said. "I make it a personal policy to never read a word in that trashy rag. Unless someone gives me a heads-up to something flattering written about me."

"I'm with you," Rachel echoed.

"I try to keep a clean mind and not judge others," Polly said.

"We're exactly alike," Rachel added.

"Yes, Laura and I may have had teensy differences from time to time—all friends do—but she was extremely important to me and to the success of our show," Polly said.

"It wouldn't have been the same without her," Rachel agreed.

Sarah added, "I'm just like both of you, I never judge others —unless they're heathens. I was behind Laura Crawford in the check-in line at the dock, and the way she treated the embarkation agent when he wouldn't give her a cabin upgrade was very disappointing."

Rachel waited for Polly's response.

"I'll bet she got the upgrade." Polly glanced at Tim and Tiara.

"Of course," Sarah said. "I overheard her say that *you* were trading staterooms with her. But isn't that just like the Polly Pepper everybody knows and loves?"

"Absolutely, the Polly that we all know and love," Rachel gushed.

"She surely didn't learn manners from you," Sarah continued.

"No manners," Rachel parroted.

"When she stepped back and crushed my foot, she gave me a look as if it were my fault I was in her way. I thought, somebody needs to be taught a lesson," Sarah said.

Polly perked up. "A lesson? Oh, for sure. A darn good one, too. She had to be taught right from wrong. What did you have in mind? Something she'd never forget. One that would make Laura Crawford realize that she'd stepped on the wrong toes, and you weren't a pushover! Maybe a threatening letter sent to her cabin? No, she'd tear it to shreds and forget about it. Something more memorable. A kick in the shins? How 'bout an old-fashioned slap on her behind? Nah. Those wouldn't do the trick either. You'd have to really show her you wouldn't be treated like a nobody just because she once was a somebody!"

Tim shot his mother a withering look.

Sarah, who was now two glasses into a champagne high, gave Polly an evil smile. "You're reading my thoughts. Of course, the Devil got into me and gave me some ideas!"

Polly reached out and tenderly touched Sarah's wrist and sang, "'Jesus loves you, this you know, for the Bible tells you so.'"

"Damn right. And I'm not responsible for what happens when that cunning fiend Lucifer monkeys around with my righteous heart..."

"... and tiny brain," Tiara whispered.

Polly's attention was undivided. Sarah, too, seemed to be drifting into a daze of clouded memory. "I prayed on this for a long while after Laura Crawford stepped all over me in public," Sarah continued. "But I know from experience that when I encounter Beelzebub's instrument of evil, it's my duty to do the Lord's work here on Earth. So, I... I..."

"You wanted to confront Laura about her behavior even though she was a famous TV star." Polly filled in the blank.

Sarah gave Polly a vacant look. "Wouldn't you?"

Polly said, "Having made a decision to teach her a lesson—er —cast out the demon hiding inside her, you frantically searched the whole ship for Laura and finally found her in the spa. You reminded her that we're living in the end times and that if she continued to treat little people like the dirt under her fingernails, she'd never be raptured up to Heaven. But you, being a true savior, could rescue her soul by destroying the evil spirit right then and there and thus set her free get into Heaven!"

Sarah forced a small smile and coughed out a weak, "Ha, ha. Sorry, but I guess I'm overly tired or have had too much champagne, 'cause I don't have a clue about what you just said."

Rachel looked at Sarah. "You have no sense of humor!" she said. "Polly Pepper is a laugh riot! Let me translate Hollywood humor. She's explaining how you killed Laura Crawford. Funny, huh?"

"It's my guess that Laura Crawford also taunted you in the spa," Polly continued. "She said that you were a mad, deranged, unhinged, a mental wacko. Am I right? And you stood in the little massage room, with the gentle sounds of harps and falling water and flickering candles and decided to pull the plug on her twisted wreckage of a person. So, you opened your *Polly Pepper Playhouse* boxed DVDs collector's edition and swiped the edge of a disc across her throat. Job done! World peace restored. St. Peter sending another soul on an eternal vacation to the Lake of Fire."

"My demon can beat up your demon, eh?" Tiara said to Sarah.

Sarah was dumbfounded.

"Demons come. Demons go. Here today, gone tomorrow—or the day we set sail," Polly continued. "So many others would have killed for the opportunity to do what you did. You stalked your prey. Confronted the devil. Then you succeeded where that adorable and sexy and totally hypocritical evangelist Ted Haggard failed. He only wanted drugs and male prostitutes.

Your sin actually has a great big commandment. Thou shalt not..."

Sarah grew wildly indignant. "Sins? The Lord took 'em all away at Calvary!"

"Convenient," Tiara sassed.

"Oh, shut up, heathen!" Sarah exploded at Tiara. Many in the bar looked in the direction of Polly's table. Sarah bellowed, "Laura Crawford got just what she deserved! She was a lousy singer, too. Her acting wasn't much better, but that hardly matters when she treated me with disdain. Miserable people like Laura have to be eliminated. I'm only sorry that I wasn't the Lord's chosen one to do something about her.

"I'd better go," Sarah said, scooting her chair back and rising. "I'll tell my husband that I had drinks, er, I'd better say a Coke, with the famous Polly Pepper. He'll think another demon has gotten sucked into me. It happens a lot. Actually, maybe it's best that I forget we ever had this meeting." Sarah shook Polly's hand. "It's been... informative," she said, and nodded to the others.

As Sarah started to walk away, she hesitated for a moment and then turned back to Polly. "I know that you Hollywood people worship that golden graven image of the false god Oscar, but I won't stand by as you blaspheme the Church of the Righteous Sinners, the one *true* religion. I don't mind being in your funny story about how Laura Crawford died—bless her damned soul—but I wouldn't want a joke like that to get around. You know how people talk, especially on the internet. If Pastor Deuteronomy hears such a tall tale, he and the church elders might keep me from coming back again on next year's Kool Krooz. And—heaven forbid—our church bulletin will suggest every Christian boycott your DVD collection. We were successful in obliterating ticket sales of *Tomb Raider,* so you know our power."

"Somehow I doubt that your congregation alone moved that flick out of theaters so quickly," Tiara teased.

After Sarah had finally disappeared out the door, Rachel took a long swallow of her drink and looked straight into Polly's eyes. "What did we *really* do for the *privilege* of having drinks with America's... um, the world's... most famous television star from the old days?" she asked.

Polly disliked being reminded that no one under the age of forty had probably ever heard of her television program. "I simply wanted to get to know a few people who I'm told appreciated my program enough to purchase the all-new boxed set collector's edition DVDs of *The Polly Pepper Playhouse*," she said. "You were just two out of hundreds who bought the new compilation here on the ship, so I wanted to autograph your discs."

Rachel, having imbibed an impressive amount of champagne, said, "I think you're full of it. So did Sarah, but she's too much of a wimp to say so. Sure, I crack up whenever I see you as Bedpan Bertha. Oh, the things you, as Bertha, used to do to poor Bill Bixby, Sherman Hemsley, Ralph Macchio, and all the other stars! Performing a pap smear on Tom Selleck was a classic laugh riot. But I think you're nuts if you really think that Sarah had something to do with Laura Crawford's death. Granted, I don't know her. But I know her type. Needs a pack of parishioners behind her before she'll commit to anything dastardly. She's sheep and needs a dog nipping at her hind legs."

"They're all on your new DVDs. The Bedpan Bertha sketches, I mean," Polly said.

"I think you're investigating the death of your so-called friend, and we're somehow suspects," Rachel continued. "Like I said, I read the *Intruder*. So, I know that you hang out with dead people and find out who made 'em that way. Just don't think for a fraction of a second that I had anything to do with anybody's death. I don't know about that Sarah chick—she is sorta possessed. As a matter of fact, I don't even have your DVDs, so you don't need to sign 'em for me."

Polly looked at Tim, who took out the Excel sheet that Tiffany-Amber had provided and unfolded the paper. "According to the sales report, you purchased *The Polly Pepper Playhouse* special collector's edition the day before yesterday."

Rachel made a face and snatched the paper out of Tim's hand. She looked at the names and turned the sheet over. "Hundreds of people?" Rachel sniggered at the short list.

Without missing a beat, Polly said, "I didn't want to carry around all seventy-five pages filled with names, dear. I won't have time to thank everybody the way I wanted to express my appreciation to you and Sarah."

Rachel gave Polly a quizzical look and took another sip from her champagne glass. "The truth is a guy came into the book store while I was there. He didn't have his Kool Krooz Swelltime Pass for shopping. He asked if I would charge it to my account, and he'd give me the $59.99 plus tax. I was just doing a good deed for another passenger."

Polly gave Rachel a wide, insincere smile. "Then he's the next customer on my list of passengers to whom I must give a great big Polly Pepper hello and autograph. What's his name?"

Rachel shrugged. "Sorta cute looking. Maybe a little tough acting."

Tim leaned in toward Rachel and said, "Neil Patrick Harris cute? Or Mark Harmon cute and tough acting?"

Rachel returned Tim's smile. "We're on the same page, sugar. This one was Colin Firth extreme."

"And you didn't get his name?" Tiara marveled.

Rachel shook her head. "I've been kicking myself ever since! I figured I'd see him around and then guilt him into buying me a drink. You know the game. I did him a favor; now it's his turn to repay. But I haven't seen him anywhere. Maybe he's spending all his time watching those darn DVDs."

"That's the only logical explanation!" Polly said. "But in the meantime, I'm keeping my eyes on Miss Vacation Bible School. Something tells me there's a serpent missing from the garden, and she knows where it's slithered to."

9

A s Polly and her posse left the lounge, they wandered to the glass elevator in the center atrium. Soon, they found themselves walking without purpose along the vast expanse of the outside Lido Deck. It was late. The air was crisp and breezy. Despite the hour and cool temperature, laughing couples were enjoying the Jacuzzi. A few other romantics were enfolded in each other's arms. "That puts me in a mood." Polly sighed as she and her team strolled passed another canoodling couple.

Polly looked at Tiara. "You have Mr. Piano Man," she said. She looked at Tim. "And you have Mr. Danger-glow. Don't ever let me go on a romantic cruise again unless I'm with Randy or a reasonable facsimile of Mr. Right."

Tim hugged himself against the cold air. "You and Randy aren't married, or even engaged. There's nothing wrong with you making a new friend—just for this week."

Polly harrumphed.

"A Kool Krooz is not elegant enough for your mama to find anyone suitable to hang with," Tiara agreed. "God knows she can't be seen sitting alone at a bar in the Coral Lounge. The *Intruder* would love a shot of that! That only leaves a one-in-a-bajillion chance encounter with an eligible man in the library or at the bingo parlor or the shuffleboard playoffs. The good ones don't play old folks' games, and they bring their own books. So, it's a lost cause."

Tim briskly rubbed his arms for warmth. "When I see D'Angelo tonight, I'll get the skinny on who's single and available. You do the same when you meet up with Lawrence," he said to Tiara.

Polly shook her head. "I can take care of myself. The only man I want is whichever of your boys killed Laura Crawford. Just hand him over to me in the morning!" Polly turned around and started back toward the warmth of the inside deck. "Get on with your love lives! And play safe!" she said to Tim and Tiara. "I'm going to my stateroom. And don't call me before nine unless you've got someone handcuffed."

"You mean with a signed and notarized statement of guilt in hand!" Tim said and gave his mother a kiss on her left cheek.

Tiara gave her a tight hug. "Sleep well," she called back to Polly as she and Tim bolted toward the glass elevator and their respective assignations.

Polly shook her head. "Who needs it? I've had my fair share." She gracefully walked along the carpeted floor to the center atrium. At the railing that overlooked all the decks, she peered down ten stories to the sparkling mirror-tiled grand piano on a platform stage. Soon the music stopped, and although she couldn't see well enough from her distance, she knew it was Tiara who closed the keyboard cover and guided her new friend off the small stage. "I guess that's a wrap," she said, and started to walk away.

"Rotten timing," said a voice from a man she hadn't noticed leaning against the balcony beside her. Polly turned and did an imperceptible double take. He was slightly taller than she, probably in his early sixties, and wore his gray hair in youthful but not immature short spikes. He smart-looking navy-blue sport coat, floral necktie, and khaki trousers. "I was going to cap off the night with a drink in the piano bar," he said.

Polly smiled as she instantly absorbed the bright white teeth behind the man's own wide smile, as well as his rimless glasses, and smooth facial skin. "There's always the Carpathia Lounge," Polly offered. "That is if you're into Gershwin, Rodgers and Hart, Porter, Coward and a smattering of the Beatles."

"Toss in a bit of Dusty Springfield, a pinch of Petula Clark, and a dash of Carly Simon, and I'm a very happy man." He held out his hand to shake. "I'm Dorian."

Polly accepted Dorian's hand. "I spoke at Dusty's funeral. So sad," she said.

After a moment in which the two absorbed each other with their eyes, Dorian said, "Let's hit the Carpathia."

"The Germans already did that."

Dorian uttered an involuntary laugh at Polly's quick wit. "A drink and a memorial toast to dead singers we've loved and lost. That may take us to dawn."

"Dawn, as in Tony Orlando *and...*"

In a fraction of an instant, a thousand thoughts about not accepting candy from strangers and never picking up hitch-hikers raced through Polly's mind. However, none of the warnings were persuasive enough to outweigh the allure of a glass of champagne with a friendly gentleman and listening to what she called "real music." The fact that Dorian got Polly's joke about the RMS *Carpathia* cinched the deal.

When Tim and Tiara knocked on Polly's stateroom door the next morning, the usual call to *"entrez vous"* didn't come. After a few more knuckles to the door, and a long gulp of coffee from a stainless-steel carafe sitting on the corridor floor, Tim used the spare keycard to enter Polly's cabin. In the pitch-blackness of the stateroom, Tiara felt along the wall for the light switch by the door. When the room was visible, she and Tim saw Polly in bed, lying in repose on her back. Her pink silk monogrammed sleep mask covered her eyes.

"It's Evita Peron in her glass coffin," Tiara cracked. "How the heck can anyone sleep as long as she does?"

"It's in the family genes. I'd still be in the sack if you hadn't barged in on me..."

"... and D'Angelo!"

"You should have arrived sooner. He's in deep doo-doo for missing his five o'clock call. I need more java."

Tiara looked at her watch. "It's way past breakfast time in the dining room, and you mom's dead to the world."

"Undead," Polly moaned, but did not move.

Tim sprang to life beside Polly's bed, channeling his inner mad scientist with "It's alive!" Although he sounded more like Dr. Frank-N-Furter than Gene Wilder. He gave Polly's hand a dramatic life and drop, as if testing gravity for the first time. "What's the scoop? Late-night bingo marathon?"

"Or did Henry Winkler swing by for a Happy Days reboot in your cabin?" Tiara quipped, eyebrows dancing.

Tim, not to be outdone, ventured, "Nah. Polly would be more likely to go for Richard Dean Anderson. I think he's actually on board."

Polly remained silent.

That's when Tim and Tiara shared a look, a gasp, and a synchronized "Oh, my God!" that could have won them an award for best dramatic ensemble.

"You two were the ones pushing for me to mingle," Polly restored, her voice flat as day-old Prosecco.

"Spill it," Tim demanded. "Who's the mystery man? The hot deck officer? Not one of the chorus boys from *Ha-Ha, Hollywood*!"

"Has to be someone with stripes," Tiara decided. "The captain, perhaps," she presumed hoping that Polly's suitor was nothing less than ship royalty.

Polly lifted the sleep mask from over one eye and squinted at the bright light in the room. "Which chorus boy?" she asked Tim.

"Never mind. What's going on?" he begged for facts.

Polly groaned as she sat up in bed and adjusted the pillows behind her back. "Obviously, I'm not going to get any sleep with you two bloggers waiting for a news headline." She looked at an uncorked bottle of champagne in the ice bucket. "Anything left in there?" she asked.

Tiara poured what little remained of the previous night's champagne into a water glass and handed it to Polly. "I'll call room service."

After a sip of what was now essentially fancy vinegar, Polly handed the glass back to Tiara. She sighed. "Yes, I met someone. Yes, he seems nice. Yes, I stayed up late. But let's keep this PG. The night was a chat-fest more than *The Bachelor*. At least as far as I can remember. Anyway, you two probably had a much hotter time."

"As a matter of fact—" Tim started to say.

"Things are interesting..." Tiara interrupted him. As she picked up the telephone to call room service, she added, "Lawrence—the piano man—has many talents. But he can't let go of Laura Crawford denting his ego. Get over it. The woman's dead, for crying out loud!"

Tim nodded in agreement. "D'Angelo is everything a shipboard fling should be, except... he spent more time telling me Laura got what she deserved instead of giving me what I deserved. I need..."

"... a security blankie." Polly chuckled. "Poor baby. You should have hung around with me a while longer last night. Like

Forrest Gump's chocolate box, you never know what you're going to find on a cruise ship."

"And a large pot of coffee, please," Tiara completed her room service order.

"Whatever happened would *not* have happened if we'd hung out with you," Tim said. "And you haven't answered our question. Who?"

Polly was now as animated as a fairy-tale princess awaking from a deep sleep and finding that the ogre had turned into Ryan Reynolds. She crossed her legs Indian-style on her bed and welcomed Tim and Tiara to sit closer to her. "He's just a guy," she said.

"Cute?" Tim asked.

"As cute as sixty- *ish* can be, I guess." Polly sniggered. "I'm sure he was more attractive forty years ago!"

"Rich?" Tiara asked.

Polly shrugged. "There was an air."

"Gigolo," Tim suggested.

"We seem to like a lot of the same things."

"Your Facebook page doesn't hold back many secrets," Tim continued. "Don't get me wrong. I'm thrilled that you finally met someone on this floating crime scene, but you've gotta be wary of good-looking, single men of a certain age. Does he wear a mustache?"

"No."

"Drats!" Tim said. "There goes my image of a greaseball slime bucket."

A sudden knock on the door sliced through the conversation. "Champagne and coffee. That was fast!" Tiara declared approvingly, as she greeted a steward flashing a friendly grin.

"Found this lurking outside your lair," the steward quipped depositing a tray on a small table and handing her an envelope addressed to **P.P.**

Tiara gave Tim the universal sign for 'cough up a tip for our smiling courier.'

Polly, with all the anticipation of a contestant on a game show, tore into the envelope. Inside, a note that read like a line from a noir films said, "You're as warm as Laura is cold." She flicked the cryptic message Tim's way with a puzzled from. "Timmy, since when did your lives turn into a crossword puzzle?"

Tim, squinting at the note, recited the ominous line. Tiara snatched the paper, her gears turning. "This is it, Polly! It's a clue hotter than a jalapeno. Someone's playing cat and mouse, and I think you're about to pounce. Maybe it *is* Lawrence Deerfield. As I was starting to say earlier, his obsession with how poorly Laura Crawford treated him is really weird. If only he didn't cuddle so well. And speaking of boxes—we weren't, but I'm changing the subject—I found the special deluxe edition boxed set of DVDs in his cabin. Guess which disc is missing? Number six! I peeked. He might be your match for murder. Just let me have a couple more nights before you have him arrested."

Tim made a face and shook his head. "I was going to say the same thing about D'Angelo. Talk about being neurotic over Laura Crawford. The guy is amazing in—"

"Save it for Grandma," Polly reminded her son.

"But my gosh, I want to hear about how adorable *I* am, not all the lascivious things he did to convince Laura Crawford to drop her formal complaint against him."

Polly looked at her son and maid and held up the note. "So, is this a threat or an indication that I'm close to solving the crime?"

"Maybe it's from your new boy toy, er grandfather joy," Tiara said. "How warm did the two of you become last night?"

"Nah. If the note came from Dorian, he'd have signed it," Polly said.

"Dorian?" Tim and Tiara chuckled in unison.

Polly laughed too. "Some parents can be mean. Imagine going through life with a name like Dorian... or Poindexter or Kal-el or Puma or Moon Unit? We had a set of twins in school named Tamara and NotTamara. Mr. Polly Pepper #1 insisted on Tim for your name because the experts at the time said that a one-syllable name was very masculine."

"Joke's on him!" Tiara teased.

Tim gave her a playful shove. "But seriously, an anonymous note is not something to take lightly."

"I don't see anything sinister about this one," Polly quipped. "Whoever sent it is probably a fan who is simply expressing what everyone knows that I'm a warm human being."

"Or maybe the writer knows who killed Laura Crawford and wants you to know that you're on the right track," Tiara added.

"But I'm not on the right track," Polly complained. "Other than your two beaux, I haven't a clue who knocked off Laura Crawford. I don't think it's Rosemary from the spa. However, I'd still like to talk to the client that Talia was supposedly massaging. I want to corroborate that at the time of the murder, she was with Daddy Warbucks, as she claims."

Polly stepped out of bed and slipped into her bathrobe. "Meet me on the upper Tundra Deck in an hour."

"Shouldn't you get some sleep?" Tim asked.

"I'm too wound up. I've gotta find out who wrote this note and have the captain arrest Lawrence Deerfield." She looked at Tim. "And perhaps *your* cutie too. So much to do!"

"One more night?" Tiara begged.

"And give him an opportunity to do to *you* what he did to Laura? Forget it!" Polly said. "If Lawrence suspects that you looked at his DVDs, it won't take him long to realize that you know he's missing the murder weapon!"

Tiara sighed. "Why is there something seductive about bad boys?"

As Polly scooted her son and maid toward the cabin door, she said to Tim, "Which chorus boy from *Ha-Ha, Hollywood*?"

Tim shook his head and gave his mother a kiss on her forehead. "Tundra. One hour."

10

"So sorry I'm tardy," Polly enthused as she arrived ten minutes later than expected at the appointed place on the Tundra Deck. "Ali MacGraw cornered me by the animal balloon exhibition for kiddies. She wanted my opinion about a *Love Story* sequel, and should she reunite with Ryan.

"I laughed too quickly and had to explain that dear Ryan has gone to the big screening room in the sky. I have to learn to keep my big mouth shut because I then spent another five minutes apologizing for quoting someone who said, 'Age mellows some men. Others it makes more rotten.' I swear I wasn't talking about Ryan or anyone in particular. But dear Ali wasn't buying it. I had to accidentally on purpose pop the dachshund balloon she was wearing on her head to escape."

Tiara waved away Polly's excuse. "Tim and I have some unsettling news. There's no one named Dorian on the ship."

"We checked at the information desk," Tim said. "Did you get the guy's last name?"

Polly looked confused. "That's embarrassing. I spent the entire evening calling him Dorian. Maybe he was just being a gentleman by not correcting me. Where on earth did I come up with Dorian? Maybe it rhymes with another name."

Tim shook his head. "Tried that. Victorian. Kerkorian. Even Ecuadorian. Nobody on this cruise has a name similar to Dorian."

"I'm sure there's a simple explanation," Polly said. "We're having drinks after the show. I'll come right out and apologize. Or demand clarification."

"We'll join you," Tiara insisted. "And don't put up a fuss; otherwise, you're not going at all!"

"Yes, Mother," Polly said. "In the meantime, I've given a lot of thought to the fact that Lawrence purchased my DVD collection on the day we sailed, and you say he's missing the disc of season six. Can you get me into his cabin? We need to find more evidence before going to the captain."

Tiara smiled and withdrew a key card from her blouse pocket. "He gave it to me. Thought I might want to surprise him one night. First, let's make sure he's on duty. He should be at the piano in the atrium."

The trio returned to the inside deck and raced to the Promenade Deck railing overlooking the wide atrium. There, ten floors below, was Lawrence Deerfield playing *Memory* from *Cats*. "Yep, we're safe. Let's get to his cabin, fast," Tiara said.

Accommodations for the ship's entertainers and staff were far below the other passengers on what was affectionately called the Derriere Deck. It was barely more suitable than a slave hold. When Tiara inserted the key card and opened the door, Polly looked at the cramped space and said, "Eww. There's not enough room for the two of you."

"You'd be surprised how little space two people need." Tiara smiled. "Plus, when I'm here, I'm not paying attention to the size... of the room. There!" She pointed to the small built-in table below the wall-mounted television. *"The Polly Pepper Play-*

house deluxe collector's edition boxed set sitting out in plain sight."

Polly picked up the box and withdrew the jewel cases in which the discs were stored. "Got him! Disc six *is* missing!"

"Careful of fingerprints!" Tim said as he plucked a tissue from a box on the floor by the bed and used it to open a drawer in the desk/makeup table. "A Bible. Pens. Passport. *Chitty Chitty Gang Bang* porn DVD." He closed the drawer and opened the closet, which was crammed with clothes. Pushing aside the hangers, he checked the shelf behind the shirts and pants. He retrieved a shoebox and removed the lid. "Disposable camera. A bunch of cocktail napkins with names of women and their cabin numbers. What's this?"

Tim set the box down on the bed and took out a theater program. "*Follies.*" He read the title aloud. "Rancho Grande Arts Festival. Isn't this the place where Lawrence got fired? Laura had him canned." Flipping through the pages, he came to a bio of Laura Crawford. Her picture had been defaced with inky black eyes, scars, and devil's horns. "I thought she was fired too."

Polly looked at the program. "Small theaters often print these things in advance of the performances." She looked further and found a paper insert. "'The role of Carlotta Campion will be played by Tracey Edison.' That was supposed to be Laura's role. Why would Lawrence keep this?"

"What's that on the back?" Tim said, noticing something written by hand.

Polly turned the page over. "Names to call LC." Polly went down the list. "Oh my! Can't say that word aloud. Or that one. Or that one!" She handed the paper to Tim, who raised an eyebrow and passed the paper to Tiara. "Where have I heard those words before?" she gloated. "Ah, yes. Through a certain adjoining stateroom wall. Apparently, they're also terms of endearment!"

"Let's just hurry and get out of here." Tim panicked.

"Not until we have more evidence." Polly frowned. "A missing DVD and a few naughty words about Laura Crawford are far from sufficient to nail this guy!"

Tiara's eye spotted something on the floor next to the overflowing wastebasket. "Looks like the housekeeping staff doesn't get around to cleaning up after the ship's performers." She picked up a pincushion that looked like a miniature plush toy of Laura Crawford. She pushed a finger into its rotund belly and made a squawking noise out of the side of her mouth. "A grown man playing with dollies?" Tiara said sarcastically. She dropped the toy to where she found it.

Tim bent down to pick it up again. "Pins! In its neck! Except for this one in the back." He withdrew the pin that held a folded fortune-cookie-size bit of paper. He unfolded the paper and read, "LC."

"A voodoo doll!" Polly announced.

Tim said, "LC equals Laura Crawford! All the pins are in her neck, which is where she was attacked."

"The initials could also refer to Lynda Carter," Tiara said, trying to find a way not to implicate her new friend.

"I'm willing to bet this is the evidence we need," Polly said triumphantly, and placed the pincushion in her purse. "Let's get out of here! Take the DVDs and *Follies* program. I've got the scary black magic doll."

As the trio exited the cabin, they looked up and down the corridor for anyone who might see them. With the coast clear, they raced to the elevators and punched the Up button with repeated jabs. Finally, the car arrived, and the three stepped in. "To the bridge!" Polly insisted. Tim pushed the button for the navigation deck. Without speaking to each other, they all had the same thought. *We've got ourselves a killer!*

Security on the navigation deck was as tight as a nuclear-power-generating station. The instant that Polly stepped from the elevator car, two ship's officers blocked her way and insisted that she and her party return to an unrestricted area.

Instantly morphing into her queen-of-television mode, Polly gave the officers her most effulgent and endearing smile. "Silly me. I know that I should have made a reservation. But it's urgent that I see the captain." After a moment of explaining that she had information about the murder of Laura Crawford, one of the officers unhooked a walkie-talkie from his belt loop and radioed the captain. In a moment, a third officer arrived and escorted Polly, Tim, and Tiara through a series of locked portals. Finally, they were ushered into a small conference room. "Captain Sheridan will be with you shortly."

"Do you think we're doing the right thing?" Tim asked. "I mean, we don't have a confession. We don't even have real proof."

Polly frowned. "What do you call a missing DVD, the same one used to kill Laura Crawford? And the voodoo doll? And the *Follies* program with all those expletives about Laura? I think we have more than enough to drag Lawrence Deerfield's skinny butt into a cell and charge him with murder."

Just then the door opened, and Captain Sheridan stepped into the room with another officer, who was bearing a digital voice recorder and a manila folder labeled **CRAWFORD, LAURA A.** "Please be seated," Captain Sheridan said. "Miss Pepper, I understand that you have information about Laura Crawford's killer?"

"Indeedy, I do!" Polly stood up and began to pace. "I'm sorry to be the one to tell you this, dear Captain, but one of your very own cruise entertainers is Laura Crawford's killer. The piano player, Lawrence Deerfield. He slashed Laura Crawford's neck in the spa on the night of May tenth, our first night at sea."

Captain Sheridan nodded. "Evidence?" he asked.

"For one thing, he purchased my DVD collection the day we

sailed. It's been established that the weapon used was disc number six. Deerfield has the collection, and that disc is missing! Also, I found this in his cabin." Polly held out the pincushion and handed it to the captain. "Notice the location of all the pins except the one in the back. Read what's pinned there."

Captain Sheridan did as instructed and raised an eyebrow when he saw the initials LC.

"Finally, there's this theater program from a show that Laura Crawford was supposed to do with Lawrence, but she had him fired. He's held hostile intent ever since. Look at the back. He even spells out how much he hated Laura's guts. I'm too much of a lady to have those words in my virginal vocabulary, but I've been in show business most of my life, so I know their definitions."

The captain swallowed hard and shook his head. "There's nothing I can do."

Polly was shocked. "You'll let a killer go free? I'm practically handing the murderer to you on a silver platter, and you're ignoring it? If you look at the fingerprints on the DVD used in the killing of Laura Crawford, and match them against Mr. Deerfield's, I'm certain you'll find that they're the same."

"That's a job for Homeland Security when we reach Juneau," Captain Sheridan said. "In the meantime, I cannot slander a member of staff with allegations. You have nothing substantive!"

It wasn't often that Polly Pepper publicly displayed any other side of her personality than what fans expected: sweet, down-to-earth, and lovable. However, this time her façade cracked. She looked the captain straight in the eyes, placed the palms of her hands on the table, and leaned her weight into her arms. "I'm not used to anyone saying *no* to me. I've been a star since you were playing with boats in the bathtub. When I want something, I get it. And I want you to arrest Lawrence Deerfield for the heinous crime of murdering my friend Laura Crawford. I don't want excuses. I want action. And I want it now!"

Captain Sheridan stood up to his full height of six feet four inches. He towered over Polly. "Would you like to be confined to your stateroom for the duration of this voyage? That's easily arranged. If I hear one more unsubstantiated accusation about one of my crew or passengers, I will have zero hesitation about posting a guard outside your door twenty-four seven."

Polly backed down. "I know my rights. Freedom of speech being one of them."

"You're in international waters, Miss Pepper," the captain said. "I make the laws on this ship."

Polly switched back to Polly Pepper mode and said, "Shall I see you at the captain's table for dinner one night?"

Polly and company were escorted not only back to the elevator, but to their respective cabins. After a half hour of pacing her own room and trying to decide her next move, Polly called Tim and Tiara and instructed them to meet her in the casino. When they were all together, Polly sought out Michelle, the cocktail waitress.

"Honey," she said when Michelle came into view, "I need a teensy favor."

"Anything for you, Ms. Pepper." Michelle smiled.

"You were such a help the other night when you summoned those two fans of mine to the lounge. Would you do that again? This time, if you would make an announcement that the legendary Polly Pepper is hosting a 'Who Murdered Laura Crawford?' party in the atrium in five minutes, and the entire shipload of passengers and crew is invited, I'd appreciate it so much."

"You've caught the killer?" Michelle asked with excitement in her eyes.

"I will as soon as you make the announcement."

"Right away!"

Tim and Tiara were both feeling more than a little trepidation at what Polly was about to do. But Polly wouldn't place her own reputation and integrity in jeopardy by making a false accusation. They figured she must know something that they didn't quite realize yet. They both shrugged in resignation and followed Polly to the atrium.

Soon, Polly, Tim, and Tiara heard the announcement calling for everyone aboard the ship to visit the atrium for a once-in-a-lifetime program featuring the iconic Polly Pepper as she announced who killed her former costar.

As crowds gathered, Tiara looked at Lawrence, who had stopped playing the piano. "What's up?" he asked. "Does Polly really know who murdered Laura Crawford?"

"She thinks so. But I can't believe it and sincerely hope it's not true."

"I guess we'll all sleep better tonight knowing that the killer has been caught," Lawrence said with a bit of unease in his voice. "Although I wasn't expecting to sleep." He chuckled seductively.

When the atrium was filled to capacity, Polly climbed up to the platform stage and pulled the microphone out from its stand on Lawrence's piano. She offered her perfect movie-star smile and welcomed her fellow passengers, all of whom she said she hoped to become intimately acquainted with during the remainder of the cruise.

"As you all know, my dear friend Laura Crawford was brutally attacked and murdered on our first day at sea," Polly began. "I couldn't let her killer go free. I simply had to find the person who did this terrible thing to her." Polly looked up and saw that Captain Sheridan had joined the group with a team of ship security personnel.

"It gives me no pleasure to make this announcement,

because the killer is someone we all know and admire. His talent is delicious. He seems so adorable and sweet on the outside..."

"It must be Cori Berman," a voice called from the crowd. It was Cori himself who made the announcement.

Polly regrouped. "That would be nice and easy, but a little too obvious. No, the person who killed Laura is..."

The atrium began buzzing during her pause. "Who is she talking about? Is this another game created by the cruise director?"

At last, Polly turned and looked directly at Lawrence. "It's this man!" She pointed. "Lawrence Deerfield. Our wonderful piano player!"

Lawrence laughed at Polly's joke.

But as a wave of incredulity swept through the crowd, and Polly became stone-faced, he started to feel uneasy.

"What are you talking about?" Lawrence demanded. "I'm not a killer. I'm a piano player."

"And you do that so well, dear," Polly said. "But facts are facts."

"What facts? I had nothing to do with Laura Crawford's murder," Lawrence said. "I swear! This is stupid. Ridiculous! I must have an alibi or something."

Polly motioned for the crowd to calm down. "We've all heard that Laura was murdered with a DVD disc copy of my famous television musical/comedy variety show, which was in the top ten for the entire twelve years that we aired and garnered twelve Emmy Awards for me, and a buncha other fun commendations. Specifically, Laura was killed with disc number six."

Polly picked up Lawrence's boxed set of DVDs. "Please drop by the All Bound Up bookstore on the main deck and purchase your very own set," she said to the crowd, as if hawking cubic zirconia on QVC. "I see that the captain has joined us," Polly announced. "Let's give him a loud and warm welcome and call him up here to inspect this box, which came directly from Lawrence Deerfield's cabin."

"What were you doing in my cabin?" Lawrence said. He looked at Tiara, who avoided eye contact.

The captain made his way through the crowd and ascended the six steps to the piano platform. He gave Polly an intolerant look. She responded with an even larger smile. "Captain, dear, would you please open this box and tell us what you find... and don't find?"

Begrudgingly, Captain Sheridan picked up the box and carefully emptied the contents on top of the piano. He looked at each disc case. One by one he inspected them and held them up for the passengers to see.

"Open the jewel cases, dear," Polly encouraged.

When Captain Sheridan opened the first plastic case, he also took out the disc. He continued to the second jewel case. And then the third. Each disc was accounted for. When he arrived at the plastic case for disc #6, he slowly opened it, looked at Polly, then at Lawrence and then held it high above his head.

Instantly, a massive roar of "Oooooh" swept through the atrium. "Empty," he said, and looked at Lawrence again.

Lawrence was in shock. "No!" he yelled. "It's got to be there! I didn't even know Laura Crawford! Why would I kill her?"

Polly spoke into the mic again. "But you did know her, sweetums. She fired you from a production of *Follies* last season. Remember? And you hated her guts and wanted her dead, so you killed her."

"Sure, she was a shrew, but I got this gig almost right away. I didn't hold a grudge!" pleaded Lawrence.

"Then what about this voodoo doll we found in your stateroom?" Polly held up the plush toy for the crowd to see. They offered the same response of incredulity as they had for the missing disc. "All the pins are in the neck, or should I say, Laura's neck? You even pinned her name to the doll!" Polly pulled the small bit of paper from the pin and read, "'LC!' Laura Crawford!"

The captain looked at Polly and then looked at the crowd, which was suddenly out for blood. He nodded toward Deerfield, and instantly four crew members in white uniforms and black epaulettes ascended the stage and took a flailing Lawrence Deerfield into custody.

Polly took a long bow and received thunderous applause from the other passengers. When she'd had enough of the ovation, Polly waved to her admirers and brought the mic to her lips. "I simply couldn't let my dear Laura die without finding her killer. I'd do the same for all of you! We're family!"

"You're the only sleuth I'd want investigating my murder," a voice from the crowd called.

Polly looked out among the throng and saw Cori Berman leaning against a faux marble column with his arms folded across his chest. "Dear Cori," she said, "I'd be especially happy to look for your killer."

Cori laughed with the crowd. "I've made so many showbiz enemies, you just might have that opportunity. But not on this ship of has-beens, please!"

Polly graciously, but facetiously applauded Cori. "Enemies? In Hollywood? Oh, no, dear. That's impossible. You'd have to *work* in Hollywood to make enemies there. Your last show was over a quarter century ago."

"So was yours!"

The crowd erupted in laughter, and Polly saw that even Cori was nodding and laughing at his own expense.

"It was fun while it lasted," Cori called from the edge of the crowd.

"The minutes fly by, don't they?" Polly retorted and waved goodbye to the crowd. Tim and Tiara both took her hands and guided her down the steps from the platform to the deck. "I'm parched," Polly said. "It's time to hit the Mermaid Lounge! There's a magnum with my name on it!"

Tiara looked forlorn. Polly reached out for her hand. "I'm terribly sorry about your stinky love life. I sincerely wish that Lawrence hadn't been a killer. But now you can get on with finding Mr. Right."

Tiara halfheartedly agreed. "I suppose it's better I found out this way instead of getting the same treatment from Lawrence. I'll be fine once we get back to Bel Air."

As the trio sipped the last of their champagne, a well-dressed crew member in white uniform entered the lounge and looked around for Polly. Upon spotting her, he approached the table. "Miss Pepper?"

Polly cast her eyes upon the handsome young sailor. "Naturally," she responded.

"Captain Sheridan has sent me to escort you to Lawrence Deerfield's cabin. Follow me."

"Lovely," Polly said, taking the sailor's hand and standing unsteadily. Tim and Tiara took over and held Polly's arms as they followed the leader down the corridor. "A medal for bravery," Polly sang, and did a little soft shoe. "At the very least, a commendation scroll. Suitable for framing! I'll try to act as humble as possible."

The quartet entered the elevator and dropped to the main deck. From there, they found another elevator that was hidden from the one used by the general passenger population. Down they went three more levels until the seaman held the door for Polly and her clan to exit.

"Looks familiar," Polly said with a grin. When they arrived at Lawrence Deerfield's cabin, the seaman knocked once on the door, opened it for Polly, then stepped aside.

The room was as it had been when they visited earlier in the day, minus the boxed set of DVDs, the voodoo doll, and the theater program. Now there was the addition of the stern-looking Captain Sheridan standing straight and steely. Suddenly, Polly wasn't feeling so giddy. She reached out to take Tim's and Tiara's hands.

Captain Sheridan was silent as he appraised Polly. He saw a woman of middle age, her hair colored an indecipherable shade of rust, her nose and chin sculpted by Beverly Hills' most experienced surgeons, and a look of trepidation cross her face. He looked away from Polly for a moment, picked up the remote control for the television, then handed it to Polly. "Turn on the damn machine," he said curtly.

"I'm not very tech savvy," Polly chuckled. "Tim's our IT specialist at home."

Captain Sheridan bellowed, "Push the On button!"

Polly's body began to shake as she looked at the control unit. Tim pointed to the power source, and Polly pressed the small bump on the remote. Suddenly, she saw herself on the screen. It was one of her finest comedy sketches. Then Laura Crawford came into view. Polly, Tim, and Tiara looked at the screen, then each other, then at Captain Sheridan.

"Very funny stuff. Now, eject the disc," the captain said in an angry tone. "Now!"

Again, Tim showed his mother the correct button. When the tray slid out from the DVD machine, Captain Sheridan instructed, "Take the disc out of the tray."

Polly did as she was told and looked at the title. She turned ashen.

"Read it aloud, please," the captain said.

"*The Polly Pepper Playhouse.*"

"What else does it say?"

"Season..."

The captain was seething. "Season what?"

Polly whispered, "Six. God, no! What about the voodoo doll and the initials LC?"

"Lawrence Casey. His passport was in the drawer. You should have looked at it. The so-called 'voodoo doll' was nothing more than a pincushion. Seems that Mr. Deerfield—his stage name—alters his own trousers to save a buck."

"But the theater program. And all those horrible things he said about Laura Crawford?"

"There's a difference between being mad and jotting down a few choice words and slicing up someone's throat."

Polly slumped onto the bed. "I was sure that I had Laura's killer."

The captain started to leave the cabin. "If I were you, I'd lie low for the rest of the cruise. When the other passengers hear about this, it's going to be humiliating for you. Oh, and surprisingly, Mr. Deerfield is not pressing charges of slander. He's a pretty neat guy if you ask me."

11

Tim and Tiara guided Polly back to her stateroom. As they walked down the long corridors to the elevator, Polly wrapped her arm around Tim's waist for support. When she was finally settled in her cabin, she was still shaking. "I shouldn't have gotten out of bed this morning. That's it. My excuse. I'm not responsible for my actions because of sleep deprivation. Tell Arnie and Tommy they'll have to cancel tonight's performance. I can't face an audience."

As Tiara laid out Polly's bedclothes, including her bathrobe, slippers, and sleep mask, she tsk-tsked about Polly having to also miss her date with Dorian, "or whatever his real name is."

Polly slipped out of her skirt and blouse and stepped into the robe. "Why would I miss my date? The fans can wait. My social life can't. We're not meeting until eleven. And don't bother accompanying me to the Lotus Lounge. Dorian, er, whoever, and I are adults. I can take care of myself."

Tiara put her hands on her hips. "At least get a plausible explanation for him lying to you."

"Nobody would lie about being given a first name like Dorian," Polly said. "Away with both of you. And hang the PRIVACY,

PLEASE sign on the door. The last thing I need is housekeeping coming in here and making those silly towel animals while I'm trying to recuperate from the most miserable day of my life."

As Tiara led the way out the door, she called back and said, "Thanks to the iconic Polly Pepper, I'm going to have to work extra hard tonight to comfort Lawrence and make him feel special. Should be a hoot."

When Polly was at last alone, she peeled off her undergarments and slipped into her jammies. She pulled back the bedsheets and made herself comfortable. Donning the sleep mask, she settled in for a much-needed nap.

Hours later, Polly awoke and felt along the wall above her head for the light switch. When she pushed the button, she slowly removed her sleep mask to avoid being shocked by the brightness of the light. She looked at her wristwatch. It was ten o'clock. Perfect timing. Polly stretched and then made her way to the tiny bathroom to shower and prepare for her meet up with Dorian.

Forty-five minutes later, Polly checked her reflection in the mirror on the cabin door. The red hair was casually brushed. Her makeup covered her flaws and accentuated her best features, which, until she'd been able to afford cosmetic surgery, were nil. As always, her smile was her best and most famous physical asset. For this night's occasion, she selected an elegant, royal-purple wrap dress with a dramatic sash tie. The couture slimmed her slightly fuller hips and thighs to stress her still shapely figure. Accessorized with an enamel swirl pendant necklace, she was ready to turn heads. Picking up her red leather clutch and dropping her key card and lipstick into the pouch, she moved to the door, turned off the lights, and stepped into the corridor.

In a matter of minutes Polly Pepper made a star's entrance at the Lotus Lounge. She stood elegantly at the hostess's lectern and was immediately met by a young, attractive woman but who couldn't have looked as stylish as Polly even if she'd had a makeover by Carson Kressley. "Miss Pepper, we're delighted to see you... again," the woman said with a wide fake smile.

"This is my first..."

"I was at your performance this afternoon."

"I canceled the show."

"Your earlier recital. The exhibition? The spectacle?"

"Hmm."

"Mr. Dawson is waiting by the piano."

Mr. Dawson, Polly repeated to herself. Polly looked at the piano player. "Where's the talented Mr. Deerfield this evening?"

"I imagine he's committing suicide. Please follow me."

As Polly wended her way through a maze of small tables, the piano music grew louder. From a distance, she could see the elegant man she remembered from the night before sipping champagne. When Polly and the hostess arrived at the table, Dorian instantly stood to greet them. He gave Polly a polite kiss on her cheek.

"You look very smart," Dorian said as he pulled out a chair for Polly to be seated opposite him. "Champagne?"

Polly smiled. "You obviously know nothing about me! Bubbles, of course! I've had the most horrific day. I'm sure you heard all about it."

"I suppose the news has traveled to every deck and state-room aboard the ship." Dorian smiled.

"What was I thinking?"

"You were thinking with your heart," Dorian said. "You wanted atonement for the utterly odious savagery perpetrated against your dear friend. You should be proud of what you accomplished today."

"Yeah, nearly ruining an innocent man's reputation. Not to

mention being told that my name will be added to the 'No Float' list of people the ship won't let on another cruise." Polly pouted.

Dorian's annulment of any wrongdoing by Polly started to heal her wounded pride. "I'm incredibly loyal to my friends and fans," Polly agreed. "I did what I thought I had to do. I shouldn't punish myself just because I got it one hundred percent wrong. At least I tried!"

Dorian raised his flute and clinked glasses with Polly's. "You're a legend. A symbol of hope for others. Never fall into the trap of believing anything negative that others may say about you."

This time Polly raised her glass to Dorian's. "You're good for my fragile ego. So, Dorian, tell me about your day. And why isn't there a Dorian listed as a passenger on the ship?"

"Caught me!" He took another sip from his glass. "This is more embarrassing than what you endured today." He hemmed and hawed for a moment. "I've been known as Dorian ever since I had the lead in my high school production of the Oscar Wilde play. It was a disastrous debut, and same-day ending, of my never-a-chance-in-hell acting career. My friends would not let me forget that I ruined the production with my lack of talent."

He held out his hand. "Allow me to reintroduce myself. Pete Dawson. And now I'm having a very good day."

"Kids!" Polly said and took another sip of champagne. "The darling light of my life but sometimes way too suspicious son had dozens of odious scenarios that starred you as someone about whom I should be wary."

"You're lucky to have someone who's concerned about you. I'm sure he's a terrific young man. How old is he?"

"Too old. I had him when I was two." Polly fussed with her hair and took another sip from her glass. "What about you? Children? Pets? A wife waiting in your cabin or who thinks you're on a business trip?"

"No and no. And not at the moment."

Polly and Dorian's conversation continued with superficial banter. They discussed the ship: "A Vegas knockoff on the high seas," Dorian said.

The other passengers: "Why would anyone pay to travel with a boatload of self-absorbed celebrities?" Polly asked.

"Are there other celebrities aboard?" Dorian joked.

Polly playfully slapped Dorian's forearm. "The entire upper Promenade Deck is crawling with more used-to-bees than at Bob Hope's funeral. Why are you on this cruise?"

"Had to get away." Dorian sighed. "Too much pressure. Found a last-minute deal that you wouldn't believe!"

Polly studied Dorian for a long moment. "Which means that you're not independently wealthy. Darn! Or you're loaded and you know how to hold on to a buck! Yes?"

Dorian laughed. "I'm afraid I'm a working stiff, just like nearly everyone else on the planet."

"A glamorous job?"

"Buster Brown shoes. I sell 'em."

"No wonder you had to get away," Polly teased. "So, you're not on this cruise to load your cell phone camera with candid pictures of Susan Dey denying that she ever starred on *The Partridge Family*?"

Dorian shook his head. "What's a *Partridge Family*? Don't get me wrong. I watch a little television. *60 Minutes, Dancing with the Stars, The Traitors.* And of course, I know who you are. But I'm too busy, and I certainly don't want to experience life vicariously. And, I didn't bother to bring my phone 'cause I'd heard the internet packages are extortionate on ships."

Polly raised her glass again. "To living." Suddenly she felt sad. "If only my old costar Laura Crawford could have lived longer and enjoyed life a bit more."

"A tragedy," Dorian agreed. "I'm very sorry for your loss. Any other leads as to who her killer may be?"

Polly shook her head. "Nope. It's a mystery. There are a couple of possibilities, but I have a feeling they'll end up the same way that Lawrence Deerfield did. Innocent."

Dorian signaled for the cocktail waitress and ordered a bottle of Dom Perignon. "I know it's late, but there's so much to talk about. I think we'll be here for hours. First, let's dance."

"I love dancing!" Polly said as she eagerly accepted Dorian's outstretched hand and was smoothly guided to a small square of parquet wood that served as a dance floor beside the piano. As soon as they stepped into the designated area, the pianist deftly completed *Blue Bayou* and immediately began playing *Long Ago and Far Away*. As Dorian held Polly close to his chest, she looked into his brown eyes. "This is my favorite song," she said, and suddenly remembered Tim's warning about how all of her personal information was available for public scrutiny on her website, her official fan site, the unofficial fan sites, and Wikipedia. "How did you know?" she asked, a bit circumspect but still pleased to be dancing with an elegant and strong man.

"I didn't," Dorian said.

"Any chance that *An Affair to Remember* is in your top ten list of favorite movies?" Polly asked.

"Just below *A Star Is Born*—the Garland-Mason version—and above *Somewhere in Time.*"

Polly's knees almost buckled. Dorian had just mentioned two of her all-time favorite films. "If we get into comedies and you say *Young Frankenstein* and *Auntie Mame*, I'll follow you all the way to your stateroom! Kidding of course! Sorta. Maybe."

Dorian drew Polly closer. Their dance movements were slow and smooth and in beat to the music, but they hardly moved. As the song ended, Dorian said, "I'll have the Dom sent to my stateroom."

When Tim and Tiara arrived at Polly's stateroom the following morning, they discovered her bed neatly made. "Yes!" Tiara said, pulling her fist down in triumph.

"I don't like this one bit," Tim hissed. "We don't know who this Dorian character is. He could be..."

"He could be the hottest thing since Ryan Reynolds. Look, your mama's a big girl. If she wants to have a night out on her own, I, for one, am thrilled. Give the woman a little leeway."

"I'm responsible for her," he said. "This ship is loaded with strange fans, not to mention a killer. When I said that it wouldn't be so bad to make a new friend for the week, I didn't think it would really happen."

Tiara shook her head. "You young people think that intimacy is reserved for your own generation."

"I didn't say that!"

"You just said that you didn't think that anyone would be interested in Polly other than as a fan. So, she's not as young as Jennifer Lawrence—who's not all that young. Well, I have news for you, kiddo. Everybody wants to be touched. I don't care how old you become; you still think about skin on skin. My ninety-two-year-old grandmother told me that once every few years she still has sex dreams."

Tim made a face. "I just want to know that Polly is safe. Of course, I hope she's having a swell time. But we need to know that she's not in any trouble."

"You're right," Tiara grudgingly agreed. "We do need to find her. If she doesn't come back or call within thirty minutes, I'll contact security. Although Captain Sheridan would probably love nothing better than to be rid of her."

"It wouldn't look good for his ship to have two murders on

the same cruise," Tim said. "In the meantime, I need coffee. I saw a carafe across the hall."

Tim opened the stateroom door, and Polly was standing at the threshold. She looked at her handsome son and nearly floated past him. "Got up early," she explained, reading the expressions on her son's and maid's faces. "Dorian thinks one should be up with the birds. He's right about one thing, the early morning sea air is so refreshing!"

"How was your night," Tiara cracked, eager for the lowdown on Polly's romantic adventure.

"If it was any better, there'd be a symphony following me around," she teased.

"Fourth of July fireworks?" Tim said, trying to conceal a smile.

"Sparklers, maybe," Polly confided. "Dorian's a teensy bit... well, the word 'snore' comes to mind."

Tiara shook her head. "I could never be with a tedious man. If he is Dorian Dullsville, why'd you stay the whole night?"

Polly thought for a moment. "You two shouldn't be the only ones having fun."

"You should have hit the road as soon as your heart rate returned to normal," Tim said. "Now he probably has expectations. He'll think you're his mate for the rest of the voyage."

Tiara grinned. "You should have these mother-son birds and bees talks more often. You're so adorable together!"

Polly gave them the backstory and explained that the evening had started out well. She recalled dancing, and that on the surface they would have passed the e-Harmony compatibility test. "Songs. Movies. Books. Plays. We share many of the same likes and dislikes. Love Angela Bassett. Don't understand Vince Vaughn. The usual. But there was something missing."

"It's called chemistry," Tim said.

"At least he has hair on his head, and he doesn't need a hearing aid," Polly said.

"Still, if he's dreary, that's a deal breaker," Tiara continued. "Monotony is not what I'd tolerate in a friendship let alone a playmate."

Polly lay back down on the bed. "Perhaps it's just me. It's possible that I expect too much from a guy. Dorian is far from the Elephant Man. He seems smart, he's sensitive, although not very worldly or sophisticated, but he passes the age-appropriate test."

Tim said, "Your problem isn't with Dorian, it's with Randy. You're feeling bourgeoisie guilt."

"Not!" Polly defended herself. "You were completely right when you said that Randy and I aren't engaged or married. So why would I feel the least bit guilty about having a little fun?"

"Because you're going steady," Tiara said. "It's high school all over again."

Polly sighed and thought for a long moment. "I'll admit that part of me was uncomfortable because I'm stuck on dear Randy. But there was something else, too. I can't put my finger on it, so let's just forget it. I promised to meet Dorian for a drink after my lecture this afternoon. Then we're going to dinner and dancing and…"

"There's no 'and' unless you're perfectly cool with it," Tim insisted. "You don't have to give a reason or an excuse for anything. Don't ever forget that."

As Polly picked up a copy of the *Daily Wave* to check the entertainment schedule, Tiara asked, "What about his phony name? Did you find out what's going on with that?"

"Dorian's a nickname," Polly revealed. "It's a nickname. His real name is Pete. But he's used to Dorian so that's the one he uses."

Tim poured more coffee into his cup. "What else is he used

to? Preying on lonely international icons from the golden age of television?"

"Yeah, he and Bob Newhart had a sloppy affair together," Polly quipped. "And who's lonely? Not me! He's just a guy. He sells shoes. He knows about contemporary art. He's a good dancer. And he wants me to stop looking for Laura's killer."

"I like him after all," Tim said. "You always get into trouble looking for killers."

Polly stepped into the phone-booth-size bathroom and turned on the shower. As Tim and Tiara waited in the cabin, they agreed that it was in Polly's best interest for them to keep her under covert surveillance, for her protection and their personal peace of mind.

Polly stepped out of the bathroom wearing one of the ship's robes. "You're still here?" she said, genuinely surprised that Tim and Tiara had waited for her. "I'm taking a mid-morning nap. I've had enough sea air for one day. But make sure I'm up an hour before my show!" She opened the cabin door and whisked her son and maid out of the room with a sleepy, "Ciao!"

12

When Polly sauntered onto the stage for her five o'clock lecture, the applause was thunderous. She visored her eyes with her hand and looked out at the audience. As the ovation continued, she pointed with appreciation and recognition to a dozen faces that she recognized, groupies who had attended each of her appearances. They were mostly older women, but a smattering of younger faces too, including Cori Berman's. "Thank you all for coming!" she said and applauded the audience. Polly then took her seat on the stage beside Tommy Milkwood and Arnie Levin.

Since the death of Laura Crawford, they had left one empty chair, a symbolic gesture to remind fans that Laura would always be part of the *Polly Pepper Playhouse* family. Gone but not forgotten.

As always, Polly, Arnie, and Tommy went through the routine of lying about how much fun they'd had for twelve seasons together on television. Film clips from some of the classic sketches as well as behind-the-scenes bloopers were played on large screens. Then it was time for the most popular segment of the program: reading audience questions. On her original hit series, Polly had started each week's program by reading a couple of letters from the mailbag. Although she and her writers had prescreened the missives and had come up with clever answers, she was now on her own. Whatever was written on a card was what she had to respond to. But no matter what her answers, it was her facial expressions, body language, and superb comic timing that made audiences scream with laughter.

Polly sat center stage on a leather wingback chair. On a low table beside her was a fishbowl filled with four-by-six-inch file cards, each with handwritten questions supplied by the audience. Everyone applauded and smiled in anticipation of stupid questions that would elicit funny responses. Polly reached into the bowl, withdrew a card, and cleared her throat. She read aloud, "If you had to choose between Hugh Jackman, George Clooney, and Brad Pitt, who would you take for a lover?"

The audience roared as Polly crossed her eyes, pushed out her lips like a fish, and slapped the backs of her hands together as if she were a performing seal begging for a mackerel treat.

From behind Polly, Arnie Levin yelled out, "She doesn't do mercy dates with unattractive men!" Everyone in the auditorium burst into laughter.

Polly looked at the audience and whispered into her microphone, "The hell I don't!" Again, the crowd wailed. Polly sighed and said, "Too bad about their looks, eh?" After a pause to let the laughter die down, Polly said, "As a matter of fact, I'm more of a Steve Martin girl. He's just as good-looking as George. What woman wouldn't want to be laughed into bed? I could feast my eyes on his big... ginormous... monumental... enviable..." Polly stopped and looked at the audience, who were howling. "What?" she asked. "I'm talking about the man's art collection, for crying out loud." Now the audience was crying with laughter.

Polly once again reached into the fishbowl. "Honestly, did you think I was talking about his big..." She stretched out each word. "Massive. Powerful." She paused. "Brain?" She'd had the audience from the moment she'd walked onto the stage, but now they could go home completely satisfied that they'd experienced Polly's famous naughty but unsullied sense of humor in person.

Polly held the next card in her hand and began to read aloud. "Laura Crawford is dead. Are you ready to join her?"

The audience was warmed up and ready for anything. They tittered self-consciously, not sure whether or not it was a joke or a sincere question. Polly, too, wasn't certain. She reread the card to herself. Deciding to make light of a mean, if not threatening situation, Polly said, "Like dear Peggy Lee sang, 'I'm not ready for that final disappointment.'" The audience applauded as Polly said, "However, if I get my hands on whoever wrote that question, they'll be swapping stories with Laura Crawford in person."

Taking a serious stand, Polly looked out into the audience and said, "Sweetums, whoever you are, you're under the false impression that I'm easily intimidated. Hell, I've worked for sociopathic numbnuts publicity executives like Stephanie Hough at Sterling Studios. I can certainly handle a psycho who thinks he, or she, is being a clever killer. I'm this close to making a positive ID, so watch this space for a big revelation very soon. I'll get you long before you get me. Guaranteed!"

An instantaneous wave of applause from the audience erupted like a geyser and washed over Polly. "It's true!" she said. "It's just a matter of time."

Polly bowed gracefully, then put her hands to her heart. "I adore all of you. Except the killer of course, who might be in this room right now. Oh, Mr. Killer," she sang, "please stand up and let us get a good look at you. Make it easier on yourself."

Again, the audience applauded, and murmurs of "Yeah! You

tell him! Polly's not afraid of anything or anyone... except critics" spread through the crowd.

Suddenly, people began to notice a man quickly leaving the small auditorium and started pointing to him. Polly saw that it was Cori Berman. She called out, "Join me for champers sometime soon, Cori."

Cori stopped and turned around. "I'm in AA and a dozen other programs. Or don't you read the *Intruder*?"

Several people recognized his voice and spread the word. "It's that child star, what's-his-name, all growed up."

"I'll join you for a cup of coffee. If you live another day," Cori said.

"Call for me at noon. Tomorrow," Polly said. "I promise to be breathing."

"I wouldn't dismiss that note card and question if I were you," Cori continued. "There are a lot of loony tunes aboard this ship. Just look around this room."

"Who'er you calling screwy?" one woman called up to Cori.

"Turn up your hearing aid, ma'am. I said 'loony.'"

"Same thing. And you're the one who was in rehab, not us loonies."

"I'm just giving our wonderful hostess a friendly warning, that's all," Cori said, and started to walk away.

A woman in the audience uttered to a friend, "He's probably the killer."

Her voice was loud enough for everyone, including Cori, to hear.

Cori turned around and demanded to know who had spoken those words. "Was it you?" He pointed an accusing finger at a gray-haired woman with a fixed pout on her lips. "Or you?" he addressed another old woman. "If I hear one more slanderous accusation from anyone, you'll wish you never booked this cruise. Remember, I'm dangerous. The tabloids say so. Which is why I never worked again on television.

"As for you, Miss Perfect Polly Pepper," Cori continued, "be careful! You should be very afraid."

When Cori had finally exited the theater, Polly looked at her audience and said with mock trepidation, "The little pisher is jealous because he was never even nominated for an Emmy, and I've got 'em crawling out of my..." Polly caught herself and said, "I'm used to tripping over them!"

As Polly left her backstage dressing room and began walking down the inside deck toward the elevator, she heard the sound of someone running toward her, and then a male voice called out her name. Polly cautiously turned around just as a good-looking young man dressed in khaki slacks and a button-down dress shirt caught up with her. Slightly out of breath, and more gregarious than Richard Simmons playing patty-cake with Martha Stewart, he said, "Hi, Miss Pepper! I'm your cruise director, Saul Landers."

Polly smiled and reached out her hand to shake Saul's.

Saul shrank back almost imperceptibly. "Sorry, I don't shake. Did you know there are about a trillion bajillion germs on cruise ships? Everybody brings something icky aboard!"

"I seriously doubt that I'm incubating anything so gross that the World Health Organization would be interested!" Polly said.

Saul laughed and then explained that he'd received great feedback about Polly's reunion show, even without Laura Crawford being alive to participate. "There is one problem, however. Can we go somewhere private to talk?"

"If this is about my darling son and his little infatuation with that hunky Italian deck officer..."

"Which one?" Saul said. "All of the Italian crew members are hunky."

"No one," Polly said. "If you're after Tiara, I know you probably have rules about the entertainers fraternizing with guests, but please don't blame Tiara. She can't help falling for guys who play piano."

Saul cocked his head. "Um, not quite sure what you're talking about, but if you're referring to the guy you dragged through the mud yesterday..."

"Never mind," Polly said. "Let's chat in my cabin. We'll have a bit o' bubbly while I unwind before dinner, and you can tell me all about this problem of yours. Although I suspect it's about to be *my* problem. Follow me," Polly said as she turned and headed for the glass elevator.

When the car arrived, Saul gallantly stood aside and waited for Polly to step inside. He then pulled a tissue from his pocket and used it as a barrier between his finger and the button he pressed for Coral Deck. Polly did her best to make small talk as the two rode to her deck and then wended their way to her cabin. "Have you been working for this cruise line for a long time?" she asked.

"Seven years."

"Do you get many murders?"

"Mainly suicides."

"Ever spot a sea monster?"

"Lauren Bacall was on board once."

"We're home," Polly said as she withdrew her key card from her clutch and inserted it into the door lock. "Don't mind the mess; the place is much smaller than I expected. In fact, Laura Crawford got the veranda penthouse suite that I was supposed to occupy. Of course, now it's off-limits. Crime scene and such. It's not as though I'd disturb any evidence. Jeez, I just want a bigger place to hang my chapeau, so to speak. Be a gent and open the champagne," she said, pointing to the ice bucket with the neck of a bottle peeking out from under a white towel. "I'll just be a sec." Polly disappeared into the bathroom and turned the sink taps on full blast.

In a moment she reappeared, drying her hands with a towel. "Now you've got me thinking about infectious microorganisms." Polly spied the two flutes of bubbly that Saul had poured and picked one up. She swallowed half the contents, poured a refill, and raised the glass to her visitor. "Now I'm fortified for whatever it is you have to tell me. Do sit down."

As Saul sat on a chair beside the combination makeup table and writing desk, Polly settled onto her bed. "Spill it," she said.

Saul took another sip of champagne and said, "I like to laugh as much as anyone else." He let out a shrill sound to prove his point. "But murder isn't funny."

"No kidding."

"It's even less funny when someone tries to exploit the dead person."

Polly gave Saul a look of confusion. "Is someone using Laura's image to promote snail-paste skin-care products or massages to die for?"

Saul reached into his back pocket and produced a copy of the *Daily Wave,* the ship's newsletter. "Luckily our editor caught this before it was circulated. I'm hoping to keep the captain out of the loop."

Polly took the newsletter from Saul. She looked at the masthead, then read the headline, which roared: **PP PISSED. IN THE DRINK.**

13

Tim and Tiara soon arrived and were at Polly's side. They listened in horror as Saul read aloud the short article. It described the fictional suicide of Polly Pepper. When Saul finished reading, he apologized profusely on behalf of the cruise line. He looked at Tim and Tiara. "I hope this matter doesn't prevent you from filling in the 'Extremely Satisfied' circle on the cruise evaluation form," he said.

"Let's think rationally," Tim interrupted. "The article must be a sicko practical joke. Maybe a crew member wrote it. That's it. Someone who contributes to the daily newsletter was goofing around, like a disgruntled secretary who sends an email to a colleague about her horrible boss, then accidentally cc's the entire company. They didn't mean any real harm. Surely the writer of this article didn't expect the copy to be picked up and printed. It was a mistake. Yes?"

"I write most of the copy," Saul said.

"Someone certainly has a wild sense of humor," Polly said. "'PP wore pearls to her suicide.' I'm not like that fool of an old woman in *Titanic*, the idiot who intentionally tossed her expensive lavaliere overboard. Dolphins may be smart enough to appreciate good taste, but sharks are as bad as scavengers in an alley Dumpster. As for the so-called eyewitnesses to my demise, my fans are not going to believe that I fell over at seven A.M. They know I don't rise before nine!"

Tiara poured Polly another glass of champagne and one for herself and Tim too. As she sipped the effervescing cure-all, she suggested whoever wrote the piece was not an innocent prankster with too much time on their hands. Rather it had to be someone connected to the murder of Laura Crawford. "Only someone afraid of Polly revealing them to be the killer would want to scare or maybe actually kill her," Tiara said. "There's no other explanation because the entire world loves Polly Pepper. She's right behind puppies and pandas."

Polly agreed, and as she took another sip from her glass, she recalled Cori Berman's threat during the lecture period that afternoon. "I'm not saying he's guilty of anything," Polly said. "But I'm not saying he's innocent either. Perhaps he wrote this silly newsletter piece. He's known for whipping up a souffle of trouble."

Tim recalled, "One of the reasons he was kicked off *Highway to Heck* when he was a teenager was because he sold a story to the *National Intruder* about the show's guest star Jane Lemour. Remember? Jane supposedly started feeding peanuts to the squirrels on the Sterling Studios lot. Then, after a few days of gaining their trust, one by one she grabbed the greedy little rodents by their neck and twisted their heads off. It was all a lie, of course! But PETA still boycotted the show until the Sterling Network execs kicked Cori off."

"Cori may also have been fooling around when he gave me a halfhearted warning today," Polly said. "The audience taunted him and suggested that he was probably Laura's killer. Oh, and one of the questions in my fishbowl was, 'Are you ready to join Laura Crawford?' Maybe he wrote that question as well."

Tim slapped his knee. "Cori's a total bad seed. Always has been! The drugs..."

"He said he's in AA," Polly reported.

"The arrests for DUI, and brawls at the Viper Room. And possession of illegal firearms," Tiara added. "Not to mention the expensive prostitutes."

"Charlie Sheen made it sort of chic to spend nearly a hundred grand on Heidi Fleiss's high-class girls," Polly said.

"It wouldn't surprise me to find that Cori Berman's the killer," Tim continued. "It's no news that Laura didn't like him. Plus, he's got an arrest record a mile long. I'm shocked that Homeland Security didn't tear up his passport."

Saul made a face. "One of my jobs is to create games for the passengers. They love the usual standbys: bingo, charades, the hairy-chest contest. As an expert, I sense that perhaps this edition of the *Daily Wave* could be a psychopath's game of truth or dare."

Polly, Tim, and Tiara were intrigued.

Saul continued. He looked at Polly. "A question in your fish-bowl asked if you were ready to join the dead actress who used to be on your show. Maybe the killer is *daring* you to come out into the open with the *truth*. Obviously, not the truth that you thought was true yesterday—the Lawrence Deerfield debacle. That was pretty lame, but perfect for the killer. Now, when you're ready to reveal the perp, no one will believe you. Then wham, the killer takes you out, quick, and easy!"

"Maybe not so quick." Tiara cringed.

"Maybe not so easy," Tim added.

"Sweetums," Polly said, "what am I supposed to be, the cornered mouse to someone's bloodthirsty cat?" She rolled her eyes and held out her flute to Tiara. "I'll find the killer, all right, but on my terms. Polly Pepper is never a victim."

"Even when she's unexpectedly slapped with divorce papers," Tiara agreed.

"The only things about that dumb headline and the bogus story that'll make me jump overboard are the prepositions at the end of the fourth and seventh sentences, as well as the grammatically challenged writer's dangling participles," Polly remarked.

Saul came to a decision. "I'll have every last copy of this blasted newsletter destroyed within the hour. I'll make an announcement and simply say that due to technical difficulties, the *Daily Wave* won't be published tomorrow. We're the only ones who'll ever know that such a mean-spirited joke was made at your expense. I promise."

"But if this isn't a joke, and Laura's killer is responsible for the article, he'll know that something went wrong, and won't come forward to make sure I jump or slip overboard, or however he plans to handle my death," Polly said.

Polly placed her hand on Saul's shoulder. "Hmm. Perhaps distribution of the *Daily Wave* isn't such a bad idea."

"The Captain'll have my head," Saul insisted. "I'd probably lose my job!"

"Where's your humanitarian spirit? I'm the one who's in jeopardy, and all you think about is your income."

"My wife and kids depend on it."

"Wife?" Polly said, and shot a look at Tim. She tried to stifle her incredulity that Saul was married—to a woman.

"Are you thinking that if someone took the time to infiltrate our press room and write spurious copy about you and your demise, they want the newsletter to be up to date when it's placed under all the stateroom doors in the morning?" Saul said.

"We might be able to catch the killer tonight if he thinks the paper's going out as scheduled," Polly protested. "I'm in favor of letting him fall into his own trap. Now that we know what's in store for me, we can catch whoever tries to do something crazy.

"Speaking of crazy!" Polly suddenly bolted out of her chair. "I'm scheduled to meet Dorian at seven." She looked at her wristwatch. "Time's up. Everybody out. I need to shower, put my face on, dress, and be ready for my date."

As Saul, Tim, and Tiara filed out the door, Saul called back, "I'll have a security detail following you all night long."

Tim said, "If Polly isn't out of Dorian's cabin by two A.M., no matter what time they get in, barge in with a faux emergency. She's getting a little tired of Dorian Dawson anyway."

Now it was Saul's turn to roll his eyes. "Oh, him."

"Him?" Polly asked.

"You said, Dorian? He's being a pest to our art gallery manager. He brought pictures of Warhols and Hockneys and wants appraisals."

"I'll give the guy an appraisal that'll make him take the leap on his own into the Pacific if he's not careful," Tiara said.

"Scoot," Polly added, and closed the door.

When Polly was dressed and coiffed and glittering with jewelry, she looked as radiant as any screen queen. She couldn't have looked any more glamorous if she were facing paparazzi on a red carpet at Cannes. Arriving at the elegant Nautilus Grill dining room, she was escorted by the maître d' to Dorian's table. As she passed the other diners, Polly left a trail of whispers.

"Psst. Mental case at three o'clock."

"Get a selfie with her before they send her to the asylum!"

Arriving at her table, Dorian put down the emery board he was using. He stood up and grazed his lips against Polly's cheek. When she was seated, the waiter, Ernesto, withdrew an open bottle of champagne and poured a glass for Polly. She looked at the glass, then at Dorian, and then at Ernesto.

"Something wrong?" Dorian asked.

Polly grimaced. "Would you think I was a dreadful diva if I made a teensy-weensy observation-slash-request? Look at those poor baby bubbles." She pointed at the few lethargic beads taking their time moving through the amber liquid to their demise on the surface. "There should be a million of those little suckers trying like hell to beat the others to the crown, like in those old-fashioned sex education films we watched in school. I really hate to make a fuss, but we sorta need to try this again. Don't you think so?"

Ernesto looked to Dorian for guidance.

Dorian nodded his head in complete agreement. "Um. Yes. A new bottle, please."

As the waiter reached for the champagne ice bucket, Polly lifted the white linen napkin that was concealing the bottle and looked at the label. "Oh, sweetums, there's the problem!" Polly said, sounding as if she just found the answer to the mystery of why Nicolas Cage is a star. "It's domestic." She looked at the table and picked up the wine list. Polly opened the folio and drew her finger down the page on the left-hand side. She stopped at *Krug, Clos du Mesnil* and pointed for Ernesto to see. Without looking at the price, she said, "Please be a very darling *garçon* and ask the sommelier to make sure the bottle is well chilled. Absolutely no colder than forty-three degrees, but no warmer than forty-eight degrees. *Si? Por favor and gracias,* señor *Ernesto.*"

Just as Ernesto was about to retrieve the unacceptable glass of champagne that he'd originally served, Polly neatly intercepted the glass. "Waste not, want not." She shrugged and took a long swallow before relinquishing the glass.

Dorian smiled and reached across the table to take Polly's hand. "The stories are true."

"Of course they are. The good ones."

"You are indeed a woman of exquisite culture and refinement."

"It's amazing what one picks up from watching old movies. Cary Grant was the best on-screen teacher. I just copied what he or Deborah Kerr did in fancy restaurants."

Dorian deftly released Polly's hand. "I'll try my best not to be intimidated by the ghosts of Hollywood legends."

"Nonsense. I learned just as many bad habits as good from the movies. I've been known to investigate strange sounds in the basement with only a candle for light when the electricity unexpectedly goes out. Dumb, I know. I suppose that during an attack by zombies, when my full magazine of ammunition doesn't stop the undead, I'd probably throw my empty gun at the beast, knowing full well that wouldn't do any good. However, I'm not a complete idiot. I never picked up smoking from watching Bette Davis."

Dorian was enchanted. "If I hadn't met you on this cruise, it would be the dreariest voyage imaginable. Ah, the champagne is here."

The sommelier arrived with the bottle of *Clos du Mesnil* and smiled warmly. "I had to meet the discerning passenger with the elegance and refinement—and bank account—to request such an extraordinary vintage," he said. "I'm delighted to find that the order wasn't a mistake or joke." The sommelier's fuss led Dorian to suddenly feel that something wasn't quite right. Either the *Clos du Mesnil* was the last bottle of champagne on the planet, or it was the most expensive one. Polly picked up on his unease. "Not to worry, sweetums," she said, patting Dorian's wrist. "I also learned from watching a Queen Latifah movie that nothing is too good for one's last night on Earth."

When the foil wrapper was removed from around the twisted wire hugging the bonnet, the sommelier poured an inch of champagne into Polly's flute and then into Dorian's. After their respective sips and nods of acceptance, he filled their glasses three-quarters of the way. The couple clinked their flutes together. "Up yours!" Polly said.

"Cheers to you, too," Dorian added. "Now, what was that remark about this being your last night? We have three more enchanted evenings to go before we dock in Juneau."

Polly looked into Dorian's clear eyes. "Never mind. It's silly. I'm just supposed to die tonight, that's all."

"You're funny. No wonder you're famous. You make me laugh."

"No joke," Polly said as she pulled a small bit of warm bread from her dinner roll and slathered it with butter. "I read my own obituary in the ship's newsletter. Pathetic, really. The writer didn't even bother to mention my record number of Emmy wins. Just referred to Polly Pepper as 'the famous celebrity.' Redundant."

Dorian was bug-eyed. "Where is this newsletter? Surely, you're being protected by the ship's security personnel."

"After yesterday's disaster, I'm not exactly on the captain's list of indispensable passengers. He'd be happy to see me disappear. The cruise director wants to keep the obit hush-hush. He's afraid of another black eye on this particular boat and is hoping it's a hoax. He said that the publicity department at the Astral Cruise Line company—which owns the Kool Krooz ships—is already working overtime on damage control following the last couple of incidents. You know, the disappearing act pulled by that old couple, and the bride whose husband claims she slipped over the railing of their terrace. And El Stupido, who was sitting on her terrace railing with a drink in hand when a gust of wind sent him sailing solo for the rest of his life. Not to mention the murder on this voyage."

The mood at the table had changed. What had begun as an evening of lightheartedness had drifted into awkwardness. When Ernesto returned to take their dinner orders, Dorian said that he was no longer hungry. "Perhaps too much champagne," he explained. He ordered an appetizer.

Polly looked at him and shrugged. "I could eat a whale," she said, and ordered the herb-crusted turbot, fennel, and leek ragout. She reached out and touched Ernesto's wrist. "Sweetums, would you please make sure there are two Amaretto crème brûlées left for dessert? Perhaps we can convince Mr. Hunger Strike here to join my palate for a teensy bit of pleasure. *Merci* and *gracias,*" she said, and returned her attention to Dorian.

Polly folded her hands on the tabletop and sighed. "My apologies for beginning the evening on such a macabre note. By now you're thinking that I'm a crazy Hollywood legend who is dazed, confused, and thinking she sees Elvis strolling the Lido Deck. I'm changing the subject, and we won't speak again of my very bizarre day and the equally weird death to follow." After a moment's silence, Polly clapped her hands together and said, "Art! I'm told that you've been visiting the ship's fine art gallery, and that you're interested in all that modern stuff. When we return to Los Angeles, you'll have to drop by Pepper Plantation for a drinky and look-see at my Warhol."

Dorian perked up. "Warhol. *Campbell's Soup*?" he said.

"If you want to call that art," Polly scoffed. "Talk about practical jokes. I mean, really. Someone paints an ordinary can of soup or a Brillo soap pad box, and it gets into a museum? I wonder who the first dork was to call it 'art.'"

Dorian took a long sip from his champagne flute. "I hear that you also have a Bachardy. And a Hockney." He appeared to be salivating.

"And one of these days, I'll get my Lichtenstein back from King Charles!"

Ernesto arrived with Polly's turbot and Dorian's crab-stuffed mushrooms.

Dorian was now more animated and decided that he was

hungry after all. "I'll have what Miss Pepper is having," he said to Ernesto, who looked perplexed but wrote the order on his pad and shuffled away.

"Art talk gives me an appetite," Dorian said, spearing his fork into a stuffed mushroom. "I thought that MOMA had all thirty-two of Warhol's cans," he said. "How on earth did you obtain one?"

Polly gave Dorian a grin. "Everybody thinks there were only thirty-two, one for each soup flavor offered by Campbell's at the time. Tomato. Chicken Noodle. Clam Chowder. Andy actually did a thirty-third. *Puree of Poo-poo Chien.* It was a joke, and obviously, it didn't fit in with the other flavors, so he chucked it."

Dorian nodded. "You know that's worth a freaking fortune! And your Bachardy is a nude. And the Hockney is one of his pools."

Polly offered a warm smile. "You're a closet case. I mean, you lead a double life. Mild-mannered shoe salesman by day, and by night you become a connoisseur of art and an expert on the private art world of Polly Pepper."

"When one has a boring job that they loathe, one must find an activity that's totally different from what brings home the bacon. I found modern art."

"This so-called 'art' found me," she said. "A showbiz colleague needed quick cash a while back and sold me a few of her treasures for pennies on the dollar. I knew she hated to lose those pieces, so I called up a friend who teaches art at Beverly Hills High and got one of his students to paint copies for a hundred bucks each. A win-win. The student made his gas money for the week, and my acquaintance could walk around her house, look at the walls, and pretend she wasn't the complete failure that she really was, and I had an instant art collection. What fun!"

Polly and Dorian finished their entrées, and soon the crème brûlées arrived. Ernesto poured the remaining champagne into Polly's glass, and Dorian made a final toast. "To bubbles! May they never burst!"

14

Dorian begged Polly to join him for a nightcap in his stateroom. She vacillated. For a moment she considered that since her time on the planet was rumored to be up in a few hours, she should take advantage of what would be a last hurrah for intimacy. However, more than desiring to be alone with a man, she wanted to make herself available to find out who, specifically, had plans to knock her off the ship.

At the glass elevator by the atrium, Polly promised Dorian that she'd do everything in her power to live another day. "Either text you in the morning, or you'll have to hire the ship's clairvoyant, to communicate with me." She laughed and gave Dorian a kiss good night. "Ciao, *bella,*" Polly said before being whisked to the Promenade Deck for a stroll under the stars.

Now, as she wrapped her arms around herself for warmth against the night air, she was intensely alert to the sounds around her: the American and *Intacti* flags slapping in the breeze above the smokestacks, the ocean as the ship cut through the surface. As she passed the lifeboats rigged to the side of the ship, she inhaled the sea air. As a sense of anxiety washed over her, she slowed down and came to a complete stop next to the metal stairway leading to the next deck.

Suddenly she spat, "Tiara! Are you wearing *my* Chanel No. 5?"

Instantly, from out of the darkness under the stairs, two sets of hands reached out and grabbed Polly by the waist and dragged her into the vise of four arms.

"As for you, Timmy, your Dolce isn't very subtle," she said.

"You're being followed," Tim's voice whispered.

"Anyone interesting?" Polly retorted.

"If you're interested in Cori Berman. And Rosemary Thyme from the spa. And D'Angelo, too."

"He's all yours, sweetums," Polly said.

"Nah, that's over," Tim said, accidentally speaking without muting his voice.

"Goody," Polly whispered without much conviction. "There's still hope you'll fall for Jason Momoa. You promised you'd at least try."

Tiara interrupted Polly's fantasy match for her son. "Dorian's hanging around the deck, too. Careful. He's getting closer. Where the hell is security?"

Polly tried to peek out from the cloak of the shadows, but she was pulled back into the fold of Tim's and Tiara's arms. The trio watched as a few pairs of passengers strolled by. When they could see Dorian approach, they held their respective breaths. Cori Berman, too, walked toward Polly's hiding place, and when he was mere inches away, he stopped, sniffed the air, and caught the scent of perfume.

"Nice night," Cori said.

Polly almost answered but was interrupted by another voice, which Polly instantly recognized.

"Skip the polite conversation." It was Rosemary Thyme's voice. "When does she cash in?"

Tim quietly wrapped his arm tighter around his mother and drew her a few inches deeper under the stairs.

"A change of plans," Cori said.

"Cold feet?" Rosemary sneered.

"A warm heart. He needs more time to get it right. But the fish has nibbled on the bait."

Cori and Rosemary moved on, and Tim cautiously peered out from their place of hiding. "All clear, I think," he said, and took Polly's hand. Tiara held Polly's other hand. They moved in tandem and retraced their steps back to the inside of the Promenade Deck. Walking briskly past the atrium, to the bank of elevators, Tim suggested that they use the stairs for a faster return to their cabins. With his mother sandwiched between him and Tiara, Tim began the descent.

"I'm in heels, dear," Polly said as she tried to keep up with her son. Tim slowed down, but when he arrived on Deck Seven, he wanted to dash for the safety of Polly's stateroom.

Just as the trio arrived at Polly's cabin door, a familiar voice bellowed down the corridor, "Polly Pepper!"

Polly and her team turned around and found Captain Sheridan, the cruise director, and two uniformed officers from the ship's security team.

Polly was dead tired. However, she turned on her smile and waited for the ship's staff to reach her. "If it's about the champagne, I don't recall any restrictions in my contract about what I'm allowed to order at dinner. You can check with my adorable agent, JJ."

"I just want to try to fathom what you think you're doing on this ship," Captain Sheridan said.

"Aside from feeling that you're a mean-spirited bully, I've been hired to perform a job," she said, shifting her weight from one leg to the other. "Frankly, your disposition has been pretty fierce ever since we arrived here. What'd I ever do to get on the wrong foot with you?" She stopped for a moment and said, "Oh, right."

Captain Sheridan looked at Polly for a long minute. "You rich and famous and pampered celebrities—"

"Icons," Tiara corrected.

"—are always looking for publicity stunts to keep your name in the public eye. Twice on this voyage you've gone too far. First with the false accusations about Mr. Deerfield's involvement in the murder of Laura Crawford. Now, with the phony obit in our daily newsletter."

Polly's smile faded. "If you continue to impugn my integrity, I'll have no other choice than to call in a few favors from my nearest and dearest in the cruise line industry. You'll be swabbing the decks instead of running the bridge!"

The captain harrumphed. He looked at Polly and flatly stated, "I intimidate the passengers. Not the other way around."

Polly laughed. "You obviously don't read the *National Intruder* or catch *Access Hollywood*. If you did, you'd know that hard-boiled studio heads cringe when they have to deal with me —or more precisely, my agent. I can play the sweet, lovable lady next door while JJ pushes publicity department senior VPs to tear off their own fingernails. But don't underestimate my own ability to handle myself in a crisis."

Tim stepped forward. "In other words, PP's JJ has titanium *cojones* the size of bowling balls."

Polly chuckled. "Timmy exaggerates."

"But not in this case," Tiara said.

Polly turned to Saul. "I thought we were going to keep the newsletter mess away from Herr Poseidon," she said.

Saul looked down to avoid eye contact with Polly. "I didn't have a choice. As a matter of fact, Captain Sheridan sent a special unit of the ship's security to keep their eyes on you. After reading the *Daily Wave,* he was genuinely concerned for your safety."

Polly's attitude melted. "Concerned? For *moi*? You're too sweet. All right. If I was slightly insane a few moments ago, keep in mind that I seldom say what I really mean. I'm really a pussy-cat. I just regurgitate dialogue from old Barbara Stanwyck movies to sound tough. Joan Crawford comes in handy too. You'd be surprised how often I can get away with lines from Alec Baldwin's famous phone call rant to his daughter!" Polly took what she thought was a tough-guy stance and quoted, "'In Sicily, women are more dangerous than shotguns!'"

Tim nudged his mother. "Um, that's from *The Godfather.*"

Captain Sheridan crossed his arms and said, "You still haven't answered my question."

Polly made a face. "Question? Oh, publicity stunts, et cetera. Let's step into my cabin. The walls out here have ears and too many cameras."

Tim tapped his card key onto the lock and led the way for his mother, Tiara, and the team of maritime personnel.

Tiara uncorked a bottle of champagne and looked at the captain. "You're out of luck. Housekeeping doesn't provide enough glasses." She then poured a drink for Polly.

"I'd share," Polly said, "but Saul was telling me all about the icky germs people bring aboard cruise ships. I wouldn't want you to come down with some hideous virus that I may have brought from Hollywood."

Captain Sheridan was exasperated. "There's always at least one passenger on every voyage I have to keep an extra eye on. This time, it's you. From the moment we set sail, you've been at the center of every storm. First your cabin wasn't big enough. Then your girlfriend was murdered. Then you started a monsoon of accusations subjecting an innocent man—an employee of the ship—to the embarrassment of having people think he was a killer. I'm forced to add another demerit to the file of one of my best deck stewards because he's spending more time playing with your son than serving the passengers. And now, our cruise director has to announce that the *Daily Wave* contained a belated April Fools' Day joke because you didn't die."

"You'd be happy to see me die?"

Tim took a sip from Polly's glass and said, "It's early yet. The paper said she goes overboard at seven in the morning."

The captain squared his shoulders. "Which brings me to why we're joined by Masters-at-Arms Ronson and Garner." He cocked his head toward the two seamen dressed in the white uniform of ship's officers. "They will be stationed outside your door. I'm confining you to this cabin until ten o'clock tomorrow morning."

Polly swallowed the remainder of the champagne in her glass and set the flute down for a refill. "I'm a victim, not a criminal!"

Tim stepped in. "Mom, I think it's for the best. You'll be protected."

"Lockdown is not the way to protect me," Polly said. "Anyway, I haven't actually been threatened by anyone."

Tiara added, "It's just for the night, Polly. You're ready to go to bed anyway. When tomorrow comes, and you're still breathing, we'll regroup and investigate Laura's killer."

"If you so much as investigate rats in the galley, you'll find yourself back in protective custody for the duration of this cruise," Captain Sheridan grumbled. "Everybody out! Go to your cabins and don't even try to return here until late tomorrow morning. Miss Pepper is going to bed!"

Tim and Tiara gave Polly a kiss good night. As the trio engaged in a group hug, Polly said, "Cori and Rosemary. Find out what they know."

15

"Polly Pepper is the most fascinating person either of us will ever know, but frankly, her detention tonight is our freedom," Tiara said as she and Tim left Polly's stateroom and walked toward the main bank of elevators.

"Some vacation. We should have known Polly would find herself in hot water," Tim said. "Wherever Polly goes, dead people spoil the party."

"And we get sucked into their final exit mess. Forget Polly's investigation," Tiara said. "I'm not spending the night on anybody's tail—other than Lawrence's. Let's hit the piano bar and have a drink while he's still playing. If you're nice, I may introduce you to the bartender."

"Been there. Done that."

As the two stepped into the elevator and pushed the button for the Promenade Deck, they talked in hushed tones about what they'd overheard Cori Berman and Rosemary Thyme say regarding Polly "cashing in." Tim shrugged and said, "We don't really know that they were talking about Polly."

"Who else?"

"Someone in the casino? I don't know."

When they arrived at the bar, it was crowded with mainly older couples dancing on the parquet floor and singing along to *The Twelfth of Never*. Tim and Tiara found seats on a long bench behind a small round table that was bolted to the floor. They were close enough for Tiara to see and be seen by Lawrence, who winked when she caught his eye. A cocktail waitress arrived and placed two napkins on the table before them. Tim looked at Tiara. "This one night, let's *not* have champagne!" he smiled.

"Right-o. A dirty martini, straight up," Tiara said to the waitress. "Gin! Not vodka!"

"Same here."

Humming along to *Bridge Over Troubled Water*, Tiara divided her attention between talking with Tim about the handsome sailors who were guarding Polly, watching Lawrence's fingers dancing over the piano keyboard—and thinking of his fingers dancing around her navel. A particularly interesting couple standing several feet away caught her eye. She nudged Tim and nodded in their direction. "Our friendly cruise director and the lovely and talented Rosemary. They seem to be having a wee tiff."

Tim and Tiara watched as Rosemary gave Saul a short but strong shove. As she started to leave, Saul grabbed her wrist and pulled her back.

"Ouch!" Tim flinched when he saw the pained expression on Rosemary's face. "Let's join the lively couple and see what's up."

Tim and Tiara made their way to Saul and Rosemary. They came up from behind the pair and arrived just in time to overhear Saul complain, "We'll all roast in hell."

Rosemary sneered, "I'll happily stoke the coals under your butt!"

"Plans for a barbeque?" Tiara squealed as she and Tim caught Saul and Rosemary by surprise. "I have a fab recipe for a chipotle and red wine barbeque sauce. It's positively de-*lish*. I'll give it to the executive chef. The passengers will mutiny for more!"

Saul looked away, and Rosemary fumbled to open a cosmetics compact to check her lipstick in the mirror. They remained quiet.

"I couldn't help noticing your darling tennis bracelet from across the room," Tiara said, pretending that admiring Rosemary's jewelry was the reason for their visit. "A present? Did the bruise come with it?"

Rosemary quickly covered her wrist with her other hand. "It's nothing," she said, and gave Saul an elbow to his ribs.

"Such a crazy day! Death always makes me thirsty!" Tim said, attempting to engage them in conversation. He looked around for the cocktail waitress. "Ah! Perfect timing," he said as she found them and set two martinis on a nearby table. "Another round here." He indicated Saul and Rosemary and handed their margarita glasses to the waitress.

The objections from Saul and Rosemary came in a simultaneous burst of "Thanks, but no thanks." However, Tim made a grand gesture of insisting on playing host and sent the waitress off to fill the order. "It'll be fun," he said. "We finally have a night without my mother." He looked at Rosemary. "Did Saul tell you she's been put away? Captain's orders. And they've thrown away the key for the next twelve hours."

Rosemary was snotty. "Probably a safety measure—protecting the other passengers. Your mother's a little... eccentric."

Tiara gave Rosemary an icy stare. "If you mean that in the same way that Saint Oprah is eccentric as she single-handedly saves the planet one free car giveaway at a time."

Rosemary made a patronizing nasal sound. "I need to go. It's been fun, but..."

Tiara did not budge. "Your drink's on its way," she said with a sharp edge to her voice. "Afterward, you can sleep like the dead."

At the keyboard, Lawrence segued from *Little Green Apples* to *Weekend in New England*. Tiara sighed and raised her glass to the pianist. She looked at Saul. "Did you ever think about what song you'd like played at your funeral?"

The cruise director gave her a look that translated to unexpected wonder at her lack of tact.

"That's a rather odd question," Rosemary said, looking down her nose.

Tiara was unfazed. "Nonsense. One should be prepared for the inevitable. I'm dying. You're dying. Saul's going too. Heck, everyone on this boat will take a final breath someday. *I'm Still Here* can't always be your theme song."

"I'm torn between *Send in the Clowns* and *Always Look on the Bright Side of Life*," Tim joked.

"I want something sad and classical, played on a harp or bagpipes, to wring as many tears as possible from the mourners," Tiara continued. *Pavane for a Dead Princess. The Meditation. Somewhere in Time.*"

Rosemary looked at the two interlopers. "Death and dying. The subject seems to hold a great fascination for you and Polly Pepper. What's the story? Is it a side effect to all the champagne that you people swill?"

The waitress returned and set the two margaritas before Saul and Rosemary. She collected Tim's Zip 'n Sip quick-track liquor card and applied the price of the four drinks to Polly's charge account. He raised his glasses to Saul and Rosemary and said, "To the remainder of this Kool Krooz adventure! May we all arrive in Juneau without anyone accidentally or on purpose falling overboard or having their lives sucked out of otherwise perfectly healthy bodies."

"Hear! Hear!" Tiara agreed and took a dainty taste of her gin.

"And for the record, we're only interested in the deaths of people we know and/or love, such as Laura Crawford, Ricardo Montalban, Suzanne Pleshette, Robert Goulet, and Vampira. Oh, and for another record, our champagne is far from swill."

Tim took a fortifying swallow from his glass and looked at Rosemary. "Yeah, even in Hollywood, we tend to like lively *living* things. The Geico Gecko is a good example. Cuter than hell, eh? If I could find an adorable Aussie with an accent like that, I'd be a happily married man."

Tim suddenly interrupted himself and snapped his fingers. "Dumbo's mother's song! That's what we should play at Laura's memorial service. I'll get Polly to ask Renee Fleming to sing."

Tiara brought a hand to her chest. "Personally, I can't watch *Dumbo*. Separation anxiety gets to me. Walt Disney was a sadist. I mean, why would anyone make cartoons about innocent forest and jungle creatures and beautiful princesses becoming orphans, for crying out loud? The horrors of those stories stay with children for the rest of their lives. But that song is perfect for sending a loved one off for their eternal sleep."

"There won't be a dry eye in the house, even among the guests who hated her guts," Tim said, "which, unfortunately, will be ninety-nine percent of those present."

"Why go to someone's memorial if you disliked them?" Rosemary sniffed.

"To be seen, of course," Tiara offered. "We're talking Hollywood C-list celebs, but they'll get free hors d'oeuvres."

Tim turned to Rosemary. "What's it like knowing that you were the last person on this ship to see a famous celebrity before she had her throat cut?"

Rosemary was surprised and miffed by the question. "How would any normal person feel?"

"I asked how did *you* feel?"

Rosemary pursed her lips. "No matter how much of a pain in

the neck a person is, they don't deserve to be driven out of this world the way Laura Crawford was. And, just so you know, I wasn't the last person to see her alive. There's the guy who did the dirty deed. Remember him? I just found the bloody corpse."

"How do you know it was a guy who killed Laura?" Tiara asked.

Rosemary shrugged.

"Any idea who?" Tim asked. "A customer? Polly said you mentioned a man getting a treatment in the next room."

Rosemary smirked. "*Treatment* is the operative word. I rather think he had other priorities than murder."

"I don't follow," Tiara said.

"Don't be naive," Rosemary sassed. "Talia, the other masseuse, provides 'special services'—for select customers. Rich ones. If you get my drift."

Tiara pretended to take a long moment for the information to filter into her head. Then she feigned shock and amusement. "This really is a Kool Krooz." She giggled. "Romance on the high seas. But not very much like the Doris Day musical film."

"Not very much like romance, either." Rosemary sniggered. "Now, I really need to leave. I have an appointment to keep."

"At this hour?" Tiara said, looking at her watch.

"Not that it's any of your business, but some of my best appointments are kept at hours later than this one, honey." As Rosemary once again attempted to leave, it was Tim's turn to keep her corralled. "What did you and Laura talk about when she arrived for her massage? What was her mood like?" he asked.

Rosemary was miffed that her exit was obstructed. "Her mood? Unpleasant. I'm quickly getting that way myself," she declared while trying to force Tim to move. "She came in with attitude. To her, I was nobody, and she was supposed to be someone. Once. A long time ago. When she arrived at the spa, I got the impression that she didn't want to talk, so I kept my mouth shut until—"

Saul listened closely to what Rosemary was saying.

"—the door to the room opened unexpectedly," Rosemary added. "Someone, a man, stood there for a moment, then said, 'Sorry. Wrong number.'"

"You saw who it was?" Tim asked.

"No. Just his form. The room was dark except for the candle-light," Rosemary remembered. "It was just a quick 'hi, bye' sort of thing. Obviously, someone made a mistake. The guy was probably embarrassed that he'd barged in on a treatment. He left in a split second. No harm done."

"Wouldn't you normally lock the door to prevent that sort of thing from happening?" Tim said.

Rosemary shrugged.

"Who would open a closed door in a spa?" Tiara thought aloud. "Everything that goes on there is private. Another reason to lock the doors to the treatment rooms. Perhaps it wasn't an accident. Maybe someone wanted to make sure that they knew where Laura was." Tiara looked at Rosemary. "You're lucky that he didn't walk in, lock the door behind him, and butcher the two of you at the same time."

Rosemary reached for her drink and took a long swallow. "So why didn't he? That is, if this guy was the killer. Why give up a perfect opportunity to do his job then and there?"

"Waiting until you left?" Tiara said.

"He couldn't be guaranteed that there would be another opportunity. I mean, even I didn't know that I'd soon leave Laura unattended."

"Perhaps he was a scout, the advance man, for the killer," Tim suggested. "He kept an eye on the victim-to-be for his boss."

"Nah." Tiara dismissed the idea. "Most killers work alone. Unless..."

"Mob?" Tim said.

"I never heard that she was in any way involved," Tiara continued. "Generally, that kind of stuff is at least hinted at along the short Hollywood grapevine."

"What about a contract?" Tim added. "God knows Laura had a lot of enemies. But come on, just 'cause you hate someone's guts doesn't mean you have them removed from the planet."

"Not unless your name is Simpson or Blake or Spector or Peterson or that other Peterson or..." Tiara said.

"So much for your 'polite Hollywood society,'" Saul said.

Tiara cackled. "*Hollywood*, *polite*, and *society* are three words not generally used in the same sentence. There's David Hyde Pierce genuine polite. Then there's Victoria Principal not-actually-shooting-the maid-that-she-allegedly-threatened-at-gunpoint-because-her-mutt-didn't-do-#2-as-quickly-as-diva lady-wanted polite. If you work as a maid for VP, you'd better feed her dog a lot of prunes, or you're out of a slave-labor job fast."

An increasingly mellow Saul took a sip from his margarita and said, "I shouldn't be telling you this..."

"Of course you should," Tiara encouraged. "We're all friends."

"Okay. A few years ago, we had a passenger who won a sweepstakes for a weeklong cruise. Turned out, his was the only name in the pot for the prize. It was set up. A phony contest. To get him on a ship in international waters. He was murdered. Shot at close range. Between the eyes. In his stateroom."

"No muss. No fuss." Rosemary continued the story. "When the killer finished his job, he hung a DO NOT DISTURB sign on the handle, locked the stateroom door from within, and no one found the body until debarkation day."

"By then, the killer had left the ship," Saul said. "I'm telling you this so you'll know that I have some experience with contract killers."

"Good to know," Tim said dismissively. "I guess expert killers have plenty of practice. They probably don't leave much of a mess. An assignment comes; the job is completed quickly and efficiently. There's a negligible amount of evidence. Then they disappear."

Tiara continued, "I'm trying to imagine a hit man coming into a spa room, and while his target has his or her face down on the massage table, he puts the barrel of a gun with a silencer to the base of their skull, pulls the trigger, and pow, it's over. So easy."

"But the person who killed Laura must have been an amateur 'cause he made a terrible mess," Rosemary said.

"The fact that he improvised a weapon by sharpening a DVD instead of using a knife or a gun tells me that he hadn't spent a lot of time planning how to get rid of her," Tim said. "He wasn't prepared."

Tiara crossed her arms and took a deep breath as she considered Tim's conjecture. "Polly always said, 'An amateur in the theater is as dangerous as a politician's brain in the Situation Room. When they screw up, they go to extremes to cover their butts.' I think you're absolutely right. We have an amateur killer running around this ship. I'll bet that Polly is closer than she thinks to finding out his identity."

"The closer she gets, the more afraid he'll become, and the possibility of him killing again, in order to save his own skin, rises," Tim agreed. He turned to Saul and said, "About the obituary in the *Daily Wave*—who has access to the computer it was on?"

Saul twisted his mouth and said, "It's the crew's communal computer. We all use it."

"Does everybody use the same password to log in?"

"It's always on. No password needed. But there's usually a long wait because everyone uses the same machine to download their emails."

"Is there a sign-in roster so we'll know who used the computer today?" Tiara asked.

"That wouldn't help. The obit was sent via text messaging from someone who wasn't a crew member," Saul said.

"To whose account?"

"Our office assistant, Julie," Saul said. "She opened it and pasted the material into the *Daily Wave* document. We've already checked on the address of the sender. But we don't have the tech support to find out where it came from. The police in Juneau will have to take on that problem."

Tim sighed. "So, Captain Sheridan isn't really mad at Polly, he's protecting her."

"Mad?" Saul laughed. "He wishes he were the captain of a seventeenth-century vessel so he could legally put Polly Pepper out on a raft and send her away. He's furious! He's had more than his share of suspicious deaths on his watch over the past couple of years. If one more dead person takes this cruise, he'll be in deep doo-doo at the main office. Captain Sheridan wants to retire with full benefits, but he'll be replaced if anything else goes wrong."

"So, he doesn't have a heart after all," Tim said. "He's doing what the amateurs do, protecting his pension."

After drinking his second margarita, Saul became more animated. He started swaying to the music, and when Lawrence started playing *Funkytown*, Saul reached out and took Tiara's hand. "Let's dance!"

Before Tiara had a chance to object, Saul pulled her to the dance floor. As they started gyrating and bumping hips, Tiara gave Lawrence a wide-eyed look and shrugged. He smiled back and nodded approval.

Although Saul couldn't quite find the rhythm of the music, he moved his arms around and bounced from the left and right. "You're a regular Fred Astaire," Tiara said, realizing it was her job to make them look good together.

Saul smiled and continued bobbing his head and flailing his arms. "After my crummy day, this is just what I needed. I'll be lucky if I still have a job when we reach port."

Tiara raised her arms in the air and bumped Saul's right hip. Then she moved to his other side and bumped his left hip. "You must have a hard job trying to please over two thousand passengers and all the so-called 'talent' aboard this ship, not to mention the captain and a demanding harridan like Rosemary."

"Every day it's like I'm getting blasted with pellets from a semiautomatic BB gun. I have to hear complaints from impatient passengers, or someone among the crew telling me I did something wrong, and then there's Rosemary. Testy. Argumentative. Has to have things her way. She and I are friends, but only because we have to work together. We're different personalities. She's hard as nails, and I'm an easygoing live-and-let-live guy. Wouldn't harm a butterfly."

"Not so easygoing on the wrists," Tiara said. "Friends don't give friends bruises."

Saul slowly came to a standstill. "She started it."

Tiara continued to bop and shimmy to the music. "Of course she did. Keep dancing. We make a cute couple. But you realize that you're both going to be in a ton of trouble if you don't do something about this situation."

"What situation?"

"I'm not dumb. I only play an idiot to throw people off," Tiara smiled. "Polly and Tim picked up on your scheme right away. I confess that it took me a moment longer. But now, I'm sure."

"Of?"

"You and Rosemary. You're completely responsible for..."

Saul clenched his jaw and curled his upper lip. He started to hyperventilate as he stared deep into Tiara's eyes. "I don't know what you're talking about."

"C'mon. You're not stupid either," Tiara brayed. "Oh, this is a good song for you," she said as Lawrence began playing *Gypsies, Tramps and Thieves.*

"I'm outta here," Saul said, and left the dance floor.

Tiara followed on his heels as he returned to where Tim was now sitting alone. "Our fourth Musketeer is missing?" she said.

"Was there too much garlic in my dinner?" Tim asked.

"Let me smell," Tiara said. "No. Anyway, Rosemary said she had important business to take care of. It's just as we suspected." She surreptitiously winked at Tim. "Saul told me everything."

"I didn't say a word!"

Other passengers, and Lawrence, began to take notice of an altercation erupting.

"Anyway, it was just fun and games," Saul said. "Nothing was supposed to happen. Laura Craw—" Saul shut his mouth and sat down at the small table. "As I said, it was that Miss Masseuse-with-a-fake-license who started the whole thing. I just tagged along for the fun of it."

"Fun?" Tiara gasped with horror.

Saul took a deep breath. "The entire crew was in on it! We've done it before, and we'll do it again if we can get away with it. But I swear, I never suspected these results. I won!"

"You call Laura Crawford's death winning?" Tim said, looking around for a security officer.

"I made seven hundred bucks."

"Is that all a life is worth to you?" Tiara bellowed.

"It would have been more if that Disney kid had died," Saul said. "Imagine if I'd said Michael Jackson! The younger they are, the bigger the payoff. Unless they already have some terminal disease. You know how it works."

"No! As a matter of fact, I don't know how it works," Tiara said as she grabbed Saul by his shirt. "Oh, sweet Jesus! Where's the captain? Where's security? Where's anyone with a phone to record what you're saying?"

Tim grabbed Saul by the arm and heaved him to his feet. "Somebody! Anybody! Get the captain!" Tim yelled. "Hurry! It's an emergency."

Lawrence stopped playing piano and jumped off the raised platform to rush to Tiara's side. A crowd encircled the quartet. Almost instantly, a team of security officers arrived and pried Saul out of Tim's clutches. Tim and Saul and Tiara were strong-armed and forced to stand against the bar. As a large crowd gathered to witness the event, the captain walked in and pushed his way through the dense throng of onlookers. He looked at Tim and Tiara. "For some stupid reason I thought Polly Pepper was the only troublemaker on this voyage."

"Don't forget that other certain menace, the person or persons responsible for the near decapitation of Laura Crawford," Tiara said.

"So, what's this all about?" Captain Sheridan demanded.

"We have one of the killers right here," Tim said as he tried to catch his breath. "It's Saul. And find Rosemary—from the spa. You'll want to get her confession too."

"Confession? You're crazy!" Saul exclaimed. "I never... What the hell are you talking about?"

Captain Sheridan cocked his head to one of his officers, who scurried off to find Rosemary and bring her to the lounge.

"Sure. Lie about it now. Cover your murderous butt." Tiara scowled at Saul. "And you're a crummy dancer, too!"

Captain Sheridan glowered at the trio.

Finally, a security officer arrived with Rosemary. She took one look at the scene and hesitated before asking, "What's up?"

"You tell me," Captain Sheridan shouted.

Crowds attract crowds, and by now it seemed that the entire roster of passengers had been drawn to the scene. An angry sea captain and a coterie of uniformed officers detaining the popular cruise director and two passengers who, someone whispered, were friends of the star of an old television series, was about as exciting as bearing witness to someone being arrested and handcuffed on the street by the police.

"May I speak?" Tiara asked.

"Someone had better," the captain thundered.

"I've heard a lot of things in my lifetime, but tonight..." Tiara shook her head in astonishment. "Earlier in the evening we overheard that television brat Cori Berman talk about Polly Pepper cashing in. And I don't think he meant poker chips."

Tim interrupted. "After the death of her friend Laura Crawford, and Polly's mock obituary in the *Daily Wave,* and the fact that she's been stalked all night..."

"And then to hear this one"—she pointed to Saul— "confessing that he and Rosemary killed Laura for a mere seven hundred dollars..."

"Kill?" Saul cried. "What are you talking about!"

Rosemary snapped, "Shut up! You greedy little pisher! You had to have the money before the voyage was over. Look what happens when we don't play by the rules. You'd better confess. Or I'll sing like a bird."

"A killing? Yeah," Saul said.

The dull clamor from the crowd nearly drowned out Saul's next words. "But it's not what you think."

"It never is," Tim said above the sounds of loud whispers and tones of disbelief. "You made seven hundred bucks, but you won't be able to spend it except perhaps on ciggies for your match made in jail."

Suddenly, from the crowd, the sound of one man lethargically clapping rose above the din of the other passengers' murmurs. As the clapping continued, the throng parted to reveal Cori Berman. In blue jeans and a white shirt with its tails out, the sleeves rolled up over his forearms, Cori proceeded to the front of the swarm of onlookers. When he arrived to face Tim and Tiara, he shook his head. "You silly people," he said.

"You're part of this too," Tim said. "We overheard you earlier this evening telling Rosemary that Polly was cashing in. Well, guess what, she's not dead, and she's not going to be dead. At least not on this cruise!"

Cori smirked. "One should never come in at the end of a private conversation and jump to conclusions."

"Saul made seven hundred dollars for killing Laura Crawford," Tiara said.

"Brains don't run in the family, do they?" Cori said. "Is it genetic and then passed on by osmosis to the household staff? Did either of you ever hear of the dead pool?"

Tim instantly said, "Clint Eastwood, Liam Neeson, Patricia Clarkson. Nineteen eighty-eight. Directed by Buddy Van Horn."

"Another notch on your idiot post," Cori scorned as laughter erupted from the mob.

Captain Sheridan wailed in disbelief. "The dead pool? You're not involved in that again!" He looked at Rosemary. "I specifically told you what would happen if..."

"With all these old celebrities ready to kick the bucket, how can you blame us?" she pressed. "The dead pool money is too good to pass up. God knows since this freakin' Kool Krooz outfit stays mostly in international waters, there aren't any minimum-wage rules. We could all use a few extra easy bucks."

"Dead pool?" Tim asked sheepishly.

Captain Sheridan shook his head and looked at Saul, then at Rosemary. "I'm outta here. You all work this out. Be in my office tomorrow morning at nine." He turned and left the horde of passengers, who were still trying to figure out what was going on.

"Dead pool?" Tiara followed Tim's query. "Where's the 'dead pool'?"

Cori giggled. "This is fun. Now everyone in the family has made public fools of themselves. You've accused two more people of Laura Crawford's murder, when all they did was ante up some *dinero* and guessed who would die on this journey."

"The dead pool!" Tim and Tiara both yelled at once and looked at each other in shocked surprise.

Cori said, "My money is still on Polly Pepper 'cashing in' before we reach Alaska!"

16

"We're a laughingstock," Tim cried as he and Tiara elbowed their way through the sniggering crowd and escaped down the corridor to the elevators.

"I can't face Lawrence let alone spend the night with him," Tiara bellowed.

"Polly'll be furious!"

"No one's as guilty of jumping to conclusions as much as she is," Tiara reminded him.

"But we're supposed to be smarter than her," Tim cried out as they rushed past passengers, a few of whom were pointing and sniggering at them. "News spreads quickly."

"Like intestinal bacteria on a cruise to Mexico!"

"Polly is many amazing things," Tim said as they ascended a staircase rather than wait for the elevator. "But her brain isn't hermetically sealed."

Tim led Tiara to her stateroom. As he hugged her good night, he said, "Call Lawrence. Trust me, he's not going to hold our stupidity against you. Blame it on me, and just have some fun."

"What about you?" Tiara asked.

"All I want is my pillow," he whined. "I'm going straight to bed. Alone. I won't even attempt to coax the guards away from Polly's door to my own." He laughed. "I'm kidding. Sort of. Actually, I should run by her stateroom to make sure everything is okay."

"This is probably the only time we'll ever be one hundred percent guaranteed that Polly is out of trouble." Tiara pushed her key card into the slot and opened the door to her cabin. "We'll talk in the ayem."

Tim made a "mwah" sound and waited until Tiara closed the door and he heard the lock pushed into place.

En route to his own cabin, Tim climbed the steps to his and Polly's deck. As he walked down the corridor toward her cabin, Tim saw that indeed his mother's door was still being guarded. However, the two ship's security men were in a heated exchange with another man. When Tim arrived, the man was yelling at the closed door.

"Polly! It's me. Dorian! They won't let me in!"

Tim looked at the two guards. "What's up?"

The three men turned and gave Tim a look that said, *What's it to you?*

"It's her kid," one guard said to the other.

Dorian's demeanor instantly changed. He beamed a wide smile and reached out his hand to shake Tim's. "I've been wanting to meet you," he said, practically wagging a tail. "I'm Dorian Dawson. Your mother speaks so highly of you—her pride and joy."

Although Tim smiled, he was ill at ease. *This can't be the guy Polly's so into. He's a nothing runt*, he said to himself.

Dorian put his hand on Tim's shoulder. "How 'bout a drink, son?"

Tim squirmed. He hated to be called "son," even by his two

fathers. However, politeness prevented him from shirking away Dorian's hand. "It's late, and I'm dead," Tim said, trying to respectfully extricate himself from the invitation. "We'll do drinks with Polly tomorrow."

"It's already tomorrow," Dorian said. "I promise not to keep you long." Dorian attempted to guide Tim down the corridor.

Tim forced a small laugh and said, "There's not much more to get to know. I'm an open book. What you see is what you get. Anyway, I'll be a better conversationalist after I get my beauty sleep. We'll have brunch."

Dorian wasn't giving up. "You hardly need any beauty sleep. Just one question. Do you think that your mother likes me?"

Tim stopped and gave Dorian a quizzical look. "Polly doesn't spend time with people she doesn't find amusing," Tim said while thinking, *Polly needs a mental tune-up.*

"That's a relief." Dorian sighed. "Women are hard to read. Don't you think so too, son?"

Tim cringed again, but he agreed that yes, sometimes women can be scary. "Why do you even have to ask if she likes you? Is there a problem?" Tim said, cloaking his hopefulness with a frown.

"From time to time we all need reassurance," Dorian said. "Polly's a very special lady, and I'm not in her league."

You're not in Joan Rivers's league either, and she's cremated!

"I don't want to do anything to jeopardize our relationship."

Relationship? Tim wanted to cry out with sarcasm. *You're nothing more to Polly than a shipboard diversion. Polly would never settle for someone like you. She already has a great boyfriend.* Instead, he said, "Yeah, Mother is unique." He made eye contact with Dorian. "We'll connect tomorrow."

Dorian patted Tim on the back in a patronizing way. "Don't do this to me, son. Did your mother raise you to reject someone who is extending a hand in friendship? I just want to have a quick drink and become your friend."

Tim had a thick skin when it came to being personally criticized about aspects of his professional work or being teased about his not-so-secret crush on *Good Morning America*'s weatherman. However, no one got away with saying anything disparaging to his face about his mother or her parenting skills. Tim brushed Dorian's hand off his shoulder and turned toward him like an angry sports team manager facing a referee. He pushed his index finger into Dorian's chest.

Dorian was shocked. He instantly backed up against the corridor wall and put up his hands to show he was harmless. "I don't understand. What did I say?" he pleaded.

"To answer your first stupid remark, yes, this is how my mother raised me. She did a damn good job, too. She always told me to be considerate of slimy things, like her agent, JJ—and an assortment of snakes. So, I'm going to let you slither away and pretend this unpleasantness never happened. Leave before I do something that Mother would *not* be proud of."

The two security guards had watched the altercation and rushed to intervene. "Break it up, guys," one said. "Passengers are trying to sleep."

Both Tim and Dorian apologized and insisted that they'd simply had a misunderstanding. "Just take care of my mother, who I'm sure is fast asleep," Tim said.

As Tim and Dorian walked in silence down the corridor toward the elevators, the guards returned to their post. When Dorian reached for the elevator call button, Tim decided to take the stairs. "I may not be able to join you for lunch or drinks after all," Tim said. "I'm sure that something more important will come up."

"Don't burn bridges, son."

"What's that supposed to mean?" Tim asked.

Dorian simply glared at Tim, and when the elevator car arrived, he stepped in, pushed a button on the panel, and the doors closed.

Tim turned and descended the stairs. As soon as he reached the next deck, he ran as quickly as he could to Tiara's cabin. He knocked softly on her door and whispered, "It's me. Open up." When the door opened, Tim was surprised but smiled brightly.

Polly, with one hand on her hip and the other high on the doorframe, said, "Perfect timing, sweetums!"

Polly Pepper smiled as she leaned in to kiss Tim's cheek and welcome him to Tiara's cabin. "We're having a little champagne celebration! Napoleon's escape from Elba couldn't have been as smooth and swift, thanks to you!"

Lounging on Tiara's bed, with a glass of champagne in her hand, and fingering her string of pearls, Polly looked at Tim. "No wonder Betty White stopped playing poker with you," she said. "Your face turns to stone. You never gave any indication that you saw me sneaking out of my stateroom."

"I was terrified that Dorian—by the way, he's a creep—or the guards would turn around before you vanished! How did you know when it was safe to open your door and flee?"

"I have an actor's perfect timing for making entrances and exits!" Polly insisted. "Also, I'd been watching those two thugs—"

"I thought they were kinda cute."

"—through the peephole all night. They were bored out of their skulls. I could hear 'em grousing about never getting to stand sentry for a *real* star. By the way, who is Jessica Biel, and what's an Alex Borstein? Anyway, I was waiting for something that might distract them. I just knew my time would come, and it did. You and Dorian came along at precisely the right moment."

Tiara looked at Polly with unvarnished distress. "Don't

blame the Grim Reaper if he reads the *Daily Wave* and realizes he has to make a quick stop here after all."

Tim nodded. "You were safe inside your cabin."

"As long as everyone thinks I'm under house detention, I'm completely secure," Polly said. "Anyway, I'm not a child who can be sent to my room because of some infraction of parental rules or curfew. I'm Polly Freaking Pepper! Plus, we're down to the wire. We have only two days left at sea. We have a mere forty-eight hours to find the killer. I can't waste time with maritime laws, or whatever phony legal statutes Captain Sheridan thinks he can use to boss me around."

Tim took a sip from his champagne glass. "Speaking of being bossed around, who the heck is this Dorian jerk? He reeks of gold digger. And he's not the slightest bit cute!"

Polly's face expressed mild surprise. "Not even a little? I think there's some Charlie Gibson there. Minus the integrity, of course."

"Not even Robin Williams sorta cuddly when he was Mork from Ork."

Polly rolled her eyes. "Okay. So Dorian isn't exactly the Gillette shaving cream guy on the commercial, but he has a certain *je ne sais quoi*. No?"

"*No!*"

Polly half nodded and half shook her head. "Actually, he's already boring the sequins off my Bob Mackies. Any man who continually uses dumb phrases like 'shows to go you' is someone I'd probably end up hurting. Physically. By the way, I heard what you said about how well I raised you. I take full credit."

Tiara took a deep breath. "You may reconsider knowing Tim, and me, after you hear the rumors that are probably circulating throughout the ship."

Polly looked at Tiara, then took another sip from her champagne glass. "Rumors. Generally, I love them. They usually hold a kernel of truth. What level of gossip are we talking here? Big stuff like Madonna's latest boy toy? Or the who seriously gives a darn about Mel Gibson's latest lawsuits, knocked-up girlfriends, and Catholic hypocrisy? By the way, I think his ex-wifey totally deserves all the dough she's getting from his hairy *Braveheart* butt."

Tim shrugged. "Closer to Madonna, I guess. We found the killer tonight."

Polly instantly sat up straight. "Who? What? Where?" Then she asked, "Wait a minute. You said 'rumor.'"

Tim nodded. "Remember Lawrence the piano player?"

"I recall someone by that name being uncooperative with me."

"Perhaps because he was innocent!" Tiara said.

"I mean, remember what you said *about* Lawrence?" Tim continued.

Polly pouted. "A minor misunderstanding."

"Minor?" Tiara huffed. "Eddie Griffin crashing a Ferrari is minor compared to what you did."

"Could've happened to anyone," Polly defended herself.

"Glad that you feel that way," Tim said, "because we played 'Polly Mistaken Identity Pepper' tonight." He nodded toward Tiara. "We were in the bar. Enjoying martinis. Suddenly we found ourselves accusing a couple of people of killing Laura Crawford."

"Martinis? That's the root of your problem," Polly said. "Stick to champagne, as I do. Keeps one's mental acuity in perfect equilibrium." She suddenly looked concerned. "Are we in trouble? Do I have to call JJ to call in a few favors from his broken-nose friends to prevent slander lawsuits?"

Tim set his glass down, finger-combed his hair, and looked at his wristwatch. "It's late. Let's talk about this in the morning."

"It's already morning," Polly said.

"So, I've already been reminded."

"Get it over with now."

"Saul and Rosemary," Tiara continued.

Polly twisted her mouth, knitted her eyebrows, and held out her glass for another refill. "What about 'em?" she said, taking a small sip from her glass.

"We sorta told everyone that they were Laura's murderers," Tiara said.

"We only *suggested* that they were guilty of one murder. Laura Crawford's, to be precise," Tim said.

Polly stood up and began to pace the small cabin floor. "I can understand how you might think Rosemary had something to do with Laura's death. After all, she had the body in her massage room. But Saul? He's an innocuous cruise director with a severe identity problem. The man hardly has enough time to race from his duties running the safety drill and the bingo games, the paintball contests, and the triple-X video rental library. When would he find the minutes needed to hack up a celebrity? Did you ever bother to ask yourselves what his motive might be? I guarantee it's not because Laura rejected sleeping with him."

When Tim and Tiara finished retelling the story of how they came to their erroneous conclusion that Saul and Rosemary and even Cori Berman had collectively become number one suspects, Polly threw her hands up and moaned. "Okay. Let's look on the perky-weather-girl bright side of things. The good news is that we can cross off three more passengers from our list of suspects. The bad news, however—"

"Is that only leaves another several thousand-plus possible killers," said Tiara.

"Way to go, kids," Polly said. "Now nobody will believe us the next time we point a finger."

Tim and Tiara were at once relieved that Polly seemed to take their faux pas in stride but upset that indeed they could hardly be taken seriously from this day forward. "I wish you could have seen the captain when he realized that we'd erred again." Tim smiled.

"I also missed Mike Tyson cannibalizing Evander Holyfield's ear," Polly said. "Thank God for small blessings! And speaking of all the things I'm thankful for, it's nearly dawn! As you know, I'm supposed to go overboard at seven. So, let's take a stroll along the Lido Deck. It could be my last bit of exercise before swimming to the Aleutian Islands. We might even encourage a killer to come out from hiding."

Tim's shoulders sagged. "I'm going to bed," he said.

"I need a witness to my murder."

"Call Dorian. He'd love to be your escort."

Tiara made "mmm-mmm" sounds and shook her head. She stood up, yawned, and stretched, and looked at Polly. "You can break out of a gilded cage and evade two uniformed security personnel with sidearms, but you'll be a dead woman before you get past me. You know that's true," she said sharply. Tiara reached for a bathrobe hanging in the tiny closet next to the cabin door. As she tossed it to Polly, she said, "Take off your clothes and put this on. Brush your teeth. And be afraid."

Polly took a defiant stance. "I've told you a gazillion times; I worked with Stephanie Hough at Sterling 'We put the sun in places where it don't even shine' Studios. They're all killers at that famously unhappiest place in the universe. Since then, I'm not afraid of anything. You're the one who should be in fear. I hold the pen that signs your paychecks!"

Tiara straightened to her full height. "Don't make me email the *National Intruder* with a firsthand account of how the famous Polly Pepper is carrying on a shipboard romance with Cori Berman. It's easy enough to Photoshop a picture of you dancing with that way-too-young-for-you child-star has-been."

Polly swallowed hard. She looked at Tim for support. When

he smirked and nodded in agreement with Tiara, Polly's nostrils flared, and she folded her arms across her chest. "You're not the boss of me," she countered. "I have so many Emmy Awards, Angela Lansbury hated me!"

Tiara said, "Trust me. I can unload those babies to private collectors for big bucks. If you want to live to worship those little gods again, you'll wash your face, tinkle, and hit the sack until Cap'n Crunch is told that you disappeared into thin air, and comes looking for you here."

"Good night, er, morning, Polly," Tim said as he tried to peck his mother's cheek, which she turned away in rebellion. "When I wake up, I'll share a great idea for recruiting your fans to help in the search for Laura's killer," Tim said.

Polly gave Tim a hurt look of betrayal. "I may not be around to discuss the idea. I could be killed at any moment, and it appears that my own army is turning its back on me."

"Remember that adorable Pillsbury dough boy we met when you were making *Detention Rules!* That stinker movie musical last year?" Tim asked.

"Duane, the security man?" Polly said.

"Sweet, obsequious, servile Duane," Tim confirmed.

"Unlike you two, he would have done anything for me!"

"Precisely," Tim asserted. "We're surrounded by a boatload of bootlickers just like him. We're not taking advantage of their starstruck idol worship. Someone on this ship knows who knocked off Laura. All you have to do is appeal to your fan base to spread out like a search party with bloodhounds and beg for their help in tracking down whatever information they can score."

Polly's eyes glistened. "Go away. I need to sleep. I've got a big day ahead of me. I have to rehearse a big scene. The one where I convince my fans that I'll probably become their best friend if they help me ferret out a killer."

17

A t ten A.M., Captain Sheridan arrived at Polly's stateroom. The two guards reported that their assignment had gone smoothly, and that with the exception of Dorian Dawson and Tim Pepper attempting to visit, the night had been uneventful.

Captain Sheridan knocked on Polly's door. No answer. He knocked again and called out, "Miss Pepper?" No response.

"Perhaps she's in the shower," said one of the security guards.

"Perhaps she's passed out from all the champagne she drinks," said the other.

"Or maybe she found the cabin too small and stuffy and decided to take a stroll for a bit of fresh air and autograph signing," a woman's voice said from behind the men.

The captain and guards turned around.

"You boys did a nifty job," Polly said, smiling at the two handsome sailors.

Captain Sheridan looked at Polly Pepper with a dumbfounded expression. "How?" he asked, then turned to the two seamen, who were at once confused and embarrassed.

"Impossible!" said one of the men to Polly.

Polly stepped forward and patted the young man's cheek. "My mother used to use that word a lot when I said I wanted to be a star." Then she tapped her card key onto the door lock. "I just stopped by to get a few things." She turned around and curtsied to the two guards. "You boys were divine. If I were the king of England, I'd certainly assign you to guard the crown jewels."

She then turned to the captain and smiled. "I know that you're just doing your job, sweetums. Protecting a famous passenger, I mean. I promise to return the favor. In fact, I'm already on the job. My divine agent is doing his best to kill a story that was leaked to the *National Intruder*. Something about a banner headline in which the entire Kool Krooz fleet of boats is accused of holding celebrity passengers against their will in the ship's meat lockers. For some reason, you're singled out as an example."

Polly saw the look of incredulity on Captain Sheridan's face. "Of course, that's a stretch. You and I know it. But the ladies in the checkout line at the Piggly Wiggly believe everything they read in that nasty tabloid. Not to worry. We'll do all we can so that your upcoming retirement doesn't come sooner than expected. After all the years of service you've given to this cruise line, we wouldn't want to give them any reason to withhold your full pension." Just as Polly was about to turn around and enter the cabin, Captain Sheridan suddenly growled and kicked at the cabin door.

Polly looked at the dented door, then at the captain and the security team, and back to the door again. She crossed her arms. "I smell a cabin upgrade," she said.

Captain Sheridan glowered, gave the door one more kick, and left in a huff. As he disappeared down the corridor, Polly called out, "I hope that the *National Intruder* story isn't too hot to retract. Good luck, sweetums!"

The two security guards were shaken to the soles of their highly polished black shoes. "He'll calm down," Polly said. "When he's in a better mood, I'll talk to him."

"Don't hold your breath waiting for the right moment," said Stephen Ronson, the shorter guard. "He thinks he's king of the world. The only fear Captain Sheridan has is that something will happen to keep him from retiring next year."

The other guard, Marc Garner, added, "He'll probably go to his grave angry that he was outfoxed by a mere celebrity. One from *television* no less! Oh, no offense."

"None taken, dear," Polly said. "Actually, being on the tube, more people have seen me than all the collective audiences on Broadway who ever saw Ethel Merman. The captain may not realize it, but he was outwitted by a very big star."

She looked at the two blank faces. "Ethel Merman. An American stage actress. Known for singing in big hit shows on Broadway."

The two men shrugged.

"Forget it," she said. "You're too young to even know that Ron Howard was once famous for doing something other than directing movies."

Officer Garner said, "We didn't fall asleep during the night, so how did you get past us?"

"Honey, stars do all sorts of astonishing things. Stick around and you might even see me fly. I was a hit as Peter Pan at the Manassas Music Tent!"

"Seriously," said Ronson. "We're in deep doo-doo. How can we explain ourselves to Captain Sheridan?"

Polly instantly felt bad for the young men. "I'll have a chat with Captain Nemo. I'll explain that while you were heroically trying to stop a fight between my son and Dorian Dawson, I slipped away. You're not at fault. I'll make him understand.

There. Done. Now, you can do something for me. What's the dish behind the death of my friend Laura Crawford?"

Both men shrugged.

"I know this is a big boat and the crew is quite large, but surely you all talk amongst yourselves, and someone must have heard something that could be used to indict the killer," Polly said. "I'm getting desperate. Tell you what, I'll send a letter of commendation about your exemplary work ethics to the CEO of Kool Kroozes if you give me just a small bit. A nibble. A morsel. Please?"

Officer Ronson shook his head. "All I've heard is that whoever murdered the actress had to be physically strong."

"Also, they were able to evade detection for one reason only: there are no cameras in the spa," the other sailor said. "We've got hundreds of hidden lenses everywhere, so either the killer got lucky by terminating the passenger's life in the spa, or he knew from firsthand experience that he'd be safe there away from the eyes of Big Brother."

"Yeah, yeah, I know all that," Polly said as she folded her arms across her chest and slipped into deep contemplation. Finally, she said, "Most passengers don't know about all the security measures that cruise ships take to prevent piracy and terrorists blowing 'em all out of the water. I never ruled out foul play by a member of the crew. Now, after seeing your lovely captain's bizarre outburst, I'm adding him to the pool of suspects."

"Captain Sheridan wouldn't hurt a fly," Officer Garner said. "However, in the absence of flies, he's more than happy to tear a new hole into anyone in the crew who disobeys an order, or who just crosses him. I've seen him go berserk if he sees a distant cloud in the sky when it's supposed to be sunny."

"In other words, he's mental like the Sterling Studios publicity execs I've had to deal with," Polly said.

Tim's voice was heard. Polly and the two crew members turned to find him and Tiara sidling up to them. Tiara added, "Everyone's left our pool of suspects. Lawrence and Rosemary and D'Angelo and Saul and every other innocent we've foolishly suspected. They're all drying off together in the cabana marked **ABOVE SUSPICION.**"

Tim pointed to Polly's cabin door. "Yikes! *Fee-fi-fo-fum.* If that's the result of a tantrum, I'd hate to be around when the giant is out for blood!"

"Yeah. Look for us in the infirmary," said Ronson. "What Captain Sheridan did to that door, he's likely to do to us, too." He looked at Polly. "There isn't anything you can do to make him see another side to the situation. All that he's able to understand is that we failed our assignment. He doesn't have an ounce of empathy in his body. There isn't room in his thought process for excuses, even if they're legit."

Polly's shoulders sagged. "Sorry, boys. I know how you feel. I used to have to tighten my sphincter whenever Stephanie Hough, that VP of publicity witch, summoned me to her office to complain about something I'd said in an interview with *Good Housekeeping* or *Redbook* or *Vanity Fair.* The only way to get back at people like Hough or your Sheridan is to find their Achilles' heel and publicly puncture their arrogance. I did it with a hidden camera in my hair and broadcast her tirade on YouTube."

"It was hysterically funny!" Tiara laughed. "Hough made Bill O'Reilly, Glenn Beck, and Michael Richards look like spoiled brats."

Polly smiled. "Ha! She forgot how beloved I am. By the time my little video, which my brilliant Timmy put together complete with the 'O-E-Yah! E-O-Ah!' chant by the castle guards of the Wicked Witch of the West in *The Wizard of Oz,* made the rounds on 10.5 million computers worldwide, she was tossed out of

Hollywood. Do I feel any remorse over having someone dethroned? Nah!"

The two security guards looked at each other. The taller one said, "I never thought of Captain Sheridan being guilty of anything so heinous as murder. But hypothetically, what if he really is responsible for something like Laura Crawford's death? What if we could help prove it?"

Polly clapped her hands together in heady excitement. "I love retribution, don't you?" She planted kisses on the foreheads of both men and said, in her most theatrical voice, "Go forth, my children! Return unto me when thou hast slain the dragon!"

Tim rolled his eyes. "In other words, reconnaissance and then let's meet up for a drink in Polly's new cabin—wherever that ends up being—at, say, seven tonight."

As they nodded and began to walk away, the two men looked as gleeful as Polly. "If you don't see us again, check the meat locker," Ronson called back in jest.

"Or the ocean," said Garner.

Polly, Tim, and Tiara watched as the men slowly disappeared down the corridor. They turned a corner and were gone from sight. "They're too cute to be in trouble," Tim said.

"I feel completely guilty," Polly added. "Those boys don't deserve what they'll probably get from that monster Captain Sheridan. Wouldn't it be marvelous if Sheridan actually had something to do with Laura's death? He's certainly strong enough to have ripped her head off. And God, he's got a mean streak!"

"I just hope that you haven't sent those two cuties to their deaths," Tim said. "Now let's see the deck steward about getting you a new cabin."

"One as gorgeous as Laura's! Restitution for all the mental trauma I've suffered," Polly said.

After supervising the transfer of the contents of Polly's stateroom to an upper-deck veranda suite, the trio set out to collect as many of her most stalwart fans as possible and invite them to meet personally with the legend herself. With each hesitation to accept the offer came the same question, "Is she going to accuse me of not tipping enough? Or of cheating at bingo?"

Following her four o'clock appearance with Arnie and Tommy in the theater, Polly raced to the Coral Lounge, where Tim and Tiara had assembled thirty of her fans for this special meet 'n' greet. Among the collection of mostly elderly women, there were also a few men. While everyone held a glass of champagne in their hand, Polly made a brief speech about her appreciation of their support over the many years of her career, and how much she valued each and every one of them.

Then Tim took the floor. He explained that as a dear friend and colleague of the late Laura Crawford, Polly had a very personal interest in finding the person who'd snuffed out Auntie Laura's life. "Therefore, would everyone please put on their thinking caps and try to remember if they saw or heard anything about that terrible night that might offer a clue as to who the killer might be." Although there was a lot of murmuring in the crowd, no one raised their hand. Tim persisted. "My mother is so distraught about what happened to her very best friend on the planet that she hasn't been quite herself since our first day at sea. You've brought Polly Pepper enormous joy and pleasure for many years, and she's done the same for you. She loves you as much as you love her. Don't we want to help the people we love? Of course we do. Therefore, even the smallest bit of information that you might have about Laura Crawford's death may mean more than you think. If you have anything to mention, even something that you think is dumb or insignificant, please let Polly know. There's a reward, too."

At the sound of the word *reward,* six hands reached into the air. Tim smiled warmly and called on the woman closest to him.

"How much?" she demanded.

Tim was taken aback. "Um, that depends on how useful the information is." He called on another woman.

"I want cash."

"Do you have information that could lead to the arrest and conviction of Laura Crawford's killer?"

"That depends."

"On?"

"Whether or not you pay me in small bills."

Tim was becoming increasingly frustrated but forged ahead. "Is there anyone here who loves Polly Pepper, and maybe even Laura Crawford, enough to be of service? Sure, there's a reward, but isn't it in our better natures to do the right thing even if there's no monetary compensation?"

The room was quiet. Tim gave up. "Thank you all for coming," he said. "I know that Polly wants to say thank you, too."

Polly stood in the center of the bar and smiled her famous overbite smile. "I certainly do adore all of you. If any little memory about this case creeps into your heads, you know where to find me. I'll be all ears. Cheers!" She raised her glass and, speaking out of the side of her mouth to Tim, said, "Little memory is all they have collectively. This was a waste of time."

As the fans shuffled out of the room, Polly, Tim, and Tiara sat down to finish off the bottle of champagne. Tiara poured, and Polly raised her glass again. "What would Jessica Fletcher do if she were in my shoes?"

"At eight fifty-five she reveals the killer," Tiara said. "We still have time to solve the mystery before the end credits roll."

From the corner of her eye, Polly could see a figure slowly

approach the table. She turned and found a shrunken woman with a widow's hump reaching out to touch Polly's shoulder. Polly smiled as Tim gallantly stood up and retrieved a chair for the woman.

"You have a very polite son," the woman said. "I'm Mrs. Hardy. I want to tell you how much I love you and your old show."

Polly put her hands to her heart and sighed. "Dear Mrs. Hardy, I can't tell you how much it means to me to hear you say those words. Don't I know you? Are you in that commercial? 'Clap on! Clap off!' No. Of course not. That old woman probably clapped off ages gone. May I offer you a glass of champagne?"

Mrs. Hardy shook her head but smiled. "I stopped doing drugs and alcohol years ago."

Polly said, "I hope you don't think less of me for enjoying a wee glass now and then."

"Heavens, no," Mrs. Hardy said. "It's your liver, not mine!"

Polly frowned. "Would you like an autograph, dear?"

"No, thank you," Mrs. Hardy said in her soft and easygoing manner. "I just wanted to unburden myself of guilt about that dear dead girl Laura who used to be on your show."

Polly straightened up and took a long sip from her flute. "What would a dear old, er, *sweet* woman such as yourself have to feel guilty about?"

"I think I sent her to her grave."

Polly, Tim, and Tiara were now facing Mrs. Hardy so closely that they could smell her dusting of lilac talcum.

"I was having dinner in the Tsunami Grill on our first night out," Mrs. Hardy continued. "I travel alone, so I'm generally seated at an orphan's table. I heard a commotion at the maître d's stand, and I instantly recognized Laura Crawford, even though she was fatter than when she was on your show. The next thing I know, she's being seated next to me! I remember she grumbled and said, 'Can't even get a decent table in this dump!'"

Tim nodded. "That's Laura."

"Anyway, the poor thing ignored dining room etiquette and answered her cell phone," Mrs. Hardy continued. "She was instantly agitated. Her hands were shaking, as if she hadn't had a ciggy in days. I asked her what was wrong, and she said, 'Roaming charges. They're killing me. And mind your own business.'"

Tiara said, "Yep."

"Finally, after taking a few sips of her Manhattan, she started to loosen up. Said she was upset by the call, and that she had some unpleasant business to attend to."

"What business?" Polly said.

Mrs. Hardy said, "Laura knocked back her drink and signaled for a refill. Then she said, 'I have to meet a man about an empty can of soup.' I patted her hand and told her to order the chicken noodle, and that everything would work out fine. She gave me a look, as though I were off my rocker, and said, 'No, it won't. My life is over.'

"That's when I suggested that she treat herself to a massage before her tryst. I assumed 'an empty can' is young-people speak for something clandestine. I said that a full-body massage would loosen her up better than alcohol. For the first time she gave me a small smile. She said I had a good idea and that she wasn't hungry anyway, she was just killing time until her appointment. Then she left the table. I watched her leave and saw that she grabbed her second Manhattan off the waiter's tray as he passed by. She drank it down and then disappeared out of the restaurant."

Polly and her team were less than enthusiastic. However, they expressed sincere appreciation to Mrs. Hardy for taking the time to share her memory of meeting Laura Crawford. Polly promised to send a complimentary special collector's edition boxed set of *The Polly Pepper Playhouse* with commentary and color photo booklet, as an expression of appreciation. When Mrs. Hardy stood to leave, Polly and her team politely stood as well.

As the old woman shuffled away, the trio exchanged looks. "Laura was a recovering alcoholic," Polly said. "A couple of Manhattans would have knocked her on her butt. But maybe she didn't care if she fell off the wagon."

"She ate junk," Tim added. "I never think of her as the type to order soup."

"But she did go to the spa for a massage as Mrs. Hardy suggested," Tiara said.

"Everyone knows that Laura was murdered there," Polly said. "It's not a stretch to think that Mrs. Hardy imagined that she and Laura Crawford shared a few moments together on the last night of Laura's life. Oh, I don't know what to think!"

Just then, Tim looked up and said, "Here's what I think— that I should be leaving. Dorian just entered the room."

"Good grief," Polly said before switching to "Polly Pepper the legend" mode. She smiled warmly and accepted Dorian's kiss on each of her cheeks. "Dear me," she said, "I think it's high time you met my lovely family. This is Tiara..."

"A pleasure," Dorian said as he extended his hand to hers.

"And my little Timmy."

Dorian and Tim stood perfectly still; their eyes locked on one another. Finally, Dorian nodded his acknowledgment and simply said, "Son."

"You're just in time to buy me another bottle of Veuve." Polly giggled.

Tim nudged Tiara and said, "We have that *thing* to get to."

"That doesn't start for another hour." Tiara smiled wickedly.

"All the good seats will be taken," Tim insisted.

Polly said, "You two run along. Dorian and I don't want to bore you with art talk, which seems to be his topic du jour every time we meet. I'm so glad that I found another passenger with more on his mind than wet T-shirt contests! Off you go."

Before Tim was out of the lounge, he called back, "Don't forget who we're meeting at seven."

"Who, dear?" Polly asked.

"Frick and Frack," Tim said conspiratorially.

Polly looked into Dorian's eyes. "By the way, Tim once decked his father #2 for calling him 'son.'"

18

"The captain's a killer!" Marc Garner wailed.

"He's a cutthroat!" Stephen Ronson cried.

"Knew it!" Polly clapped her hands as she eagerly ushered the two men into her elegant new veranda suite stateroom. She handed them both flutes of chilled champagne. "Of course, I suspected it all along. That ratty rug of curly hair on his head. The dumb mustache over his thin lips. Those deep-set beady brown eyes. He's a dead ringer for a police sketch I once saw of a serial killer!" Polly turned to her maid and extended a hand with her empty glass. "We'll open another bottle to celebrate finally pinning down Laura's nefarious butcher. Captain 'Ahab' Sheridan!"

Stephen and Marc exchanged horrified looks. "No!" Stephen shrieked. "I mean, yes, the captain's an executioner, but I'm not saying he slaughtered anyone. Just our careers."

"And egos," Marc added. "I've never seen Captain Sheridan angrier. He's relieved us of duty."

"Fired?" Polly said.

"He's holding us personally liable for any witness or evidence tampering that may have occurred during the hours that we were guarding your cabin. He said he suspects that you have something to do with Laura Crawford's death, and he's calling the Coast Guard to question you when we reach Juneau."

"Of course, he would accuse someone of note," Polly said, "especially if he's trying to divert attention away from himself. 'He who smelt it dealt it!'"

Tim grimaced. "Or words to that effect. What exactly happened when you met with the captain?"

"It was ugly," Stephen said. "My ears are still ringing. I didn't know if I should hold my sphincter or my tears."

"In a nutshell, sweetums," Polly encouraged. "Less visualization."

"Um, other than we're idiots, he said what we already knew, that a killer roams this ship. He also said that he suspects Polly Pepper of somehow being involved. By the way, he's going to monitor each of you and your every move until we reach port," Stephen said. "We're to be tailed, too."

"We're under surveillance?" Tiara said. "Then the captain is sure to know where you are right now and with whom. Maybe you are idiots. Kidding. Sort of."

Polly was suddenly and uncharacteristically enraged. She stood up from the cheap knockoff of a Barcelona chair on which she had strategically seated herself to be the center of attention. Grabbing her head of red hair with both hands, she stepped out on her balcony and screamed maniacally into the sea air. "You want my blood? Take my blood!"

The room became deathly silent as Stephen and Marc looked on in shock and surprise at the woman whose legend for being a great star was matched by her reputation for always being as pleasant as Flo, the Progressive Insurance commercial girl. They were equally surprised to see Tim and Tiara quietly sipping champagne, oblivious to the meltdown taking place.

Polly returned to the living area and paced the room. After a moment of watching her, Tiara lethargically clapped her hands and dryly said, "Brava, diva. When in doubt about what to say in any situation, there's always a quote from a movie."

Tim said, "That was Polly's impersonation of Samuel L. Jackson. From *The Negotiator*. She does a great Sly Stallone. And Schwarzenegger, too." He looked at his mother. "Say 'California' the way the Governator does."

Polly plopped herself back down in the chair. "I'm frustrated with this case and angry that Captain Sheridan dares to impugn my integrity and character." She looked at Stephen and Marc. "What else did that nautical Neanderthal say? Anything that might suggest that he's hiding something or protecting someone? Maybe himself?"

Stephen and Marc exchanged looks. "He mostly yelled and called us words that we can't use in front of ladies," Stephen said.

"Ain't no ladies here," Tiara teased.

"Get this," Marc continued. "After we were dismissed, we went to the infirmary."

"To throw up," Stephen said.

"And to score a couple of Xanax," Marc said. "While we were there, we overheard Dr. Girard saying something like, 'Of course she's locked up, sir. Tight as a witch's—'"

Stephen abruptly nudged his colleague.

"Sorry, Miss Pepper," Marc said.

Polly waved away the apology. "Tiara's the prude."

Tiara harrumphed. "I watch *South Park* religiously!'"

Stephen added, "The doc also said, and I quote, 'A little freezer burn, but otherwise, as fresh as the day we rolled her into storage.'"

"Oh, and he said something about a memory card being safe," Marc said.

Stephen looked at Marc. "What do you think he meant when

he chuckled and said, 'You'll make another killing with that, sir'?"

"Sounds incriminating to me," Polly said and took a sip of champagne. "Especially the killing part."

Tim hedged. "A murder victim is in the crisper section of the fridge to keep her fresh for the autopsy. The captain is right to make sure the body is under lock and key."

"What about the reference to *another* killing?" Polly said. "And what's a memory card? Another nauseating Hallmark birthday memento?"

Tim reached for his digital camera that he'd left on the coffee table and withdrew an object the size of a foil-wrapped chocolate mint square. "This is a memory card," he said. "It's what digital pictures are stored on." He passed it over to Polly.

As she examined the tiny article, Polly shook her head in amazement. "All those party and vacation pictures you take are on this little thingamajig? Anything from last week's pool soiree at Mark Harmon's? I'd like to squeeze *his* Charmin."

Tim snatched the memory card out of his mother's hand and quickly reinserted it into his camera.

"What if... Stephen started to say, then changed his mind.

"What if what, dear?" Polly encouraged. "There are no stupid questions. Only stupid people."

Stephen gathered his nerve. "What if the captain took pictures of the dead celebrity and has plans to make money by selling 'em to the *National Intruder*? Therefore making 'another killing' as Dr. Girard said."

Polly shook her head. "It's a fabulous idea, but I don't think it'll fly. Captain Sheridan's not a complete moron. To do something so sinister, repulsive, and unethical would be to jeopardize his entire career. By the by, can you scam a couple of Xanax for me?"

"The captain's career is already in jeopardy," Marc said. "He's certainly not foolish, and if I were in his position, facing the possibility of getting booted out of my job just before retirement, I'd keep something of value around for insurance. Either something to sabotage the company I've given my life to, or something that would provide an annuity of sorts."

Stephen said, "What would be better than dead celebrity pictures, fresh from a brutal crime scene? There's always a market in any number of tabloids. Or on gossip websites. Perez Hilton or TMZ would probably cough up a fortune. If they pay multimillions for the rights to publish pictures of celebrity babies coming into this world, it stands to reason they'd pay a bundle for pix of celebs leaving the planet. Especially if it's in a particularly ghastly way."

Polly wondered aloud, "Hypothetically speaking, if Captain Sheridan indeed had photos of a dead Laura Crawford and wanted to sell them, wouldn't he think that such material might somehow link him to her death? Or if he actually was the killer, why would he keep photographic souvenirs? Maybe to prove to someone that he knew a celebrity—dead or otherwise."

For a few moments the stateroom was quiet as everyone considered the previously unthinkable possibility that Captain Sheridan, a lifelong sailor and dedicated commander of cruise ships, might have had a hand in the murder of Laura Crawford, or at least in reaping rewards from her death.

Polly cleared her throat. "Let's think about this rationally. What would be his motive for killing Laura? They didn't even know each other. On the other hand, if anyone could get in to any room on this ship, including the spa, without attracting suspicion, it would be the captain. But why would he risk his career?"

Tiara added, "Don't forget the murder weapon. It doesn't make much sense that Captain Sheridan would have the new boxed set collector's edition DVDs of *The Polly Pepper Playhouse*."

Polly gave her an indignant look. "I have ardent admirers in every social station of life."

"If he was such a fan, why would he take one of his precious discs and sharpen the hell out of it, then leave it in Laura's neck?"

Polly raised an eyebrow.

Tim leaned forward and picked up the champagne bottle. He refilled his mother's glass and Tiara's and then filled his own. Marc and Stephen waved a pass. "Before we waste time trying to figure out if the captain had a motive for killing Laura, we'd better make sure he's a legitimate suspect. We've got to find the memory card and see if Laura's dead body is in any of the frames."

Marc looked at Tim. "You know how small that memory card is. You're looking for the proverbial needle in a haystack."

Tim nodded. "First things first. We've got to get in to see Dr. Girard. Find out what he knows."

Polly coughed, then felt her head for fever. "I'm getting dizzy," she moaned. "I have an earache, too."

"Mm–hmm." Tiara nodded. "All the symptoms of *infectiouschronicosis!*"

Tim looked at Marc and Stephen. "You don't need a vaccination. But we'd better get Polly to the infirmary, pronto."

Dr. Girard was short, pudgy and wore what was left of his gray hair in a comb-over. His teal-colored V-neck scrubs top couldn't conceal his stomach, and the short sleeves of the shirt showed off thin forearms. Polly and her troupe tried to explain the symptoms of the star's faux malaise.

As Polly kept Dr. Girard occupied with taking her temperature, feeling the glands in her neck, swallowing, sucking in deep breaths for the stethoscope, and giving a list of medications she was currently taking for high blood pressure and cholesterol, Tim and Tiara surreptitiously scoped out the clinic. Although they didn't know where to begin, they felt the pockets of white lab coats, opened desk drawers, picked up stacks of papers, and even opened the instrument-sterilizing machine. Nada.

Suddenly, Tiara had a scheme. She opened the door to the private examination room and announced, "You've saved a star's life! Bless you, Doctor! I'll make sure that she gets rest and drinks plenty of fluids."

Dr. Girard was startled by the intrusion and annoyed that Tiara, followed by Tim, would barge into the examination room while he was performing a medical checkup on a patient. Tiara buttoned Polly's blouse and helped her off the exam table. "Miss Pepper would love to have a photograph of the two of you together," Tiara said. "And I'm sure you'd love one too, for your wall of fame, which I see you don't have yet. But what better legend to start with than the one highest on the heap!"

Tim quickly caught on. "Oh, darn," he said in a theatrical tone, "I left my camera and my phone in my cabin. Whatever shall we do?"

"Dr. Girard must have a good digital camera on hand," Tiara said. "You never know when a passenger might come down with werewolf syndrome, or bubonic plague makes a comeback, and you need photographic evidence to email to the CDC. Yes?"

"Hardly," Dr. Girard declared testily. "I don't need pictures of passengers with a case of Montezuma's revenge."

"Of course, that would be creepy!" Tiara continued. "But please let us thank you with an autographed picture! She doesn't have any recent eight-by-ten headshots on hand, so we'll have to play photographer. Timmy's an expert. He shoots a lot of Hollywood A-list stars."

Polly played along. "Do let me have a picture of the man who saved my life," she said.

Dr. Girard gave Polly a suspicious look. "There's nothing wrong with you."

"Because you're a great healer! You should have seen me an hour ago! You are Mayo, Johns, and Hopkins all rolled into one great medicine man."

Weary of this trio, Dr. Girard sighed and said, "I'll get my camera." He left the examination room, and Tim slyly shadowed him as he retreated through the main infirmary and into his private office. From a distance, Tim watched as Dr. Girard withdrew a key fob from the top drawer of his desk and selected a key to a filing cabinet. He opened the drawer and withdrew an ultrathin chrome-colored camera. Tim quickly backed up and raced to his mother's side, arriving seconds before Dr. Girard.

"Ever use one of these before?" Dr. Girard asked Tim, hesitant to let a novice use his expensive camera.

"Just like the one I have," Tim said. As he arranged his subjects side by side, in front of a poster depicting the human heart, Tim pushed the On button. "Um, what am I doing wrong? It's not working. Are you sure it's charged?"

Dr. Girard sighed and stepped forward to take the camera out of Tim's hand. "I thought you knew how to work this!" As he attempted to turn on the camera, he discovered that it really wasn't working. "There goes our picture," he said, making no attempt to hide his lack of distress.

Tim snatched the camera out of Dr. Girard's hand. "I had this problem last week. Yeah, my memory card was full, and I had to replace it." Tim opened the slot for the chip and said, "Just as I suspected. Empty. You're as forgetful as I am."

Dr. Girard rolled his eyes and left the room. As before, Tim shadowed him to his private office. This time, a key on his chain unlocked a heavy metal box that Dr. Girard picked up from the floor and placed on his desk. He looked around before opening the lid, quickly took out a memory card, then locked the box again and proceeded back to the examination room. Dr. Girard took the camera from Tim's hand and inserted the memory card into the slot. "Now try it," he snapped. "And let's get this over with fast. I'm a busy man. Lots of patients to see."

"Absolutely," Tim said as he again arranged Polly and Dr. Girard side by side with the big plump heart as a backdrop. Tim found their images in the LCD frame, said "Smile big"; then pushed the Shutter button. "Excellent!" he said, looking at the image in the LCD. "One more for insurance!" He shot another picture and showed it to his subjects. Then he pushed the Off button and turned around to leave.

"Thanks again for taking such good care of Polly," Tiara said as she hugged Dr. Girard, who stiffened but accepted the gesture.

"From me too," Polly declared, and gave the doctor a long tight squeeze.

"Am I next?" Tim asked, handing the camera back to the unsmiling physician.

"Toodles, sweetums," Polly called back as the trio left the infirmary, and Tim said, "Run!" The threesome dashed back to Polly's veranda suite. When they were safely inside the room, Tim locked the door. "Better open another bottle," he said. "I'm to be congratulated." He reached into his pocket, held out a fist, turned it over, and opened his palm. There, resting on his deep lifeline, was a digital camera memory card.

"I knew you'd do something clever!" Polly squealed with delight as Tiara opened another bottle of champers and poured three flutes. "Bravo, my love!"

Tim exchanged memory cards in his own camera and viewed all the new images. "Oh, gross! I'm going to vomit!" He finally put the camera down.

"I don't want to see her in that state," Polly declared. "I can't bear to look at a squashed cat on the road let alone a colleague butchered by that horrible man!"

"No, it's not Laura," Tim said. "It's Captain Sheridan in a Speedo bathing suit."

Polly snatched the camera off the table and looked at the LCD screen. "It's always the people who shouldn't remove their clothes in public who do," she said, with nausea that matched Tim's. "Have another glass of champagne. It'll keep down whatever's in your stomach."

After taking a fortifying sip, Tim looked through the rest of the photos. "Uh-oh. It's not pretty."

"Captain Sheridan posing in the nude?" Polly said.

"Laura Crawford in a body bag."

19

Tim ran to his cabin and quickly returned to Polly's suite with his laptop computer. He connected the USB cable between his camera and the computer, uploaded the images of Laura Crawford, and saved them in a new file folder that he named "IRS Audit." He figured that if anyone accessed the computer, they would never think to look for photos in a file with the bone-chilling title "Internal Revenue Service." When the upload was complete, he said, "How am I supposed to get this memory card back to Dr. Girard without him knowing that I pocketed the little sucker?"

Suddenly there was a loud knock at the door. Polly panicked and said, "Sweet Lord Jesus, he's here!"

Tim slapped the top down on the computer, disconnected the cable, and placed the machine under a cushion on the sofa. In an instant, he exchanged Dr. Girard's memory card in his camera with his own. "Sit tight. Here are your roles: obsequious hero worshipers," he said to Polly and Tiara.

Another more impatient knock occurred. "It's Dr. Girard. I'm checking up on Miss Pepper's recovery."

Tim opened the door and gave the doctor a wide smile. "A house call?" he said. "That's so Kool Kroozy of you."

As Dr. Girard gave Tim a suspicious look, he walked into the room and was greeted by Polly's famous loud singsong voice, "He's hee-ere!"

Dr. Girard was immune to special attention from a celebrity, but he forced a smile. "I wanted to make sure that my patient is comfortable and on the road to recovery."

Polly raised her glass. "I'm as good as new, and we're celebrating!"

"Birthday? Anniversary? Our special photos?" He looked at Tim.

Polly said, "To the great good fortune I had to be treated by a talented physician who must have been first in his class at Stanford or *ER* or *Grey's Anatomy,* and who will probably go on to invent a cure for that sweet girl I read about who has dozens of orgasms every day, or that poor Indonesian man who has a fungus that's turning him into a tree. I watch *The Discovery Channel.* Between your medical magic and the natural healing properties of Mr. Champers here"—she lifted her glass— "I'll definitely live another glorious day."

"No doubt," Dr. Girard said with an edge to his voice.

Tiara went to the wine cooler and withdrew another bottle of Veuve. She popped the cork, poured a glass of champagne for the doctor, and topped up Polly's and Tim's glasses, as well as her own.

As Dr. Girard looked around the massive veranda suite and nodded his approval of the accommodations, his eyes stopped and focused on the glass-top coffee table. "I thought you left that at home," he said, pointing to Tim's camera.

"Um. Er, I meant this is home," Tim said.

Dr. Girard picked up the camera and noticed the cable still attached to the port. His eyes scanned the room, looking for a computer, which had to be nearby. "Same as mine," he said, looking at the brand and model. He pushed the On button, and the lens automatically emerged from its casing. He pushed the button again, and the lens retracted.

"Yep, we could exchange cameras, and neither of us would be the wiser."

"A switched-at-birth scenario, eh?" Polly giggled. "By the way, how is my dear dead friend Laura Crawford's body holding up?"

"Non sequitur," Tim sang between clenched teeth. "Danger, Will Robinson."

Dr. Girard grinned. "How do you think a body that's been lifeless for four days is holding up?"

"It's a simple question," Polly said, perturbed by the derisive tone in Dr. Girard's voice. "What I'm getting at is, did her head come off, or is she in one piece? I haven't been given the opportunity to visit the dearly departed, so I don't know what shape she's in."

Dr. Girard softened his attitude. "The body, er, Miss Crawford's remains look as well as can be expected. The trauma was severe, but the attack was so brutal and probably occurred so fast that she was unaware of what happened to her. For that, we can be grateful."

Tiara scoffed. "Small comfort. I'm actually shocked that our intrepid captain hasn't returned to port, or that the Coast Guard hasn't been aboard to investigate Laura's murder. OJ promised to spend his life tracking down Nicole and Ron's killer but did about as much as the skipper of this Kool Krooz is doing to find Laura's murderer. What's he hiding?"

Dr. Girard took a long swallow from his champagne flute, then set the glass down. "Don't blame the captain. He has a lot on his plate."

"But I *do* blame him," Polly retorted. "When we dock in Juneau, the killer may disappear into the disembarking crowd."

Dr. Girard acted as though he hadn't heard Polly's response. He wandered toward the balcony. "Mind if I step outside for a bit of fresh sea air?" he asked, not waiting for an answer.

"Give him a push!" Polly whispered to Tiara as they watched the doctor gazing at the sea.

When Dr. Girard finally turned around and stepped back into the room, he said, "They don't make many days as beautiful as this one. I feel like taking a walk around the Promenade Deck until I have to report back to the infirmary."

Polly stood up and again told Dr. Girard how grateful she was for his attention to her medical problem. "When I have my next emergency, I'll know precisely who to call."

As Tim opened the cabin door and said goodbye, he looked at what Dr. Girard was holding in his hands. "You do have one of your own."

"Huh? Oh, your camera!" Dr. Girard said as he handed the camera back to Tim. "See you around."

"I do not get a good vibe from that man!" Tiara said.

"He's also a thief," Tim added, looking at his camera and the open flap of the memory card compartment. "He stole my photos!"

"He obviously figured that you stole his, so he came to get them back."

"Ha! I switched out the cards. I still have his. When he finds out that he's taken the wrong memory card, he'll be back, and we'll be in deeper trouble than before. I think he also knows I've uploaded the images to my computer. I saw his eyes focus on the USB cable."

Polly shrugged. "So why don't you just give him back his thingamajig?"

"Because I don't want him to know that I took his 'thingama-jig' in the first place! Darn. He's in for a big surprise. Thank God he's a doctor. When he looks at what's on my card and sees all the anatomy, he shouldn't be too shocked. Well, at least not until he gets to the files of... Oh, damn! He could make more money from the tabloids with my pix than the dreary ones of dead Laura!"

"Am I in there, too?" Polly asked, concerned that Tim's constant fooling around with his camera and getting candid shots of her without makeup or in her bubble bath or asleep on the couch with half a dozen empty champagne bottles by her side might be seen by the public.

Tiara moved to the couch and withdrew Tim's computer from under the cushion and placed it on the coffee table. As Polly and Tim looked on, Tiara lifted the desktop screen and pushed the On button. She typed in a password, selected a file, then double-clicked on an icon. She said, "Mm–hmm. With stuff like this for the good doctor to select from, you don't have to worry your pretty dyed-red head about Polly Pepper being caught in a candid moment of disrepair."

Polly and Tim moved to the coffee table to see what Tiara had brought up on the screen. Polly instantly burst out laughing. "Is that...? And the other one?" She laughed again. "The execs at the Disney Channel will have one big collective stroke if they see their latest and most expensive moppet singing superstar in the tabloids doing *that*!"

Tiara giggled. "Oh, Tim's got a million that are even more hysterically amusing and ripe for blackmail!"

Tim, on the other hand, was not so giddy. He looked at Tiara. "How do you know my password?" he asked. "I change it frequently."

"It isn't hard to figure out," Tiara said. "RicosTheOne. TaylorsTheOne. JasonsTheOne." Tiara ticked off the names of

Tim's crushes over the past six months. "It didn't take an Enigma machine to break your puppy-love codes."

Tim was visibly miffed. "Is there no privacy anymore?"

Tiara rolled her eyes and shook her head. "It's not as though I check your emails from those online dating sites, for crying out loud. By the by, you should do something about your username: 'BigLegendsSon' is a bit self-aggrandizing. Even Jason Gould's is more subtle. Oh, and your profile has a few errors. For instance, you're not twenty-two years old!"

"It's called online dating years. Everyone lops off five years. And I'm not excusing you for disturbing my personal space!"

"Sometimes I just need to look at the pretty celebrities and wannabes who drop their clothes at the parties you go to," Tiara said. "It's the voyeur in me."

Tim folded his arms across his chest and smirked. "As a matter of fact, I know darn well that you peek at my pictures file. I don't need photographic mementos of models and young TV stars splashing around together in Kim's pool. I've seen them so often that I'm inured. They no longer excite me. I take those shots expressly for you!"

"I know that you know," Tiara bragged. "Very much appreciated, too."

Polly closed the cover of the computer and said, "When was I going to be included? I do all the work, and you two have all the fun."

Tiara waved her hand dismissively. "It's just a game that Tim and I play. We have to do something in between our sporadic Mr. Rights. You have Randy Archer, Beverly Hills police detective extraordinaire. We can't keep a guy hanging around for more than a few weeks."

Tim lifted the computer monitor lid again. "Be my guest," he said to Polly. "Have a long look-see. Just don't die laughing when you see some of your old friends, or their spoiled rotten kids, displaying their inappropriate behaviors at Malibu beach house parties. But if those shots get out to the showbiz rags, we'll have to leave the planet!"

Polly refilled her champagne glass and sat down on the sofa to consider what the sailor boys Marc and Stephen had said about Captain Sheridan, as well as the behavior of Dr. Girard, and how they might be tied together to produce a real live murder suspect. "Who's the biggest gossip in town? I don't mean Tinseltown. Is there someone on the ship who should know all the best stories about both the passengers and crew?"

"What about Saul, the cruise director?" Tim said. "He's gotta be up on all that's going on."

"We should have brought along Nina, the girl who does your manicure at Swag," Tiara said. "She's the human equivalent of Google Gossip, with the latest facts and information on every romance, prenup, marriage, affair, divorce, divorce settlement, who's sleeping with the nanny, and/or personal assistant. Isn't she fab?"

"Tiara!" Polly said, snapping her fingers. "You and I are going in for salon. Call the spa. We'll get the floating version of Nina to paint our toes and a picture of whodunit! But we'd better get the oldest operator in the joint, someone who remembers my show and knows that I'm an icon. She'll kiss up and tell us whatever we need to know."

Seated side by side in the manicure salon, Polly turned to Tiara and whispered, "This one's the oldest? She's twenty-one if she's a day."

"Double up on your famous PP persona, and make her fall in love with you," Tiara encouraged.

Ligaya, whose name tag said she was from the Philippines,

introduced herself and said that she'd heard that Polly Pepper was a celebrity. "We have a lot of you people on board this cruise." She smiled. "Which one of you is the one my supervisor said is a living legend?"

Polly glanced at Tiara with a look of defeat.

"It doesn't matter. I treat all of my customers like stars," Ligaya continued. "I heard that someone named Shelley Long is here. I think she was on TV. And a Jamie Lynn Spears person who was on a kids' television show." Ligaya leaned in close to Polly and Tiara and whispered in one long run-on sentence, "I heard she did the naughty with her BF, who was supposed to be damn hot, so who could blame her, really, but she ended up a teenage mother and living in Louisiana, which is, like, totally weird since she had a glamorous Hollywood life and a famous sister and all—imagine anyone actually living in Louisiana on purpose..."

As Ligaya chattered on, Polly looked at Tiara and said, "I think this one'll do."

"Oh, I'll do anything!" Ligaya said. She exfoliated Polly's hands with a mixture of salt that she claimed was imported from the Dead Sea, and liquid soap. "It's made from something organic that one of the masseuses created," Ligaya said.

"Another of Rosemary's concoctions?" Polly asked. "Isn't she amazing!"

Ligaya sniggered, "I wouldn't have the stomach to make this stuff. I'd tell you where it comes from, but I've been sworn to secrecy; plus, you'd puke."

"Gee, it feels like snail pulp."

Ligaya looked up in horror.

"Just a guess, dear. You didn't say a word to me," Polly insisted.

"I think I've been aboard this ship for far too long because when I finally have interesting customers like you, I just want to chat, chat, chat," Ligaya continued. "We're at sea so much of the time that I don't get to watch my favorite American shows like *Entertainment Tonight,* or *E!* or *Access Hollywood.* I love that handsome Billy Bush who used to be on one of 'em until he got caught laughing at something a big dumb-ass politician said. So cute. Don't you think so?"

Polly gave Ligaya a big smile and lied that she agreed completely.

As the young manicurist moisturized and massaged Polly's hands with scented oil, she yammered on about how she could tell that Polly was probably a very rich lady; she knew by looking at hands whether or not their owners lived a pampered life or one of hard physical work. "Yours are so delicate and not at all in need of attention or a manicure." Then she looked over at Tiara. "I'm going to have to work extra hard on yours. I think someone is giving you too many chores to do around the house."

"I work in a diamond mine in Bel Air," Tiara teased, and gave Polly a look of satisfaction.

"Really?" Ligaya said with deep interest. "Makes sense that there would be jewelry mines in such a ritzy place." As Ligaya talked about how few men she was able to meet on cruises— mostly because they're with their wives or girlfriends—Polly took action to avoid being dragged into a one-sided conversation. She had information to pick from Ligaya's brain, and she wasn't going to let the opportunity pass.

"Have you joined the dead pool yet?" Polly asked.

Ligaya stopped kneading Polly's palm and gave her a quizzical look. "That's over. Our cruise director cashed in."

"Oh, but there's a new one," Polly pretended. "One must guess who kills me."

Tiara leaned toward Ligaya. "My money is on Captain Sheridan."

"Madam Destiny, the psychic, is the one I'd bet on," Polly

said. "She and I had quite a chat, and she seemed to know far too much about the killer. What about you? Any guesses?"

Ligaya resumed her duties and blithely said, "I could use the extra bucks if I win. Passengers are lousy tippers."

"I'd bet you have a good idea who might kill again?" Polly said hopefully.

"What makes you think that?" Ligaya said warily.

"Just a hunch. I'll bet you pick up a lot of interesting gossip in your job."

Ligaya picked up a white towel and wiped Polly's hands of excess oil. She then set an abalone shell filled with warm water on a tray in front of Polly. "We'll soak for a few minutes to soften your cuticles." She then moved to Tiara and began the same treatment that she had performed for Polly. As she was exfoliating Tiara's hands, she said, "If I correctly guess who killed Laura Crawford, then it'll be a three-way tie, and I wouldn't have all the money to myself."

Instantly Polly's hands jumped out of the abalone shell, an involuntary reflex.

"Not that I'm greedy. Soak a little longer," Ligaya said, placing Polly's hands back in the shell.

"I never gamble," Polly insisted. "I have a ton of money and intend to keep it that way. So, I'm definitely not in competition to win the dead pool. It's all yours. Who killed, er, who do you *think* killed Laura Crawford?"

Ligaya washed and dried Tiara's hands and then applied moisturizer. "I had an interesting customer the other day."

"More interesting than the Charlie's Angel who's on board?" Polly prodded.

"Almost," Ligaya said. "This one was an art historian. She was in desperate need of a manicure. The nails on her left hand were ripped and jagged. She was fussy, too. She insisted that I clean and file and buff each nail three times. I was just a little bit suspicious, because it seemed like I was cleaning dried blood out from under her nails." Ligaya leaned in for a whisper. "I kept a bit of her cuticle and nail trimmings in an envelope in case anyone wanted to test her DNA for a match with the dead woman."

She and Tiara looked at each other as if to say, "This one's no dummy."

"What day was that?" Polly asked.

"The second day out. The day they found the actress's body over there." She pointed to a closed door in the spa. "It's locked, of course, waiting for when we reach port for the police to investigate. Gives me the creeps to be so close to that room, knowing what happened." She shuddered.

As Ligaya wiped Tiara's hands clean from oil and instructed her to place them in another abalone shell of warm water, she returned to Polly with a cuticle stick. Although there was very little cuticle to push back, she made a show of doing her job professionally.

Polly nonchalantly said, "After all your hard work on that woman, I hope that she left a decent tip."

"Not!" Ligaya snorted. "The English are terrible tippers."

"British, eh?" Polly said. "And an art dealer. Perhaps she gave you an intangible tip instead, like advice about buying a Rembrandt or Picasso?"

"Who needs art?" Ligaya said. "I'd much rather have the dollars!" She took out her emery board and began to shape Polly's fingernails.

Although Polly was attempting to be subtle, Tiara was having none of it. "What was this woman's name? What did she look like? What was she wearing? Pierced ears or not? Shade of lipstick? Long hair? Short hair? Rings? Wedding band? Any distinguishing features other than her accent?"

Ligaya batted her eyes at Tiara. "It was four days ago. I've had a hundred other clients since then. I'll have to think hard and get back to you."

Polly interrupted. "Darling, if you're going to win the pool, you'll have to think fast. The drawing is tonight. How 'bout if we play coach and try to help you remember?"

Ligaya's eyes sparkled when she thought of winning the dead pool. "How much money did you say was in the kitty?"

"I didn't. It depends on how many passengers are playing. According to Saul, the cruise director, the pot is up to about thirty thousand dollars!" Polly lied.

Ligaya's emery board slipped, and she filed across Polly's nail plate, causing her to grimace in pain.

Ligaya didn't seem to notice that she'd injured her client, as she stared into her future and imagined what she could do with that much loot.

Tiara continued, "Young? Old? Tall? Short? Think of a movie star that she looked like."

"Maybe she was a real movie star," Ligaya said. "There are so many of you people on this cruise, and maybe she was lying about being an art dealer so she wouldn't have to talk about Hollywood."

"Are you kidding?" Polly pooh-poohed Ligaya's assumption. "Any semi-celebrity on this ship would be thrilled to spend an hour telling you every show they ever appeared on."

"She did seem more sophisticated than the usual Hollywood types I've had as clients," Ligaya said. "Maybe if we had a police lineup, I might be able to pick her out."

Polly suddenly sat up straight. "We can arrange that! Sort of! Come with me!" Polly insisted as she pulled off her smock and got out of her chair.

"I'm still on duty!" Ligaya insisted.

"I promise to leave you a great big tip," Polly said as she

helped Tiara out of her chair and threw her a small towel to dry her hands. "This way!"

In moments, Polly, Tiara, and Ligaya were racing toward the glass elevator in the main atrium. When they arrived at Polly's luxurious stateroom, Tiara automatically brought out four champagne flutes and unwrapped the foil surrounding the cork of a bottle of Veuve. Polly picked up the telephone and pushed 0 to reach the operator. "Tim Pepper, please and thank you." Soon after, there was a knock at the door. "Is it you, sweetums?" Polly called.

"'Tis I." Tim assumed an affected voice.

When he was ushered into the room, Polly introduced Ligaya. "Game time!" she declared. "Ligaya may have had a special movie-star client the other day, and we need to find out who it is. Here's a copy of the *Daily Wave*," she said, handing the paper to Tim. "There's a list of every celebrity lecturer on this boat. Google 'em and let Ligaya see if she can pick out the one who didn't leave such a hot tip."

Tim smiled. "Ah! Revenge of the stiffed!"

Polly watched as Tim opened up his computer and signed on to the internet. "We're trying to help this talented young woman win the dead pool. Just bring up the female celebs."

"Dead pool?" Tim asked, looking at Polly. "I'll do what I can to help." As Tim ran down the list of celebrities who were aboard the *Intacti,* he Googled their names and brought up official web pages or fan sites, which included mostly old photographs from the time when they were somebody semi-important in Hollywood.

With each name and each photograph, Ligaya shook her head. "Maybe that one?" She finally fingered a photo.

"Loni Anderson's too likable," Polly said.

Ligaya pointed to another picture. "She looks familiar."

"That's Faith Ford. She never worked with Laura; hence she wouldn't have a motive."

"What about her?"

"Laurie Metcalf? Pul-eze! If she didn't murder Roseanne during all the years of hell on that show, she probably wouldn't kill a cockroach."

"It's hard to tell," Ligaya complained, and withdrew an emery board from her pocket. She buffed her nails as she continued to view photos. "In real life they're in living color."

"What about the name?" Polly said. "If you saw the name again, do you think you'd remember if it belonged to your customer?"

Ligaya shrugged. "She came in without an appointment."

"Let's try," Polly begged. She picked up the *Daily Wave* and started to run down a list of guest lecturers who were experts in such fields as origami, and the art of bending forks into fine sculptures, and raising centipedes for fun and profit.

Finally, when she read, "'My Five-Year-Old Can Paint Better Than That!' A discussion of modern art in contemporary culture by internationally renowned archivist from the Leeds-Upon-River Kite Museum of Pop Culture in Upper Crosstone, England. Amelia Aimsburry,'" Ligaya's eyes popped.

"That's her! That's the one!" she exclaimed. "I'd know that name anywhere!"

"And yet you couldn't think of it a moment ago," Polly said. She continued reading—then looked at her watch. "Ms. Aimsburry has a lecture in twenty minutes. Grab your sketch pads. We're attending class!"

Despite intense objections from Tim and Tiara, both of whom whined that they would rather learn how to raise centipedes for fun and profit, Polly took one last sip from her champagne flute and headed out the door. Naturally, the others followed.

20

In anticipation of low passenger interest, the cruise director arranged for the art lecture to be held in the relatively small space of the ship's library. As a matter of fact, when Amelia Aimsburry introduced herself from the librarian's desk, the audience consisted only of Polly, Tim, Tiara, Ligaya, and two old women who looked as though they'd wandered in because they had absolutely nothing else to do before the next round of bingo.

Tiara nudged Polly and said, "I know you're turning over every rock to find Laura's killer, but this sparrow of a thing doesn't look strong enough to hold a paintbrush let alone the head of an overweight so-called actress."

As Polly hushed Tiara, Amelia offered a long list of professional and academic credits in the art world that qualified her to deliver a lecture on what she called "a misunderstood aspect of pop culture." As she prattled on about the boredom she'd suffered as a child being taught about classical art followed by her studies of the Impressionists, Postimpressionists, the Cubism movement, and nonrepresentational art, Polly stifled a yawn.

Amelia looked at Polly with a small smile. "I quite agree with you, Miss Pepper," she said. "I, too, found it all a great challenge to understand why anyone would want to look at haystacks and lilies when they could be looking at this!" In that moment, with the push of a button on a remote control, a slide projector filled a home movie screen with an image of a white unframed canvas on which one red pinstripe was painted across the bottom width of the artwork. "Would anyone like to tell me why this master-piece, *Mother and Child,* is one of the most important artistic contributions to the contemporary canon?" Amelia said. She looked around and saw only blank expressions and one of horror from Tiara. "Because it speaks!"

One of the two old ladies said to the other, "It's saying, 'I'll bet some damn fool fell for the joke and paid a fortune for that piece of crapola!'"

Polly couldn't control an involuntary surge of giggle. Although she instantly caught herself, it was too late. Amelia Aimsburry stopped her lecture and, with arms folded across her chest, stared at Polly fiercely. Polly forced a cough and pointed to her throat.

After a moment, Amelia continued, *"Mother and Child* repre-sents the never-ending journey of not only the artist, but the universe. As you can see, one's eye is instantly drawn to the deceptively simple bloodline, which symbolizes the inter-minable and enduring hopelessness of our existence."

One of the old women got up and said to her friend, "This is interminable and hopeless. Let's find a game of darts and stab out our eyes."

As they left the room, Amelia looked crestfallen. She turned to Polly and company. "I'm afraid that my talk isn't very inter-esting to most people," she said. "I thought that if I had a little fun with the title, people would drop in instead of out."

Polly stood up and walked the few feet to Amelia's side. "As a matter of fact, the title, 'My Five-Year-Old Can Paint Better Than That' is one of the reasons we came to hear you. It's quite fun. All you need is a little showbiz pizzazz. Open with a joke. 'Um, what do you call a snail who cut off his own ear? *Escar Van Gough! Ha! Ha! Ha!*' Get your audience wrapped around your little finger and wham! You'll have a hit!"

Amelia shrugged. "I haven't a funny bone in my body. Even my knock-knock jokes never get laughs."

Polly smiled. "I do have a home-team advantage when it comes to talent. But I still had to hone my skills. With a little practice and a lesson in timing, you too can have people slapping their knees. Try this. Knock, knock."

"Who's there?"

"Who."

"Who who?"

"Is there an owl in here?"

Polly laughed as loudly as if she'd just heard Joan Rivers's famous joke that Madonna's armpits are so hairy that when she lifts her arm, it looks like Tina Turner is trapped there.

Amelia offered a vague smile. "Shall I continue with the lecture?" she asked.

"Perhaps another time, dear," Polly hurriedly suggested. "We're taking you down to the Coral Lounge. We'll help you practice your 'who who.'" As Polly linked her arm with Amelia's, she said, "Please meet my son, Tim, and my maid and BF, Tiara. You've already met Ligaya. She scraped your cuticles the other day."

Amelia smiled and shook hands with each of them. She then showed off her manicure and said, "I've received compliments!"

As Polly and her team strolled through the Promenade Deck toward the bar, Tiara said, "No offense, but a five-year-old really did paint that red line on a canvas, right? The artist's kid got into his studio, and he had a deadline for a commission and said, 'Screw it, this is what I'll turn in.'"

Amelia said, "As a matter of fact, it's an Eelz." She looked at blank faces. "Gregory Eelz? Hmm? Well, he is to contemporary art what Ben Tyler is to modern literature, and he's equally reclusive. He's an artist's artist."

"Which means he doesn't make a dime, and nobody will ever hear of him," Tiara said.

Amelia nodded. "That's the way it is in the art world. Unless you're Thomas Kinkade, you only make money *after* you're dead."

As the leader of the pack, Polly escorted her troupe into the Coral Lounge. The hostess greeted the group warmly and led them to a small table. "I'll have a bottle of champagne sent over right away," she said, as aware as everyone else that Polly Pepper lived for her bubbles.

Polly smiled and affectionately touched the hostess's arm. "I'll depend upon you to make sure it's something nontoxic."

"I've read that you can't get Andre past your lips. I understand." The hostess grinned. "I feel the same way about my husband."

As the quintet awaited the arrival of their libations, Polly held court and talked about how much fun she was having aboard the *Intacti*. "The food is decent. The drinks don't keep me sober. And my audiences have been grateful for my appearances. I should cruise more often."

"Polly always has a good time when there's a murder to be investigated," Tim said. "It's too bad that this time the victim is a family friend."

"Please accept my condolences," Amelia said as she withdrew an emery board from her purse and unconsciously began filing her nails. "You're holding up pretty well, considering..."

"Considering that I'm not the one who had a razor-sharp

DVD saw through my neck, I guess I am doing well," Polly said as a champagne bucket was placed beside the table and a cocktail waitress uncorked a bottle of Dom Perignon. Polly kept track of how many glasses were filled and decided there wouldn't be anything left for seconds. "I guess we'd better have another one right away," she said to the waitress, who had turned the empty bottle of Dom upside down in the ice bucket.

After a long swallow, which drained half the champagne in her glass, Polly made a contented sigh and reached out to take Amelia's hand. She admired the nails and nodded to Ligaya. "Lovely job, dear. We'll get back to mine a bit later." She looked at Amelia and said, "Try not to chew your nails anymore, sweetums. You'll get poisoned by the polish."

Amelia looked at Polly and said, "Ick. Never. That's a nauseating practice. I generally keep them well maintained." She blew on her nails and put the emery board back into her purse.

Polly looked at her own unfinished nails. "They were a disaster when Ligaya got hold of them."

Amelia examined Polly's nails. "I can see that she still has a ways to go."

"I mean *your* nails," an embarrassed Polly said, placing her hands on her lap. "Ligaya said that your nails looked as though they'd gone through the garbage disposal."

Ligaya put down her drink. "I was simply bragging about my ability to handle tough projects."

Polly continued her line of questioning. "How did your poor little nails come to resemble something that had been run through a woodchipper?"

Amelia flushed. "I hardly think..." She looked at Ligaya.

"And you had dried blood embedded..." Polly continued.

Amelia picked up her champagne flute with a shaking hand, took a long swallow, and set the glass down. "Blood?" she said cautiously.

"Human blood," Polly guessed, but made it sound as though she were one hundred percent certain.

Amelia took another sip from her glass. "The truth is... my suitcase."

"Suitcase?" Polly jumped in.

"A carry-on. Cheapie. The zipper was stuck, and I had to wrestle with the damn thing. I pulled back and forth on the zipper until, finally, I got it to move. But my fingers were in the way, and when it came free, the teeth ran over my nails. My index finger bled like crazy."

Polly deflated. The story made sense. She'd had her own suitcase zipper problems in the past and had seen how easily Amelia could be injured. "Darn! It wasn't Laura Crawford's blood under the nails."

Amelia was jolted. For a long moment she stared at Polly. "I should have known the moment you walked into my lecture that people like you weren't interested in art!" Amelia stood up and knocked over her chair. "On this cruise I've seen what happens when Polly Pepper gets involved in a murder investigation. Innocent people, with no more relationship to the crime other than the fact that they may have breathed the same air as the victim, have their lives ruined by innuendo!"

"Please, dear, sit down and finish your drink. Dom Perignon is like a mind... It's a terrible thing to waste," Polly insisted.

Amelia started to walk away, then turned and said, "If we'd had a little more time together, I might have told you about a man who came to one of my lectures. Yes, he was quite the chatterbox, too. Your name came up several times during our conversation, as did Laura Crawford's."

"Who?" Polly asked.

"Is there an owl in here?" Amelia laughed with disdain. "You'd like a name, wouldn't you? Well, I'm not about to let some other innocent passenger find himself the center of your aberration. From what I've heard, and now seen firsthand, in your world everyone is guilty until proven innocent. You'll keep making false accusations until, through the process of elimination, a shipload of passengers and crew is humiliated. Even then, you may not find your killer. There is such a thing as the perfect crime."

Amelia then walked away. When she reached the exit, she bumped into Dorian, who appeared distraught. Polly watched as Amelia pointed to Polly. Dorian nodded and headed for Polly's table.

"Oh, happy day," Polly said facetiously as Tim, Tiara, and Ligaya followed her gaze.

"Who is it?" Ligaya asked.

"Someone who wants to be Polly's new beau," Tim joked.

Ligaya made a face that read, "You must be kidding."

21

"Call me crazy," Polly said.

"Loco!" said Tiara.

"Bananas!" said Tim.

Polly held out her string of pearls for Tiara to help fasten around her neck. "Dorian's harmless. You heard the poor man. He's genuinely sorry that he caused you the slightest bother outside my cabin." She looked at Tim. "If I'm willing to forgive and forget... Heck, we only have another two days."

Tim rolled his eyes. "Do you remember when I was dating that stud from *Desperate Housewives*?"

"Which one?" Polly asked impatiently.

"Um, the one you invited to the Plantation for dinner..."

"Oh! The one with the Teri Hatcher fetish. Or so I'd hoped. But all he did was kneel at the altar of Marcia Cross."

"I didn't want to listen when you and Tiara told me to break it off with him ASAP."

"He wasn't stimulating," Tiara said.

"That's what you think!" Tim smiled.

"Plus, he had ulterior motives for hanging out with you."

Tim nodded. "I thought that I was enough. I couldn't see that what he was really after was a chance to try on one of Polly's Bob Mackie gowns."

"You're so naive," Polly cooed, and tickled her son under his chin.

"The thing is," Tim continued, "Dorian gives off a strong negative vibration."

"There's definitely something odd there," Tiara agreed. "I don't trust overly polite fans. They don't have opinions of their own. They never dissent from what you say and have to agree that 19 *Kids and Counting* was quality television when of course it was shameless exploitation! The truth is, he makes my skin get all itchy."

Polly checked her hair in the mirror and smiled to see if any lipstick had smudged her teeth. "See Dr. Girard for a bottle of calamine lotion," she said. Polly turned around to her family. "I know that Dorian is a nerd and a bore, but I can tolerate him for a little while longer. I can't very well be rude to a man who venerates me."

"Fine," Tim said in resignation. "But try this when you see him. Tell him how much you adore demolition derby's."

Tiara reached into her bra and withdrew a wad of cash. She placed a twenty-dollar bill on the coffee table. "I'll wager that Dorian says demolition derbies are his passion."

Tim matched the wager and gave his mother a good night kiss. "I'm staying up until you get back!"

The Polar Bar was jammed when Polly arrived. Dorian was already seated, and he waved from across the room. Polly wended her way past couples who were dancing and others who were pointing at her. Dorian was standing when she eventually made it to his side.

"Perfect timing," he said, and offered a continental air-kiss to each of her cheeks. Then he held out the chair for Polly to be seated. "The champagne is just the right temperature," he said, and poured too much into her glass. It frothed and spilled down the side of the flute. "I'll get the hang of it someday."

Polly gave a tolerant smile, raised the glass to her lips, and took a tentative sip. "Another domestic bottle, eh?" she said as she simultaneously thought, *No. He'll never get the hang of it.*

Dorian frowned. "Sorry. I should have ordered something more expensive." He raised his hand to signal a cocktail waitress, but Polly stopped him. "This is absolutely fine, sweetums," she insisted. "One of the important things to know about my nature is that I'm very flexible about almost everything. I'm trying very hard to realize that not everyone on the planet has my heightened sensitivity and aversion to mediocrity." She took another sip from her glass. "Yummy," she lied, and tried to ignore the jarring antiseptic taste. "Tell me, what did Miss Art Creature say to you earlier in the Coral Lounge?"

"Amelia Aimsburry? She just gave me directions to your table."

Polly nodded and looked into Dorian's eyes. "She was certainly upset with me."

"Who could be angry with you?" Dorian said. "She was probably having a bad day. I'm sure that she didn't mean to be indignant with a star of your caliber."

As Dorian regurgitated stories about how well-liked Polly Pepper is, and how she might have misinterpreted Amelia's temper, Polly thought about what Tim and Tiara had said about Dorian being a disingenuous lackey eager to please her just because she was a celebrity. "Unfortunately, I think Amelia is right about me."

"There's always that possibility, too," Dorian agreed.

"Perhaps I should forget about finding the person who

murdered Laura Crawford and just leave it to the police," Polly said. "After all, I've had zero success, and I've made terrible accusations about innocent people."

"*Presumed* innocent," Dorian corrected. "You had your reasons for calling out Lawrence and D'Angelo and Saul and Rosemary and whoever else has been on your list of suspects. You did what you thought was best. No one can blame you for that. But maybe it is time to just enjoy the rest of the short time we have left on this voyage, and let the dead take care of themselves."

"By the by, how do you know the dear art expert?"

"I attended her lecture yesterday. She's quite the brainiac when it comes to contemporary art," he said.

"Did she show you that five-year-old's painting?"

"That's an Eelz!"

"So I heard."

Dorian paused for a moment. "I'll bet if you saw something more representational, like his iconic series titled *Watching Paint Dry*, you'd rush to include anything by the master in your own contemporary art collection. I had his *Nails on Chalkboard*—actual human fingernails glued to a blackboard! But I had to let it go."

Dorian suddenly fell quiet and Polly cooed, "If you love this artist so much, I'm sure you'll eventually find the funds to buy another piece."

Dorian smiled. "Absitively. Posolutely. Somehow, I've always had the ability to get what I want. Right now, I simply want to have fun with you. Shall we take our drinks to the Promenade Deck and look at the stars?"

Polly picked up her champagne flute and her clutch purse. "Since I didn't die this morning when I was scheduled to, I guess I'm safe."

Dorian escorted her out of the lounge to the glass elevator.

When they stepped out of the car and onto the deck, the sea breeze played with Polly's hair and ruffled her sparkling bugle-beaded blouse. "I should have brought a wrap," she said, and instantly wished she could take her words back as Dorian wound an arm around her and pulled her close to his side. She stiffened, but Dorian didn't seem to notice.

"Isn't this romantic," Dorian purred as he slowly guided Polly along the deck. "It just shows to go you that in America, anyone can grow up to meet Polly Pepper and spend time on an intimate ocean cruise with the legend herself."

Wedged tightly between the vise of Dorian's arm and the side of his body, the position made it impossible for Polly to walk casually. Her rigid body was growing more uncomfortable with each step. Finally, she shrieked, "Oh, look! A shooting star!" She extricated herself from Dorian's grip and dashed to the railing along the edge of the deck. "Darn, you missed it."

"You're the only star I want to see," Dorian said as he sidled up to Polly at the railing. "I hope your invitation to visit Pepper Plantation is still a go. I'm eager to see your famous home. And your art collection."

"Ah, the not-so-famous soup can," Polly said. "I don't know why you'd care about such a dreary subject for a painting."

"Far from dreary!" Dorian objected. "If you don't like it, maybe I can take it off your hands."

"I'd have a difficult time explaining that to my decorator," Polly said. "She designed the entire room around it. Matching cushions on the sofa. Even the rug was made especially to pick up the colors of the canvas. I'm afraid it's staying right where it is."

"I was kidding, of course," Dorian said, not sounding too convincing. "But maybe when I visit, you'll have a dinner party and invite David Hockney to join us, so he can tell me all about that painting of his that you own."

"Mmm," Polly said vaguely. She yawned and said it was time for her beauty rest and would Dorian mind awfully if she called it a night. "We'll have brunch tomorrow."

Dorian looked at his wristwatch, obviously disappointed. However, he said, "Absitively. Posolutely."

Polly shivered at hearing that ridiculous phrase again, but pretended it was the chilly night air that caused her to shudder.

Dorian began to walk Polly back to the inside deck when she insisted that he stay out and enjoy the star-filled night. "I can certainly find my way back alone."

Suddenly, Dorian became testy. "Are you tired of me? If you are, it's fine. You can be tiresome too. But I'd like to know where I stand."

Polly gave Dorian a blank look. "It's been an exhausting day. I had very little sleep last night, you may remember. Also, Polly Pepper is many things, but *never* tiresome. She's—rather, I'm—the life of the party."

Dorian instantly checked himself. "I'm so sorry, Polly. That didn't come out the way I intended. Of course you're *never* tiresome. I have to face the fact that we're from two different worlds, and compared to your exciting showbiz friends, I don't have very much that's interesting to talk about. I hope you'll forgive me."

"There's nothing to forgive," Polly dismissed his apology. "One can't help being a fireman or a computer programmer or—a shoe salesman. Just as I can't help being an internationally acclaimed, multi-Emmy Award-winning superstar with a new DVD collection of all-time greatest hits musical/comedy sketches from my long-running television variety series, which is syndicated in forty-two countries."

Dorian leaned in to give Polly a kiss, but she turned her cheek to his lips. "I have done something to change your mind about me," he said coldly. "Will you keep our brunch date, or blow me off with an excuse that you have a headache or some other such transparent lie?"

"Sweetums, I have no idea what you're talking about," she said with mock sincerity. "You're a lovely man, and I'm happy that we've had this opportunity to get to know one another. I'll definitely see you at brunch."

Polly turned and disappeared into the ship. She rode the glass elevator to her deck and quickly moved along the corridor to her deluxe veranda suite.

As she was about to tap her keycard onto the door lock, a voice from behind startled her. "Don't turn around." A man with a New England accent spoke. "I have a message for you, Miss Pepper."

Polly wanted to say, "Not Miss Pep-*pa*. It's Miss Pep-ER."

"It comes from the grave. Laura Crawford's grave."

"She's in cold storage, not in a grave." Polly found the nerve to speak.

"Splitting hairs," the voice retorted. "Do you want this information or not?"

Polly didn't answer.

"Laura Crawford said to tell you that the man who killed her is probably…"

"Probably?" Polly scoffed. "The dead are supposed to be omniscient. Doesn't she know for sure who killed her?"

"Jeez, lady, do you mind if I talk?" The voice lost its accent. After a moment, the accent returned. "The killer is probably a man she double-crossed…"

"Ugh! She was always doing something stupid to tick people off."

"Before you interrupt again, no, it's not a fan she snubbed or a celebrity she had a fight with."

Polly kept her back to the voice but folded her arms across her chest. "Laura Crawford seems to be sending you a lot of vague signals. Can you be more specific about what she did to make someone so angry that they'd slice and dice her?"

"I'll say this much. A fragile ego seeks revenge."

"An actor?" Polly guessed.

"Don't you listen? I said he wasn't a celebrity!"

"Excuse me," Polly said in a sarcastic tone. "Maybe the killer was jealous of one of her lovers."

"With all the weight she'd packed on, do you really think she had a stream of men flowing in and out of her life?" The voice was now impatient. "Forget it. In fact, forget that I tried to help."

"No!" Polly begged. "I'm at my wits' end and need all the help I can get to solve this crime. What else do you know?"

"Laura Crawford wants me to tell you that if you're not careful, you'll die for the same reason that she did. Be wise."

"Is that really Laura giving me a warning, or are you simply trying to scare me and redirect my investigation, or stop it altogether?" Polly demanded.

The voice stammered, "Look, I'm sorry. I had nothing to do with Laura Crawford's death, but I think I know who did."

"Tell me! I promise I won't tell a soul. About you, I mean. You won't be in trouble," Polly implored. "I'll protect you."

"You can't promise that! Anyway, I'll be considered an accessory for not coming forward. I just can't speak on the record. You're going to have to find out for yourself!" The voice cracked in fear. "But you're closer than you think."

"Please, please, please!" Polly begged. "At least give me a hint. A really good one 'cause I'm not so hot with riddles."

A loud but resigned sigh came from behind Polly. "What can I say that won't implicate me? Okay. Um. Maybe this will help. A book. A movie. I guess a play, too. Oh, and an Oscar nomination for A.L."

Polly rolled her eyes. "How can I play charades if I can't see your signals? A book? How many words in the title? How many syllables? Sounds like? You have to tell me if I'm getting hot or cold. This is totally dumb. Why don't we go to the Polar Bar for a drink and sort this out?"

Silence.

"The champagne is on me."

Silence.

"You can't pass up champagne! Oh, but you're right. We can't be seen together. But I can't let you into my cabin either because, for all I know, you may be the killer, and you'll do to me what you did to Laura."

Silence.

"Are you the killer? Would the real fiend who murdered Laura Crawford as she prepared to have a relaxing massage please stand up. Please?"

Silence.

Polly slowly and tentatively moved her head to look over her shoulder. The corridor was empty. She turned around and looked up and down the hallway. She turned back to her door and tapped her cardkey against the lock once more. "Damn. Maybe I do talk too much."

"To yourself." Tim's unexpected voice gave Polly a start.

Tiara said, "Why so jumpy? Dorian's frightening, but..."

"I was just talking to... Did you see anyone in the hallway as you came down?"

Tim and Tiara looked up and down the corridor. "Just us chickens."

"That's me." Polly sighed. "A chicken talking to a ghost." She pushed the door open and entered her stateroom.

"Ghost? Anyone we used to know and like?" Tim mocked.

"I'm serious!" Polly said, expecting a glass of champagne to be placed in her hand right away. "Thank you, dear," she said as Tiara fulfilled her duty. "I was outside the stateroom, just about to unlock the door, when the voice from the

Pepperidge Farm commercials spoke to me. He had a dire warning."

"That the Keebler elves are baking something illegal into their cookies?" Tim teased.

Polly gave him a scornful look. "He had a message from the grave. Laura's grave."

"She doesn't have a grave," Tiara said.

"That's what I said. He said he thought he knew who killed Laura!"

"Who?" Tim asked.

"He wouldn't say."

"Jeez. You'd think the spirit world would repay the living for all the people who help guide the losers into the light," Tim said.

"A prankster who was having fun at your expense," Tiara said as she poured herself a glass of champagne. "He was probably getting back at you for all the finger-pointing that turned out to be false."

"I'm not so sure." Polly defended her phantom. "There was something legitimate in his voice."

Tim took Polly's glass from her hand and took a sip, then handed it back. "We're on a ship filled with actors. Any one of them could have changed their voice, slipped into ghost character and, as Tiara said, had a big ol' laugh at spooking Polly Pepper. Look for it on *The Intacti's Funniest Kool Krooz Videos*."

Polly swallowed the remainder of her champagne and waited for a refill. "Now I'm depressed. I'm at the end of my rope. Like David Carradine. But without the added entertainment of auto-erotic asphyxiation."

"Or as much behind-the-corpse sniggering," Tim teased.

"The voice. No, I never saw who it belonged to." Polly answered the question before it could be asked. "However, he said that Laura double-crossed someone, and that if I wasn't careful, I'd die for the same reason that she did."

"We've been hearing that all week." Tiara snorted. "You were supposed to go overboard hours ago. Look who's still drinking."

Feeling devoid of any hope that she would ever find the killer among the thousands of passengers, Polly sighed and folded herself onto the sofa. "This has not been a very good vacation. Not to speak ill of the dead, but it's all Laura Crawford's fault. As usual. Right from the moment she got me involved in this cockamamie scheme to earn a few extra bucks, and up to the moment she got herself ripped apart, it's been a nightmare for me. And God knows I haven't sold nearly as many DVDs as Laura promised I would!"

"It hasn't exactly been a Carnival Cruise for Laura either," Tim reminded her.

Polly shook her head. "In some ways, she's better off. At least she doesn't have to live with my guilt."

Tiara heaved a heavy sigh of frustration and then tried to comfort Polly. "The only thing you're guilty of is calling my beau a sociopathic serial killer who, if not immediately locked up and kept under tight security, would have every celebrity aboard this Kool Krooz slaughtered before he finished playing the Rodgers and Hammerstein songbook."

Tim agreed with Tiara. "Add a heaping scoop of guilt for scaring away my one and only true love-of-the-week. Without D'Angelo, I'm an old maid at twenty-seven, with absolutely no hope of finding everlasting love on the high seas during the last forty-eight hours of this voyage. You'll be paying for years of therapy for me after this."

Polly looked at her family with the condescension they deserved. "I'm talking about the guilt of not being able to solve the murder for Laura. I'm a failure!"

The room remained quiet for a long moment as the trio

sipped champagne and thought about the ordeal they'd all endured over the past five days. Finally, Polly said, "Who's up for a game of charades?"

"It's too late," Tim said.

"We don't have enough people," Tiara added.

Polly stood up. "My ghost and I were playing when he suddenly vanished." Polly opened her palms and held them up.

"Oh, Lord, we're stuck in game mode," Tim said.

Tiara gave in with a loud moan. "A book," she said, recognizing the charade clue to indicate a book title.

Polly nodded in excitement. She then curled her fingers to her thumb and made an O, which she brought up to her eye while using her other hand to pantomime cranking a handle.

"A movie," Tim said halfheartedly.

Again, Polly nodded effusively. She then stretched out her arms and placed the backs of her hands together in front and pushed them in opposite directions.

"Swimming!" Tim said. *"Swimming with Sharks!"*

Polly shook her head.

"You're parting something," Tiara said. "Tall grass, like in the savannahs of Africa. Pushing away grass to see a lion."

"The Lion King! Out of Africa!" Tim wailed excitedly.

Polly shook her head firmly and tried another clue. She held out her palms and raised them up as if lifting a heavy object.

"Levitation!" Tiara said.

Polly shook her head. She then clenched her fists around an invisible rope and acted as though she were straining to hoist a heavy pulley.

"You're raising a flag!" Tim said.

Polly shook her head.

"Hand over fist!" Tiara said, getting into the fun. "A book from a movie that brought in money hand over fist!"

"What's the clue for a play?" Polly said.

"You're not supposed to talk!" Tiara snapped.

Polly gestured zipping her lips. She thought for a long moment and then stood perfectly rigid and as still as a statue.

"A guard at Buckingham Palace!" Tim said.

Polly pinched her thumb and forefinger together.

"Small!"

Polly nodded.

"Miniature guards. Toy soldiers!"

Polly frowned. She pretended to place something heavy in the crook of her arm and cradle it.

"Rosemary's Baby!" Tim shouted.

Again, Polly looked through the O of her fingers while turning a crank.

"Movie. Baby. *Toy Soldiers.*"

Polly was clearly frustrated and repeated looking through a viewfinder, standing rigid for a moment, placing something in the crook of her arm.

"Oscar!" Tim suddenly called out loudly.

Polly excitedly pointed to her nose.

"A book that became a movie and a play and won an Oscar," Tiara said. "We'll be here all night."

Polly would not give up. She pinched her thumb and fore-finger together again.

"A short word," Tim said excitedly. "A. And. The."

Polly shook her head and pinched her thumb and forefinger still again.

"Smaller word?" Tiara asked. "Initials?"

Again, Polly tapped her nose.

After Tim and Tiara had finished going through the alphabet fifty-two times, they finally had the correct initials.

"Well?" Polly finally spoke.

"Well, what?" Tim said. "What does A.L. stand for? Abbreviation for Alabama?"

Polly shrugged. "All the clues that my ghost—oh hell, the idiot who was trying to scare me—gave me were book, movie, play, Oscar nomination, A.L."

"Come again?" Tiara said, irritated. "You don't even know the answer yourself!"

"Why do you think I started playing this stupid game? I was hoping you two would figure it out. Name movies with the initials A.L."

Tim instantly said, *"Amityville...* something. *Alien...* whatever, *Avalanche... Lane... Lodge... Lake, Auntie Mame.* Close but A.M., not A.L." Tim went to his computer and checked the Internet Movie Database, as well as Rotten Tomatoes, The Razzies, and even the TCM website. "Your visitor is an idiot, all right! There's not a single movie with an A.L. title! Are you sure that's what this specter said?"

Polly shook her head. "I don't know now. It's been too long, and it's all your fault anyway."

"My fault?" Tim protested.

"You scared him away!" Polly said. "I was just gaining his confidence. He would have given me the killer's name and address, and I could have solved the mystery if you hadn't come along when you did. In fact, I'm surprised you didn't see him when you pounced on me."

"Perhaps because ghosts are invisible to we mere mortals." Tiara defended Tim. "And we didn't pounce! We saw Dorian wandering the Promenade Deck by himself and figured he'd either thrown you over, or you escaped back to your stateroom."

"Rather than make any unfounded accusations, the way some people around here do, we thought we'd better check on you first," Tim said.

"You're welcome for our concern," Tiara cracked.

Polly slumped down onto the sofa and sighed. "I've screwed

everything up. I'm the boy who cried wolf or would be if I had Chastity Bono's operation."

"Try the star who cried murderer," Tiara said. "If someone hasn't called the *National Intruder* by now and filed a story about Polly Pepper's lunatic ravings en route to Alaska, I'll be surprised."

"Gossip was so much easier to control before cell phone cameras and the internet made everything immediate and traceable," Tim said. "All it would take is for one passenger to snap a picture or stream a homemade video of the squeaky-clean Polly Pepper accusing harmless law-abiding people of killing a fellow passenger and email the pictures to *TMZ* or Perez Hilton or *Access Hollywood,* and you're on YouTube for eternity."

Polly looked dejected. "In my rush to find a killer, I've become my own personal Salem witch hunt."

"Or a Duke University stripper filing false charges against the lacrosse team," Tim added.

"Good grief! Make me feel even worse!" Polly cried. "Next you'll be calling me the lame-ass Limbaugh of the *Intacti!*"

Tim and Tiara sat down on opposite sides of Polly and put their arms around her. "Everything will be all right," Tiara cooed. "You're under a ton of stress, and you haven't had much rest. Shall I put you to bed and sing a lullaby? Maybe Tim will rub your feet."

Polly calmed down. "What would I do without you two, my fame, and a bottle of champagne? We need another. I'd be lost. That's where I'd be."

With one hand, Tim kneaded the back of Polly's neck. "You're tight."

"I haven't had *that* much to drink."

Tim playfully squeezed harder. "I mean you have a knot in your neck, silly. And I'm sorry for comparing you with that Duke U. tramp."

Polly tilted her head back and enjoyed Tim's strong hands on her neck while Tiara massaged her fingers and hands. As she closed her eyes and let the healing energy permeate her soul, Polly's thoughts drifted. She thought about Laura Crawford and the terrible way she died. Images of the people who, over the course of the past few days, had seemed to be ripe for arrest, but who turned out to be blameless, accumulated in her mind, as did eyewitness accounts of Laura's last night alive.

Polly thought of Talia and the acrimonious telephone call that she claimed Laura had made prior to her massage with Rosemary. Then she thought of old Mrs. Hardy and her recalling that Laura received a cell phone call during dinner. Suddenly, Polly sat up straight, which jolted Tim and Tiara, who followed suit. Polly looked at Tim. "What did you say about cell phones?"

"That they could spread gossip faster than Page 6."

"Why didn't we think of this before?" Polly said triumphantly.

Tim and Tiara were too tired to ask questions. Instead, they simply listened to what Polly had to say.

"Rosemary and that other masseuse said that Laura was having an argument on her cell phone when she came to the spa. If we can find her cell phone, we can probably find the number of the person she was talking to. I'll bet all of my People's Choice Awards that the person she spoke to is the killer."

Tim and Tiara were intrigued by Polly's idea. "All of Laura's personal effects are in storage," Tim said.

"You've burned your bridge to the captain," Tiara reminded her. "He'll never give you permission to go anywhere near Laura's things."

"I'm Polly Pepper. I don't need a permission slip from the

principal's office to look through the lost and found department."

22

Within minutes, Tim and Tiara were reluctantly following Polly down the corridor to the glass elevator. "It's nearly midnight," Tim complained. "You'd better be surprising me with a visit to Anderson Cooper's cabin!"

Stepping into the elevator car, Polly said, "Galleon Level, dear."

Tim pushed the button. "The infirmary again? You're finally going in for a much-needed lobotomy."

When the car stopped, the trio stepped out and found themselves in a quiet corridor. Polly pointed to a red arrow under the universal sign for hospital. She took a deep breath and reached into her clutch for a Kleenex. "How do I look?" she asked Tiara.

"Like a woman who hasn't had much sleep in a week."

Polly smiled. "Give me more of that methamphetamine insomniac look."

Tiara mussed Polly's hair and made her look as distraught as she was tired.

"Follow me," Polly said. "And pray that Dr. Girard doesn't

work twenty-four seven." As Polly led the way toward the infirmary, she started to cry.

"Oh, I get it," Tiara said with zero compassion.

At first Polly merely sniffled, by the time she reached the door to the clinic, her chest was heaving with deep distress, and her mascara was running in rivulets down the creases in her face. She stood outside the door and sobbed into her son's shirt as he embraced her.

In moments, a woman came out to see what was causing all the noise in the corridor. Wearing blue scrubs with a name badge that said PAT SMALLEY, R.N., the woman said, "Poor baby. What's wrong? Tummy hurt?"

At the sound of Nurse Smalley's voice, Polly's blubbering became louder.

Tim looked at the nurse. "Mother... Polly Pepper... has been this way for the past few days. We're hoping you have something to calm her down."

Nurse Smalley instantly recognized Polly and the reason for her distress. She ushered the trio into the infirmary and insisted that Polly take a seat on the leather chair beside the desk. She poured a glass of ice water and handed it to Polly.

Polly nodded in appreciation and took a small sip. She began to cry again. Through her tears and sobs, she said, "I... miss... my... Lau-ra!" And again, she broke down.

Nurse Smalley reached out her hand and patted Polly on the shoulder. "I know, dear. It's difficult to lose friends. But she isn't the first, and she won't be the last. Soon, you'll be gone too."

Polly sniffled and gave the nurse a wary look. She agreed that intellectually she understood the circle of life, but that it didn't ease her pain. "Perhaps if I could just see Laura one last time and say a proper goodbye," she said, almost begging.

The nurse reached out and gently brushed strands of hair away from Polly's forehead. "Oh, honey, that wouldn't be a very good idea. You want to remember the way she looked the last time you saw her. Or at least the last time she wasn't so overweight."

Polly brought her now-damp Kleenex to her eyes and dabbed at the flowing tears. She sniffled between words and said that seeing Laura again would help her to put closure on the fact that she would never again have an opportunity to say face-to-face what she felt in her heart.

Nurse Smalley was understanding, but adamant that Polly could not see the body. "In fact, the drawer is locked," she said. "Only the captain has the key."

Now Polly was inconsolable. She crossed her arms over her stomach and bent forward as if she were going to be sick. "I'm sorry," she wailed. "I'm usually so strong. I guess the stress and grief has done me in."

The nurse insisted that Polly should have a cup of chamomile tea and went to the mini kitchen. She filled four mugs with water and set them in the microwave oven. Then she brought out a box of tea bags. "We'll all have a cuppa," she said.

In minutes, the tea was steeping, and Polly was calming down. "I know that I'll never see my beautiful and talented costar again," she admitted, "but may I please see the evening gown that I bought for her? She was supposed to wear it to the Northern Lights Ball tomorrow night. It's a beauty. I paid ten grand for Michelle Obama's designer to create something just for Laura—so she'd feel like the star she never was." She lied.

As Nurse Smalley removed the tea bags from each mug, she passed around a tray with the four cups. "I'm sure it's stunning," the nurse said as everyone enjoyed their tea. "I'd like to see it too, but all of Miss Crawford's belongings have been placed in storage." She pointed to a door next to the one that said **REFRIGERATION ROOM. KEEP OUT.**

Polly started to cry again. "I have to touch something that

belonged to Laura. I simply must! What possible harm could there be in me holding something—anything—that was actually a present from me to my friend?"

Nurse Smalley stopped and thought for a moment. She looked around as if to see if anyone was watching her. "There are cameras everywhere."

Polly said, "Anyone monitoring the infirmary is probably doing so looking for drug addicts. We're lovely, quiet, and very famous passengers. Please, dear sweet healing woman, I can tell you've got a gold-plated and generous heart. Please help me. Grant this living legend one teensy, but oh-so-important request."

With a deep sign of apprehension, Nurse Smalley walked over to a key rack attached to the wall above the spring-water dispenser and lifted a fob off a cup hook. "Will five minutes work?" she asked. "I'll be in deep trouble if anyone finds out that Miss Crawford's personal items have been disturbed. Everything may be evidence to help the police find her killer."

Polly slowly got to her feet. "Thank you, dear Nurse Smalley. You're a latter-day Sister Kenny—without all those polio cripples. You won't get into any trouble, and I promise to leave my Rolls-Royce to you in my will."

The nurse smiled. "Promises, promises. I've had dozens of patients say the same thing. I've never inherited anything more than my louse of an ex-husband's bills and a going-away gift of STDs."

"Flowers always make lovely parting gifts," Polly said, confusing STD with FTD.

"I would have preferred Casablanca lilies to chlamydia," Nurse Smalley said as she unlocked the door to the storage room and flipped on the light switch. Polly was instantly devastated. The three large boxes, all marked **CRAWFORD, LAURA/PASSENGER LC-8727,** were stacked on top of each other and completely encased in shrink-wrap. "I'm sorry," the nurse said. "If we rip that off, the police in Juneau will know that someone tampered with the boxes."

Polly began to sob again. As the nurse turned around to escort the trio out of the room, Polly begged, "May I just stay here alone for a few minutes to meditate? I feel Laura's spirit here, and I know that she wants to tell me all the things that have been on her mind for years—the personal thoughts and feelings she should have said to me while she was alive and able to appreciate my forgiveness."

Nurse Smalley nodded. "Of course. I suppose there's no harm. It's the least I can do. I'll have your maid make another cup of tea for us."

Tiara gave Nurse Smalley a scathing look, but for Polly's sake, she instantly corrected herself and curtsied. "I shall prepare the tea, mum." She spoke with an affected English accent. "Direct me to the scones and crumpets, *s'il vous plait.*"

The moment the door closed, Polly opened her clutch purse and withdrew her autograph pen, a sleek Montblanc that was given to her by the crew of *The Polly Pepper Playhouse* to commemorate winning her first Emmy Award. Terrified that the door would open before she fulfilled her mission, Polly pulled off the pen's cap and eyed the thickness of the clear plastic film that stretched over the boxes. Sidling up to the cargo, she held the pen like a scalpel and punctured the wrapping. However, the seal easily fell away; someone else had already cut through the cling film but had sloppily rewrapped it. As quickly as possible, she exposed the boxes. She lifted the first box off the tier and cautiously placed it on the floor.

The box, too, which had apparently been taped closed, had been sliced open with the precision of a razor. Polly put away her pen and then opened the wings of the box top. Blindly reaching down into the container and feeling around, she rapidly came to the conclusion that only Laura's clothing filled the box. "Drats!" she complained as she closed the box and pushed it aside.

In the second box, which also had been taped and opened, Polly discovered toiletries, a wig, and several vials of pills for high blood pressure, bladder control, depression, and a herpes treatment. "Ick!" Polly said and tossed the pharmaceuticals back into the box. "Please, dear Lord, let the damn phone be in the next box," she prayed.

Peering inside, she found a heap of what appeared to be miscellaneous odds and ends from Laura's desk and suitcases. Among the sundry articles were a digital camera, several books, an iPod, and the new collector's edition DVD boxed set of *The Polly Pepper Playhouse*. "May as well take this," she said, and set the collection aside. Peering deeper into the carton, she suddenly called out, "Yes!" She located Laura's cell phone. Grabbing it from among the other items, Polly took only a moment to examine the shiny titanium casing.

As she held her golden chalice, Nurse Smalley's voice snapped in her ear, "Meditation time is over, thief!"

Polly was startled and dropped the phone back into the box and instantly dropped herself to the ground in a heaving pile of grief.

"My God! You've unwrapped all the evidence!" the nurse cried as she stepped over Polly's body to examine the damage. "We agreed that you wouldn't touch anything!" Nurse Smalley said.

"Technically, I didn't unwrap anything," Polly said. "Someone else beat me to it."

As Tim and Tiara helped Polly to her feet, Tim insisted that his mother's only reason for visiting Laura's possessions was to have one last moment where she felt the presence of her friend. "You have to understand how close they were," Tim said to Nurse Smalley. "Only Ellen and Portia are closer to each other."

Nurse Smalley gave Tim a suspicious look but admitted, "I did see your mother on *Ellen* once. It was that eco-themed show. Polly was the spokesperson for solar bras. I almost bought one when she said that undergarments could help save Mother Earth while generating enough electricity to charge my iPhone."

Tiara looked at Polly and admired the way she was able to turn on the tears. "Yes, hon, we'll have another bottle of... er... cup of tea when we get back to your cabin."

As Polly continued faux weeping, Nurse Smalley took pity on the star and promised that she wouldn't report the incident. However, she said that if asked by the police who had opened the sealed boxes, she would have to tell the truth. Polly nodded and sniffled her way out of the room. When the door was closed behind them, and they bid good night to the nurse, Polly allowed Tim and Tiara to support her as they left the infirmary. Although Polly continued weeping, the waterworks turned into a trickle. By the time they reached the elevator, Polly stood up straight. "Of all the rotten luck," she hissed. "We have to go back! I had the phone in my hand! Nurse Nosey came in, and it fell back into the box."

Polly looked at Tim. "You knock her out. Tiara, you tie her up. I have to get that phone!"

Tim heaved a deep sigh. "You're lucky the nurse didn't call security! Heck, she's still bound to put our names down as patients. There'll be a record of our being near the body and Laura's personal effects. We can't be seen there again."

Tiara agreed. "She's onto you, Polly. If you return to the scene of your crime, you'll be hanged."

"I'll be hanged if I don't get that cell phone!" Polly demanded. "I'm sorry to do this to you, Timmy."

"I'm getting used to it," he said.

"No, this." Polly reached out and said, "Hold still. You've got something in your eye."

"I've got what?"

Before Tim realized what Polly was doing, she quickly grazed her index finger over his eyeball and removed his contact lens.

"Oh, my God! That hurt! I can't see!"

"You'll look cute in glasses," Polly said as she tossed away the lens. "My hands are filthy from digging among Laura's panties and such. Better run back to the nurse and have her wash your eye out. In the meantime, look for your lens. You probably lost it in the storage room."

Tim was seething. "You've become Medea! I'm doomed! Run for your life, Tiara!"

Polly rolled her eyes. "Don't be a baby, like Rob Schneider. Simply go back to Nurse Smalley, tell her the truth—"

"That Polly Pepper is a maniac?" Tim said.

"—that you're blind—"

"I'm beginning to see you more clearly."

"—without your contacts, and you have to find them or risk falling overboard and suing the Kool Krooz company. She'll buy that."

"At least I'll be telling the truth for the first time tonight," Tim said, and resigned himself to going back to the clinic. "Someone has to play guide dog. I'm liable to fall over the atrium railing."

Polly turned around and began to leave. "Drop by my suite the moment you have the phone."

"Whoa!" Tiara called and reached out to stop Polly. "You're not getting away with this. It's your fault that you freaked out when Nurse Smalley caught you rummaging through Laura's personal stuff."

Polly tsked and said, "You said yourself that the nurse is onto me. I can't show my face there again tonight. But I need the phone! You two are my only hope. I've taught you everything I know about getting VIP treatment. So go and sell it!"

"Sell what?" Tim hissed.

"Our souls to the devil," Tiara said.

Polly looked contrite. "You know I wouldn't ask you to do anything that I wouldn't do myself. If I could help, I would."

Tiara huffed. "Let's go, Mr. Tim. Turn on the waterworks like your mama taught you."

"The only lesson I've learned is to never take another vacation with the legendary Polly Pepper," Tim spat, and allowed Tiara to take him by the arm and lead him to the elevator. "If Justin Timberlake is on this ship and I miss seeing him, I'll never forgive you," he said to Polly as he and Tiara walked away.

23

W hen Tim and Tiara arrived at the infirmary, Nurse Smalley was nowhere in sight. "Probably getting her head examined for allowing Polly access to Laura's stuff," Tiara said. "This is a good time for you to toss that stolen photo memory card!"

Tim crept into Dr. Girard's office and placed the card on the floor next to the filing cabinet. "He's not stupid enough to think he dropped it, but at least he'll know that I don't have it anymore," Tim whispered to himself.

When he stepped back into the main room of the clinic, Tiara was surreptitiously peering into the adjoining storage room. She felt Tim's presence and slowly turned around with her finger to her lips. Tim looked over Tiara's shoulder and almost couldn't control his reaction. There, rummaging through the open boxes, was Nurse Smalley. She held Laura's shimmering bugle-beaded gown against her body and swayed as if dancing in the expensive dress. She then lifted Laura's satin-lined jewelry pouch from one of the boxes and placed it on an eye-level step of a ladder leaning against the wall. When she opened the small sack and looked inside, her eyes grew wide with awe.

As Tim and Tiara stayed as far back as possible, they saw Nurse Smalley slip a diamond tennis bracelet over her wrist. She then selected a diamond and platinum butterfly brooch and pinned it to her white coat. Next, she accented the middle finger of her left hand with a large topaz ring and held out her hand to admire the bauble.

As the nurse returned the remaining items of jewelry to the sack and laid the pouch inside the box, she was suddenly startled by a small noise. Tim and Tiara leaned back as Nurse Smalley's eyes darted to every corner of the room. However, she quickly realized that the sound was made by the temperature-control system kicking in. Tim and Tiara backed away and left the infirmary.

When they were safely at the end of the corridor, Tim and Tiara exchanged evil smiles.

"I'm missing an eye, but I think I just saw Nurse Smalley robbing the dead," Tim said.

"Suddenly, getting Laura's cell phone doesn't seem so difficult," Tiara acknowledged. "We're going back to the infirmary, have your eye washed out, and then tighten the screws on her sticky fingers."

In advance of their arrival at the clinic, Tiara called out, "Yoo-hoo! Nurse Smalley? We need medical attention, *por favor.*"

"You sound just like Polly," Tim said.

As Tiara led Tim into the infirmary, Nurse Smalley was locking the door to the storage room. She turned around and uneasily gave them a wide smile. "So soon again?"

Tiara said that although Polly Pepper was recovering, Tim Pepper wasn't doing as well. "He dropped a contact lens. His eye is getting infected."

"I'm completely blind!" Tim cried. "Haven't been able to see anything since I left here!"

As the nurse escorted Tim to an examination chair, she opened a cabinet and withdrew a bottle of eyewash. She donned a pair of gloves and magnifying spectacles and shone a light in Tim's eye. "You'll live," she said, and poured the eyewash solution into a small eye-shaped cup. "Lean forward and hold this tight against your eye. Then tilt your head back."

After a minute, Nurse Smalley looked at the eye again. "I've saved your sight. You owe me big time," she joked. "I'll call Dr. Girard and have him take a look at it."

"No! No!" Tim insisted. "It's late. I'm fine now. But I'm out of lenses. I need to find the one I lost. I'm sure it came out when I was in the storage room." He leaned forward and slid out of the chair. "I'll just take a quick look," he said, reaching for the doorknob. "It's locked."

"Notice the sign," Nurse Smalley said. "AUTHORIZED PERSONNEL ONLY. Anyway, I've cleaned the room and didn't find a contact lens."

"Not surprising, considering how small it is."

"Even if it had been there, I probably swept it up and dumped it in the trash."

Tim looked around the room. "Where's the trash?" he asked.

Nurse Smalley pointed to a white container with a foot pedal.

Tim lifted the lid. "It's completely empty," he said. "I really need my lens."

Nurse Smalley shook her head. "I told you, it's not here."

Tim pondered his dilemma for a moment before turning to Tiara. "Isn't it funny how one good eye compensates for one that's not so good? I guess my right eye is doing double duty 'cause I never noticed that gorgeous ring before." Tim pointed to Nurse Smalley's hand.

Instantly, Nurse Smalley hid her hand in the pocket of her white lab coat. "I'd better call Dr. Girard now."

Tim and Tiara simultaneously crossed their arms and moved toward the nurse. "While you're at it, call the captain," Tim said. "Or better yet, just hand over the key to the storage room, and we won't utter a peep about Laura's amazing and benevolent bequest to you."

"I don't want this gaudy ring anyway," Nurse Smalley fumed, and removed it from her finger. She placed it on the counter next to the eyewash and faced Tim and Tiara with a defiant smirk. "Now leave, or I really will call Dr. Girard. And the captain, too!"

Tim and Tiara stood their ground. "There's the phone." Tim pointed to the white wall-mounted touchtone telephone. As Nurse Smalley moved to pick up the handset off the cradle, Tim said, "I have a photograph of Laura Crawford taken the day we embarked, and she's wearing that same butterfly brooch. You both have good taste, but I'm afraid it looked much nicer against her lavender cashmere sweater than it does against your stark white coat."

"Tim teaches creative accessorizing at Saks," Tiara said. "He could show you a few tricks."

Nurse Smalley stood still for a moment. Then she said, "You probably know that the ship has hundreds of surveillance cameras. If you aren't out of here in two seconds, I'll do something that will irrefutably prove that you're intruders."

Tiara shook her head and clucked. "When those same tapes are reviewed and they see that you weren't wearing jewelry before you went into the storage room, but you came out looking like you've just been on a shopping spree at Tiffany, who do you think security will want to investigate?"

Tim said, "Frankly, all we want is to borrow Laura Crawford's cell phone. She has a few numbers in her contacts list that Polly doesn't have. If you'll just unlock the door, I'll grab the phone, and we'll be on our way."

Nurse Smalley was silent for a long moment as she considered her next move. Finally, she said, "Just the cell phone? Then you'll leave and never come back?"

"Not unless a shark attacks me in the pool," Tim said.

Smalley reached into her pocket and withdrew the key to the storage room. She held it in her hand for a moment and then gave a reluctant sigh. "It's all yours," she said, placing the key on the counter.

Just as Tim was about to reach out to retrieve the key, Tiara held him back. "You'll be shown on the surveillance tape opening a locked AUTHORIZED PERSONNEL ONLY door," she said. "Nurse Nincompoop here will have our nuts in a vise."

"Oh, for crying out loud," Smalley snapped. She picked up the key and inserted it into the door lock. "Have at it! I'm turning my back. I'll honestly be able to say I didn't see anything."

"Nuh-uh," Tiara demanded. "You lead the way. I'm not letting you say that we entered the room without permission. If we get into trouble, you'll be right by our side. Now, move it."

The nurse pulled open the door and stepped inside the storage room. Tim and Tiara followed. "You call this clean?" Tim said as he went straight to the tower of cardboard boxes. He lifted the first one off the stack and placed it on the floor. He set the second box on top of the first one. Tim then opened up the third box and immediately retrieved the cell phone. "Exactly where Polly said it would be."

"Don't forget the charger," Tiara reminded him.

Just as Tim was about the close up the box, the trio heard a voice calling out for Nurse Smalley from within the infirmary.

"Damn!" Tim said. Just as he shoved the phone into the waist of his pants and tried to cover it with the tails of his shirt, he looked up to find Dr. Girard standing in the doorway, his mouth agape.

Tiara tried to cover for them. "You'd think this was Tut's tomb," she said. "Some reprehensible person had the audacity to break in here and trash the place. Probably looking for dead celebrity souvenirs. I'll keep my eyes on eBay!" She reached out for Tim's hand and started to leave.

Tim looked at Dr. Girard and shook his head. "I'm appalled that you don't have better security on this ship," he said as he and Tiara moved toward the door. Feigning outrage, Tim added, "The captain had better have made an inventory of Laura Crawford's possessions. If there's anything missing, I'll personally see to it that her estate sues his butt! By the time the attorneys are through with Kool Kroozes, Laura's niece will own the whole damn ship!"

Dr. Girard leaned against the doorframe. He looked directly at Tim. "Is that a cell phone in your pants, or are you just happy to see a sexy doctor?"

The phone had slipped down to Tim's upper thigh. He unconsciously reached down to adjust it. He looked up and said, "Sexy doctor? Where?"

Dr. Girard offered an arrogant smirk. "In all my time aboard this ship, I've never had passengers—with the possible exception of Faye Dunaway—who are as beastly as you and your mother and her showbiz friends."

"Polly Pepper is far from beastly!" Tim demanded. "And Faye is a pseudo family friend. She may be a witch to some, but to Polly she's always been more of... well, more like a flea that can be eradicated with an application of *Frontline*."

"Beastly? Quirky? Bizarro? Whatever word you choose, Polly Pepper is still a nut," Dr. Girard insisted. "She and that Cori Berman dude should do a nightclub act together."

Nurse Smalley added, "There's a pathetic duo."

"Cori Berman?" Tim repeated. "Why bring up his name? What's he got to do with anything?"

Dr. Girard looked annoyed. "That has-been came in a few days ago, begging to say goodbye to Laura's body. I told him to get his Hollywood heinei out of the infirmary. He pleaded with me to at least allow him to spend time in here talking to the dead celebrity's spirit, which he insisted occupied every object in these boxes. More Hollywood mumbo jumbo."

Nurse Smalley said, "Must have worked because he left on cloud nine."

Dr. Girard looked at the nurse. "How would you know?"

Nurse Smalley swallowed hard. "Um..."

"Damn it!" Dr. Girard wailed.

"He was only here for a few minutes."

"When?"

"Wednesday. Just before Sarah Michelle Gellar, and right after Scott Baio."

Tim looked at Tiara and said, "Cori and Sarah didn't even get along. Why the heck was he here?"

Nurse Smalley said, "Everyone's turning religious on this cruise. Rosemary, the masseuse, wanted to pray at the box shrine of Laura Crawford too. They only knew each other for a few minutes. As for the others, William Katt and Joan Van Ark, I figured they'd worked with Laura and just wanted to pay their respects. Non-celebs didn't have a chance with me."

Dr. Girard was in shock. "When were *they* here?"

Nurse Smalley shrugged. "Throughout the week. I'm a sucker for people who are grieving, okay? Plus, they're kinda like stars. Or used to be. Celebrities are harmless."

Tim and Tiara laughed. "Not counting the tantrums of Roseanne Barr," Tiara teased.

"I figured it couldn't hurt to let 'em say a prayer over Laura Crawford's boxes of junk, for crying out loud."

Tim looked at Tiara. "Laura worked with all of 'em, but I can't imagine why they'd care enough to make a point of paying any sort of tribute to her," he said.

"Maybe to make sure she was really dead." Tiara chuckled.

Dr. Girard bellowed, "Out! All of you! As for you, Smalley, this is your last cruise."

Nurse Smalley instantly stopped in her tracks. "You've never liked me," she said to Dr. Girard. "I'm an excellent nurse. I have everything that patients appreciate: compassion and *empathy*. And I pretend to be stupid about your unethical practices. Taking pictures of the dead! You should be ashamed!"

Dr. Girard crossed his arms and gave Smalley a look of contempt. "You'd better be careful of any attempt at character assassination."

"Character?" Nurse Smalley sniggered. "You don't have any. As I said, I'm stupid about a lot of things. On purpose. However, my IQ goes up and down on an as-needed basis. I sense a 130 coming on. When it reaches 175, I'll have figured out why I saw you taking pictures of the dead actress."

"I suggest that you not expose our valued passengers to your delusions." Dr. Girard cocked his head toward Tim and Tiara.

Dr. Girard stood as close to Nurse Smalley as possible without touching her. "Your IQ is smaller than a gnat's. Now, get out," he said. "You're off duty. Forever."

Tim stepped in. "Nurse Smalley isn't any more of a thief than you are."

"Or you!" Dr. Girard said, turning to look at Tim.

Tiara said, "Is everyone on this ship a liar, a cheat, and a potential killer?"

"Who's talking about killing?" Dr. Girard said.

"I didn't even know the woman!" Smalley shouted. "But everyone who has come to see about viewing her remains and/or seeing her stuff was at least an acquaintance."

"Point taken," Tim said. "But you said you turned some people away. Who were they?"

"Fans, maybe," Nurse Smalley suggested. "Looky-loos? Some people just like to check out other people's misfortune. If they didn't have a Google entry, I sent 'em back to the all-you-can-eat fried mayonnaise balls bar." Smalley thought for a moment. "There was one..."

"One what?" Tim said.

"The one who said he was Laura Crawford's brother."

"Except for a niece, Laura's family are all dead," Tiara said.

"I know," Smalley continued. "I checked out her bio online. This sucker was way too assertive, too. First, he wanted to visit the body. I told him to come back when he had a better story."

Nurse Smalley stopped and looked at Dr. Girard. "I told you about that guy."

Tim looked at the ceiling. "You didn't get his name, but the surveillance cameras would have captured the scene."

Tiara said, "Isn't there a law against impersonating a dead person's family? Even if there isn't, anyone claiming to be kin to a murder victim has to be up to no good."

Tim heaved a heavy sigh and shook his head. "Let's start over. We don't like each other. But can we call a truce for our last full day at sea?"

Dr. Girard and Nurse Smalley looked at each other. Slowly, they shrugged and nodded. "Sure," Girard said.

"Whatever," Smalley agreed.

Tim reached out his hand to shake Dr. Girard's and Nurse Smalley's. "We need to get the video surveillance tape from the day that *Mr. Laura Crawford* came in."

"I think I can arrange that," Dr. Girard said. "But I'll have to get Captain Sheridan's permission."

Tim said, "Not if you go to Officers Stephen Ronson and

Marc Garner. They hate the captain's guts. Tell 'em Polly Pepper personally asked for their help."

Tiara looked at her wristwatch. "The sun will be coming up soon. This is our last full day on ship. We'd better move fast if we're going to get this guy and find out what he was really after."

As Tim and Tiara began to leave the infirmary, Tim turned to the doctor. "I'm sorry I took your memory card. I've left it on the floor in your office."

Dr. Girard offered a stern shake of his head but then gave Tim a sly smile. He reached into his pocket and withdrew Tim's memory card and handed it back to him. "I'm keeping the pool shots of Jessica Alba and Cameron Diaz. Oh, and Aaron Eckhart and Ryan Reynolds, too."

Tim gave the doctor a knowing look as he and Tiara left the infirmary.

y the time Tim and Tiara returned to Polly's veranda suite, they found her sound asleep in her evening clothes. "You strip her, and I'll get her PJs," Tim said. Polly was in a deep sleep and didn't stir when Tim and Tiara laid her out on the bed and covered her with the silk top sheet. As they quietly left the stateroom, early risers were beginning to step out of their cabins to start their final full day at sea.

As Tim and Tiara walked down the corridor, he saw a carafe of coffee outside another cabin door and picked it up as if he were homeless and had found a half-empty can of beer on the street. "Get a couple of hours' sleep," he encouraged Tiara. "I can hang on. I've got java and Laura's cell phone to keep me occupied. Figuring out who she last spoke to will keep me busy."

When they arrived at Tiara's cabin, she said, "Your mama will be pissed if we let her waste the last day sleeping."

Tim agreed and wandered off toward his own cabin. In the quiet of his room, Tim drank a cup of coffee and then another and another. Finally getting a second wind, he looked at Laura's cell phone and carefully studied the features. He turned it on but found that the battery was dead. Plugging the charger into the wall, he inserted the head of the cable into the charging port. Knowing it would take a while to have enough juice to function, Tim stretched out on his small bed and promptly fell asleep.

A loud knock on his door brought Tim back to consciousness. The knock grew louder as Tim got up and reached for the door handle. "Who?" he called.

"Doo-doo! We're in a heap of it!" It was Polly.

Tim opened the door to find his mother and Tiara standing outside. They both looked disheveled, and as though they hadn't slept for days. "Oh, my gosh! What happened?" Tim said.

Polly said, "God, I'd kill for a Bloody Mary!"

Tiara looked at the cell phone being charged. "What'd you find?"

"The battery was dead. I closed my eyes for a second. Which became hours."

"Let's have a look," Polly said, picking up the phone.

"Careful!" Tim cautioned. "Don't make any calls."

"Like to who?" Polly said. "I'm never speaking to JJ again, and I don't have Brad Pitt's number, so it looks as though I have to spend an hour of my last precious day on ship at that dumb art auction I agreed to go to with Dorian."

Tim removed the phone from Polly's hands and pushed the On button. As it went into activation mode, the phone made the glissando of a harp. "All charged," he said. "Let's go into Laura's call log." As Polly and Tiara looked over his shoulder, Tim pressed a few more buttons and found Laura's call history. He looked at the time stamps. "She talked to the same number, one, two, three..." He counted six entries, beginning early the day of embarkation up until just before the time that Dr. Girard suggested she was killed.

"That number belongs to the murderer!" Polly said and pulled the phone out of Tim's hands. "I'm going to call the son of a bitch right now!"

Tim instantly retrieved the phone. "You can't do that!"

Polly attempted to snatch the phone away, but Tim held it high above her head. "He's got to know that we're onto him!" Polly pleaded. "I want the killer to know that we have his number. Literally."

"Tim's right. You can't just call someone up and accuse them of murder," Tiara said. "Although we've done a pretty good job doing just that to a few innocent people this week."

"Allegedly innocent," Polly reminded her. "But we don't have any time to waste! We dock tomorrow morning, and we still don't have Laura's killer. This may be our final chance!"

"And what would you say if someone answers?" Tim asked.

Polly thought for a moment. "That I'm the ghost of Laura Crawford and I'm back from the grave to seek revenge for taking my life away."

Tiara harrumphed. "That was dialogue from your Mexican movie, *Crawling Eyeballs II: The Vision Returns*."

Polly stuck out her tongue at Tiara. "Can you think of something better?"

Tim shook his head. "Just because Laura spoke to the same person a half a dozen times that day doesn't mean that she was speaking with her killer. She could have been on the phone with her real estate person. You know she's been trying to unload her dump of a condo in North Hollywood. She could have been chatting with anyone. A new boyfriend..."

"Ha!" Polly sneered.

"Her agent. Maybe she was up for a part?"

"She would have bragged to me," Polly scoffed.

"Drug dealer. Cat sitter. Computer tech support person in New Delhi. Who knows!" Tim said. "We just can't presume that the call was made to her killer."

Tiara nodded in agreement but added, "I'm not saying that Laura was chatting all day long with a madman, but we do have to take that possibility into consideration. Does her caller log show the same number on other days?"

Tim scrolled through the list and made a face. "Yikes! She made and received calls to and from the same number as far back as three months ago," he said. He looked at Polly. "What was going on in her life back then?"

Polly shrugged. "Laura was always having one problem after another. Three months? Hmm. I remember she called to tell me how much fun it was watching me as a judge on *I'd Do Anything to Be Famous*. I know she was incredibly envious. She went so far as to say, 'The rich get richer.'"

"She was also having financial problems," Tiara said.

"The woman lived way beyond her means," Polly added. "I bailed her out as often as possible, but I had to put an end to being 'Pepper Savings and Loan.' Accent on 'loan.'" Polly slipped into deep contemplation. "Do you remember when I bought her Warhol?"

"Years ago," Tim said.

"Laura was having another financial meltdown then. I felt a little bad about buying her precious pieces for such low prices. It was Tiara's bright idea to have an art school student make an exact copy as a gift to Laura," Polly said.

"The same with her Hockney and Bachardy," Tiara added.

"I vaguely recall that Laura called me up about three months ago and asked how much her old originals had increased in value. I made up a low figure. She would have died... well, she did anyway... if she knew what they were really worth. I pretended that if she'd kept the paintings, she'd have enough dough to see her through until she could collect Social Security."

Tim looked confused. "Why'd she want to know the value of artwork that didn't belong to her? It could only make looking at her copies intolerable."

Polly thought back and said, "I remember joking that the copies were so good she could probably palm them off as genuine. That is, if she found a rich sucker who didn't know any more about art than I do about hip-hop music, and they just wanted to fill their home with expensive things. Hell, put a high enough price tag on anything and people jump to the conclusion that it's worth every cent. How else can you explain the amount of money that Charlie Sheen got for his TV show?"

Tiara elbowed Polly and reminded her that she'd better get showered and made up quickly if she was going out in public with Dorian. She looked at Tim. "In the meantime, why did we even go to the trouble of stealing Laura's phone if it's no good to us?"

Tim shook his head. "I was hoping that whoever Laura was speaking with during her last few minutes alive would be named in her caller ID log."

"Too easy," Polly huffed. "But check out everyone else in her directory. If anyone in the address book is aboard, we might have a lead." Polly turned around to leave. "Otherwise, we're screwed. When we arrive in Juneau tomorrow, it's over for us. God knows the *National Intruder* will have something to say about Polly Pepper making a fool of herself on an Alaskan cruise and this being the beginning of the end of her illusion that she can outfox non-celebrity killers. Hell, I don't think I even sold enough DVDs to pay for the extermination service at Pepper Plantation. We'll have to live with rats in the pool cabana."

Tim scooted Polly and Tiara out of his cabin. Before he closed the door, he said, "See if there's an appraiser at the auction. The sale of your fake Hockney could keep us rodent-free for a while."

As Tim submitted to the quiet of his stateroom, he shook his head. Laura Crawford's killer was going to get away scot-free unless the police could come up with a DNA match to a previous felon. Polly didn't stand a ghost of a chance of finding her former costar's killer. Whoever it was had done their job and moved on. Now it was time for Polly to do the same thing.

Although it was early afternoon, Polly, the consummate dressed-to-impress celebrity, arrived at the ship's art gallery wearing a beaded chiffon halter dress, with her red hair styled in a trendy bob with bangs. There was no competition for admiring glances as she walked beside Dorian, and together they picked apart the art that was soon to go on the block. "This is what passes for art these days?" Polly sniped as quietly as she could. She looked at the bidding start price and nearly laughed out loud.

"You'll see," Dorian said. "This is a Kadok. If it goes for under twenty K, it's a steal."

"Who's stealing from whom?" Polly quipped.

After making the rounds and eyeing the paintings and sculpture, it was time for the event to begin. Polly followed Dorian and found seats in the second row of folding chairs in front of a Lucite lectern. The room was more crowded than Polly had expected. She looked around and thought, *These people don't look as though they could afford a poster of* The Scream *let alone original art.*

Soon a prim young woman walked to the platform and welcomed the guests. "As I was wandering around, I heard your enthusiasm for some of these magnificent pieces." She looked directly at Polly. "So, let's begin."

Two handsome ship's stewards in white uniforms with black and gold-braided epaulettes carried a cloth-covered painting to an easel next to the lectern. They removed the covering to a wave of whispered "oooohs."

Not wanting to make any expression that might be construed

as a judgment, Polly sat perfectly still. Just as she asked herself, *What is it*? the auctioneer said, "I don't have to tell you who this artist is. Feast your eyes on the visual content! Admire the defiance in the subject matter. This canvas is called *Hoax*."

Polly couldn't control a loud snigger and instantly pretended that she was coughing. As other passengers looked on and made not-so-quiet comments about the lack of intelligentsia in Hollywood, Polly whispered to Dorian, "At least the artist has a sense of humor."

Dorian was not amused. He sat stoically as one passenger after another bid on the painting.

When the gavel came down and proclaimed that the canvas had sold for $5,000, Polly was dumbfounded. "The moment I get home, I'm going to start painting!" she said.

As the afternoon continued, a PowerPoint presentation on a large screen showed several enormous pieces of sculpture, which were apparently at their sculptors' homes or workshops. As one image after another appeared on-screen, Polly tried to keep from shaking her head in disbelief. But with each piece, Dorian became more excited. Polly witnessed what to her was nothing more than a large nut and bolt standing side by side. Then there were two humongous metallic squiggles jutting out of what looked like a giant birthday cake. The piece de resistance was a rip-off of the woodchipper in the film *Fargo,* in which a bloody leg is protruding from the hopper. When Dorian nudged Polly with the excitement of a five-year-old spotting Mickey Mouse on Main Street at Disneyland, she instantly decided she no longer found Dorian to be the least bit amusing.

Although there were no bids for the sculpture, when the lights came on and another canvas was carried up to the front of the room, Polly leaned over to Dorian and said, "This is really BS. I'm going for a much-needed glass of champagne."

"Just a few more items," Dorian pleaded. "I promise you'll

love what's coming up." He opened the catalog of auction pieces and pointed to a photograph of a bust of Eleanor Roosevelt. "Made entirely from found toothbrushes!" Dorian said with awe.

Sucking up her annoyance, Polly refused to pretend to be interested when another canvas was unveiled and revealed a collage of pictures of blond celebrities Anna Nicole Smith, Marilyn Monroe, Farrah Fawcett, Jayne Mansfield, and Jennifer Aniston.

"Something's not right with that collection," Polly said.

Suddenly, just as the auctioneer said, "Going twice..." to the blond mix, a cell phone rang with the ringtone of the theme song for *Jeopardy!* In the otherwise quiet room, all eyes instantly turned and looked around, glaring.

Dorian quickly reached into his pocket and withdrew his cell and automatically whispered, "Hello." Silence. Looking at the caller ID number, he made an involuntary gasp and pressed the Off button. He stared into space as the gavel came down and pronounced a sale. "We have to go now," Dorian said as he stood up and made his way down the aisle of chairs. Polly followed close behind him.

As they left the art gallery, Dorian said he felt ill.

"I've felt that way since you dragged me in here," Polly said. "I almost lost my stomach when that painting on velvet of Margaret Thatcher was unveiled. I have nothing against painting on velvet. But that should be reserved for Elvis and Mother Teresa."

Dorian was distracted. Barely able to maneuver through the crowds strolling the inside deck without bumping into people, he said, "I'll meet you at the bar. I need to use the little boys' room."

Polly watched as Dorian scurried down the concourse past the restrooms and ducked behind a faux-marble column.

Deciding to stalk him, Polly found Dorian in the Tundra Bar, quickly downing a shot of whisky. "And they say I have a problem!" Polly growled to herself. When Dorian seemed satisfied, he turned around and headed back toward the Coral Lounge. When he arrived, Polly came up behind him and said, "The little girls' room was jammed." When they were seated, Dorian's attention was still divided between Polly and his private thoughts.

After a full glass of Veuve, Polly gave up. "I suppose I should leave you two to be alone together. You and whatever's taking up ninety-nine percent of your brain neurons. I'll head back to my suite."

Dorian apologized. "Speaking of calls, I think you should have your Warhol appraised again. For insurance purposes."

"Hell, if the junk we saw today can fetch big bucks, I'll bet Laura's art is worth a thousand times more!"

"Laura's art," he said distantly.

Polly took another long sip from her glass. "My art used to be hers. Sometimes I forget it's now mine, free and clear. I saved her heinei a couple of times by purchasing the pieces she had collected for a rainy day. She got soaked, all right. But it's not as though I took advantage of her. I gave her what she asked for."

Suddenly there was a gleam in Dorian's eyes. "Allow me," he said, pouring another round for Polly and himself.

"After witnessing the shocking prices of those unimaginably horrendous pieces today, I bet I'm sitting on a larger fortune than I ever dreamed of," Polly said.

"You own all of Laura's collection? Then what was hanging on her own walls? I saw her condo in a magazine. She showed off her Warhol and a Bachardy. And a Hockney, too. But you say they're really yours."

Polly raised her glass and clinked against Dorian's. "El fake-os!" she sang. "I had an art student reproduce them for her. I gave Laura the copies so she wouldn't feel so bad about losing her originals. Hell, they looked identical. I doubt that even Las Vegas superman Stevie Wynn with his eagle eye for art could tell the difference. Actually, I should call up ol' Steve-o. He's just the man to see about the value of my stuff."

Dorian stared at Polly for a long moment, clenching his jaw and the vein in his temple pulsating.

Polly felt almost as disturbed by the vibrations emanating from Dorian as she did watching art collectors bid on a canvas of painted underwear labels. The catalog titled it *FruitoftheCalvin-HanesDieselJockeyNavyLoom.* Suddenly, Dorian stood up. "I need to be alone with my thoughts."

Polly answered, "My sentiments exactly. Have to pack. I can't count on Tiara to take all the amenities that housekeeping leaves in the bathrooms."

When Polly returned to her suite, Tim and Tiara were waiting for her with a freshly opened bottle of champagne. "Did you know that there's a huge market out there for crap in a frame?" she said as she accepted a flute of bubbly and took a long swallow. "Whodathunk? I know I'm behind the times. When it comes to pop music, I don't know Daffy Taffy from a Lil' Willy, except when they're in the news for getting beaten up by boyfriends or riddled with bullets and stuffed into coffins. I swear art has gone the same way as music. Mediocrity rules!"

"An enlightening afternoon, eh?" Tim teased. "We've got something that might cheer you up."

Polly settled onto the sofa with her drink in her hand. "I have news too," she said. "I think ol' Dull Dorian's an alcoholic. I found him drinking during the day."

"What color is your kettle?" Tiara smirked.

Polly looked askance at her maid and best friend. "I never touch spirits, especially while the sun is shining!" She took another sip of Veuve and sighed. "I'm a failure as a sleuth. We dock in the morning, and Laura's killer goes free."

"That's our news, too," Tiara added. "Timmy was monkeying around with Laura's phone, scrolling through her directory of incoming calls. Figuring he had nothing to lose at this late date, he pushed Redial."

"What do you know? Someone picked up!" Tim said.

An excited Polly took another long swallow of her drink and said, "Who was it? What did they say? Anyone we know?"

Tim suddenly lost his look of elation. "Um. I didn't exactly talk to anyone. I just heard a man's voice."

Polly's enthusiasm died. "You found the killer, and you didn't get him to tell you his name?"

"We don't know that it was the killer who answered," Tiara said, standing up for Tim.

"Who else? The Prize Patrol?" Polly simmered for a moment, then snapped her fingers at Laura Crawford's phone.

Tim picked up the cell phone and handed it to his mother. "Push Redial."

"I know what to do," Polly said testily. "I didn't become an iconic legend of stage and screen by being an uninformed Luddite. I'll get a confession out of whoever answers."

As Polly pressed her manicured thumb on the Redial button, she sat with a petulant look on her face, listening to the sound of ringing. Suddenly, Polly sat up straight, her mind completely focused on what was occurring on the other end of the signal.

A weak voice whispered, "You're next!"

Polly's confidence abandoned her. She hadn't rehearsed what she would say. Instead of a simple introduction, Polly suddenly lost control and ranted, "Killer! Murderer! You took away Laura Crawford. I know who you are! You'll pay! You'll get the chair! I'll personally push the lever or drop the cyanide or inject the lethal!"

When she stopped to take a breath, the voice on the other end said, "And I know who you are, too."

The call ended, and Polly repeated, "Hello?" several times before putting down the phone. "I guess I told him!" she said triumphantly. "He knows what's what and should be shaking in his boots 'cause his time is just about up."

After a moment, Tim said, "You've just accused someone else of killing Laura. Do you really know who it is? A number in a cell phone call log is not evidence."

Tiara poured Polly another glass of champagne and said, "If you did just speak with Laura's killer, and even if you don't know who he is, he now thinks that you know. No killer would be cornered like a bear without fighting back. You've practically given him carte blanche to nail all of us."

"He did say, 'And I know who you are, too,'" Polly recited.

Tiara slapped her knee. "I said I wanted to have sex one more time before I die. I didn't think I'd be dead so soon afterward!" she said.

"There's time for at least one more," Tim joked, looking at his watch. "I'm over D'Angelo, but I sorta liked Ronson and Garner, too."

Tiara reached over and took away Polly's champagne flute. "Seriously, it's time we stopped putzing around and went to the captain."

"And tell him what? That lunatic Polly Pepper—I know that's what he thinks of me—really and truly knows who the killer is this time?" Polly shook her head. "I don't know who it is. Tim's right. A number is not a name. So, it won't do us any good to bring him into this mess."

"We blew that opportunity a couple of suspects ago," Tim agreed.

"I'm a failure," Polly said. "I have no talent. Well, at least not for picking out a killer from a passenger manifest of four thousand people."

Neither Tim nor Tiara argued with Polly. Tim said, "I suppose you could call the killer back and tell him to meet you at the piano bar in the atrium. Tell him you'll make some sort of deal. I'm joking, of course."

At that moment, Laura's cell phone rang. Polly grabbed the unit and looked at the caller ID. She tapped on the screen and said, "So you think you'll get away with Laura Crawford's murder, do you? Not while there's a breath left in my body. You'll be dragged off the ship tomorrow morning wearing handcuffs and an electric dog collar. I'll see to it!"

Polly listened for another moment. Her complexion turned from pink to white. She swallowed hard and said, "Right back at ya, fella!" Then she ended the call. "What a jerk!"

"Threats?" Tim asked.

"Defamation of character lawsuit?" Tiara added.

"He wants my autograph. In blood. I think I recognized the voice. Cori Berman. Or Robert Wagner. Or Kathleen Turner."

Tim instantly picked up the room phone and dialed the operator. "Connect me with Captain Sheridan, please."

"Hang up," Polly said. "There's nothing he can do. This killer thinks he's Wyatt Earp, and this is his personal OK Corral."

"All the more reason to get protection for you, and for us!" Tiara said. "Don't sit there and think we're going to let you strike out against this nut on your own. You're a comedienne, not Dirty Harry in a Bob Mackie gown!"

"I have a reputation to consider."

"Absolutely!" Tim said. "You're a legend, and your public wants you around for a long time. We're going to the captain, tell him everything, and hope he has our backs."

Polly frowned. "I appreciate how you put my vocation before

my avocation, dear, but I'm not sitting around waiting for this creepy maniac to make me disappear. You know me better than that. Here's my plan."

25

P olly gave cruise director Saul Landers an air-kiss beside his cheek. "I'll tell a couple of jokes, maybe sing a song. Although I do feel a tad sorry for the act that follows me."

"If you've seen one Charo impersonator, you've seen too many," Saul said. "Don't worry your famous red head over cuchi-cuchi."

"You're a love," Polly cooed as she made arrangements to be the opening act in the *Ha-ha, Hollywood* musical stage extravaganza. Backstage, together with Tim and Tiara, she met the other dancers and singers, all of whom were far too young to remember Polly's days as a superstar. Although they knew that they were in the presence of someone famous, it could just as easily have been Ray Charles or Barry Manilow. Although most of the show kids didn't have a clue who those giants were either. Still, they pretended to know about the celebrity in their midst and made her feel important.

"I'm barging in on your little show," Polly said in a tone of contrition.

"Whew! Now we get to cut that ridiculous musical tribute to

Colonel Sanders," said one lithe young chorine doing stretching exercises.

"Trust me, I can happily spend a night without wearing that dumb-ass extra-crispy-chicken-breast costume and singing about how finger-lickin' good the Colonel was to his chicks," said a chorus boy who was not succeeding in his attempt to keep his eyes off Tim.

Polly blew air-kisses to everyone. "Good grief," she said, "it's almost showtime." She turned to Tiara. "How do I look?"

"Like Polly Pepper. The madwoman," Tiara said.

Polly looked at Tim. "Are we all set to snare us a big ol' front-page headline?"

"Just remember," Tim warned, "if we get ourselves killed with this stunt, you'll never get a send-off like Michael Jackson's."

"I'm more than happy to let that sweet, talented, misunderstood soul steal all the thunder of a million dead stars," she said. "Now, go to your stations. I'm about to put my life on the line as the warm-up act for the Kool Krooz Krazies."

As Tim and Tiara left the backstage dressing area, Polly checked herself in the makeup mirror. As she was fluffing her hair, she could hear Saul through the backstage PA system speakers. He was listing the credits of the great Polly Pepper and telling the audience they were in for a rare treat. "If we give the great lady a warm round of applause, perhaps we can coax her into singing her hit signature song, *For New Kate*."

After tepid applause, Saul announced, "And now, the legend herself, the one... the only... Polly... *Pep-per!*"

More halfhearted applause drew Polly to the center of the stage, where, under a bright spotlight, she bowed and curtsied and made the sign of the cross. She milked the attention by lifting the hem of her dress to show off her still shapely legs. Polly nodded her own approval and expected the same from the crowd. With her hands caressing the curves of her chest, she pretended to self-admire her breasts. Catcalls ensued. She then set her hands on her hips and said, "I've still got a *hull* of a ship shape." With the audience now under her spell, Polly pouted, "I was expecting romance on the high seas this week. But none of you darling men bothered to cast your nets my way. And I'm well worth the trawl! No mercury in this catch!"

While the audience applauded their approval, Tim and Tiara fanned out through the theater, keeping their eyes peeled for each of the week's suspects, and anyone else who appeared to be a threat to Polly. Tim was waiting for a cue from his mother.

Polly told a few more jokes, then said it was her nature to be a sentimental old fool. "God knows I lost a dear friend the first day on this otherwise divine Kool Krooz," she said. "You all know who I'm talking about. The lovely and talented Laura Crawford. Someone on this very ship cut her life short. Literally. Perhaps I've passed him in the corridors of this great big boat. Maybe he's danced on the floor right next to me. It's possible that, at this very moment you're sitting beside that awful beast. Look around. Does anyone seem suspicious to you?"

The audience was starting to get restless. After all, they'd come to be entertained; they weren't interested in hearing about death and dying. Polly instantly switched course and began telling her famous chicken jokes. They were lame, but with Polly's perfect comedic timing, the punch lines still received titters if not roars of laughter. "And now, for my next trick..."

Tim heard his cue and dialed Laura Crawford's cell phone. Suddenly, a cell phone rang out in the audience. Polly shielded her eyes against the spotlight and said, "Whoever it is, tell 'em you're seeing Polly Pepper live onstage. You'll call back."

As the phone continued ringing, and the audience looked around, annoyed with whoever hadn't had the courtesy of turning off their device, Polly laughed. "Ha! It's me!" She held up the phone. "Would you all excuse me for just a teensy moment-o?"

The audience laughed.

Polly opened the phone and looked at the caller ID. Then she turned to the audience and said, "I'd better take this. It's from Laura Crawford's killer."

The audience squealed with laughter.

"Seriously," Polly said, and held up the telephone. "See? It says '1-800-Kiler4U.'"

Again, the audience sniggered and applauded mildly until Polly frowned and said, "Drats! We've lost the signal. That's a huge problem on this ship. God knows dear Laura herself lost her signal for good!"

From the back of the theater Tim disguised his voice and yelled out, "Redial!"

"Brilliant idea!" Polly replied, and for a moment built suspense by pretending not to know how to accomplish that simple task. She held up the phone to the audience and asked, "Which button?"

One of the chorus boys dashed out from the stage wings and sidled up to Polly. He looked at the cell phone and pointed to the button clearly marked Redial. Polly looked with appreciation at the dancer, who was wearing his practically nonexistent costume of sequined footless ballet tights and a glitter-dusted muscled bare chest for the upcoming "Salute to Liberace" production number.

The audience laughed as Polly pretended to have a difficult time weaning her eyes away from the attractive young man. When she finally faced the audience, she tsked, "He'll need years of therapy someday when the glitter is all tarnished. Thank God he's tech savvy. He'll have a trade." She looked back at the dancer, who was smiling and eating up the attention. "I have a lot of equipment at home," she said to him. "With all your bells and whistles, I'm sure you could click my browser and download a blog or two."

As the audience continued to be amused by Polly's naughty but harmless nature, she finally said, "Looky! I'm redialing. Let's find out what Mr. Killer wanted to say to me." Polly surreptitiously went into Laura's call log and selected the number that Tim had dialed earlier. She found the number and pushed Dial. "One ringy-dingy, as my darling Lily Tomlin used to say."

Suddenly a ringtone could be heard in the audience. Everyone froze and became silent as they tried to determine where the sound was coming from. As the ringing continued, Polly could see two dark shadows in the audience tussling. She yelled into her mic, "That's the killer! Turn up the house lights! Where's security? Someone, get those men!"

In an instant, Tim, along with a couple of unexpected volunteers, grabbed the men and dragged them, flailing and shouting, to the stage. With a strong thrust, they were set at Polly's feet.

"We've got him!" called out one of the men who had subdued the passengers.

"You're a love," Polly called out.

By now the cast of the show had assembled around Polly. The theater house lights went up and flooded the venue. Polly gasped. There before her were Cori Berman and Dorian Dawson. Cori was still holding the phone. "I should have known," Polly said with disgust. "Cori Berman. Child star and infamous troublemaker grows up to be a has-been hell-raiser!"

The audience surrounded the stage for a better look at the man who killed Laura Crawford. "He's been a bad seed since day one," a woman called out. Another said, "I stopped watching *Highway to Heck* because the *Intruder* said that your every other word started with an *F*!"

As Cori continued to kneel at Polly's feet, he said, "You're making another huge mistake. I wrestled the phone out of this guy's hand." He pointed to Dorian.

"Tell it to the captain and the chief of security," Polly said as she saw Captain Sheridan being escorted to the stage by a team of men in white ship's officers' uniforms.

When the captain took center stage with Polly, he gave her an angry look. Just as he was about to open his mouth with a reprimand, Polly spoke out. "This time I have the real killer," she said, pointing to Cori. "I can prove it."

"How?"

"With this. Laura Crawford's cell phone."

Captain Sheridan snatched the phone from Polly's hand. "How did you...?"

"Never mind how I got hold of it. You're just lucky I did. You should be thanking me for saving you the embarrassment of letting a killer off your ship."

Tim and Tiara made their way to the stage to stand beside Polly. Tim said, "When I checked Laura's call log, I discovered that she'd been talking to a certain number over and over, almost right up until the moment she was killed. So, I dialed it myself. And guess which phone it turned out to be? This one!" he said, taking the cell phone away from Cori.

"Stand up!" the captain ordered Cori. "Is this your phone?"

"Of course it is," Polly declared. "Possession is nine-tenths of the law!"

"Physical possession does not necessarily mean ownership," Cori stated. He reached into his pocket and withdrew another cell phone. "555-2803," he said, reciting his telephone number.

"Then who owns this phone?" the captain demanded as he held the other cell in his hand. He looked at Dorian.

Dorian shrugged.

The captain looked at Tim.

Tim presented his own phone.

Polly chuckled. "Timmy's an elitist when it comes to technical toys," she said. "He'd never be caught dead with any gadget that wasn't up to the minute. *That* phone looks to be at least six months old." Polly suddenly took a good look at the cell phone. Then she looked at Dorian. "Sweetums, this *is* your phone."

"Nope," Dorian said.

Polly took a longer look at Dorian and said, "I saw it today at the auction."

Dorian huffed and said, "Um, mine fell overboard this afternoon. A wind came along and swiped it out of my hand."

"Convenient," Cori snorted.

Suddenly, Polly froze. "Oh, my God. I've made another huge mistake. I'm so sorry."

Dorian smiled. "Not to worry, my dear. You're under a lot of stress. You can't find Laura's killer, and it's driving you nuts. No hard feelings."

"But what I've done is unforgivable," Polly cooed. "Once again I've accused the wrong man of killing Laura." She turned to Cori and said, "Over the years, the hot studio klieg lights have burned holes in my brain. It's my only excuse. How can I ever get you to accept my apology?"

As the gathered crowd collectively looked at Polly with suspicion, Dorian chuckled softly and said, "Why are you apologizing to a killer? Let Captain Sheridan take over. You and I will go out for a bottle of champagne, to celebrate that you cracked the case, as well as our last night out at sea."

"This is your phone," Polly said to Dorian. Then a loud whisper began to roll through the crowd.

"No, it's not," Dorian stammered. "I'm insulted by your insinuation. If you don't drop this foolishness, I'll sue you for everything you're worth, including the Warhol, Hockney, and Bachardy!"

Polly looked at Dorian. "You keep bringing up those damn

paintings," she said. "What's up with my art collection?" She turned to the captain. "Dorian and I were at the most god-awful art auction this afternoon. At three thirteen he received a call on his phone. I know the exact time because I was bored and looked at my watch." She turned to Dorian. "I was also surprised that you had a cell phone. You previously claimed you didn't bring one because you didn't think it would work at sea. The call you received came from my son, Timmy."

She turned to the captain. "If you'll look at the incoming calls on that phone, I suspect you'll see Laura's number displayed over and over, but most recently at three thirteen and five forty-five, just before my call a few minutes ago."

The captain took a deep breath. "I swear to God, Miss Pepper, if this is like the missing DVD disc or the dead pool, I will not wait for the police in Juneau. You'll be in the brig so fast..."

Polly was suddenly ill at ease. Another false accusation could not only find her facing charges of slander, but the tabloids would have a field day reporting how she'd sailed away to the shores of Looneyville.

As a thousand thoughts collided in Polly's brain, Tiara whispered in her ear and pointed to Cori. All eyes followed Tiara's finger and focused on the V of Cori's open-neck shirt.

Cori became self-conscious and touched his hand to a gold braided choker he was wearing. Before Polly could say one word about it, Cori shouted, "Okay. I confess! It belonged to Laura Crawford. It was in a box among her personal things. But I swear I had nothing to do with killing her! I took it as a remembrance."

Polly looked confused.

"I persuaded the nurse at the infirmary to let me into the storage room where Laura Crawford's things were being stored. I lied and said that Laura and I were old friends, and that I wanted to meditate for a few minutes while near to what she left in this world. I didn't think anyone would notice if I took one small item. A memento. Laura was important to me."

Polly laughed. "That didn't work both ways. Laura Crawford was only important to Laura Crawford."

"What was important was the example she set."

"How to alienate friends and lose a career by being hostile to directors and producers and fans?"

Cori nodded. "Exactly. By watching her behave so poorly toward others, I realized that I was the same way. Ever since appearing on your show and seeing how mean she was to everyone, including me, I've tried to change my ways. I didn't want to end up a bitter old has-been like Laura Crawford."

"And yet you still stole from the dead," Polly said.

As everyone was staring at Cori suspiciously, the cell phone rang. While Polly and Cori were having their discourse, Captain Sheridan had pushed the Redial button on Laura's phone, and the ringtone from the other echoed out among the crowd. The captain looked at Dorian. "I checked the call log. Miss Pepper is right. This phone received a call at three thirteen and five forty-five. It lasted all of twelve seconds."

Dorian suddenly looked uneasy. "So? Just because I received calls at the same time that someone called Laura's phone doesn't mean anything. Just a coincidence."

"Then this is your phone?"

Dorian was silent.

Captain Sheridan said, "Let's take a look at the text messages, shall we?" He scrolled through several pages and stopped to read a particular entry. "Someone who used this phone texted Saul dot Intacti at Kook Krooze dot org. It says, *'Daily Wave.* Headline. PP PISSED. IN THE DRINK.' It's dated the day before yesterday. It's the phony obituary."

Dorian shook his head and said, "I'll be in my stateroom. I won't endure any more of this Hollywood-style harassment and insinuation." He turned to Polly. "I thought we were friends. You're nothing more than a diva... without the talent!" Dorian turned and began to walk away.

"Hold it, Mr. Dawson," Captain Sheridan ordered.

Dorian turned around with a sneer on his face. "If you so much as whisper an accusation about me being involved with a murder, so help me, I'll have your commission. I may look like a humble little shoe salesman, but I have friends in places that would make you cringe with fear."

Captain Sheridan glared. "I simply wanted to tell you to enjoy the rest of your cruise. We're placing Mr. Berman under arrest."

Cori Berman railed, "I'm not a killer!"

"You're at least a thief!" Captain Sheridan yelled. "An admitted one at that. If nothing else, I'm holding you for stealing Ms. Crawford's personal property. And for tampering with evidence in a murder investigation." He turned to his security detail. "Take him away."

Polly, Tim, and Tiara watched as Cori Berman was led from the stage, down the steps, and up the aisle to the theater doors. His last words before they disappeared out the door were, "A.L. stands for Angela Lansbury!"

26

"The show must go on!" Captain Sheridan demanded of the crowd. "Git!"

As passengers filed back to their seats, and the small band began to tune up, the cruise director picked up the microphone and joked about the unexpected excitement that can happen in live theater. "You never know what to expect." He laughed. "But now, it's back to *Ha-Ha, Hollywood!*"

As Polly, Tim, and Tiara made their way into the stage wings, they were followed by the captain. When they were safely out of the spotlight and away from the possibility of their voices being heard over a microphone, the captain stopped and faced Polly. He stood with his arms tightly folded over his chest. "Perhaps this time you're right. Maybe Cori Berman is the killer. He has a reputation. His motive for killing Miss Crawford is flimsy at best, but he did steal her choker and maybe destroyed evidence. I don't know. I'll leave this investigation for the police when we dock in the morning."

Polly mimicked the captain and crossed her arms as well. "I'm no longer sure," she admitted. "Maybe he's too obvious. Maybe Dorian did drop his phone overboard. He is a klutz pouring champagne. But I would have sworn that when his phone rang..."

The captain shook his head and said, "Save it for the police and the Coast Guard and Homeland Security. The only reason I feel comfortable holding Mr. Berman is because he confessed to stealing Laura Crawford's personal property.

"Do me a favor," Captain Sheridan continued. "Get out of my sight and don't let me see you again until TCM shows one of your old movies. Then I can turn you off."

Tim reached out and placed a comforting hand on Polly's shoulder. "Let's go drown ourselves. I notice *Krug, Clos du Mesnil* is on the wine list."

"Lead the way," Polly said, cinching her arm around Tiara's waist as they followed Tim to the backstage exit. When Tim pushed the bar handle on the fire exit door, it opened up onto the upper Tundra Deck. The trio unexpectedly found themselves outside. It was a cool night, and Polly leaned in closer to Tiara for warmth as they made their way toward the inside deck.

Polly looked up at the stars. "I wonder if Laura is looking down at me and laughing at the mess I've made of my investigation."

Tiara hugged Polly closer. "It's about time that shrew had a good laugh. Maybe if she'd watched *Frasier* and *Road Runner* cartoons, she would have been happier. Let's face it. Sad as this is to say about anyone, she won't be missed."

Polly nodded. "Imagine being given a small talent and many opportunities and not being grateful for it. Right now, I'm feeling very sad for her. Oh, not because she's dead. She probably doesn't care about that. But she wasted a perfectly good life."

Tim said, "I think you should be feeling happy for her. Thanks to you and *The Polly Pepper Playhouse,* she actually left a legacy and a body of work. She'll be remembered not for the intolerable witch that she was, but for making audiences laugh."

Polly said that she thought Tim was probably right. "You two run along to the Polar Bar and order that bottle for us. I'll be along shortly. The stars are so bright. I sorta want to be alone for a few minutes to gaze up to heaven—not that Laura is anywhere near that place—and say my own version of farewell to her."

"Don't freeze to death," Tim said. "And what did Cori mean by 'A.L. stands for Angela Lansbury'?"

"Cori's crazy," Polly said.

"Say a prayer for me, too, while you're at it," Tiara said. "Tell Him I need my tummy rubbed by Lawrence one last time before we reach Juneau in the morning."

Polly smiled as she left her family and strolled along the brightly lit wooden deck, the sound of flags slapping in the breeze putting her in a meditative mood. As eager as she was to return to her mansion in Bel Air, she was disheartened that she was unable to bring Laura Crawford's killer to justice.

As Polly walked into the shadows between two lifeboats, she sighed. "Laura. Laura. Laura. Who did this awful thing to you? If you hadn't needed money, you wouldn't have been on this cruise in the first place, and you wouldn't have died the way you did. I feel guilty because we could have worked something out financially."

Polly leaned against the railing and looked down at the white waves flooded with light from the ship. She then looked to the sky. Polly closed her eyes and shook her head. "Laura, dear. I have a very funny story for you. You're probably someplace hot and sticky right now, and you could use a giggle. Remember the paintings you loved so much? The Warhol, Bachardy, and Hockney that I bought from you for next to nothing when you were broke? Guess what? I got what I paid for. Nothing. You sold me fakes, just like the ones I had reproduced for you. I knew almost from the beginning but figured they still looked good and were cheap, so why make a fuss and have to pay a fortune in insurance premiums. And I've lied all these years telling people that they're genuine. Hell, I've impressed hundreds of guests. Isn't that too funny?"

Suddenly, the scent of fresh sea air shifted, and Polly picked up the fragrance of men's cologne. She sniffed the air, turned away from the ocean, and gasped as she found herself staring directly into Dorian's fierce and blazing eyes.

"Interesting conversation you're having with the dead," Dorian said.

"At least she can't talk back to me anymore."

"Confession time?"

Polly nodded. "I suspect you didn't like what you just heard."

"On the contrary. I wanted confirmation of what Laura told me with her last breath," Dorian said. "My guess is that Laura counted on you keeping your trap shut all these years. If the *Intruder* got wind of the story, she would have looked like Bernie Madoff, and you one of his hapless victims. Of course, she'd have cried shock and embarrassment and explained that she didn't know anything about art and had obviously been duped herself. You could afford to keep quiet about her deception. I can't."

Polly rubbed her arms against the evening chill and said, "You were swindled. She cheated you the way she cheated me and probably others. So, you killed her. When did you find out they were fakes?"

"Too late," Dorian said. "I stupidly thought that since she was a pseudo-celebrity, she'd be on the up-and-up. I had the canvases appraised *after* I paid her $175,000."

Polly laughed. "Sweetums! Haven't you ever heard the saying, 'If it sounds too good to be true...'"

"The Andy Warhol Art Authentication Board denied the

authenticity of the silk screen," Dorian interrupted through gritted teeth. "They laughed at me. Then, I demanded my money back from Laura, she laughed too and had the gall to say, 'All sales are final.' She had an insolent, imperious way about her."

"I remember the look," Polly said. "It was an attitude that made you want to strangle her."

"I paid her every cent that I had, for Christ's sake!" Dorian looked deep into Polly's eyes. "The last thing she said to me was, 'Get them from Polly Pepper.'"

"She sold *me* what she sold *you*—worthless junk. I just didn't make a stink about it. I never believed her tale of Warhol's lost can of soup. What a crock." Polly smiled. "But I was able to help a fellow thespian who needed money, and I let her go on thinking that I was as much of a moron about art as she was about musical comedy. Funny, eh?"

"Never mind," Dorian spat. "Laura ripped me off. I got chummy with you in order to get my hands on what was rightfully mine. I think you're lying about their authenticity."

Polly stared Dorian down. "How did you plan to get them out of my possession? Did you think I'd simply hand over my Hockney?"

"In a manner of speaking." Dorian reached into the inside breast pocket of his sport coat and withdrew a trifolded piece of paper. He held it under his nose like a cigar and pretended to inhale the aroma. "A change to your will." He smiled.

Polly blanched. "Tim had you pegged as a nut from the beginning. In the future, I'll pay more attention to his intuition."

Dorian repeated, "In the future..." and offered a hollow laugh. Opening the folded document, he explained what he'd done. "I love the internet. There's a website for everything—Sick 2 death dot com creates wills for only $9.95. I made a codicil to yours. You'll sign it, and I'll be very happy to receive your generous bequest of three of your most important pieces of modern art."

"You wasted your money," Polly said.

"After you're gone, no one will question your gift because we've become such chums during this week. Our mutual love for modern art is now well established. At least by the passengers who saw us together at the art auction. It was especially lucky that my cell phone went off. It called further attention to us."

Polly nodded. She thought Dorian's plan was actually a pretty good one. "Ah, but if I leave the planet via a dunk in the ocean, you'll have to wait ages—decades maybe—to get your mitts on my canvases 'cause without a body, it'll be a while before I'm declared officially dead."

Dorian nodded. "Everyone feels they have more time left on Earth than they actually do. Every breath could be our last. Accidents happen in the blink of an eye. Poof! Gone and soon forgotten."

"I'm not accident prone," Polly said. "I survived those snarling beasts at Sterling Studios; now nothing can harm me. And there's no sense in signing some stupid will that you downloaded from the Net, 'cause even if the artworks in question are real, I wouldn't give a boring man like you the satisfaction."

Dorian sniggered and shook his head. "All actors are liars."

"We play roles," Polly corrected.

"Right now, you're playing the role of an innocent who was taken advantage of by Laura Crawford, just as I was," Dorian said. Suddenly he was in Polly's face. "Bullshit!"

Polly tried to step back but was stopped by the railing along the side of the ship.

"You do have my art! Maybe they're the pieces on your wall, the ones you insist are forgeries. Or maybe they're tucked away in a vault."

Polly could hear the roar of the ship's engines and the sound of the vessel slicing its way through the Pacific Ocean. And she could see murder in Dorian's terrifying eyes. "Why would I lie about being moronic enough to buy phony art? Do you think I want my fans to know how absurd I am about culture? I swear, the only things of any value in my home are my Emmy Awards, the People's Choice Awards, of course the lovely Peabody—oh, and I have a soft spot for the Grammy I won all those years ago. Of course, I want an Oscar and a Tony, too. My friend Chita had all those prizes and a freakin' Kennedy Center honor. If she hadn't been so damned nice, I'd..."

"Stop droning!" Dorian hissed. "I've hated every time you do that!" He made such tight fists that the document he held was crushed. "You don't get to be a star by being half-witted," he said. Dorian withdrew a ballpoint pen from his coat pocket and thrust it at Polly, along with the addition to her will. "Just sign and date the damn thing and it'll be over."

"You're going to throw me into the drink whether I sign this silly paper or not because, first of all, I can identify you as Laura Crawford's killer. Second, you need me dead to collect your entirely undeserved inheritance," Polly said.

Dorian took a deep breath. "You're right that if you go missing from this ship, it'll take years for the courts to rule that you're legally dead. That's too long to wait for my reward."

"You're damn right, and in the meantime, my Timmy will loan the works to a museum. It'll be near impossible to get them back once I'm officially not being resurrected."

"I have it all figured out," Dorian said with an arrogance reserved for those with an answer to any question. "And thanks for just now admitting that you do have the paintings."

"I meant *if* I had them. For crying out loud, I'm under a little bit of pressure here." Polly squared her shoulders and demanded to be allowed to leave the scene. "I'm not signing anything, so you're wasting your time."

"You have my art! I paid for it!" Dorian demanded. "How many other buyers did you and Laura scam? It was a really clever shakedown, selling so-called masterworks to suckers. You haven't made big bucks in television or movies in a long time. It takes a lot of moola to keep that Pepper Plantation place running, not to mention all the champagne you swill. Now that I think about it, I'd say you and Laura had a good game going. Suckers are born every minute."

There were tears streaming down Dorian's face. "Laura took advantage of me. I hate when people do that! I'm too nice. I'm a stupid pushover! It's happened all my life."

"I don't think you're too nice," Polly scoffed.

Dorian continued in a voice mimicking past insults: "'Dorian won't mind if you walk all over him. Dorian likes being a door-mat. Dorian's too sweet to complain about getting his teeth kicked in. Dorian plays well with others.'"

"Laura was the final straw. Is that it?" Polly asked.

"She acted as if I were a nuisance for politely informing her that she unknowingly owned forgeries and had sold me knockoffs." Dorian sniffled. "I tried to be a decent guy to give her the benefit of the doubt. She claimed she didn't know that the paintings were fakes. But she said she didn't owe me anything. That was all BS! She took advantage of me. Now, God damn it, you're doing the same thing!"

In that moment, Dorian reached into his pocket and pulled out a DVD disc. He held it up close to Polly's eyes. "Recognize the title?"

"I'm farsighted."

"Season five. One of your best."

"Something tells me that you don't want me to autograph it for you," Polly quipped. "I think I'd rather go overboard after all.

I don't like blood. Especially my own. And that disc looks all jagged and sharp."

"If you don't sign this amendment right now, you'll get the same thing that Laura Crawford had coming to her."

"I'm damned if I do, and damned if I don't," Polly said. "But like you, I don't appreciate being pushed around. So, get out of my way, or I swear I'll fight you until one of us is dead. Be the nice man that people see on the outside and let me go."

Dorian began to hyperventilate as he clutched the paper in one hand and felt a sticky dampness on the other. He took his eyes off Polly for a split second to look at the hand that held the DVD disc; he was bleeding. He had gripped the sharpened edges of the disc too tightly. Dorian gasped and dropped the disc.

In that nanosecond, Polly took advantage of the moment and tried to bulldoze her way past Dorian. He grabbed Polly's dress and nearly ripped it off as he dragged her back and threw her to the deck.

"'Cry me a river,' as the song goes," Dorian hissed, and picked up the already bloodied DVD. He kicked the pen toward Polly and reached out to hand her the amendment to her will.

Polly looked up at Dorian and said, "The probate court will find it very odd that there's blood all over a will. When some smart detective does an analysis, they'll discover it's *your* blood. Although I'll be long gone, and apparently there won't be any eyewitnesses to what you're about to do, all the pieces of the puzzle will fit together, and you'll end up spending two life sentences in a cell with someone named Big Bowser or Roach or Sidewinder!"

Polly took the folded and wrinkled paper from Dorian and picked up the pen that lay beside her leg. She scrawled "Screw you!" where a line for her signature was drawn and scribbled a date late in the future. She handed the paper back to Dorian.

He didn't bother to review the paper but simply placed it in the inside pocket of his sport coat.

Polly looked at the DVD that Dorian was once again holding. "Did you decide to kill Laura Crawford with season six for any particular reason?" she asked.

Dorian cocked his head and said, "The commentary section. Laura came across as a sweet Mary Tyler Moore. But I knew better. She was a dragon. It seemed the most appropriate disc to use."

"Why season five for me?" Polly asked.

"I hadn't sharpened the others." He held up his bloodied hand. He then retrieved the pen and threw it overboard. "As little evidence as possible," he said. "God, you were a handful this week. No wonder men can't stay married to you."

Then suddenly he lunged for Polly. In quick succession, he grabbed her by the hair with one hand and yanked her head back. "This'll only take a few moments," he said as he held the DVD close to Polly's neck.

Polly's self-defense survival instincts suddenly kicked in, and she began to fight for her life. "It's men like you I can't stay married to," she said as the two struggled. As Polly flailed and kicked and screamed, she knocked the DVD disc out of Dorian's hand. It was instantly picked up by a strong gust of wind and carried into the air. Dorian automatically dropped Polly and reached up to grab the disc as if it were a football about to be called out of bounds.

However, as he made a slight jump for the shiny disc, his sport coat filled with wind, and as he reached for the DVD, he was thrown off balance. Suddenly, with a loud cry of fear and confusion, his eyes met with Polly's for an instant before he disappeared over the side of the ship.

Polly was in wide-eyed shock as she saw Dorian look back at her in disbelief about what had just happened to him. In a fraction of an instant, he was absorbed into the water. He was gone.

Polly stood staring into the ocean. She couldn't move. Her eyes kept searching for Dorian. "Didn't you just say, 'Everyone feels they have more time left on Earth than they probably do.' And 'Accidents happen in the blink of an eye.' You were right."

Suddenly an elderly couple stepped into the shadows with Polly. "Lose something, dear?" the woman asked. "We heard a scream. I hope you didn't drop anything important overboard."

Just as suddenly Tim and Tiara appeared from out of nowhere, heaving breathlessly from a mad dash to find Polly. Tim yelled, "A.L. Angela Lansbury! Oscar nomination. *The Picture of Dorian Gray!* A portrait in the attic! Your ghost gave you the clue that the killer was Dorian!"

"No kidding," Polly said, in monotone, as she tried to come to terms with what had just occurred.

Tim and Tiara both reached out to steady Polly, and in that moment, the captain and several members of the ship's security detail rushed to Polly's side.

"It was an accident. He tried to kill me!" Polly said.

"Where is that son of a bitch?" Tiara barked, ready to throttle Dorian Dawson.

"Too late," Polly said. "He's taking a swim."

Polly looked at Captain Sheridan, and suddenly she was fuming. "You should be brought up on security violation charges for not keeping your passengers safe from killers! I was almost—"

Captain Sheridan raised his hands to put an end to Polly's tirade. "It's all recorded on our security monitoring system," he said. "That's why we're here. We watched the entire incident."

"So, you were waiting for a commercial break before coming to my rescue?" Polly charged.

Polly just as suddenly smiled. "I was right after all."

Captain Sheridan made a face. "You haven't been right once this week. Tonight, you said that Cori was the obvious killer."

"I clearly remember telling you and everyone in the theater that Dorian Dawson was the one you wanted, not sweet, darling Cori Berman."

Tim rolled his eyes at Tiara. "I'll back up Polly's story."

Polly looked at the ground and pointed to the DVD. "You'll find Dorian Dawson's blood all over that thing. Mark it as exhibit A." She drew a deep breath and looked around at her family, the crew, and a horde of passengers who had suddenly appeared as looky-loos. "I think I deserve a reward," she said, meeting the captain's eyes. "The only thing that will do, aside from money, is a bottle of *Krug, Clos du Mesnil.* Pick up the tab, won't you, sweetums?" Polly said as she patted the captain's cheek and walked hand in hand with Tim and Tiara toward the Polar Bar.

27

Morning arrived like an unwelcome guest, barging in with the subtlety of a brass band. As Tim and Tiara trudged their luggage to Polly's suite, ready for the great debarkation, Tiara spotted an envelope skulking by the door, stamped in the upper left-hand corner with the Kook Krooz logo like a tacky tattoo. "Lord, not another threatening letter," she begged as she retrieved it and rapped her knuckles on Polly's door.

"Entrez vous, por favor," *came Polly's mangled mix of French and Spanish.*

Tim snatched the envelope with the finesse of a magician revealing is final trick. "Bet you ten bucks this is another curveball in our Agatha Christie cosplay," he quipped, dramatically pulling out a sheet of paper and scanning the document. "Holy plot twist, Batman! It's worse than a cliffhanger!"

Tiara took the paper from Tim, her eyes bulging. "It's a *bill!* Three thousand smackeroos for all those bottles of *Krug, Clos du Mesnil,* at $625 each! Laura told us that this was an all-inclusive package! Dorian didn't succeed in killing Polly, but this'll definitely shorten her lifeline!"

When Tim and Tiara entered the suite, they found a radiant Polly Pepper looking every inch the glamorous legend that she was and exuding the haughty aura of one who had won a grand prize—and blissfully unaware of the financial iceberg she'd hit. "I was just reminiscing about our fun voyage, she said, dismissing the looks of bewilderment from her troupe, who were obviously thinking that Polly must have been on a different cruise.

"I only wish Randy had been here to share in the thrills." Polly sighed as she handed Tiara a few articles of clothing, expecting her to pack the suitcase.

"Trade ya," Tiara said, exchanging the envelope for Polly's silk bathrobe.

"My paycheck?" Polly squealed.

"Someone's," Tiara clucked.

The moment that Polly opened the envelope, her smile flipped from sugar to vinegar as she scanned the invoice. "Laura Crawford's ghost is haunting my bank account! Or maybe this is the work of Dorian Dawson?"

"It was your idea to order pricey champagne to impress Dorian with your good taste," Tiara jeered.

"Polly Pepper doesn't impress anyone," the legend pouted, and quickly realized that the words hadn't come out right. "I mean I don't have to go out of my way to make an impression. If we switch that story around, we can easily convince anyone that Dorian needed to impress *moi,* then stiffed me with the bill. That'll be my take. JJ can use it to have this charge expunged," she said.

"Pity the poor accountant who picks up the phone when JJ calls," Tim tsked.

As they lounged, watching the debarkation process on the television's CCTV channel like it was the hottest reality TV show —*I'm a Celebrity, Get Me Off This Ship!* —and expecting the passengers on their deck to be summoned at any moment, Polly said, "If the *Intruder* spins a juicy tale about my masterpieces being the star of Laura Crawford's whodunit, maybe they'll finally fetch more than a pity bid at a character auction. I'll bet they'll finally be worth something." She turned to Tiara. "Kinda like that insane auction where Matt Dillon's jacket went for the price of a small island."

"Damon's jacket. The younger Matt," Tiara corrected. "The one who actually has an Oscar to use as a doorstop."

Polly, unfazed continued. "With a little luck, we could be swimming in cash. We might just come out ahead after all," Polly brayed.

"Ahead is where you'd better stay, or you'll be sued for copyright Infringement," Tim suggested.

"Stick to the story you've told for years," Tiara said to Polly. "You unknowingly bought forgeries from Laura and were shocked to find out the truth. But Good Samaritan that you are, you not only forgave her, but you replaced her fakes—with other fakes."

"If Laura hadn't had the knockoffs in the first place, she wouldn't have been killed for her larceny," Tim said.

"And stupidity," Polly added. "I'm only responsible for cleverly escaping from getting *myself* murdered in an effort to find Laura's killer!"

Tim leaned over and hugged his mother. "If Dorian had succeeded in doing to you what he did to Laura, I'd be going to jail for murdering him, to avenge you. And thank God for the law of aerodynamics! I know I'm heartless to say this, but I sorta giggle every time I picture Dorian's coat blowing open and filling with sea air. I can see your description of him rising like the flying nun before being whisked overboard and dropped into the drink!"

Polly barely muffled her giggle, her eyes twinkling with

mischief. "I'll be cackling in my crypt, seeing Dorian doing his best Wile E. Coyote impression—wide-eyed and gobsmacked, hanging in thin air like he's forgotten gravity exists, right before the desert floor and a grand piano labeled 'ACME' introduce themselves."

Whirling around to her team with a dramatic flair, she whispered conspiratorially, "And for the record, Dorian and I never sparked. When I said 'fireworks,' I meant the kind you buy for a buck that fizzle out before they even start. The only fling happening was in your overactive imaginations. I'm too smitten with Randy Archer. It's like he's the only channel my heart's remote is programmed to."

Tiara, barely containing her laughter, nodded. "Oh, we figured. You're quite the performer, Polly, but your *smitten kitten* routine wasn't very well rehearsed. I've known you a long time. When you're truly enchanted, it's less like *bells ringing* and more full-blown *symphony* with a laser show."

While watching the television and the stream of passengers filing out to the gangway, Tiara reminded her, "You have an appointment with the police as soon as we set foot in Alaska."

"A quick interview and a few selfies," Tim said.

"Nonsense. They'll give me a commendation for bravery and actions above and beyond the call of duty," Polly said confidently. "After all, I did them a huge favor by finding Laura's killer."

Over the ship's PA system, the announcement was finally heard that passengers on Polly's Veranda Deck could queue up for the debarkation process. "Next time, let's try someplace posh, like the *Queen Elizabeth II,*" Polly said as she looked around for anything she might have neglected to pack. She spied a candy dish of chocolate mints and handed it to Tiara, who slipped the candy *and* the dish into a side pocket of her suitcase. "Did you get all the soaps and shampoos?" Polly asked.

"Every last one. And the extra complimentary bottles of champagne, too."

Polly took a last look at her beautiful stateroom, then made her way out the door and down the corridor.

When they finally arrived on the main deck, Polly, Tim, and Tiara merged into a tributary of other passengers moving toward the exit at the speed of a clogged drain. The Kool Krooz Swelltime Passes and Zip 'n Sip liquor card were collected. Then they moved down the gangway and descended into the cruise ship terminal and into yet another queue. There, Homeland Security guards were checking passports and transfer documents.

Suddenly, Polly's eyes automatically locked on the open double doors in the distance, and she excitedly took a deep intake of breath. She eagerly called out to Tim and Tiara, and everyone else, "My Randy's here! He's come all the way from Beverly Hills, California, to surprise me!" With her eyes trained on her attractive boyfriend, who was standing outside with a bouquet of cellophane-wrapped flowers, Polly waved wildly and slipped out of line. She pushed past other passengers and ignored uniformed border security guards demanding she "Halt!"

Polly was deaf to all but the affectionate sounds she was imagining she would soon hear from Randy, until she was abruptly sidelined by four whistle-blowing officers shouting her name. Polly was where she ordinarily preferred to be—the center of attention—but this time she was flummoxed by the commotion.

"Yes, we're well aware of your celebrity, Miss Pepper," said one officious officer, in response to Polly's look of surprise. "We've been assigned to drive you to police headquarters. There's a matter of a murder."

"Not just any murder," Polly insisted. "The murder of a dear and trusted friend of mine. A used-to-be, almost star."

As Polly nodded her readiness to spill the beans, Randy flashed his badge like he was unveiling a golden ticket, darting to her side. Their embrace was so tight, you'd think they were trying to squeeze orange juice out of each other. Randy then stepped back, his grin wide and genuine. "So, let me guess," he teased, "you were just lounging around, innocently sipping bubbly, when out of nowhere, a kamikaze seagull dive-bombed a corpse right onto your pedicure?"

Polly made a dismissive snort, giving Randy a nudge that could start a pinball game. "Oh, please! Everyone knows it's storks are the only birds that drop bodies. But oh, how I wish you'd been there to see my murder investigation prowess in action!"

Randy's eyes twinkled with mock astonishment. "A murder, you say.

Tim and Tiara exchanged smiles as they listened to Polly's revisionist history of how, apparently, she alone had cleverly pieced together the clues to find the killer.

"Not just any body!" Polly continued. "A semi-celebrity body that soon will be more famous than when it was walking around making trouble for the living. Her head was missing."

"Not quite," Tiara sassed.

"Let me tell *my* story *my* way!" Polly hissed.

As Polly and her posse were escorted with much police fanfare toward the building's exit, Lawrence Deerfield stopped on his way out and gave Tiara a hug goodbye and handed her his business card. Then he turned to Polly and said, "You know I adore you, Miss Pepper, just as everyone else does. But being accused of murder was the last thing I ever expected to happen in my lifetime. In lieu of court action, I'll be writing to you for a letter of recommendation to secure a gig for me at the Pasadena Playhouse. You owe me big time."

"I hear you, Mr. Talented Fingers." Polly laughed, trying to pretend that Lawrence's farewell was a private joke just between them.

As Lawrence shook his head and stepped out of the terminal, Deena Howitzer and Cori Berman, their arms linked together, walked up to Polly. Deena gave the diva a peck on her cheek and said, "If it hadn't been for all of your false accusations about who killed that Laura C.—darling Cori being among them—I might never have found the love of my mid-life." She turned to Cori and gave him a kiss on his lips. "Yeah, I'm like 'em young, so sue me," she giggled. "Cori's been *remanded* to my custody," she cooed in a sultry whisper. "*Remanded.* Isn't that the most seductive word you've ever heard?" she giggled and added, "We'll need your help getting that dopey charge of pilfering from the dead removed from his record. I think you owe him that much."

Cori, too, gave Polly a kiss on her cheek. "You never complimented me on my New England accent?" he said. "And jeez, lady, you were right when you said you weren't good at solving riddles. I gave you tons of clues about Dorian that night outside your cabin door!"

Polly looked at Cori. "You were my ghost!" Then she corrected herself. "I knew it but wanted to hear it from your own lips. And you knew that Dorian was the killer because you overheard him talking to Laura on his cell phone."

"No. I was at the spa with Talia the night that Laura was murdered. We finished our um, er, *treatment*, and as I was leaving, I saw a man enter the therapy room next door. I heard him swear and shout Laura's name. He called her a double-crossing tramp. Laura yelled something back and I clearly heard her say 'Polly Pepper.' I didn't catch the rest and didn't think any more about it until the next morning when I learned that she was dead. Then I saw you and Dorian together and added things up. I decided you might be at risk. I tried to warn you, but God, you're so obtuse!"

"Why didn't you tell the captain what you saw?" Polly asked.

"Because you were already doing a damn good job of casting aspersions. And I decided I might end up looking as foolish as you."

Deena interrupted. "We have to file statements with the authorities, too, and my Cori will tell all. Mind if we join your police escort?"

As the security team continued to lead Polly and her troupe toward the exit, two women approached. "Remember us? Rachel and Sarah? We bought your dumb *Polly Pepper Playhouse* discs in the gift shop. We wish we could say it was a pleasure meeting you, Miss Pepper, but the truth is that you burst our bubble. Celebrities do that at their own risk. If you're Julie Andrews, we expect a nun. On the other hand, if you're Russell Crowe—well we don't expect too much of him. But you're Polly Flipping Pepper, and we're very disappointed with your phony baloney act! You're not the saint that Betty White was."

Sarah made a face and clutched the crucifix around her neck. She babbled something unintelligible before moving away.

"Tongues?" Tim asked.

"Expletives in pig Latin," Tiara answered.

Polly cinched her arm into Randy's and linked the other with one of the Homeland Security officers'. "Wait'll I tell you all about this appalling Kool Krooz and the nut jobs I've met this week," she said. "It'll make a great chapter in my book!"

"Speaking of which"—she turned to one of the security officers — "please make a note that I'm writing my memoirs and need a copy of my police deposition for the chapter titled 'A Bonnie Body Lies Over the Ocean.' God knows I don't want The Smoking Gun or *Oprah* accusing me of exaggerating or fabricating my stories!"

Outside, Polly and her entourage hit the pavement like they were strutting down a Hollywood red carpet, only to be swarmed by a gaggle of news vans and reporters. Polly beamed and greeted them like they were long-lost relatives at a family reunion.

With the grace of a gazelle, Polly broke free from her Homeland Security escorts and waltzed over to the media circus. "Listen up, buttercups," she announced, "as a common courtesy to the brave men and women in blue who earn their pay with our taxes, I can't discuss details of my involvement in this murder investigation. However, I will say that despite the lovely and talented Laura Crawford being beheaded on the boat, I sold a *ship*load of the brand-new *Polly Pepper Playhouse* boxed set collector's edition of DVDs. They're available everywhere, and I know your TV audiences will want to know that Laura is heavily featured on these discs. So, get 'em while she's still hot. As a commodity, I mean. Of course, the real Laura is pretty darn cold."

A reporter called out, "Polly! Are they booking you a suite at the Graybar Hotel?"

Polly rolled her eyes. "Please! I'm the heroine of this saga, not the villain. I'll be sipping champagne in a five-star hotel by sundown, celebrating my sleuthing skills along with my adorable Plus One, Detective Randy Archer." She pointed to Randy, who seemed reticent to accept any acknowledgement.

"Polly!" another voice called from among the reporters. "Is it true that your old costars Arnie Levin and Tommy Milkwood hired a hit man to kill Laura Crawford?"

"Sweetums, that was twenty years ago!" Polly laughed. "This

time it was Laura who got herself in trouble and couldn't get out of it."

One of the Homeland Security officers rushed to Polly's side and whispered in her ear. Polly blew kisses to the reporters and the crowd that had gathered and said, "I'm being told that I've said too much, and I have to save the really juicy stories for my deposition. I suppose it'll be available on the internet by tonight. Feel free to quote me as often as you like. But pretty please, be kind to this living legend and use decent pictures. Ta, sweetums!"

"One last question, Polly!" an intrepid reporter called out. "What's your next movie or TV gig? We miss you!"

"Miss you more!" Polly shouted back. "Watch this space for some very big news coming soon. My agent is putting me up for the new Woody Allen project."

"Sorry to hear that," the reporter called back. "I guess we can look forward to reading your memoirs soon, too."

"Something great will come along for me, I assure you," Polly trilled. "You know that Polly Pepper always lands in clover!"

THE END

ALSO BY RICHARD TYLER JORDAN

Polly Pepper Cozy Mystery Series

Final Curtain

A Talent for Murder

Set Sail for Murder

Remains to be Scene

A Corpse in the Castle

Shadows at Midnight

Murder and a Missing Manuscript

LGBTQ+ Titles

Strangers in the Night

Overnight Sensation

Gay Blades

One Night Stand

Breakfast at Timothy's

ABOUT THE AUTHOR

RICHARD TYLER JORDAN began his career in Hollywood, spending 30 years as a senior publicist at the Walt Disney Studios, where he worked on marketing campaigns for more than 500 feature films. He later turned to writing novels and is the author of the Polly Pepper cozy mystery series, including *Murder and a Missing Manuscript, Shadows at Midnight,* and *A Corpse in the Castle* and several more. He is also the author of the novels *Breakfast at Timothy's, Overnight Sensation, Strangers in the Night, Gay Blades*, and *One Night Stand*, among others. He also wrote the non-fiction book *But Darling, I'm Your Auntie Mame!* Jordan is an American expat writer living in a 500-year-old stone cottage in England. For more information about him, visit www.RichardTylerJordan.com.